THE FAKE OUT FLEX

HOCKEYMANCES BOOK 1

ASH KELLY

Copyright © 2024 by Ash Kelly

All rights reserved.

No part of this book may be reproduced in any form or by any electronic or mechanical means, including information storage and retrieval systems, without written permission from the author, except for the use of brief quotations in a book review.

ABOUT THE BOOK

He's a guarded pro hockey player.
My brother's best friend.
My high school crush.
And now...my fake date to my ex's wedding.
What could possibly go wrong?

After my breakup on live TV goes viral—yep, I'm *Breakup Sneeze Girl,* hi!—I *cannot* go to my ex's wedding alone.

So my totally non-meddling—*cough*, yeah right—brother ropes in his best friend as my date.

The only problem is, Fraser and I share a history. He was my high school crush...until he left without even saying goodbye.

But that was seven years ago, and I am completely, *one thousand percent*, over it.

One fake date with Fraser? No problem. I can handle that.

Until one date turns into me being his fake girlfriend.

The more time we spend together, the more I catch glimpses of the Fraser I knew back in high school. Under his gruff exterior, he's kind. Protective. Encouraging. He's also got the most intense blue eyes and cutest smile I've ever seen.

And yep, okay, my crush is back with a vengeance.

Only this time, it doesn't feel so one-sided. Fraser buys me my favorite flowers. He flies across the country just to check in on me. And when he gazes into my eyes, there's something simmering between us I can't deny.

But will Fraser leave again, or can our fake relationship turn into something real?

The Fake Out Flex is a closed-door pro hockey romance with plenty of banter, fast-talking friends, truth fries, the granddaddy of grand gestures, and a heartwarming happily-ever-after. It's the first book in the **Hockeymances** series and can be read as a standalone.

The Fake Out Flex is PERFECT if you love:

- Pro hockey sports romance
- Fake dating
- Brother's best friend
- High school crush
- Boy-obsessed
- Cozy small-town feels
- Chosen family
- Closed door romance

1

Evie

"Now, you know I don't like to meddle in your life, right?"

Wrong.

My brother, along with everyone else in Comfort Bay, loves nothing more than to meddle. It's the town's unofficial favorite pastime.

I cut off a decent chunk of Camembert from the charcuterie board, plonk it onto a cracker, and take a bite. Something tells me this conversation is going to require cheese and carbs.

"But I've come up with an awesome solution to your problem."

I'm tempted to ask which of my two major life crises he's referring to but instead opt for a cautious, "Go on."

Levi rests the ladle against the side of the saucepan, then turns and focuses his full attention on me. With his skinny jeans and faded Fall Out Boy T-shirt, he could easily be mistaken for a rock star, when in reality he simply manages the hottest pop act on the planet—WHAT NOW. Yes, in all caps because that's apparently a thing bands do now.

"It's to do with the, uh, unfortunate incident."

Ah, so we're on to discussing my love life now.

My cursed love life.

I'm not superstitious, but a string of three boyfriends in a row breaking up with me just before we reach the one-year anniversary mark? Come on. That can't just be three unfortunate coincidences. Is there an unauthorized *How to Date (and Break Up With) Evelyn Freeman* handbook floating around somewhere that I'm not aware of?

"And by *unfortunate incident*, you wouldn't happen to be referring to Bryce dumping me on live television, having the video go viral, and forevermore being known as Breakup Sneeze Girl?"

Levi frowns. "I liked my words better."

"Hey. It happened." Two hundred and forty-seven days ago, to be exact. But who's counting? "There's nothing I can do about it but move on."

I scoop up a few blueberries and hope that the whole *move on* bit sounded believable.

Levi assesses me with the same hazel eyes we both inherited from Dad.

"Yeah, see, I don't fully believe you, Ev. Which is why I've come home for the weekend, forced to activate concerned-big-brother mode."

I plop a blueberry into my mouth. "Remind me again how that's different from meddling-big-brother mode?"

"Let's not get buried in the details." He grabs a spoon, dips it into the sauce, and then extends it over the breakfast bar toward me in a bold and brazen attempt to distract me with chili shrimp sauce. "Here. Try this."

It's piping hot, so I blow across the top before taking a nibble. "Mmm. That's really good."

"Too much chili?"

"Pfft. Never."

One thing that unites my family? Our love of spicy food.

We've been known to make a game of it, seeing who can handle the hottest dish. It's not a real Freeman family dinner until we're all red, sweaty, and crying. It's nice to blame the tears on food and not decades of unresolved psychological trauma.

"I know the heat level is fine for you and me, but would it be too hot for a...normal person?"

"What normal person?" What's he talking about? "It's just you and me for dinner."

Levi averts his gaze.

I sit up taller. "It *is* just you and me for dinner, isn't it?"

He wipes his hands on his jeans. "Not exactly."

"What are you up to?"

"Before I answer, let me remind you of the immunity afforded to me as part of concerned-big-brother mode. No threats can be made against me, nor can my physical safety be put into jeopardy."

"I make no promises."

A few beats pass.

"As I'm sure you're well aware, Bryce's wedding is coming up in a few months," Levi says delicately, the teasing gone, replaced by full concerned-big-brother mode activation.

It's in two-and-a-half months—seventy-one days, to be exact. Not that I'm counting.

"I'm aware. And I am totally fine with it."

I bypass the cheese knife, pick up a whole mini-wheel of Brie, and shove it into my mouth to prove just how totally fine I am.

Levi tries not to look horrified at my display of fine-ness. "Right. So, um, look. There's no easy way to ask this."

"Jushhh ashhhk."

He shakes his head, biting back a grin. "Do we need to go over this again, Ev? Chew, swallow, *then* talk."

I finish eating. "Just ask whatever you're going to ask."

"Okay. Fine." He flattens his palms across the countertop. "Are you still planning to go to the wedding?"

"I am."

People might think I'm crazy, showing up at my ex's wedding after the very public—and very humiliating—way we broke up, but I have my reasons for why I want to attend.

Levi rolls his eyes. "I still think that's kinda crazy, but whatever."

The Fake Out Flex 5

Reasons I haven't shared with anyone else, which is why he, the rest of my family, and my friends have all been trying to talk me out of going.

But, when needed, I can be just as stubborn as our mother, and I *will* be at that wedding.

"Do you have a date yet?"

"I don't."

"Just as I suspected."

"Your point?"

His lips stretch. "I have someone."

"Someone for...?"

"You. To be your date. To the wedding."

"You're setting me up? No. Levi, that's a terrible idea." I inhale some more cheese, but this time I chew, swallow, *then* ask. "Who? Please don't tell me it's someone from WHAT NOW. I'm sure they're lovely guys and all, but aren't they, like, twelve?"

It couldn't get much worse than attending Bryce's wedding solo...unless I showed up on the arm of a minor.

"They're in their early twenties, they just look—"

"Underdeveloped?"

"I was going to say, young. But anyway, no, that's not who I locked down for you."

"Please don't use the term *locked down* in the same sentence as my dating life. I know I've had a run of bad luck when it comes to love"—*understatement of the decade*—"but I'm not resorting to locking anyone down."

"Fine. I won't use that term again. Consider it banished."

"Thank you." I hesitate, almost too afraid to ask. "So, who, then? Not some slimeball music exec friend of yours."

"My music exec friends aren't slimeballs, thank you very much. I'm very discerning about who I associate with in LA, and my friendship circle is filled with plenty of fine and upstanding—"

"Stop rambling, and just tell me already."

"Okay. Fine." Levi smirks, lifting his chin. "Fraser."

The blueberry I just popped into my mouth goes down the wrong pipe, sending me into a coughing fit. Levi watches in amusement as I try to regain my composure.

Between sputters, I hear him say, "I was wondering if you still harbored a crush on the guy, and now I *berry* much know you do."

I grab a peanut and toss it at his stupid face because good people cannot leave bad puns unpunished.

Annoyingly, he ducks out of the way.

Even more annoyingly, he's now laughing.

I take a sip of water, square my shoulders, and level my brother with my most serious look. "I *do not* still have a crush on Fraser. My feelings for him are where I left my bangs, my anxiety about failing algebra, and my love of bracelet-making. In. The. Past."

"So that whole coughing fit was, what, your attempt at slapstick comedy?"

"I hate you." Then I point to the pot and smile sweetly. "Your sauce is boiling over."

"Oh no!" he cries, dashing over to the stove. He lowers the heat and begins cleaning up the overflow.

While Levi's dealing with the mess, I pile some more cheese onto a cracker—because blueberries are clearly a health hazard; point taken, universe—and take a minute to process the host of emotions Fraser's name has stirred up.

Yes, it's true. I developed a teeny-tiny crush on Fraser when I was a sophomore in high school and he was a senior.

We got close over a few months in the spring. Nothing physical ever happened. Fraser was a complete gentleman.

We just talked.

And not just about hockey, which was what our conversations normally revolved around whenever Fraser would come over and be forced to wait for Levi who, to this day, takes longer to get ready than my sisters or I do.

We *really* talked.

Fraser opened up and told me what was going on with him and his family. How much he hated filming the reality TV show his parents had signed them all up for. How he couldn't wait to get away, make it to the major leagues, and leave Comfort Bay for good.

Well, his dreams have come true.

He's playing in the NHL. He's one of the highest-scoring forwards since my dad. And he's just as reclusive and mysterious as ever. He only ever returns to Comfort Bay for the obligatory family holidays.

But I meant what I said to Levi—I am over my silly high school crush.

And the fact that Fraser left without saying goodbye, without so much as acknowledging the bracelet I made for him?

Yeah. I'm over that, too.

He probably did us both a favor, bypassing one epically awkward conversation.

Listen, Evie, thanks for the bracelet. It's really nice of you, but I don't want things to be awkward between us. Not with you being my best friend's little sister and all...

Because that's all I've ever been—and all I will *ever* be—to Fraser.

His best friend's annoying little sister who bugged him incessantly about hockey since the day his family moved in next door to us and who made him a bracelet to show how much she liked him which he probably threw out as soon as he got home.

And I'm okay with that. There isn't enough cheese on the planet to show how okay I am with that.

With the sauce under control, Levi wanders back. "So. Fraser. What do you think? It's genius, right?"

"Genius is a stretch."

"I disagree. Anyway, thoughts, feelings, observations?"

"About taking Fraser as my date to the wedding?"

He nods. "It shouldn't be a problem, right? Unless you *do* still have a crush on Fraser?"

I fold my arms. "I do not."

"Great. In that case, since you've got no lingering feelings for him—as well as no other options—*and* since for some inexplicable reason you are determined to attend Bryce's wedding, it looks like you've scored yourself a date, courtesy of the world's greatest brother."

"*Fake* date. It would be a fake date," I correct, before quickly adding, "Not that I'm agreeing to anything."

"Sure, sure."

I hate it when he smirks at me in that annoying older brother way, like he thinks he's got the upper hand. Do they ever grow out of that?

"Think about it, Evie. Fraser is…safe."

"Safe?"

"Yeah. We know him. I trust him with my life. He won't ever do anything to hurt or embarrass you."

Unlike a certain ex of mine…

Levi doesn't say those words, but I can tell that's what he's implying.

"Because if he ever did anything wrong by you, he knows I'd inflict a slow and arduously painful death on him."

Levi stares at me.

He's kidding, obviously, but there's something else going on behind his eyes. Something I need more cheese to help me process.

I pick up a cube of Jarlsberg and, as I start chewing, give his suggestion some more thought.

Maybe I should go with Fraser?

He does tick all the revenge arm candy boxes a girl could want when going to an ex's wedding to prove to him—and the world—she's over what happened and has moved on with her life.

Successful sports star? *Ding.*

Famous? *Ding.*

Rich? *Ding.*

Ridiculously attractive? *Ding ding ding!*

I swallow.

And then I have to swallow a few more times.

Why are my windpipes conspiring against me tonight?

While my crush on Fraser has diminished somewhat over the years, his attractiveness hasn't.

At all.

He's one of the hottest players in the NHL.

In high school, Fraser was tall and athletic, but he had a certain gangliness to him. Today, that gangliness is gone, replaced by a well-defined chest, broad shoulders, and powerful legs, essential for agility and speed on the ice.

His jawline has sharpened, his bright-blue eyes are more intense than ever, and he's picked up a small scar on his left cheek from an ugly high-sticking incident with an opponent two seasons ago, which, if you ask me, makes him even hotter.

I'm stating all of this objectively, as someone who is completely over her crush. These are simply the facts, people.

"Wait." I tap on the counter. "Aren't we forgetting something here?"

"Like what?"

"Like the small matter of asking Fraser about this?"

Levi smirks.

The doorbell rings.

Levi's smirk grows smirkier.

My stomach drops. "Don't tell me you invited Fraser here to spring this harebrained idea of yours on him? Because that would be a terrible thing to do to the guy, putting him on the spot like that."

"I agree, and I'm a nice guy who would never do that to his best friend," Levi replies, moving to answer the door. "Which is why I called him last night and cleared it with him."

"You've already discussed this?"

"I have."

"Your honor, the prosecution seeks to strike any mention of my brother not meddling in my life off the record."

"Overruled."

"Hang on, hang on, hang on." I push to my feet. "You spoke to Fraser about this and he...agreed?"

"No, Ev. He didn't. And I've invited him here to duke it out with you gladiator-style." Levi rolls his eyes. "Of course he agreed."

"And he's here right now?"

"He is. Standing on the other side of that door, probably wondering why I'm taking even longer than normal to answer it."

"Get out of my way."

I shove past my brother and race over to his refrigerator. It's brand new and one of those super fancy ones that has full-length mirror doors. I teased him about it when he bought it, but now, I couldn't be more grateful for his vanity. I'm going to need every precious second I have to do something about the horror show staring back at me.

If I'd known we'd be having company, I would have worn something other than my dad's old hockey jersey, black leggings, and a pair of Ugg Boots that my boss bought me on her yearly family visit to Australia.

And if I'd known *Fraser* would be joining us, I would have done something to tame my hair and at least put on lip gloss. Maybe even some blush.

Levi stares at me like I'm crazy as I frantically run my fingers through my frizzy blonde locks. I let out a tiny shriek when my fingers come across something that is very much *not hair*.

I untangle the stick and wave it in my hand once it's freed, glaring at my brother's reflection in the mirror.

"Why didn't you tell me I had this in my hair?"

"Because I didn't notice it. It was in the back." He grins. "How did you get a stick in your hair, anyway?"

"I went for a jog in the park after work."

"That doesn't actually answer my question. But whatever. Why are you freaking out? It's just Fraser. The guy you *don't* have a crush on, remember?"

I ignore that last comment as I start tying my hair into a ponytail. "I'm not freaking out. I'm making myself presentable...because I'm considerate like that."

"For Fraser?"

"For a fellow human being who will be forced to look at me for the next several hours."

"Okay, let me see if I've got this right. You're perfectly happy walking around with part of a tree lodged in your hair when it's just you and me, but you make yourself presentable for others?"

"Correct."

The doorbell rings again.

"I'm going to answer that," Levi says, grinning. "Unless you need more time? I only ask because I'm considerate like that."

I need more time.

Some makeup.

A new wardrobe.

But Fraser is here *right now*.

"It's fine. Go answer the door. Just don't walk too fast."

"Got it."

Levi makes a show of taking a giant stride in slow motion toward the door as I focus on the task at hand.

Hair is…passable. And stick-free, so that's a bonus.

Now onto my face.

This will need a minor miracle.

Maybe she's born with it, maybe she's a girl standing in front of her brother's mirrored refrigerator frantically pinching her cheeks to bring some color into them while her former high school crush is standing outside after agreeing to her brother's crazy idea of taking her to her ex's wedding.

I straighten.

There. Done. *Ish*.

My cheeks do have a bit more color in them, so I'm taking the win.

I glance down at what I'm wearing and release a long, resigned sigh. There's nothing I can do about my outfit other than smooth out the jersey a little.

My sigh turns into a groan when I take in my Ugg Boots. Why did I wear them tonight? From this moment on, I'm renaming them to *ugh* boots and vow to never wear them outside of my apartment ever again.

I shuffle my *ugh*-boot enclosed feet toward the dining room and duck behind the wall so I have a clear line of sight to the front door.

Levi's almost there, about to open it.

My heart starts to race.

And no, it's *not* because I still harbor feelings for Fraser. Those days are well and truly behind me...I'm, like, ninety-nine percent sure.

No.

I'm on edge because this is all happening so fast. Levi drops this bomb on me, and boom, thirty seconds later, Fraser rocks up.

Give a girl a little time to process.

Also, I may have possibly overdone it on the cheese.

As I hold my breath, waiting for Levi to open the door, a question suddenly springs to mind.

Despite being one of the most successful and famous players in the NHL, Fraser hates the limelight.

He's notoriously private and guarded and does everything he can to lie low and not draw any media attention.

He's even pulled back from the team's hospital visits these past two seasons, which makes no sense because he's always had a soft spot for kids.

So why on earth has he agreed to this?

2

Fraser

I stand outside Levi's apartment, wondering how long it will take him to open the door. If I had a dollar for every time he's kept me waiting while he gets ready, I'd be rich.

Well, rich*er*.

But Evie's in there with him. I spotted her car—a lemon-yellow Mini Cooper is pretty hard to miss—in the visitor parking lot. So I have no idea what's keeping him.

I glance down at my hands and can't help but grimace.

The flowers were a mistake.

But it's too late to ditch them now.

So yeah, I'm going to be the guy who gets his best friend's sister a bunch of yellow roses because when I saw them, I remembered they're her favorite.

I'm an idiot.

I shuffle on my feet, regretting having said yes to Levi yesterday.

Not because I don't want to help Evie out. I witnessed what that jerkface did to her eight months ago. Heck, the whole world saw it. So if Evie needs me by her side at his wedding, that's where I'll be.

Glaring.

Scowling.

And doing my best to suppress the instinct to punch him in his smarmy face for what he did to her, even though I've never done a violent thing in my life.

So my regret at having agreed to be her date has nothing to do with not wanting to help Evie.

It's more complicated than that.

For the last seven years, I've had to keep two big secrets.

One about my family, the other about Evie.

The family secret will stay safe. There's no way I'd ever let that slip.

But my Evie secret?

The one I've kept ever since senior year?

That one could totally blow up in my face.

Because even though Evie is my best friend's younger sister.

Even though she has every right to be mad at me for how abruptly I left, without even saying goodbye or properly thanking her for the bracelet she made for me.

Even though she's probably never once even considered me in any sort of romantic light at all.

I can't say the same.

The truth is—the truth that no living soul in the world knows—I am truly, madly, deeply, head-over-skates in love with Evelyn Freeman. I have been since senior year.

I never acted on my feelings back then because, hello, she was a sophomore and way too young.

I had too much respect for her to ever try to take advantage of her in any way. I would never do that.

Not to mention Levi.

Nope. Evie was totally off-limits.

I always tried to keep some distance between us. It would have looked bad enough if I'd been caught sneaking into her bedroom late at night. The last thing I needed was for them to jump to the wrong conclusion.

The thing is, I only realized how deep my feelings for her were a week before my family's world changed forever, and I got whisked away to a training camp, ending my close connection with Evie.

We've both moved on with our lives.

I made my way through juniors, to the AHL, to now playing

in the major leagues, while Evie graduated high school, went to UCLA, and then returned to Comfort Bay, where she landed a reporting role on a local morning show two towns over.

For seven years, I've kept a lid on my emotions.

No one suspects a thing.

Not Evie.

Not Levi.

No one from our families.

Even the Comfort Bay *Stick Our Noses into Everyone's Lives* committee remains blissfully unaware.

But now, with this one decision to accompany Evie to her ex's wedding, I risk ruining everything.

Reining in my feelings is easier when I'm not here. When I'm not around her. When it's not just the two of us. Alone.

She'll be classic Evie—upbeat, witty, gorgeous—and I'm going to have to pretend like...like I'm immune.

Like she's just my best friend's little sister. Someone I used to know and spent some time with all those years ago.

How am I meant to do that when the truth is, no one I've met or dated since has even come close to making me feel the things she made me feel?

The door swings open, snapping me out of my thoughts. I plaster on a smile. "Hey, buddy."

"Fraser. My man."

I hug my best friend. "It's good to see you. You're looking well. Have you lost a few pounds?"

"LA passed an ordinance banning carbs, remember?" He smiles, then his eyes drift to the flowers. "Aw. You shouldn't have."

I shake my head, chuckling. "They're not for you, bozo."

"Really? I'm devastated. How will I ever get over it? Oh, wait. There. I'm over it. Come on in." He raises his voice, speaking louder than necessary. "Evie's spying on us from the dining room."

My eyes flick over to the dining room, and I catch the tail end of her ponytail as she zooms out of the room.

By the time Levi and I reach the kitchen, Evie's perched at the breakfast bar, scrolling through her phone. Which I'm pretty sure she's holding the wrong way around, if the upside down cats on her phone case are anything to go by.

She looks up and smiles. "Oh, hey, Fraser."

"Hey, Evie."

She drops the phone and moves toward me.

Now, I can do a spin-o-rama on the ice, rotating three hundred and sixty degrees while maintaining control of the puck, but I cannot for the life of me get my feet to move right now.

So I stand frozen in place, my eyes raking over her as she approaches. She's wearing her dad's famous *81* jersey and looks like she always does—effortlessly beautiful. Minimal makeup, with just a faint rosy hue in her cheeks. Her wavy blonde hair is pulled into a ponytail. And she's smiling that smile that makes my chest tingle.

A subtle floral scent hits my nose as she walks right up to me, lifts on her toes, and plants a small peck on my cheek. "It's good to see you," she says, her voice sounding a little airier than I remember.

"It's good to see you, too."

We stare at each other for a few beats.

Apart from occasionally running into each other after a home game, we don't hang out together anymore. The hockey season sees me traveling for eight months of the year, and even though we both have places in Comfort Bay, most of the time, when Levi and I catch up, it's in LA since we both have our reasons to avoid coming back here.

Unlike Evie.

She's a small-town girl through and through. Even in high school, she always said she'd be back here after college.

When I left, I knew it'd be for good. I didn't know where I'd end up settling down, I just knew it wouldn't be here.

Seven years later, I still haven't found a place I can truly call home.

She smiles at me.

I smile back.

Her gaze drops.

To the flowers.

Oh. Right. I forgot I was holding them.

I extend my arm. "I got these for you."

Levi bites back a grin and moves into the kitchen to check on dinner.

Evie takes the bouquet from me, her hazel eyes twinkling in delight. "Yellow roses. My favorite." She studies the bright petals for a moment, then brings them to her lightly freckled nose and inhales deeply. "Ah, I love this smell. They're so beautiful."

I squash down the urge to say something stupid like, *I remembered how much you like them and would always have them in your room*, and instead go with, "I saw them and thought of you."

"That's so sweet. Thank you."

She's still smiling as she heads toward Levi. "Vase?"

"Second shelf on the right."

I pull out a stool from the breakfast bar and watch her as she finds a vase, fills it with water, and then arranges the flowers in it.

Okay. So far, so good.

Operation *Keep Things Normal* is on track.

She thinks the flowers are sweet. I've regained control of my legs. Levi's staring at me.

Wait.

Why is Levi staring at me?

Did he catch me gawking at his sister?

Okay. Maybe I'm not as stealthy as I think I am.

I shoot him a friendly smile and deflect by asking, "Whatcha making there, buddy?"

"Spicy shrimp linguine."

I groan. "How spicy?"

The Freemans have a thing for spicy food. And not just a little spicy. I'm talking *melt your tongue, make your eyes cry rivers of tears* spicy.

"You should be fine," Levi says, cocking his head. "Unless you're a baby."

Another thing about the Freemans? They're all super competitive.

"Says the guy who lost the chili dog eating contest at the Comfort Bay Fair four years ago," Evie says, her eyes gleaming.

See? Competitive.

Levi bristles. "You cheated."

"Did not. You devoured the hot dogs like a madman, tiring out way too early. I had a clear strategy in mind, eating steadily and methodically, focusing on maintaining a consistent pace rather than speed. The results speak for themselves."

I chuckle as it hits me how much I love their fast-talking banter.

I've got two older brothers and one younger sister. We're all close, but I'm especially close with Dawn. She's just as guarded as I am, though, so while we do open up to each other, we're nothing like these two. When Levi and Evie get together, they generate enough energy to rival a wind farm during a tornado.

"So," Evie says, leaving a sulking Levi and plonking down

on a stool next to me. "I've re-watched all your games from last season, and I have some notes."

"Of course you do." I drag a hand down the side of my face. "But take it easy on me. I'm still reeling."

Evie's expression softens. "From the breakup?"

"Yeah," I say, mainly because it's the right thing to say.

I don't want to sound like a heartless jerk who wasn't that upset when Tori broke things off with me. But we were incompatible. It wasn't going to work. The writing had been on the wall for a while.

The real reason I'm reeling?

"There's the breakup, but then that was followed by losing six consecutive games."

Talk about a bad run.

"The second half of the season was a trainwreck," Evie agrees. When she notices my pained expression, she throws in, "Sorry. Gentle. I'll try."

She'll try. She'll end up failing.

Like always.

Outside of people actually involved in the game, she's the most hockey-obsessed person I know. She puts the *fan* in *fanatic*.

She watches every single game of the season.

She drives three hours to all LA home games, which is essentially Comfort Bay's home team since it's the closest city with an NHL team.

And I know for a fact she still compiles a spreadsheet of team statistics, covering everything from shots on goal to power play opportunities to time of possession because as she starts talking, she pulls out her phone and opens up said spreadsheet, referring to it every so often.

After every game I play, she very kindly emails her notes for me to ponder.

It all comes from a good place, even if she sometimes gets carried away by it. She forgets that big dumb hockey players have feelings, too. But she's a lot better these days than she used to be. She was *harsh* back in high school.

I wait until she's done sharing her thoughts, including encouraging me to work on my shooting techniques in training because apparently my wrist shots have been letting me down. She's actually right. That's something I have been working on in the offseason.

"You know, I think you've missed your calling," I say.

"How so?"

"You'd be an amazing coach."

"I don't think so."

"Why not? You've got expertise in the game. Great insights. Killer analysis."

"And you're super bossy," Levi supplies. "An important quality in a coach."

I frown at Levi. "That's not necessarily a bad thing," I say to him before turning to Evie and lowering my voice. "And you're not really that bossy."

"Thanks." For a split second, she looks like she may be considering it before shaking her head. "No. No. That's crazy. I'm not coaching material."

"Weren't you tossing up between being a reporter and a teacher in high school?" I ask, the conversation we had lying on her bedroom floor, staring up at the ceiling, drifting back to me. "Being a coach isn't that far off from teaching."

"I was also tossing up whether fanny packs should make a comeback." She smiles at me. "Which, for the record, they should not."

"Okay." I raise my hands. "I'm dropping it."

"Food's up," Levi announces, and we make our way to the dinner table.

"This smells great," Evie says, taking a seat.

"And not too overpowering," I happily add.

"Thanks. Dig in, guys."

We fall into an easy conversation.

I haven't seen Levi in over three months. He traveled with the band he manages on the European leg of their world tour, so he regales us with a few backstage stories.

"And how are your folks?" I ask.

Levi's demeanor changes instantly. "I'm still a huge disappointment to Dad for not following in his footsteps and becoming you, basically."

"And I'm still a huge disappointment to Mom for not moving to Washington and taking up, what she calls, *a real reporting career*," Evie says from across the table.

"Right. Glad I brought that up. Let's move on. How's your work, Evie?"

Evie stops eating. "Fine. For the most part."

Levi and I exchange a look.

"What's going on?" he asks.

She sighs. "Everything's fine."

"Yes, because that was definitely a happy-sounding sigh," Levi presses. "Very common thing for people to do when communicating good news. Like, sigh, I won the lottery. Or, sigh, I landed my dream job. Or, sigh, I'd like to thank the academy for this awar—Ow."

A breadstick strikes the side of his face.

"Evie." I try to make my voice sound stern. "Please don't throw food at your brother."

"But it shut him up."

I tap my chin. "Fair enough. Continue."

"Okay, okay, I'll stop," Levi says, before Evie can peg anything else at him. He rubs his cheek. "But talk. Tell us what's going on, Evie."

"It's just...numbers."

I frown. "Numbers?"

"Yeah. My segments aren't generating the kind of numbers the network expects."

Levi stops rubbing his cheek. "Why not?"

"Because bad news sells, and good news doesn't," she replies despondently.

Evie is the good news reporter for KCFB's morning show, *The Morning Buzz*, and she is easily the star of the show. In fact, if they don't make her co-anchor soon, I plan on launching a complaint with the FCC for the network failing to give the viewers what we want.

"I really liked your piece on crafts with a cause," I say, twisting a strand of linguine around my fork. "It's such a great way for the elderly to stay connected and do something fun and creative. And your story about the dog who survived a house fire and is now training to be a therapy dog for burn victims was really touching. Oh, and the one about that old lady who scrolls through social media looking for posts about independent restaurants that are struggling and then goes there, orders lunch, and posts rave reviews about it online. She's so awesome. I wanted to reach into my screen and give her a high-five."

Evie's eyes widen. "You...you watch *The Morning Buzz*?"

Only for you.

The words threaten to spill out of me, so I shove some shrimp into my mouth and reply with a nod.

"*How* do you watch?" Levi asks, raising an eyebrow. "You're hardly ever in town."

"There's this thing called a cell phone, and on it you can download these things called apps. And have you heard of this thing called streaming?"

He rolls his eyes.

I continue. "I downloaded the network app. That way I can watch"—*Evie*—"the show when I'm on the road."

"You're more dedicated than I am."

I glance across the table. Evie's eyes are brimming with an unspoken curiosity. Her cheeks seem a little redder, too.

Is it weird that I watch her show? Weirder than bringing her flowers, or about on par on the Fraser weird-o-meter?

I keep my mouth shut to avoid escalating the awkwardness already filling the room.

So of course, that's the precise moment when Levi decides to step in with, "So, should we talk about my genius idea?"

Evie's eyes dart between me and her brother, and yeah, her cheeks are definitely getting redder.

"Thanks for agreeing to take this one to her ex's wedding," Levi says. "I owe you one, man."

Tightness bands around my chest.

I realize Levi's just messing around and doesn't mean anything by what he's saying, but I don't like the way he's making it sound like I'm doing him a favor. Like it's a chore. Or something I'm doing out of obligation.

It's not any of those things.

There's nothing I want more than to spend time with Evie.

Despite the danger.

I've deliberately avoided spending time with her alone all these years. Don't I deserve just one day with her? A few measly hours when I can let my imagination run wild, and who knows? Maybe I'll be able to shake her out of my system.

Yeah, you keep telling yourself that, buddy.

"You don't owe me anything," I clarify to him, then turn to look directly at Evie. "It's an honor to escort you. Even if I am a little surprised you actually want to go in the first place."

Evie forces a smile. "I wouldn't say I want to go, but it's the right thing to do. Half of Comfort Bay is going to be there, and if I don't show up, everyone will whisper in hushed tones about poor Breakup Sneeze Girl who got dumped on live TV and was so traumatized by it, she went into hiding, spiraled, and by the time she hit thirty, lived with at least that many cats named after members of eighties punk bands."

Levi chuckles, but I simply stare at Evie.

She's trying to be brave about this, but I know it's taken a toll on her. Levi told me she didn't leave her apartment for a whole month after the story broke.

As someone who already has a very low opinion of the media, they managed to sink even lower in my estimation. Why is someone's pain considered newsworthy? I'll never understand that. Just like I don't get why Evie's segments aren't more popular. They're the best part of the show. What is wrong with people?

"No one's going to think any less of you if you decide not to go," I say.

"But I need to go," she says, determination rising in her voice. "I don't want to be Victim Evie anymore. I want to be Revenge Evie, who shows up at the wedding with a guy who's ten times hotter than Bryce."

I can't help but grin. "Ten times hotter, eh?"

"At least." Evie grins back. "Right, Levi?"

Levi gives me a once-over, then shrugs. "If you're into wildly successful athletes with huge trust funds who've got that whole mysterious, broody vibe going on, sure. I guess."

"Remind me again why we're best friends?"

"Because I'm one of the very few people who can put up with you." Levi stands. "Seconds, anyone?"

"Not for me. I think I've reached my heat limit."

"Sure," Evie says. She hands him her plate, then smiles teasingly at me. "Because I'm not a baby."

Levi leaves, and then it's just the two of us.

Alone.

Evie's smile fades.

She leans in and lowers her voice. "Listen, thank you. For taking me. I really appreciate it. And sorry for Levi springing this on you. If it's any consolation, he sprung it on me, too. On the upside, I'm no longer walking around with a stick in my hair."

"Excuse me?"

"Never mind." She blows out a heavy breath. "This whole situation is such a mess. I feel so stupid about it."

"You have nothing to feel stupid about."

I reach across the table and take her hand in mine. Her skin is so soft. I brush my thumb slowly, steadily, trying not to show any outward signs that indicate my heart is clanging wildly against my ribcage at this unexpectedly intimate moment.

Keep a lid on it, Rademacher.

"The only dumb person is jerkface for letting you go. What he did to you was cruel, Evie, and I am more than happy to do whatever you need me to do to get back at him."

"Really?"

"Absolutely. Feel free to use me in any way you see fit."

She perks right back up, pulling her hand out of my grip. "Can I pick what suit you wear?"

"Of course."

"Can I order you to break into his house and steal random stuff like the microwave turntable or one shoe from every pair of shoes he owns?"

"No."

"Okay. Forget the microwave turntable and the shoes. What if you break into his house..."

"No."

"Steal his beloved PlayStation..."

"Still no."

"Pawn it..."

"I *know* you can hear me."

"And use the money to sponsor a pig at the local petting zoo, which we'd name after him?"

I suppress a smile. "We are not doing any of that."

"You're no fun." She pouts, but she's trying not to smile, too.

I peer over into the kitchen. Levi's almost done plating up seconds. I don't have much alone-time left with her.

So I take Evie's hand in mine again and say, "You are not defined by what that guy did to you, okay? We are going to that wedding, and you will show him and everyone else there that you are a brilliant, vibrant, beautiful woman who has moved on with her life."

Her hazel eyes meet mine, and I give her hand a reassuring squeeze.

"Because I promise you this, Evelyn Freeman, I will do everything I can to be the best date you've ever had."

3

Evie

"You busy, Evie?"

My boss's commanding voice startles me. I snap my laptop shut—hoping she didn't catch a glimpse of what I was about to view for the eighty-seventh millionth time—and swivel around in my desk chair to face her.

"Never too busy for you." I lift my gaze and offer a smile. "What's up?"

Margo glances around the cubicle farm. "Come on. Let's walk and talk."

"Okay."

I tuck my laptop under my arm and join her as we commence one of her infamous 'walk and talks' around the office. It's a step up from her impromptu, *oh you're in the next cubicle, let's have a chat in the ladies' restroom* meeting.

"I need your top three reasons for why I should *not* get a tattoo," she says in her thick Australian drawl as we commence our walk. "Go."

"Um, okay..."

Margo Bailey.

My boss and the formidable executive producer of *The Morning Buzz*.

A one-woman powerhouse, responsible for my ever-growing collection of *ugh* boots.

And also my personal hero for a bold decision she made in her life. One that inspires me, especially on days when I'm dealing with my mother.

Upon joining *The Morning Buzz* straight out of college, I quickly learned that conversations with Margo can splinter into a million different directions, so you have to be prepared for anything she might throw at you.

The Fake Out Flex

"I need some more information to work with," I say, keeping pace with her. "What sort of tattoo are we talking about, and where would you put it?"

"On my back. Something massive and tacky. Will mortify my kids when we go to the beach."

I tap her arm. "And *those* are your top three reasons right there."

A smile spreads across her face. "I knew I hired you for a reason, Freeman."

We take a sharp left by the photocopier.

"So, you wanted to talk to me?"

"I do, and I'll warn you now, this isn't going to be an easy conversation."

My breath hitches, but I'm not entirely surprised. I had a feeling this would be coming. "Is it about my latest numbers?"

"It is, hon."

"Thought so."

The network runs a series of focus groups to assess what our audience likes and dislikes. Ratings are still the most important metric, but they only tell us how many people are tuned in at any given time. They don't reveal what the audience thinks about what they're watching, or why they choose not to watch certain shows or segments.

Every few months, a group of randomly selected people is brought in, led into a viewing room, and shown a variety of segments from the show. They receive a knob and are instructed to dial it as they watch. The scale goes from zero to one hundred. Zero means they have no interest in what they're seeing, one hundred means total interest. They also have an option to 'click off,' which would be the point when they would change the channel or choose to stop watching the show if they were at home.

The most recent testing took place last week, and I've been dreading finding out the results.

After an initial burst of interest when I first joined the show—*oh, how novel, someone not shouting that the world is on fire and instead reporting on positive, uplifting, interesting stories*—my numbers have been on a slow, steady downward trajectory ever since.

Except for one notable bump, but it doesn't count because it was for all the wrong reasons.

We migrate toward the back corner of the office, where it's quieter.

"Let's start with the positives."

"There are positives?"

"Of course there are. Quite a few of them. People adore you, Evie," she says, giving my forearm a gentle squeeze. "You've got the highest number of social media followers out of all the on-air talent, apart from the leads."

I knew this already. "I've been getting chilly vibes from Mandy the weather girl lately, ever since I overtook her on Instagram."

"Yeah, well, her forecast isn't looking that great based on the latest testing, so brace yourself for some arctic conditions coming your way. She's falling, you're gaining."

"Noted. Avoid driving in icy conditions."

"Now, on to the focus groups."

Here it comes.

"First, the good news. Viewers love you as a person. You scored off-the-charts for likeability and relatability. Your upbeat optimism resonates with people. People feel like they can trust you. That's important—and increasingly rare in the current landscape."

She's building up to a *but*. I can feel it.

"But..."

Knew it.

"When it comes to your segments..." She gives me a double thumbs down.

"Wow. One thumb wasn't enough?"

"'Fraid not, hon. It's pretty bad."

"They tune out?"

"In droves."

"Okay. Um. Wow. I actually repel people enough to get them to turn off their TVs or watch something—anything—else but me."

"*You* don't repel people. A small, but crucial, detail I want you to remember. This isn't personal. It's about the content."

"But *I* create the content, so it is very much personal."

"I've been in this game for over twenty years, Ev. Trust me. If it were personal, we wouldn't be having this conversation. You'd be at your desk packing your belongings into a box."

"Really?"

"Really."

We've reached the wall of windows overlooking the parking lot. I smile at Daisy. She's my car, and I refuse to apologize for giving her a name because naming inanimate objects is totally a thing more people should do.

And if anyone has a problem with it, they can take it up with Pop-Up Pete, my toaster. I should warn you, though—you don't want to mess with him. Pop-Up is currently embroiled in a long-standing feud with Microwave Mike, and it isn't going well. Pop-Up eviscerates the poor guy every day, reducing him to toast. *Ba-da-boom.*

My eyes shift to Margo. "Can we walk and not talk for a moment? I need a moment to process."

"Of course, hon."

Margo takes her phone out as we swing back in the

direction we came from. My thoughts drift back to something Fraser brought up over dinner at Levi's last week.

I didn't always want a career in journalism. For a while, I was seriously contemplating teaching.

Well, actually, my *real* childhood dream was to coach a pro hockey team, but that dream is about as likely to happen as growing up and becoming Taylor Swift.

What finally tipped me over the edge to choose journalism was thinking I could reach more people this way than I could in a classroom.

Guess I misjudged that.

And...I thought becoming a reporter would make Mom happy.

I misjudged that one, too.

She's got a contact in Washington and has been on my case for me to leave *The Morning Buzz* to pursue more hard-hitting stories. What she doesn't understand is that I don't have that drive, the ruthless ambition you need to succeed in such a cut-throat environment. That's not how I'm wired.

Sure, I can be weirdly—some might even say obsessively—competitive and passionate about certain things––like hockey and beating my brother in chili dog-eating contests––but I don't have that same sort of energy when it comes to my reporting career.

And I never wanted my job to take me away from the place I love, the place where I grew up. I moved back to Comfort Bay after college because I couldn't imagine living anywhere else. Some people might view returning to their small, quirky hometown as a failure, but it's not for me.

I'm a small-town girl through and through, and Comfort Bay is a very special small town.

It's nestled right on the ocean, so it's got a laid-back coastal vibe. The world-class marina attracts plenty of impressive yachts, making it a logical headquarters for Fraser's Dad's family business.

Main Street is like something straight out of a Hallmark movie set, with brick-paved sidewalks, an array of charming boutiques, a cozy bookstore, a florist, and a quaint diner, run by a guy we call Bear because a) no one knows his real name, and b) his main forms of communication involve pointing, grunting, and the occasional monosyllabic word.

We're three hours north of LA, which means we avoid getting swamped with tourists on the weekends and holidays, but we're close enough to attract some mega-rich or mega-reclusive—or both—Angelinos. Rumor has it there's a two-time Oscar-winning A-lister living in the hills.

The artistic community here is thriving, we're close to the mountains—and some great hiking trails in the national parks—there's some incredible wine country farther inland, and the weather is decent for most of the year.

Why would I want to live anywhere else?

But most of all, my friends are here—Hannah, Beth, and Summer. Collectively, we're known as the Fast-Talking Four, for reasons which become evident to anyone who spends more than thirty seconds in our company. Those girls mean the world to me.

"You need more no-talking time, hon?"

I need a few more weeks of no-talking time, but I've kept her waiting long enough.

"I'm fine. Let's discuss my numbers. I'm tanking. People would rather read their phone's terms of service than watch me. But it's not personal. I know, I know. So...what next?"

We wait until Delta from accounting passes us, then Margo says, "The network execs have you on their watch list."

"I'm assuming that's as ominous as it sounds?"

"Pretty much. You've got their attention, but in a bad way.

They'll be looking at your next numbers very closely, and, well..." She blows out a breath. "I'm afraid if there isn't a marked improvement over the next few months, we could be having this conversation at your desk while I help you pack your stuff."

My head drops. "Got it."

"You need a big story, Ev. Unfortunately, the last huge story you were involved with had you in the main role."

"I remember."

Oh, I remember all right.

It feels like every single media outlet in the world picked up on my very public, very humiliating dumping.

It even boosted *The Morning Buzz* ratings for a few weeks when I returned from my month-long off-air hiatus. People were actually tuning in just to watch my segments.

But then, like all viral fame, the interest and attention dissipated as quickly as it had come. People moved on to the next thing, and my numbers dropped again.

Margo stops by a wall of empty cubicles and leans against the partition. "I heard that nitwit ex of yours is getting married."

"He is."

"When?"

"Next month."

She cocks a brow. "And you know this information how?"

"Your honor, the prosecution is leading the witness."

Margo lifts her hands and concedes, "Okay. So I may have heard some rumblings around the office that you'll be attending. But you know me, I like to fact check thoroughly. Are you really going?"

"I really am."

"Alone?"

"Uh..."

"You have a date!" Margo raises her fists. "Fantastic. Go, you. Please tell me he's an incredibly hot, panty-melting date."

"I have a date." I look around to make sure no one's within hearing range. "But I refuse to utter the words *panty-melting*... Apart from just now when I said them only to point out that I will never be saying them ever again."

Margo laughs. "You're one of a kind, Evie. Who is he?"

"You don't know him."

"Try me. What's his name?"

"He's a friend. Well, he's my brother's friend, actually. We were neighbors growing up. It's a bit...complicated."

"His name, Evelyn." She persists in a tone that tells me she's not going to let this go anytime soon.

I cough into my hand. "*Fraserrademacher*,"

"Sorry. I didn't catch that."

Sighing, I repeat, "Fraser Rademacher."

"Why does that name ring a bell? Is he a singer?"

We resume walking.

"No."

"Is he the actor in that series, the one who won an Emmy? He had a fling with his co-star. That actress I can't stand. You know, the one with the bony Ozempic shoulders."

"He's not an actor. Nor does he date bony-shouldered actresses."

Ballerinas, gymnasts, and yoga-instructors-turned-influencers are more Fraser's style, if his dating history is anything to go by.

"Is he—"

"He's a pro hockey player," I cut in, putting an end to what could easily be another five minutes of relentless questioning.

Margo jumps out in front of me and grabs me by the shoulders, her eyes dancing with excitement. "Are you joking? Is this a joke? I need to know right this very second if this is a joke, because if you're just toying with me, I will be seriously mad about this. I may even fire you on the spot."

"It's not a joke."

Keeping one hand firmly braced on my shoulder, her other hand slides into her back pocket. She produces her phone and furiously taps away, running a Google search on Fraser, I assume.

"It's Fraser with an *s*," I supply.

Her mouth falls open, and she brings the screen to within an inch of her face.

"This him?"

She spins the phone around.

There's a full-screen image of a shirtless Fraser and his former girlfriend—Tori, the infamous yoga-instructor-turned-fitness-influencer—taken on a yacht during their sailing trip in the Mediterranean last summer.

In the photos, Fraser's dark hair is wet, his skin is golden and glistening, and his impressive physique of sculpted muscles and chiseled contours is on fine display.

Full display, I mean.

And before anyone accuses me of stalking, I only knew his whereabouts because I follow all of my favorite hockey players on social media.

Except…this wasn't posted on Fraser's Instagram. Because Fraser doesn't have an Instagram account.

But Tori, his now-ex, does.

And yeah, okay, it may have been *sliiightly* stalkerish of me since I don't usually follow players' girlfriends on social media.

I peel my eyes off the screen. "That's him."

"This is perfect!"

Margo's enthusiasm draws the gaze of a few people, so we retreat to the more sparsely populated side of the office again.

"I was hoping your date would be a solid six. Maybe a seven," she continues. "But this guy is...is..."

"More than a seven?"

"Yes." Margo laughs. "Definitely more than a seven. Evelyn, this is your chance to come out with a massive story and reverse your numbers."

"Whoa, whoa, whoa. What are you talking about? What story?"

"A story about you and your wedding date. Hello. This has all the ingredients you Americans love. Redemption. Revenge. And the sweet girl rocking up to her ex's wedding with a hot hockey player."

"I can't do a story about Fraser."

"Why not?"

"He doesn't do press."

"He's an athlete. Surely he does interviews?"

I shake my head. "Nope. He avoids the media like the plague."

"What about this photo I just pulled up? Doesn't exactly scream *avoiding the media* if he's posting images of himself strutting around like some Greek god come to life in the form of a hockey star."

"He didn't post that photo. His ex did."

I have a feeling that could be why things ended between them. She craves the spotlight, he detests it with a passion.

"And you know this, how?"

Uhhh. "Because I'm a reporter," I shoot back. "It's my job to know...things. Fraser is the most private, publicity-shy person I know. Trust me. He won't agree to a sit-down interview."

"See, you say that, but all I'm hearing is that in addition to being off-the-charts good-looking, he's mysterious and possibly hiding something. Two key ingredients of an incredible story-in-the-making." Margo turns her attention back to her phone. "That is one *obscenely* attractive man. Those cheekbones. Are they even real?"

"They're real. So are the eyelashes and the lips, in case you're wondering."

She studies the screen intently for a few more moments before pulling her gaze to me. "I finally get why hockey is so big in romance."

"It is?"

"Have you been to a bookstore lately?"

"Yeah. One of my friends, Beth, runs The Cozy Corner bookstore in Comfort Bay."

"Oh, I've been there. I love that place. Have you spent any time in the romance section?"

"Not really. I only really pop in for a chat or to drag her out to get some food with me."

"Well, have a look next time you're there. You'll see what I mean. Sports romance, particularly hockey romance, is huge at the moment. For the longest time I didn't understand why." She drops her gaze again. "But I do now."

"Can you please stop checking him out?"

She lifts her head, a smile teasing her lips. "Oh. So it's like that."

"Like what?"

"You like him?"

"Of course I like him. I've known him for years. He and my brother are basically like brothers, even if they are nothing alike. It's odd. But I find most male friendships slightly weird, don't you?"

Margo smiles at my rambling. "No. I mean you *like him* like him."

I roll my eyes. "Fact check says *not true*."

"Uh-huh." She tucks her phone away. Her smile stays,

though. "This could be huge, hon. And if he's as media-shy as you say he is, that's even better. You'll have an exclusive."

"I won't have an exclusive because I'm not doing the story. I can't. Fraser would never agree to it."

I don't even have to ask him to know this is a non-starter. Plus, I already feel like it's a huge imposition having him come to the wedding with me.

Asking him *this* would be too much.

He's just being a decent guy doing a nice thing by stepping up and helping his best friend's sister out of a jam.

But then...why can't I get what he said at dinner out of my head?

I will do everything I can to be the best date you've ever had.

There was a sincerity in his voice, a determined glint in his intense eyes, and a protectiveness in the way he held my hand that felt nice and confusing at the same time.

Nice because I can't remember the last time a guy has ever vowed to be my best date—probably because it's never happened. I don't seem to attract *best date vowing* guys, I'm more of a magnet for *let's dump Evie one year in* guys.

And it's confusing because, well, it's Fraser. He's a terrific guy, but let's be real here: He's doing Levi a solid.

Nothing else. Nothing more.

Although...if he is simply doing this as a favor to Levi, why didn't he say something practical like, *When is the wedding?* or *Would you like me to punch Bryce in the face before or after the ceremony?*

I may not read hockey romances, but even I know that what he said was a totally swoony, romance-novel-worthy thing.

Or am I reading too much into it?

Margo's phone buzzes. "I have to take this. But listen, hon. I want you to succeed. I believe in the stories you're telling. But this is no joke. If your numbers don't improve significantly, your head will be one of the first on the chopping block."

"Thanks for the gross visual."

"I don't want it to come to that. Believe me. But you're about to take a smoking-hot hockey player, who I'm guessing hordes of women are dying to know more about, to your ex's wedding, the same ex who dumped you in a now-infamous viral video. That's a story right there. A big one. Just think about it, okay?"

"Leave it with me."

Margo takes the call, and I head back to my desk.

Via the snack station.

Where I swipe a pack of walnuts.

And by *pack of walnuts* I mean a chocolate bar because I have feelings that need to be eaten.

Five minutes later, I'm sitting in a toilet stall with my laptop open, munching on a Hershey's Cookies and Creme Bar, re-watching the single most humiliating moment of my life, which happened two hundred and fifty-three days ago. Not that I'm counting or anything.

The video starts with Mark Merril, the anchor of the show, throwing to me. "So, Evie, we hear it's your birthday today."

We were doing a live in-studio segment. I knew the birthday bit was coming. It had been discussed in the pre-show meeting. I thought they'd maybe wheel out a cake or sing a horribly off-key rendition of "Happy Birthday."

I had no idea they'd invited Bryce to the studio.

The second I saw him, I knew what was about to happen.

Ha. I *thought* I knew.

He's going to propose.

How could I have been that naive?

I was so giddy with excitement, I didn't even notice he was holding a colorful bouquet of chrysanthemums.

The one and only flower I'm allergic to.

Mark introduces Bryce who gives me the flowers before answering a few softball questions. I stifle a sneeze and hold the flowers away from me. If I wasn't trembling with nerves about my upcoming proposal, I would have paid more attention to not letting the flowers make contact with my skin.

But I was nervous. A jittery tension thrummed through me, and I was focused on trying not to show it.

Or sneeze.

Because I was on live TV.

The segment continues on my laptop.

Bryce turns to me. That gives me a chance to drop the flowers and place my hands in his.

"Evie, our one-year anniversary is next month..."

Actually, it's next week but this is a big moment. An easy mistake to make in the circumstances. He's probably nervous, too. His first time on live TV, and all that.

He starts talking about all the wonderful times we've had together.

Okay, this is it. He'll be dropping to his knee any minute now.

"I've been giving this a lot of thought..."

Yep, any second now...

"You're an incredible person, Evie. One of the best people I've ever met..."

Okay. Late knee-to-floor launch. That's okay. No need to panic. He's probably overwhelmed by the whole situation—the studio lights are ridiculously bright for anyone not used to them—and has forgotten to do the knee drop. That's okay. A standing proposal it is, then.

He lets go of my hands.

He's getting the ring. HE'S GETTING THE RING!

"...but this isn't working."

Gasps fill the air.

I turn in shock to Mark, who is doing a double take. My hands fly to cover my mouth, and I inhale sharply.

"I think we should break up."

Think *that* was the moment of peak humiliation?

Nuh-uh.

Stay tuned, because it's coming up...right now.

As I breathe into my hands, my mind spinning in disbelief, the flower residue I have on my fingers filters into my nose.

I sneeze.

Uh-oh.

Once.

Twice.

I drop my hands.

Somehow, through the haze of shock, my brain snaps into gear, warning me to get my chrysanthemum-stained fingers away from my breathing passage.

But it's too late.

The damage is done.

And that's how, right after getting dumped on live TV, I fall into an unstoppable sneezing fit.

I can't bring my hands to cover my face because that would only make it worse.

I've got nowhere to hide because I'm in a studio with three cameras pointed directly at me.

All I can do is stand there, face uncovered, with the studio lights beaming down on me, open-mouth horror-sneezing over and over and over again.

No wonder it went viral.

It was the most memeable, GIFable, instantly shareable trainwreck thirteen seconds of live TV since that actor from *Ted Lasso* forgot his own name in a late-night interview and inexplicably jumped up and started doing some Irish folk dancing.

The story blew up.

Meet the sneezy breakup girl everyone's talking about

Have you seen the sneezing breakup sensation who's all over the internet?

There's something sneezy about Evie

And that's how #BreakupSneezeGirl was born.

I snap the laptop shut and get up.

A sickly feeling skitters in my belly as I pace.

Well, try to pace.

I'm in a toilet cubicle, so it's more like I take two steps, spin on my heel, take two steps, and repeat.

I feel horrible.

And a little dizzy.

And I am so over feeling horrible about this. My relationship with Bryce wasn't exactly healthy. There were a bunch of red flags I was ignoring. Was I excited about getting married to him, or by the prospect of the proposal?

It was the latter. Definitely the latter.

"What am I doing here?" I mutter to myself. "This isn't healthy. I have to let this go."

"Everything okay in there?"

I let out a scream.

I'd been so in my head rewatching that stupid video, I didn't hear anyone come in. "I'm fine," I reply to my cubicle neighbor.

"I just heard something about not being healthy and needing to let it go, and since we are in a toilet, I thought you might be a little backed up."

Physically, no.

But emotionally? Quite likely.

"I'm all good." I gather up my stuff, vacate the stall, and make a beeline for the door. "Thanks for your concern, though," I call over my shoulder.

By the time I make it back to my desk, I've made a few decisions.

One, no more talking to myself in toilet stalls. That is officially banned.

Two, I'm done with watching that video and being stuck in that moment.

It happened.

It's done.

I *need* to move on.

That can't be something I just say anymore. It needs to be something I *do*.

And three, I'm not bringing up the story idea with Fraser.

I can't. It's a total non-starter.

My mind is made up.

Despite the ratings juggernaut I know it would be.

Fraser has good reasons to despise the media as much as he does. They invaded his life once. He never wants to go through that again.

I get it.

I respect it.

I'd never put him in that position because I know how much he'd hate it.

Which means...

I'll just have to find some other way to increase my numbers and save my job.

4

Fraser

The clock ticks down, deep in the third.

The scores are tied at two apiece.

It's the third game in the preseason. We lost the first two, unable to shake whatever funk we got into last season.

But tonight's game is different.

Despite the locked score, this is the best we've played in a long time.

It's the best *I've* played in a long time, too.

One of the two goals was mine.

We need this win.

Even though the preseason scoreboard doesn't count toward the main season, that doesn't mean these exhibition games don't matter.

They do.

Coaches are keenly eyeing all the players to see who's strong, who's weak, and weighing up trade possibilities. I've played for the LA Swifts my entire pro career. Three years. It's my hometown team. I don't want to get traded out.

My back is drenched with sweat. With less than a minute remaining, we line up for the faceoff. Slater passes to Donovan, who sends the puck to me. The star forward. In theory, at least.

My performance hasn't been that stellar of late.

Until tonight.

Focus, Rademacher. You got this.

I weave through the defense, faking out two opposition players and drawing the goalie out of position.

Just as I'm about to be cornered by a third defender, I fire off a powerful wrist shot at the goal. The same wrist shot I've been working on during the offseason. The same wrist shot Evie pointed out I needed to work on.

Twenty thousand people in the stadium hold their breath.

I hold my breath.

The puck sails over the goalie's glove, sneaks in under the crossbar, and hits the back of the net. The goal light flashes, and the fans go wild, leaping to their feet, cheering and clapping.

Relief swamps through me as my teammates converge from all sides, burying me under a wall of hugs and back slaps.

The Suns regroup for one last attempt to equalize in the remaining seconds, but our defense holds strong. The final buzzer sounds, and the arena erupts in a deafening roar.

Through all the elation and the noise, all the pressure and doubt that had been smothering me for months finally shifts.

At least temporarily.

I scored twice, so I should be safe from getting traded.

For now.

Should be enough to get the media off my back, too. They've been having a field day with story after story about my form going south since Tori and I broke up.

I can't even look at a woman now without someone snapping a photo, posting it on social media, and beginning a relentless campaign to get me to bring her to the game to end my bad luck streak.

Which only ends up drawing more women who *want* the attention. It won't work because after dating Tori, I am done with publicity-seeking, fame-hungry women.

It doesn't mesh with who I am and the type of life I want to share with someone. I value privacy, not likes on posts of what should be private moments—like on a vacation. I still fume when I think about all the photos Tori uploaded from our time in the Med last year. What was she thinking?

But I don't want to stew over what happened in the past, I want to savor the win. I take a victory lap with the team, acknowledging the loyal fans who came out to support us.

As always, I bypass the media contingent and head straight for the locker room to cool down, shower, and change.

"You comin' to celebrate?" my teammate Culver asks, joining me by my locker, where I'm packing up my gear after a shower. "Everyone's headin' out for food and drinks."

"Can't. I'm heading home tonight. Got a red eye to catch in..." I glance at my watch. "Whoa. Soon. I need to get going."

"When's the wedding?"

The wedding of the guy who dumped Evie so brutally. So publicly.

Part of me can't believe she wants to go. The other part of me tells me to shut up, mind my own business, and do the one thing I said I'd do.

Be the best date she's ever had.

"Tomorrow."

Culver drops his gym bag onto the floor and leans his back against the wall of lockers. "Normally, I'd guilt you about not coming out with us, but look, I get it."

"Get what?"

He angles his face toward me. "Dude. Come on. You really think I'm that blind?"

"Blind to what? You're not making any sense." I hastily toss the rest of my stuff into my gym bag. "Just spit it out, man. I've got a flight to catch."

"Fine. I'll make this nice and simple for you."

He pushes off the lockers and lifts his right index finger into the air. "You."

He lifts his left index finger. "Evie."

He smooshes his fingers together. "Clear enough for ya?"

I close my locker and stare at the floor. All these years, no one's suspected anything.

Or so I thought.

My eyes remain glued to the ground. "How long have you known?"

"Well, let's see. We both joined the team three years ago..."

"All this time? Seriously?" I groan. "I thought I've been doing a good job hiding it."

"You have been. I don't think anyone else has picked up on it. But I'm your hockey bro. I notice things. And you have tells."

"What kind of tells?"

He points at what I'm dangling between my fingers. "Like that."

My good luck bracelet. The one I kiss three times before and after each game, no matter what.

Culver grins, lifting his chin. "She gave it to you, didn't she?"

"Well, yeah..." I cast a glance his way and smile sheepishly. "She made it for me."

"Aha. So she likes you, too."

"It's not like that. She's my best friend's—"

He clears his throat.

"She's my *other* best friend's younger sister."

Point of clarification. Levi's my non-hockey best friend, and this guy is my hockey bestie. Think guys don't get weirdly competitive about this type of stuff? Trust me. They do.

"Evie used to make bracelets in high school." I pause for a moment, curious if she still makes them today. "She probably made them for everyone. It doesn't mean anything."

At least not to her.

I glance down at the bracelet, its three leather bands braided together secured with a sturdy metal clasp. It's a little too fashionable for me, so not something I'd wear out, but I couldn't imagine being on the ice without it.

"It must mean something to you if you've still got it after all these years."

If only he knew how much.

But I don't have time to take him on a journey aboard the *Fraser Loves Evie but It's Never Gonna Happen* express.

"How are things with you and Hannah?"

Culver slow claps. "And the award for most epic deflection of the decade goes to...drum roll please...Fraser Rademacher."

Okay. So I wasn't exactly subtle, but Culver is best friends with one of Evie's closest friends, Hannah, and even though I know it is theoretically possible for a man and a woman to be *just friends*, I've always had a gut feeling there could be something more there.

"Do we really need to go over this again? For the millionth time, there is no *me and Hannah*. She's my best friend, that's all."

It's my turn to clear my throat and act like I'm all put out.

"I see what you're doing, but fine." Culver chuckles. "She's my best *female* friend. There. Happy?"

"Deliriously so," I deadpan.

"Good. Now we can get back to what we were talking about?"

"I'd rather not."

He overrides me anyway. "Have you told Evie how you feel?"

"It's not that simple, man."

He pauses for a beat, assessing me. "Judging by your closed-off body language, as well as having known you these past three seasons, I take it you're going to leave a brother hanging on that mysterious note."

"Got it in one."

"Fine. I'll drop it. But if you ever wanna talk..."

"Thanks."

"No problem. Also, before I drop it for real, you might want to think about talking to her. There's a rumor going 'round that chicks dig guys who can talk."

"That so?"

He nods, grinning like a goof.

"That's interesting because I recently heard something, too," I say.

"Oh, yeah?"

"Yeah. That only baby chickens should be called chicks, not women."

"Fair point."

I sling my bag over my shoulder. "I gotta jet."

"No worries. Have fun at the wedding tomorrow." We exchange fist bumps. "Don't do anything I wouldn't do."

Ha.

If only he knew about *that*.

Another area where Tori and I—and every other previous girlfriend I've had—were incompatible.

I kiss the bracelet three times, then slip it into the tiny compartment lining the inside of my gym bag.

As I make my way out of the locker room, my thoughts drift back to that night all those years ago when my feelings for Evie first started to change.

∼

Seven years ago, outside of Evie's bedroom...

I let out a low grunt, straining as I attempt to shove the window open, but it refuses to budge.

It's shut.

And locked.

Which is strange since Levi usually leaves it unlatched.

He's also grounded, which means he should be inside, but even though the lights are on, his bedroom is completely empty.

Why didn't he mention he was taking off when we texted earlier? I would've gladly gone with him. Anything to get away from this place.

Muffled sounds emanate from the other side of the fence that separates our house from the Freemans'. I shouldn't be here, so I retreat from the window and duck into the lilac bush outside Levi's room.

It's probably just the crew, but I doubt they're looking for me. They always sneak out behind our pool house to have a smoke, thinking we don't know what they're up to. Mom has apologized to Mrs. Freeman so many times for the cigarette butts that get flicked into her yard.

I consider my options. My *way more restricted* options now that my best friend has bailed on me.

I don't want to go back home, that's for sure. They're filming, and yuck. No way. Mom gave me an out tonight, and I intend to take full advantage.

But I'm exhausted after practice, which rules out doing anything too active.

I suppose I could call up some buddies to see if anyone wants to hang out. But that will require me driving, and how am I meant to sneak out in Dad's Range Rover without any of the crew noticing? They've got cameras everywhere.

Maybe I'll see what my younger sis Dawn's up to? If she's in a people-talking mood and not in her usual people-killing one.

My gaze travels to the golden glow spilling through the window from the room next to Levi's.

I take a few steps toward it. Levi likes to joke about how annoying Evie is, but he's totally got a soft spot for his little sister.

I reach her window and peer inside. Evie's sitting at her desk, an LA Swifts scarf dangling from her shoulders. All sorts of materials are scattered around her. She's got headphones on, and there's a hockey game playing on the TV in the background.

I lean in to get a better look and smile when I realize it's the 1997 Stanley Cup final—the last game her father ever played. Bet she's watched it a million times. It's where her love of the game comes from. Alex Freeman is one of the all-time greats. One day, I'm going to be as good as he was.

The voices from over the fence fade away, so I guess the coast is clear for me to make my way back home.

Just as I start to leave, the window opens behind me.

"Freeze! Put your hands where I can see them! I have a weapon!"

I stop, raise my hands into the air, and turn around.

Slowly.

"You call that a weapon, Mary Poppins?"

Evie lowers the bejeweled pink umbrella she's clutching and squints into the dark. "Fraser?"

"Yeah. It's me. Please put your weapon down so no one gets hurt."

"Oh, my goodness." She sags against the frame. "You scared me to death."

Some shadowy figure creeping around in the dark outside her room? Yeah, I can see that.

"Sorry. I didn't mean to frighten you."

She ditches the umbrella. "What are you doing here?"

"I came to see Levi."

"He's grounded."

"He may be grounded, but he's not in his room."
"He isn't?"
"No. But you didn't hear that from me, okay?"
"Uh, okay."
"Any idea where he might have gone?"
"No."
"Cool."
"Cool."
"So, I should probably—"
"Wanna watch the game with me?"
"Huh?"
"Or would that be weird? It's probably weird. Yeah, it's definitely weird, judging by that weird thing your face is doing and how much I'm rambling. Forget it."

"To be fair..." I move in a little closer. "Your current rambling is pretty much on par with your normal, everyday rambling."

"I'm officially rescinding my invitation."
"Rescinding. Fancy word. I'm impressed."
"Actually, I'm rescinding it for another reason."
"Being?"

"Your performance last week. You totally blew it. You missed two chances to score. And your deke? Don't even get me started on that. You need to work on your change of direction. Way too slow. You were unfocused and a step behind the whole game."

Ouch. Can't ever accuse Evelyn Freeman of not saying exactly what's on her mind.

"Your sensitivity is...non-existent."

She winces. "Sorry. I get a little carried away sometimes. I watch too many games with Dad. You should hear some of the stuff that flies out of his mouth." A small smile appears. "At least I don't swear like he does."

"Points for that." I slide my hands into my pockets. "So, where do we stand on the double rescinding of the invitation? I'm confused."

She drums her fingers lightly against her chin. "I'm rescinding the rescindingnation."

I'm ninety-five percent sure *rescindingnation* isn't a real word, but I'm not confident enough to call her out on it.

"Meaning?"

"You can come in. If you want?"

I look between Evie in the window and my house. "S'pose watching one game can't hurt."

She moves out of the way as I hoist myself into her room. Standing so close to her makes me take in details I normally don't notice about her.

Like how nice she smells, sweet without being sickly sweet, and with a hint of vanilla.

Or the light freckles playfully scattered across the bridge of her nose.

Or the mesmerizing blend of colors in her eyes, swirls of green and brown that seem to shift and change with the light.

And whoa.

It suddenly hits me.

Optics, man.

I'm a senior. She's a sophomore. My best friend's sister, no less. And I've just snuck into her bedroom in the middle of the night.

I shuffle away, creating some physical distance between us, and take a moment to eye her room. I've never really given much thought to what her room would look like, but it's very her.

Framed posters of hockey players and album covers adorn the walls. A massive vase filled with yellow roses sits atop her desk. Against one wall there's a queen-sized bed, and on the other side of the room, there's a seating area with a plush two-seater sofa, a couple of bean bags, and a large flat-screen TV mounted on the wall that's currently playing her dad's final game,

"Your room is so..."

"I know, I know. It's messy."

"I was going to say clean. Compared to Levi's."

And mine. But I leave that out.

"And it smells so..." I sniff the air.

She approaches me, a grin spreading across her face. "Not boy?"

"Yeah. That's exactly it. *Not boy*. You know, I heard that was going to be the name of the new Calvin Klein fragrance until they changed it at the last minute."

"Changed it to what?"

"Girl."

Her grin grows into a smile, and it's a really pretty smile.

Maybe a little too pretty for someone I've known since she was ten. I jam my hands into my pockets, feeling bad for noticing.

Because yeah, there's no denying it. Little Evie is growing up. She's almost sixteen. Cotillion is coming up soon. I wonder who she's going with.

Another thought I probably shouldn't be having, so I sidestep past her and wander over to the wall lined with framed posters. They're a mix of hockey players—the current crop mixed with a few from her dad's era—as well as...huh, well, what do you know?

I spin around to face her. "When Levi told me he got you into punk music, I thought he meant, like, Avril Lavigne."

She rolls her eyes, takes off the headphones from around her neck, and shoves them into my hands. "Listen to this."

I place the headphones over my ears, then rip them off almost immediately. "What on earth was that?"

"That was punk music." She lifts her chin, smiling proudly like she's just scored a victory over me.

"I think use of the term *music* is debatable. My ears hurt."

"Would you like to listen to some Avril instead?"

"Not funny."

"Then stop being a baby."

"Who are these women?" I ask, tapping the last frame on the wall.

Evie comes up and points them out one by one. "That's Dani Rylan Kearney, founder of the National Women's Hockey League. That's Kim Davis. She's just been named the Executive Vice President of Social Impact, Growth Initiatives & Legislative Affairs for the NHL. Here we have Hayley Wickenheiser, one of the most decorated female hockey players of all time. And rounding things out, this is Heidi Browning, Senior Vice President and Chief Marketing Officer of the NHL."

"Cool. You ever thought about playing?"

"Those who can, play, those who can't, yell from the sidelines, take notes on their phone, and share them with their neighbor whenever they see him."

"I've noticed. What about coaching, then? You know the ins and outs of the game better than most players."

She presses her fingertips to the glass, a wistful smile curving her lips. "How many coaches do you see here?"

"You could always be the first."

"Yeah. Because Mom would love that. No. I think I'll have to find a different career path to disappoint her." She points to the TV. "We can watch another game, if you like. I've got this one committed to memory."

She doesn't want to talk about it. That's cool. I'm not going to push. I hate it when people try to make me open up.

My eyes flick to the game. "Nah. I'm fine with it."

"Cool."

Evie settles into her desk chair, so I claim a spot on the couch, far enough away from her that should her parents walk in, they won't get the wrong idea about what's going on here.

"Whatchya making there?" I ask, pointing to her desk.

"Oh, it's nothing."

"It doesn't look like nothing to me."

"They're just bracelets." She lifts up a few of them for me to see. "I enjoy making them. It relaxes me. They're not very good or anything."

"They're nice."

"Moving on." She drops the bracelets onto her desk and swivels in her chair to face me. "How did you escape?"

"Huh?"

"The whole street is clogged up with camera vans. Aren't you meant to be filming?"

"I am, but I told Mom I wasn't up for it, so we staged a fight. I got sent to my room, which gets me out of having to do anything. At least for tonight."

Evie shifts her gaze between me and the TV screen, then says, "Levi mentioned something about you not being a huge fan of the show."

"Would you like to have a TV crew in your house recording everything you and your family say and do?"

"Absolutely not. That sounds like a nightmare. Worse than that nightmare where you're giving a speech and suddenly find yourself naked. Or is the audience naked? Whatever, it doesn't matter. Public nudity is involved, which is definitely the stuff of nightmares. As is rambling, which I'm doing again. Sorry."

I swallow a grin. "Don't be. You're fine."

I've gotten used to Levi talking fast, but Evie, man, she takes fast-talking to a whole other level.

A few moments pass.

"Can I ask you something?"

"Sure," I say.

"Why is your family doing it?"

"The show, you mean?"

"Yeah."

I lean back into the sofa and hook an ankle over my knee. "Dad thinks it'll be good for his business."

Evie smirks. "Tough times in the luxury yacht industry?"

"It's the economy," I reply. "The multi, multi, multimillionaires are struggling at the moment."

Evie keeps a straight face. "They really are the silent victims."

We share a smile.

"He thinks it'll be a good exercise in branding. You know, like the Kardashians or the Hiltons."

"*That's* his benchmark?"

"Tell me about it."

"What about your mom?"

"She's going along with it because she wants to revive her acting career. The offers have dried up, and whatever does come in are usually mom roles."

"But she is, you know, of mom-age."

"Don't *ever* let her hear you say that. You won't get out alive."

"Noted."

Sometimes I think about how different Mom and Dad are. They're from two completely different worlds—Dad from old-school money and five generations of proud yacht-making,

Mom from Orange County. Her family had nothing, but she always dreamed of becoming a star.

Yet when it comes to some things—like fame, money, and power—they couldn't be any more alike.

I've also never seen two people more in love. It's a beautiful thing. Except for the constant PDAs. They're vomit-inducing. You'd think after being married for almost thirty years, they'd be over it. But nope. They're still very much into each other.

"What about your brothers? And Dawn? What do they think about doing the show?"

"Trace"—oldest brother, total Dad clone—"just goes along with whatever Dad wants."

"Right."

Dad's grooming him to follow in his footsteps and take over the family business someday. I have no issue with that. My problem is that Trace needs to stand up to Dad once in a while. He needs to be his own person outside of who Dad wants him to be.

"Meanwhile Clayton"—second oldest, human equivalent of a fireworks display—"he's loving the attention. Lapping it up like there's no tomorrow. Mom's always been disappointed that none of her kids have any acting talent."

"But Clayton does?"

"Not actual acting talent, but it's good enough for reality TV. He loves the spotlight. Thrives in it. Almost as much as Mom."

"I thought he was into woodwork?"

"He is. But being famous versus being a carpenter? Not much of a contest. It also sucks that he and Trace have had to move back home to film the show."

"They have? Why?"

"So it looks like we all live together and are one big happy family, even though they're both in their twenties. I thought I'd finally gotten rid of them."

Evie smiles. "And what about Dawn?"

"Ah. You've saved my angsty, guarded little sister for last, I see."

Evie opens her mouth as if to say something but decides against it at the last minute.

"What were you about to say?"

She smiles bashfully, then tucks a loose strand of hair behind her ear. "I was going to say it reminds me of someone else I know."

Me. She means me.

Because yeah, I'm not exactly renowned for my openness. This conversation with Evie is the most I've opened up to someone—apart from Levi—um...ever, actually.

Why is talking to her so easy?

"Guess Dawn gets that from me," I continue. "But she overtakes me in the *angry at the whole world* department. I'm at a moderate five, she's at eleven...million."

"I've...I've tried to reach out to her."

I know she has. Multiple times. "Don't take it personally. Humans are social creatures who are wired for connection with others, and Dawn isn't human."

Evie laughs, then covers her mouth like she shouldn't have found that funny. "You're terrible."

"Hey. I love my sister to pieces. That doesn't mean I can't point out her...I won't say faults. What's a better word?"

"Idiosyncrasies?"

"Yeah. Her dislike of human interaction being one of them."

"Let her know if she ever wants to hang out or anything, I'm here."

"I will." I uncross my legs. "Listen, it's getting late. I should probably get going."

Evie gets up. "Of course. Thanks for scaring the life out of me."

I head toward the window. "You made me listen to punk music, so I think we both feared for our lives tonight."

She smiles. Which makes her eyes sparkle. Which makes my stomach flutter in a funny way.

"Thanks for the chat," I say, climbing into the window.

"No problem. You know..."

I turn my head back to her.

"If you ever want to talk...and Levi's not here...and the world is burning down and my room is the only safe haven on the entire planet, you can...come here. And we can, like, watch a game. Or whatever."

She holds my gaze—me, lodged in her window, her, standing there, rubbing her arm and looking uncharacteristically unsure of herself.

"Sure." I smile. "Thanks for the chat, Evie."

She gives a little wave. "Anytime, Fraser."

5

Evie

"What are you doing in there, Evelyn?" The irritation in Mom's voice is evident as she raps on the bathroom door. "You're taking longer than Levi does to get ready, for Pete's sake."

"Who's Pete?" I call back, smiling as I picture her annoyed face, while I continue fixing my hair into an updo.

"That's not funny. Hurry up, please. Fraser will be arriving any minute now."

Ugh. Why did I agree to get ready for the wedding here?

Mom brought it up over dinner last week, slipping it into the conversation so casually that it seamlessly evaded the usual internal defensive line I activate whenever I'm in Mom's presence. These imaginary guys in my head have one job and one job only: to protect me from my mother's incoming barbs.

Or at the very least, warn me they're coming to give me time to plan a counteroffensive.

Clearly, they took a break sometime between mains and dessert, so I was caught off guard. I found myself nodding and the words, "Sure, I'd love to," flying out of my mouth.

So here I am.

In my parent's house.

In my old bathroom.

Getting ready to go to my ex's wedding.

With Fraser as my date.

"I'll be right out, Mom."

I ignore her muffled huff of annoyance on the other side of the door, finish adjusting my hair, and eye the dress I agonized over for months.

Choosing it proved tricky because while I want to look good, at the same time, I don't want to overshadow the bride. As much as I'm looking forward to sticking it to Bryce, this is

Mercedes's big day, too. She's done nothing to deserve an ex-girlfriend swanning in and stealing the attention that very much belongs to her today.

So I hunted for a dress that didn't scream *center of the universe*, but whispered *elegance and grace* and *shove this where the sun don't shine, Bryce*.

Tough assignment.

I finally settled on a one-shoulder chiffon lavender midi dress with an asymmetrical neckline.

Occasion appropriate. Classic. Fashionable. And not too showy.

I open the door and step out into my old bedroom.

Mom's inspecting the posters on my wall. On her nose-scrunching disapproval scale, she's somewhere in the four-to-six range—she doesn't mind the hockey players, but it's evident she doesn't approve of or understand any of the album covers. She barely pays any attention to the women in the final frame.

As always, she's the epitome of elegance and sophistication, her meticulously styled hair coiffed to perfection. She's smart with her makeup, always opting for neutral tones that enhance her features. And even when she goes for a casual, around-the-house look, she remains more polished than I could ever hope to be, dressed in a pastel-blue silk blouse with a cashmere cardigan draped over her shoulders, crisply tailored navy-blue trousers, and stylish leather flats.

I clear my throat.

She spins around, and her face lights up. "Oh my, Evelyn. You look beautiful."

"Wow. A compliment."

I regret it the second the words fly out of my mouth.

Hello, defensemen? Where are you?

Granted, I hadn't run any drills with them to be on the lookout for praise, but still, twenty-three years as Meredith Freeman's daughter has taught me we need to be prepared for anything.

"Don't sound so surprised," Mom says, walking over to me, her eyes raking over every detail. "I compliment you all the time."

When? I want to scream but decide against it. I don't want to get into a fight with Mom before the wedding. I'm already on edge as it is.

Ah, we made a logical decision. Thanks, defensemen. Teamwork makes the dream work.

"But not too beautiful, right?"

Mom raises an eyebrow. "Is that a trick question? You seem to be under the false impression that I don't compliment you enough, and now you want me to, what, walk it back?"

"It's not a trick question, Mom. I just don't want to pull the focus away from Mercedes, you know? It's her big day, not mine."

Mom rolls her eyes and *tsks*. "What sort of a name is Mercedes, anyway? Who names their child after a car?"

"You don't like it?" I direct a warm smile at her. "I was thinking of Silverado for a boy, Camry for a girl."

"Does that mean I can expect grandchildren sometime this century?"

Ouch. Well played, Mom. Well played.

Side note: Camry for a girl. It grows on you. Give it a few.

"You do realize I'm the youngest of the four children you birthed. Do you badger them as much as you badger me?"

"I don't badger anyone, Evelyn," Mom says, picking at one of the pleats on my dress. "And for the record, you look just the right level of beautiful."

The doorbell rings.

"I'll get it," Dad yells out.

"And I'm sure Fraser will agree with me." Mom smiles, and it's a little too smiley for my liking. "He's become quite the strapping young man, hasn't he?"

"Ah, yeah, about that."

I haven't gotten around to explaining to her that Levi roped Fraser into going with me, and that's all this is—him doing me a favor. Mom is under the impression that this is an actual date.

After having failed to move to Washington to become 'a real reporter,' in second place on Mom's list of *things I wish Evie did with her life* is marrying well.

And by *marrying well*, she means marrying into money.

And you can't marry any more *well* than the Rademachers. They're one of the wealthiest families in Comfort Bay, which is really saying something, given the numbers of Lexuses and Cadillacs you see driving around town.

"Listen, Mom—"

There's a knock on the bedroom door.

"Ah. That'll be him."

She gives me a final once-over.

I'd say *approving final once-over*, but I don't have much practice with those words in relation to Mom.

"I'll leave you to it."

She flashes another too-smiley smile before spinning on her heel to open the door.

"Fraser," she greets enthusiastically. "How wonderful to see you."

"It's great to see you, too, Mrs. Freeman."

She gives him two air kisses, whispers something into his ear I can't hear, and then she's gone.

And Fraser is here.

In my bedroom.

Entering through the door and not the window, for a change.

He steps in, his eyes darting around the space, and I wonder if he's having the same sense of nostalgia I am.

Probably not.

Why would he?

Absolutely nothing ever happened between us. He just needed a place to escape filming and vent, and my bedroom was that place.

The bedroom. Not me.

Important distinction.

His intense gaze rolls around to me. "Wow, Evie. You look...breathtaking."

"Don't lie. You prefer the hockey jersey and Ugg Boots, don't you? You can admit it. I won't be offended."

"I'm so relieved," he says, wiping imaginary sweat off his brow. "Any chance you can get changed? It's going to be torture for me, looking at you in that dress all day."

"You're not the only one who's going to suffer. Look at you in that suit."

Yes.

Can we please take a minute and *look at him* in that deep-navy-blue classically tailored suit? How it accentuates his broad shoulders and muscular physique? The crisp white dress shirt underneath contrasts perfectly with the dark hue of the suit, and the electric-blue tie brings out his summer-sky blue eyes.

His hair, usually tousled and damp under his helmet during games, is styled neatly. He's clean-shaven, which makes the scar on his cheek more prominent.

And he's got a confident ease about him, like he's dropped the guarded, brooding persona he adopts on the ice and is letting his natural charisma shine through.

Like this is who he really is. The person he let me see all those years ago.

But that's in the past now.

Today, he's simply in *handsome revenge-date man-candy* mode, just like he promised he'd be.

He produces something from behind his back.

Flowers.

Yellow roses, to be precise.

Again.

Which is twice more than Bryce ever did. Not that I'm keeping score.

"I seem to have developed this bad habit of buying flowers for you."

"You're a monster. Where can I report you?"

He lets out a light chuckle. "Is your vase in the same spot?"

"Uh, I assume so."

Mom has kept my room pretty much how I left it when I went away to college.

Fraser strides over to my desk, crouches down, and reaches behind it. Smiling, he produces the vase and lifts it onto the desk, setting the flowers down beside it.

"I'm impressed," I say.

"By the flowers?"

"No. That you remember where the vase is stored."

He slides one hand into his pants pocket. "I have a knack for remembering random details."

"I'm tucking that little nugget away for trivia night."

He observes me with an amused warmth, then knocks on my desk. "I also remember you sitting here making your bracelets. Do you still do that?"

"Not really. I didn't have time in college. I took it back up after the breakup video went viral and I went into hiding, thinking it would relax me like it used to."

"Did it?"

"No. It doesn't seem to have the same effect anymore."

"Why?"

"No reason."

Big reasons. But I can't exactly tell him that it's his fault.

One, that would sound illogical.

Because two, it is illogical.

But three, that doesn't make it any less true.

After Fraser failed to acknowledge the bracelet I made him —*and* disappeared the very next day without saying goodbye— let's just say, it put me off bracelet making altogether.

In my head, it had become intertwined with his late-night drop-ins, and I was trying desperately to put that behind me. So I packed up all the beads, leather cording, clasps, jumping rings, and other bits and pieces I'd amassed and threw them all away.

"Hmm." He wanders over to the wall. "Remember that time you committed violence against me?"

"Excuse me?"

He spins around, a smile curling his lips. "You made me listen to punk music."

"That's right. I'd forgotten your taste in music is as poor as your tolerance for spicy food. Unless that's changed in the last seven years?"

"'Fraid not," he says. "You would still easily beat me in a chili eating contest."

"That's purely speculative." I place my hands on my hips. "There's only one way to find out if it's actually true."

"Ha. Not happening." He chuckles. "Are you ready to go?"

"I am. I just need to put on my shoes and find my purse."

Spotting my purse on the bed, he goes over to collect it. I slide on a heel but almost topple over as I put on the other one.

Fraser magically appears and extends his hand.

I take it gladly, slipping my fingers into his large palm to steady myself. "Thank you."

"You know..." He leans in, his voice getting low, almost husky. "I get that the dress has to stay, but it's not too late for the Ugg Boots."

I slap him away with a giggle. "I wish. No. I've officially banned myself from wearing them outside my apartment. I've also renamed them to *ugh* boots. Remember that, because if it catches on, I want all the credit."

He reaches out, lightly grazing my cheek with the backs of his fingers. "You're an intriguing woman, Evelyn Freeman."

My heart stutters at the unexpected closeness, at the unexpected touch, at the unexpectedly sultry smile he's aiming my way.

Perfect fake date material, I remind myself. *That's all.*

"Thanks again for doing this," I tell him as we make our way out.

"No need to thank me," he says. "I've been looking forward to this for a long time."

∽

Well, this is a fizzer.

"You okay, Evie? Can I get you something else to drink?"

I throw a glance at the four barely-touched glasses on the table in front of me. Fraser, in total perfect-date mode, got me every one of those drinks, but nothing is hitting the spot.

I feel restless.

And agitated.

And like I'm the world's biggest fool.

Again.

No amount of alcohol can fix that.

"No. I'm fine. Thank you."

"All right." Fraser bumps his foot gently against mine under the table. "We'll resume sitting here in stone-cold silence thinking about ways we can plot our revenge on jerkface that don't see us getting twenty-five to life behind bars. Oops." He lifts his fingers to his lips. "Did I say that out loud?"

That manages to draw a tiny smile out of me. "For the record, that's not what I'm doing."

"What sort of name is *Bryce* anyway?" he continues. "Do you think he was actually meant to be called Bruce, but someone at the hospital accidentally typed *y* instead of *u*?"

I bring my napkin to my lips to hide my growing smile. "Stop it."

Fraser stops, his expression turning serious. "Well, what is it, Evie? You haven't been yourself all day. Tell me what's wrong."

"How do you know something's wrong?"

He takes a sip of his whiskey. "Because I've got eyes."

Great. I'm that obvious.

I thought I'd been doing a good job concealing whatever weird funk I fell into the moment we got here.

I wished the bride and groom all the best, and, surprisingly, it wasn't even that awkward.

I mingled with the other guests who, in all honesty, were more interested in talking to Fraser and taking a selfie with him than they were in me.

I've been making pleasant conversation with the people at our table, listening and nodding politely as we somehow veered to the topic of foot health and Mr. Mariano's horrifying story about how he names his corns.

The only thing I haven't done is take Fraser up on his offers to dance.

Yes, *offers*.

Plural.

He's asked seven times, which I'm sure he's only doing to fulfill his date obligation and make it look like we're a couple, as opposed to what we really are—a pity date called in as a favor by his best friend to help said best friend's loser sister out of a jam.

Besides, I'm a terrible dancer. The last thing I need is someone recording me and earning myself a second viral moment.

Move over, Breakup Sneeze Girl, and make way for Dance Floor Bambi.

I scrunch the napkin up and toss it onto the table.

So much for showing up to Bryce's wedding and sticking it to him. What was I seriously expecting would happen?

"This sucks," I mutter, lifting the champagne flute. "This really sucks."

"The ceremony was a tad on the long side," Fraser agrees, not missing a beat. "And the chicken was dry."

He's trying.

He's been trying so hard all day to be here for me.

He hasn't left my side.

He's been checking in with me and getting me drinks.

He's been great at handling all the attention coming his way when I know it's precisely one of the reasons why he avoids social situations like this.

He doesn't like peopling at the best of times, but I guess he hates disappointing his fans even more. So he's been the perfect gentleman, smiling and listening as people gave him pointers and unsolicited advice about how he can fix his game, despite last night's thrilling win.

Who do these people think they are? Me?

In short, Fraser has been nothing but wonderful.

The problem isn't him.

"I don't mean the wedding sucks," I say with a sigh. "I mean...me. Coming here. I didn't think it through properly."

"What specifically didn't you think through properly?"

I take a sip of champagne. Okay, maybe it's more of a gulp. Then I push the flute away from me. I refuse to be the ex-girlfriend who gets wasted and does something embarrassing, like topple into the wedding cake.

"I mean, I got so fixated on being here. On showing up. On proving to everyone that I wasn't the loser sneezing girl they saw online, that I never really considered what I'd do once I got here."

"You have been remarkably well-behaved."

I let out a small hiccup, the bubbles from the champagne percolating in my chest. "I never intended to cause a scene."

"You really should have disclosed that upfront. I thought I had front-row seats to a romcom situation here, where you'd interrupt the speeches or maybe get down with one of the groomsmen, engage in some wildly inappropriate dancing."

"Sorry to disappoint you."

"You haven't." He reaches across the table and pins me with a heated look. At least, I think it's a heated look. Or maybe the champagne's messing with me? "You *couldn't*."

I hold his gaze for a moment before blowing out a breath and looking at the wedding scene unfolding around us.

People are swaying on the dance floor, children scamper between tables, and everyone else is mingling and laughing and having a great time.

Everyone except for me, it seems.

And because I've been such a Debbie Downer, I'm sure Fraser isn't exactly having the time of his life, either. Bet he's regretting going along with Levi's silly idea now.

Another thing for me to feel bad about.

Great.

"Mercedes seems lovely. Bryce looks happy. But I'm just... lost. Floundering. Like I have no idea what I'm doing."

"Like me in the second half of last season?" Fraser says, injecting some humor into his voice.

"That's not funny. Also, leave the critiques of your game to the experts."

"And by *experts* you mean..."

"Me."

"Thought so."

I manage a smile, and he grins right back at me.

"I'm sorry for dragging you here and forcing you to sit through the tediously long ceremony. If it's any consolation, the fish was really chewy."

"I'll be able to sleep soundly tonight knowing that." He drags his chair closer to me, cups my hands in his, and says, "What do you say we get outta here?"

"You want to go home?"

"Who said anything about going home?"

"Where do you want to go, then?"

There's a mischievous glint in his eye. "Do you trust me?"

"Absolutely not."

"I'm taking that as a yes. Come on. Let's say goodbye to everyone and do something fun. You deserve that."

"Uh. Okay. I guess."

I mean...why not? I don't want this day to be a complete bummer. I owe it to Fraser to do something enjoyable.

As I shift to get my purse, I spot Bryce standing by himself at the bar. "Can I meet you out front?"

Fraser follows my gaze. His jaw clenches. "Want me to go with you?"

"No. It's fine. I just need a few minutes."

"Okay. I'll be outside."

Fraser stands, glares in Bryce's direction, then leaves the table.

I quickly check my makeup, then make my way over to Bryce and accidentally-on-purpose bump into him. "Hey. How dry was that chicken? Am I right? You'd think they would've forked out a bit more for proper catering—Oh, it's you. Sorry, Bryce."

"Evie." Bryce turns, then looks around. "Where's your bodyguard?"

"Restocking his weaponry."

"That guy has been giving me evil looks all day."

"No, he hasn't. That's just his face. Some people have a lazy eye. He has a mean eye."

"As I experienced so many times during our relationship, I have absolutely no idea if you're being serious or not."

Yeah. We weren't exactly compatible in the banter department.

Or the flower department.

Or, as it turns out, in the *what we want to do with our lives* department, either. I've heard that Bryce and Mercedes will be relocating to New York. So much for wanting to settle down and live a small-town life.

"Thanks for coming today. I know it couldn't have been easy for you."

"Thanks for going with peonies and not chrysanthemums, otherwise it wouldn't have been easy on anyone standing within ten feet of me."

Bryce at least has the decency to look bad. "I'm sorry about the flowers. And the, you know…"

"Humiliating breakup on live TV that went viral and forced me to go into hiding for a month?"

He exhales deeply. "Yeah. That. I honestly never meant to

hurt you. It had been building inside me for a while, and I guess it just...came out."

"It's fine."

It isn't.

It was, and will always be, a rotten thing to do to someone.

Note to all the men out there who may need to hear this—breakups should be a private thing, not an on-live-TV thing.

"I'm okay, really. Doing heaps better, and for what it's worth, I am over you."

Now *that* is unequivocally true.

We had issues in our relationship that I put up with because I was making Bryce 'put up' with something, too.

Looking back on it, I see how wrong it was of me to frame it that way. I was up-front about everything right from the beginning. He knew what he was getting into from the moment we started dating.

"I'm really, truly over you," I repeat, my gaze flicking over his shoulder. "So you can tell that bridesmaid-zilla over there that she can stop death-staring me."

Bryce turns around and gives her a discreet thumbs up to chill her out a bit.

"I know you have a million people to get to, so I won't keep you. I just wanted to say..." A tightness grips my chest. "Thank you."

"Thank you?" Bryce looks understandably shocked. "What are you thanking me for?"

In the aftermath of the story going viral, the press hounded Bryce for more information. Why did he *really* break up with me? There had to be a juicy story there, right?

"Thank you for never mentioning—"

"Ah. *That.*"

For once, he catches my drift without me having to spell it out for him.

Because believe me, while being the Breakup Sneeze Girl was bad, being the *Virgin* Breakup Sneeze Girl would have been a thousand times more mortifying.

To his credit, Bryce turned down every interview invite and kept his mouth shut until the story blew over.

"Evie, I would never..."

"I know. Deep down, you're a decent guy, Bryce. That's why I'm here. That's why I really do wish you and Mercedes all the best."

I feel lighter as I say the words, and it hits me.

This is why I needed to come today.

It wasn't to prove anything to him or anyone else, it was to help me put this whole saga behind me and finally move on.

And I have. I really have.

"Take care. Have a great life, Bryce."

"Thanks. You, too, Evie."

6

Fraser

I pace back and forth, waiting for Evie outside.

I've put my sunglasses on and am keeping my head down, hoping to keep a low profile and not get recognized right now. That's the last thing I need. I am not in the mood for any more chit-chat.

Or smiling.

Or selfies...

I'm irritated.

It bothers me that Evie's inside talking to that guy. I would never challenge her on it or stop her from doing it. She's free to talk to whomever she wants to talk to. But it doesn't mean I have to like it.

A group of people exit the venue. I hide behind some bushes, wait until they're gone, and then duck into the entry. I scan the bar searching for Evie. But the place is too crowded. I'm unable to spot her.

I step back outside and resume pacing. Throw in some grumbling under my breath for good measure.

Let's break it down.

Pros about today:

One.

Evie knocking the breath out of my lungs when I stepped into her old bedroom.

As if the memories of the time I spent there flooding back weren't enough, the way she looked...

Man. *Beyond* sensational.

Although, if I'm being honest, Evie's just as much a knockout in leggings, an old hockey jersey, and Ugg Boots.

Correction. *Ugh* boots.

But still, with her hair swept up, her shoulders exposed,

and that lavender dress hugging her body in all the right places, it took everything I had in me not to sweep her into my arms and never let her go.

Two.

Spending time with her.

I meant what I told her as we were leaving her parent's place. I've been looking forward to this day ever since Levi first brought it up. And that was over two months ago.

Because let's face it. This is it. My one and only shot at getting to spend some time alone with her.

There's never any other reason for just the two of us to hang out. I might see her occasionally after a home game if she sticks around, but Levi and a million other people are always milling about.

And I might stumble into her in town when I'm back visiting family, but that's never planned and never for longer than it takes to exchange a few pleasantries and for her to recap whatever latest feedback notes she'd emailed me.

I've had weeks to prepare myself for today and mentally compartmentalize everything in a way that makes it possible for me to enjoy spending this time with her without doing anything stupid like blurting out my feelings and turning what's already bound to be a tough day for her into a complete disaster.

Evie deserves to be with a great guy. Someone who not only treats her well—base requirement—but who also has emotional intelligence and the ability to communicate. As Tori liked to remind me during our many, many fights before we broke up, I'm a prickly, closed-off robot with the talking skills of a cactus.

There must be something wrong with me because I just can't do it. I've had a few relationships, and every time, it's the same issue.

Me.

For some reason, I don't seem to be capable of opening up to anyone.

The thing is, I know I can. I do it around Evie without even thinking about it. After spending even a few seconds in her presence, I'm all aboard the Evie Banter Bandwagon.

It's easy.

It's fun.

It's natural.

So why can't I find whatever that is and apply it when I'm with someone else?

Because I'm damaged, that's why, and I don't deserve to be with someone as great and special and funny and smart and beautiful and hockey-obsessed as Evie.

I just don't.

So yeah, one day. That's all I get with Evie. That's all I can allow myself to have.

Which is why I need to salvage what's left of it and make good on my promise.

I look toward the entry. Still no sign of her.

Okay, resume mental dissection.

Let's move on to the cons about today:

One.

Seeing her miserable.

That alone instantly wipes out the pros.

Despite putting on a brave face, Evie hasn't been herself all day, and I hate that I haven't been able to make her feel better. That was my job after all, wasn't it? And I've failed.

I may not know her reasons for coming here, but it obviously means something to her. Maybe closure? Maybe revenge? Maybe to prove something?

Whatever it is, she clearly didn't get what she needed to get out of it.

And I clearly didn't step up and fulfill the obligation I made. I told her I'd be the best date she's ever had. I've done a pretty lousy job of it so far.

Two.

Watching that smarmy jerkface getting his girl while hurting my gir—er, Evie. While hurting *Evie*.

Three. The way too long ceremony.

Four. The crappy food.

Five. The crappier band.

Six. The inane small talk. I really could have done without hearing all about Corny, Kernel, and Pop, aka Mr Mariano's corns which, for some unknown reason, he actually names. I've heard of people naming inanimate objects, but that's taking it a step too far.

I could go on listing negatives because, believe me, there are plenty more sucky things about today.

But none of those things are as bad as seeing Evie upset.

I don't want her memories of this day to only be bad ones, which is why as soon as she comes outside, Operation Un-Badify Today begins.

I turn back to the entry, and my eyes land on the vision in lavender standing there. Evie looks around. Once she spots me, she smiles, gives a wave, and hikes up her dress to make it easier to walk over my way.

I meet her in the middle. "Hey."

Studying her, I look for any signs of what she might be feeling. Is she angry? Sad? Did jerkface say something to upset her? Is it time for me to go in there and rearrange his face?

She smiles. "Hey. So, Bryce is dead. Long story. But it involves a rogue butter knife, a voice in my head daring me to do it, and another voice reminding me that you're here and that I could put you and your crazy big muscles to use helping me bury the body. I just need a shovel. Or shovels.

Plural. I don't expect you to do all the grunt work by yourself."

"I've got two shovels in my trunk for just this very thing."

"Excellent. Lead the way."

I extend my arm and clarify. "Just so you know, I'm leading us away from the scene of the crime and toward the fun activity I have in mind."

"But what about the body?"

I crack a grin. "I really shouldn't encourage you, should I?"

"You really shouldn't."

Evie wraps her slender fingers around my bicep as I usher us along a gently sloping trail that winds down to the beach. I have so many questions for her, but I hold off. She might need some time after speaking with her ex.

The important thing is that she's with me, and I am a man on a mission—make Evie happy, or die trying.

The salty air mingles with her perfume. It's a different scent from whatever she wore in high school, but that same trace of vanilla is there.

High school.

Still can't believe that was seven years ago. It feels like a lifetime.

Sometimes I wonder what would have happened if, after returning from what would be my final late-night chat with Evie, my family hadn't ambushed me in the living room.

Everything changed that night.

We had a family meeting, talked about all the options.

Then we decided.

We agreed as a family to double-down and do everything we could to protect Dawn.

To immediately cancel filming that awful reality TV show midseason.

To pull back from all interviews and press.

To never tell a single soul outside of the family what had happened, even when people made up all sorts of nasty stories about us.

Over the years, some of the rumors have filtered through to me.

Mom went to rehab. Or had a botched facelift. Or went to rehab *after* her botched facelift.

There was gossip about my brothers and me, too. That we'd gotten into trouble with the law. That there was some big cover up. That we were on drugs.

All of it is nonsense.

But the worst rumors, the ones that hurt the most, were the ones about Dad. Especially the ones about him cheating on Mom.

That man loves Mom the way I want to love my wife someday. He would never, *ever* look at another woman, much less do anything to hurt Mom.

We braced ourselves, preparing for the inevitable blowback of doing what we were about to do. And we agreed as a family that no matter how bad it got, no matter how much mud they slung at us, we'd never cave.

And we haven't.

All the years later, we've kept our mouths shut and stuck to the plan.

For Dawn.

And now, for Oakey. My favorite little dude in the world.

Evie tightens her grip on my arm as the path becomes sandier.

Needing a break from my thoughts, I take in a few deep breaths and allow myself to picture this moment but in a different scenario.

One in which we're not escaping her ex's wedding, but

instead Evie's my girl, and we're going down to the beach because it's something we both love to do.

Maybe we've got a couple of dogs—big dogs, because I'm a big dog guy—and they've raced ahead of us and are splashing as they run through the water.

Maybe we've just spent the entire weekend together. I would have made her breakfast in bed. She would have insisted we move to the kitchen since it allows me to keep producing more pancakes to feed her.

She would have dragged me to the Comfort Bay Farmers' Market, and I would have pretended to hate it.

We might have gone for a hike through Cuddle Cove Cliff at the crack of...two in the afternoon—Evie has never been a morning person.

I may have surprised her with a cozy movie night at home, complete with blankets, popcorn, and a selection of romcoms, because yes, they're secretly my favorite movies. But that stays between us, okay?

No telling Levi.

Or Culver.

Or even Evie, for that matter.

I'm not sure what her current taste in movies is, but she likes punk music, so there's a chance her taste in film could be equally questionable, and she would just love to tease me about it.

Maybe I'd have spent the entire weekend with a fluttery, nervous feeling ticking away in my belly, waiting for the right moment to get down on one knee and—

Evie loses her balance, letting out a small yelp. Her nails dig into my arm.

"Sorry," she says, looking up at me and easing her grip. "Sand and heels."

"You're fine." I'm the idiot who didn't even think it might be difficult for her to navigate the sandy path in a tight dress and heels. "I've got an idea."

"Fraser, what are you doin—*oomph*."

"There." I scoop her off her feet and carry her, bridal-style. "Better?"

For possibly the first time in her life, Evie is speechless. After a few seconds, she adjusts to being cradled in my arms, looping one arm around the back of my neck, the other pressing into my chest.

"Better," she says so softly it almost gets lost in the breeze.

Silence envelops us as I amble on, loving the way her body feels against mine, loving the feel of holding her.

Protecting her.

I suppose I could have offered to help her take her shoes off, but I like my way much better, thank you very much.

"Are you comfortable?" I ask a few moments later.

"A pillow would be nice. Maybe a blanket. Is there any way to make my seat recline some more? And I have some thoughts about the in-flight entertainment."

I can't help but grin.

How can one woman be so perfect?

"The captain has just turned on the fasten seat belt sign due to some expected turbulence," I reply, keeping a straight face. "But I'll return with everything you asked for as soon as it's safe to do so. And I can't wait to hear your thoughts about the in-flight entertainment. I trust you've been taking notes."

She throws her head back and lets out a laugh. The radius of the joyous sound stretches out around us. My heart blooms in my chest.

It's the first time she's laughed all day.

Forget hockey. I've got a new job now—making Evie laugh.

We reach the beachfront, but I imagine walking in heels on

fine sand will be a challenge, so I keep her in my arms and head closer to the water.

"As we prepare for landing, please make sure your seat belt is fastened, your seat back and tray table are stowed, and your window shades are open."

She eyes me with an amused expression. "When are you planning to put me down?"

Never.

"Once the captain turns off the fasten seat belt sign and the aircraft has come to a complete stop at the gate," I reply, totally nailing my flight attendant voice. "Until then, please remain seated."

She laughs again. "I know I joked about your crazy big muscles before, but aren't you getting tired?"

"Nope. Not at all."

Okay, so I am getting *slightly* fatigued. But why ruin the moment?

We reach firmer sand.

"I'm all out of plane talk," I announce as I carefully ease her down.

"That's okay. I'll be sure to leave a positive review on the Rademacher Airlines website, despite the criminal lack of romcoms offered."

Ah, so she *does* like them. Good to know.

"Thank you, ma'am. Your feedback helps us continuously improve our service and better meet your needs."

Laugh number three. "You're a doofus."

"Guilty."

The gentle murmur of waves brushes against the shore as the sun dips toward the horizon line, casting a warm glow of tangerine and soft pinks over the tranquil beach.

At least I think it's a tranquil beach.

As far as I'm concerned, there's no one else here apart from Evie and me.

I unbutton my jacket and set it down as a makeshift blanket on the sand. "Are you okay sitting down in that dress, or do you need some help?"

"I should be *fiiii*—"

She crashes straight into me.

"Were you about to say *fine*?" I tease, securing my arms around her back, holding her in place.

She tries to straighten, but it must be hard to rebalance in heels, so her body remains pressed against mine. And yeah, no complaints here.

She chuckles lightly. "I was."

I take hold of her arms and help her get steady on her feet. Once she is, her gaze meets mine. Wordlessly, I guide her down onto the sand, staring into her eyes the entire time.

With Evie seated, I let go. She tucks her legs to one side and scooches over.

"There's room for one more," she says, patting the jacket.

"It's fine, I can just sit on the sa—"

She flicks my calf with her purse and yanks me by my shirt sleeve. I land beside her with a heavy thud.

That's one way to get me to sit next to her.

We both stare out into the ocean for a few moments.

It's funny how something so simple, so mundane as sitting next to someone can make me feel so at peace. I've always felt good being around Evie...and it looks like I still do.

"How are you feeling about jerkface?" I eventually ask.

"Better, actually." She darts her gaze to me and smiles. "How come you don't say his name?"

"Excuse me?"

"You hardly ever refer to him by his real name."

"Who? Jerkface?" I retort. "I thought that *was* his real name.

I found it quite handy actually, how it's both his name and it captures his whole personality."

"You really don't like him, do you?"

That's putting it mildly. "Nope," I say, popping the *p*.

"Why?"

"Who breaks up with someone on live television?" I spit out, then, noticing the surprise on her face, tone it down a notch. I shake my head. "That's not a real man."

"Ah, so that's where I've been going wrong this whole time. I've been dating fake men."

"Maybe you have."

"So how would a real man break up with me?"

I turn so I'm angled toward her and lift her chin so that our eyes connect. "A real man would never break up with you in the first place, Evie. A real man would be smart enough to realize what a precious gift it is to be with you. A real man would do whatever he could to keep you happy and safe and would always keep two shovels in his car for any unexpected no-questions-asked moments that might arise."

She laughs—number four, by my count—making her hazel eyes glimmer in the late-afternoon light.

Something passes between us.

I can feel it. And I think she does, too.

Compartmentalize, man. That's the plan, remember? It's a good plan. A solid one. But a plan only works if you actually stick to it.

I need to control my feelings.

I need to lighten the mood.

I need to show her a good time...remember? That's what I promised, and it's time to deliver.

"You know," I begin, "I'm actually a little upset with you."

She frowns. "Why?"

"You rejected me."

"I did? When?"

"Today. Seven times."

"Seven times? When did I reject you sev—? Oh." Her frown softens once she cottons on. "The dancing."

I nod. "The dancing."

"I thought you were doing that as part of the whole *we're a real couple* ruse."

"Nope. I was doing it as part of the whole *I really want to dance with the prettiest girl at the wedding* non-ruse."

"I'm sorry." She rubs my arm apologetically, then, with a hint of a smile, continues, "Consider yourself lucky. I'm a truly terrible dancer. You dodged a bullet, believe me."

"That won't do." I aim my most serious look her way, hoping the squinting doesn't come off as some weird eye condition. "I can handle being rejected seven times. But eight? That's a bridge too far."

She looks in the direction of the reception hall. "But we've missed our chance."

"No. We haven't."

Leaning forward, I unlace my shoes, slide them off, and then remove my socks.

"Fraser, what are you doing?"

I lift myself up, brush the sand from my backside, and offer her my hand. "I'm asking the prettiest girl at the wedding if she'll dance with me."

"Here? On the beach?"

"No. Not on the beach."

I shift my gaze to the ocean.

Evie's eyes widen. "No way."

"Way." I roll my pant legs halfway up my shins and jog the few steps into the water. "Come on in. It's warm."

"Fraser! I can't."

"I'm sorry. This version of Fraser software doesn't recognize that word. To update to the latest version..." I drop the robotic voice and smile at her. "You're gonna have to come here and say it to my face."

"Yeah, right. The second I move closer, you're going to splash me."

"Oh, Evie." I prop my hands on my hips. "It's cute you think I can't splash you from here."

I make a move as if I'm about to kick some water her way. She covers her face and shrieks, "Don't you dare! This dress cost seven thousand dollars."

I stop mid-kick. "I'll buy you ten more dresses."

She uncovers her face. "Wait. You believe me?"

"Well, yeah. You look incredible in that dress, so I assume it's expensive. I'm also assuming seven thousand dollars for a dress is expensive. I don't really know much about fashion."

Evie pulls herself onto her knees, then heaves herself into a standing position. She takes a few cautious steps toward me. "I bought it online for two hundred bucks."

I don't know how to respond to that. What can I say? She makes it look like a seven-thousand-dollar dress.

"Is that your way of telling me you don't mind if it gets wet?"

"Absolutely not. It's my way of telling you I have nothing else to wear, and even though it's lavender, I'm worried that if it gets wet, it'll become see-through."

"Fair enough. Good thing I've got a backup plan."

I step out of the water and stalk toward her.

"I'm getting nervous," she says as I get closer.

And closer.

Until I'm standing right in front of her.

So close that her vanilla fragrance infiltrates my nose.

So close that I notice the freckles on her nose are gone. Because I'm assuming that makeup has the power to make freckles disappear, right?

So close that as the sun begins to set, I can see every fleck of brown and green and gold swirling in her beautiful eyes.

"Trust me," I murmur. "I won't get your dress wet."

"Um..."

"Say yes, Evie."

She sighs out a quivery breath. "Okay, yes."

"I won't get your dress wet," I repeat. "But I am getting my dance with you."

And with that, I bend over, lift her in my arms again, and carry her into the water. "You can't be serious. This is how we're going to dance?"

"It sure is. Now, I've got something in my back pocket," I say.

"Bet you say that to all the ladies."

I chuckle. "My phone, Evie. Could you take it out please?"

"Why do you need your phone right now? I thought you didn't do social media."

"I don't," I reply. "And I don't want to take a photo. Call me crazy, but I need music to dance to."

"Oh. Right." She shifts her weight. "I'm going in. No funny business, mister."

"You're the one about to grope me. I'm innocent," I say, smiling.

"For the record, I am not groping you."

Is it wrong that I wouldn't mind if she did?

With her tongue poking out the side of her mouth in concentration, she reaches behind me. Her hand slips into my back pocket for barely a second as she retrieves my phone.

"Your phone's locked," she informs me. "Do you have face ID?"

"No. Only fingerprint or code. And since my fingers are otherwise occupied, I'll give you my code."

Evie looks at me like I just told her I'm quitting hockey to fulfill my secret lifelong rock star ambition and will be joining the band Levi manages.

She blinks hard. "You'll give me the code to your phone? Just like that?"

"I trust you. Besides, I have two shovels in my trunk, remember? And I'm ninety-five percent sure you're not some sexy enemy double agent, or worse, an undercover reporter."

"Technically, I am a reporter," she points out.

"Technically, you're the only good one."

She laughs. Number five, is it?

"What's your code?"

I tell her the numbers, and she types them in.

"Scroll down, and you should see Spotify."

"Yep. Got it. I'm in the playlists section. Now let's see, what do we have here? The *Fraser Loves the Ladies* playlist. The *Rademacher Burt Bacharach Hour of Love* playlist. Catchy title. Ooh, I like this one—the *I Secretly Love Taylor Swift* playlist."

I grin. "You're making it all up. Those playlists aren't there."

"True. But I have two questions."

"Go ahead."

"How good is *Rademacher Burt Bacharach Hour of Love*? That just came to me. Completely out of the blue."

"That one was definitely my favorite."

She smiles. "And question number two. I need to know... are you a Swiftie?"

"Well, I do play for the LA Swifts."

She narrows her eyes.

"And yes, I'm a Swiftie."

Her eyes narrow some more. "Taylor's versions?"

"Naturally."

She pats my head. "Good boy. Now, what song would you like me to pick?"

"Okay. I'll pick the song, but first, you have to tell me—Bacharach or Swift?"

"Taylor. And just so you know, I will be judging your decision for months, possibly years, to come."

"Gee, well, good thing there's no pressure. Give me a minute."

"Your time starts now—"

"'Sweet Nothing,'" I say before she can begin the countdown.

"That was fast."

"It's a great song. Do you know it?"

"Of course I know it. It's just...Why do you like it?"

"It's a soft, sweet song," I begin, feeling a little self-conscious as I delve deeply into this. I haven't really given it all that much thought. I just like it.

But then I remind myself it's Evie I'm talking to, and from out of nowhere, the words just come.

"It's a love song that's not about big moments but about the ordinary, beautiful, everyday aspects of being with someone. It's about finding your person and feeling safe. Settled. Like you're enough exactly the way you are. I...I like those lyrics, and the whole song feels like a soft kiss on your forehead from a person you love. Sorry. That was probably too sappy."

"No, it wasn't." She searches my eyes. "It was just the right amount of sappy."

She finds the song, and it starts to play. Her head rests against my shoulder, and I stand there, holding Evie in my arms, cherishing having her this close to me.

The sun goes down.

The water laps at my feet.

I close my eyes for a moment and wish this was real.

That despite being standoffish and not great at talking,

with my heart enclosed by the Great Wall of China, I could be a man worthy of her.

She pulls back slightly so we can see each other.

My breath hitches in the back of my throat as the rightness of the moment barrels into me. I'm looking into the eyes of the woman I've spent the past seven years in love with.

No other woman compares.

No other woman even comes close.

Which makes me hate myself a little since I never meant to hurt or string anyone along.

But I can't help it.

No other woman is Evie.

I lean down.

She tilts her head up.

Evie and I are about to kiss.

I pull back slightly.

Wait. If this happens—and believe me, I want it to—it has to be because *she* wants it.

Evie presses down on my shoulder to lift herself a little higher.

Okay, seems like she wants it.

The tips of our noses touch.

It's happening, people. This is not a drill.

Our breath mingles.

Her eyes flutter to a close, and...

"OMG! Is that Fraser Rademacher?"

"No way! It is! And is that...is that the Breakup Sneeze Girl?"

"Hey, Fraser! Fraser! Over here!"

Evie wriggles in my arms, and I fight to keep her from falling out of my grip. Once I've got her securely snuggled against my body, I glare at the two idiots on the beach who just broke into our private moment.

Two idiots who are pointing their phones directly at us.

"What are we going to do?" Evie whispers.

"Don't worry. I've got you. You're safe."

She tucks her head into my shoulder, and I stomp out of the water, keeping Evie shielded from view.

I've seen my brother Clayton handle this situation the wrong way enough times to know how to handle it the right way.

Don't engage. Make a swift exit.

That's it.

Simple but effective.

And so, keeping my back turned to our unwanted intruders, I block Evie as well as I can from them. I may not be able to go back in time to un-take whatever shots they've already got of us, but I can do my best to ensure they don't get any more.

We collect our things, and I carry Evie back toward the reception hall, her body pressed against mine the entire way, leaving behind the kiss that got away.

7

Evie

"We need details."

"We need *all* the details."

"Agreed. Don't leave anything out. We want the teeniest, tiniest, nittiest, grittiest little morsels of information."

I stare at my friends Hannah, Beth, Summer, and Amiel, whom we just met since Hannah invited her to join us on our morning walk, and say nothing.

Collectively, we've been dubbed the Fast-Talking Four. Normally, I'm a fan of the cute moniker.

But there's nothing normal about this morning.

Because it's the morning after the wedding.

The morning after Fraser carried me to the beach and held me in his arms as we danced in the water to "Sweet Nothing."

I'd warned him I'd be judging his Taylor song selection for years—possibly decades—to come, and yeah...he has nothing to worry about. He couldn't have picked a more perfect track.

And that almost kiss?

Because we were just about to kiss, weren't we?

And that right there, folks, is the biggest abnormality of them all.

I was about to kiss Fraser Rademacher.

Me.

Evelyn Freeman.

The girl who has, up until this point in my life, always strictly enforced a *no kiss until the third date* rule.

The girl who, up until yesterday, was ninety-five percent sure her feelings for Fraser were in the past.

The girl who stupidly agreed to a sunrise walk, only to be grilled by my three besties and one newcomer who doesn't know where to look or what to make of us.

All. Without. Coffee.

My friends pick up on my not-okay-ness and start talking like I'm not even here.

"Oh, no. She's got that look."

"This is bad, you guys."

"The diner is one block away. Do you think she'll be able to hang on?"

Whatever the *hangry* version of *needs caffeine* is, I've got a major case of it this morning. It must be showing on my face. It's probably seeping out of my pores.

"We have no other choice. Come on."

Hannah slides one arm through mine, Beth takes the other side, and Summer shoots out ahead of us.

"I'm texting Bear," she says over her shoulder. "I'll get him to meet us out front."

"Of course she is," Hannah says under her breath, and I giggle.

Everyone in Comfort Bay knows Bear has a thing for Summer. Everyone except for Summer, that is. She's a high-powered lawyer a few years older than me, and she divides her time between her life in LA and caring for her sick father here. Maybe she's too busy to notice Bear stealing glances her way or how he hangs on her every word.

Beth gives my forearm a squeeze. "Hang in there, girl. We got you. Coffee will be hitting your bloodstream in less than a minute."

"I should be able to last, but I make no promises."

My mind flashes back to that moment on the beach when Fraser realized we were being photographed.

The determination in his eyes as he held me tight and close. The protective way he shielded me with his back, sidestepping through the water to block their view of me. The way he took off away from them.

I didn't like what was happening, but I *did* feel safe. Fraser made me feel safe.

Summer skips ahead when she sees Bear, aka Monosyllable Man, stepping out of his diner, flannel-clad, with his sports cap on backward, as always. Seeing him holding a tray of to-go cups, my mouth waters. I can almost taste the coffee on my lips.

Forget the sunrise, *this* is the best sight I'll see all morning.

"Thank you," Hannah and Beth say in unison as Summer starts handing out drinks.

The second I snatch mine, I bring it to my mouth like a baby does a sippy cup. Ahhh...I can feel myself booting up.

"You're the best, Bear," I say after taking a few sips.

"No sweat."

His gaze lingers on Summer for a moment. She's oblivious, of course, focused on the Great Dane who's basically walking her. Because in addition to being a lawyer and a carer for her father, she also volunteers at the local animal shelter, and because she can never say no to an animal in need, she often ends up fostering them at home.

Bear gives Summer a wave she completely misses as the Great Dane yanks her away, and we keep heading for Cuddle Cove Cliff, our favorite place to watch the sun come up.

The girls try to do this walk once a week. Not being the morning-est of morning people, I join them whenever I can, usually every few weeks. You'd think that working on an early morning show would acclimate me to early starts...but you'd be wrong. And the last thing I want to do on a day off when I can sleep in until noon is get up in the dark. But it's worth it to spend some time with these girls.

"So, Amiel," Beth says to our newest friend. "Hannah mentioned you're new in town."

"That's right. I've been in Comfort Bay for two weeks."

"And you work in the bakery right next door to Hannah's flower shop, right?" I ask, one hundred percent because I'm interested in getting to know her and zero percent because I'm hoping to keep the topic off me and yesterday's wedding for as long as possible.

"I do. I'm so lucky I got the job. I've been baking since forever."

"You bake *and* you have that waistline?" Beth says, giving Amiel a thorough once-over. "I officially hate you."

"You'll get used to her and her 'sense of humor,'" I say to Amiel, putting the words *sense of humor* in air quotes.

"It's true. I'm all bite and no bark," Beth concedes with a friendly smile.

"And what do you do?" Amiel asks Beth.

"I run The Cozy Corner bookstore. Do you like to read?"

"I haven't had much of a chance lately with how busy and stressful the move has been, but I'd love to get back into it."

"Favorite genres?"

"I'm afraid I'm kinda boring. I mainly like YA and clean romance."

"Boring? Hardly," Beth says. "The best people in the world read those two genres. Come in one day, and I'll hook you up."

"That sounds great. I will."

"It's so funny," I say to Beth. "How you're all in on reading romance, but in real life, you're the most anti-love person I know."

Beth grins. "I am a complex and nuanced individual."

"You can say that again," Hannah says before giving me a nudge. "So, now that you're caffeinated..."

Uh-oh. I can feel the conversation steering back to me. Where's the eject button?

"Clue us in, Evie. There's only so much to be gleaned from social media stalking."

And that sets off the morning's first proper round of fast talking.

Summer: "How was the ceremony? Did they write their own vows or go traditional?"

Beth: "Was Bryce floored when you showed up with Fraser? I bet he was. I would have loved to have seen the look on that mousy little face of his. No offense to mice."

Hannah: "The band looked super crappy. Were they super crappy?"

Beth: "Did you go all revenge romcom crazy ex-girlfriend on them?"

Hannah: "I saw the bride's dress on Insta. I wanted to hate it."

Summer: "I saw it, too. And same. I tried to make myself hate it. I just couldn't. That girl's got good taste."

Beth: "Except when it comes to men."

Summer: "One hundred percent agree."

Beth: "But anyways, back to you, Evie. Details. All of them. Spill. Now."

Hannah: "And start with Fraser. Everything else can wait. How dreamboaty was he?"

Ladies and gentlemen, The Fast-Talking Four. I did warn you.

I lengthen my stride as we start climbing the hill. "Fraser was great. He couldn't have been a more perfect wedding date. He checked in on me to see how I was doing the whole time. He kept getting me drinks even though I couldn't settle on anything. He stared at Bryce the way a sniper surveys their target. He asked me to dance seven times."

Beth's eyebrows shoot up. "Seven times?"

"Uh, yeah," I pant. "To, you know, make it believable. Keep up the pretext that we're a real couple."

These girls are my besties. There's no way I was going to hide that this was all for show with them.

I glance over at Amiel. "What happens on this sunrise walk, stays on the sunrise walk."

She grins and nods in agreement. "Understood."

I like her already.

Hannah: "Uh-oh. She's got that look on her face."

Me: "What look? I don't have a look. This is just my normal *I have a face* look."

Summer: "But she's caffeinated."

Hannah: "Oh, this isn't her *I need coffee or else there will be murder* look. This is her *I'm not telling y'all something* look."

Beth: "How can you tell the difference?"

Hannah: "I've known her since elementary school. I know all her faces."

"I do not have faces," I retort, schooling my face into... dammit, probably another face for my closest friends to dissect and analyze.

"But there is something you're not telling us, right?" Hannah probes, softening her words with a smile.

"There is."

"I knew it. Spill."

The incline is getting steeper. "Can I spill once we reach the top?" I huff out. "I'm out of practice."

"Well, if you joined us more often..." Beth teases. "Fine. But don't think we won't be on your case the second we reach the peak."

"Wouldn't dream of it," I grumble.

These walks were her idea. She's a morning person, but since she's so awesome and snarky and one of my closest friends, I'm prepared to overlook her one fault.

When we reach the summit, the sky is still a canvas of deep, muted blues and purples, gradually lightening at the horizon where the first hints of morning are beginning to emerge.

Humans are not designed to be up and active this early in the day. This is a hill I am prepared to die on.

Beth checks her watch and smiles. "Perfect timing. The sun is due to come up in two minutes."

We sit down at our usual bench, each taking swigs from our water bottles.

Hannah bumps me with her elbow. "Well?"

"Wouldn't we all like to watch the sun come up in peace and quiet?"

My friends look at me like I've sprouted a second head.

"Fine. I'm spilling."

As the sun comes up over Comfort Bay, I fill them in on everything, starting from the moment Fraser picked me up in my old bedroom and ending with Fraser taking me down to the beach.

I omit the fact that he carried me to the beach.

And insisted on dancing in the water.

To a totally underrated but brilliant Taylor Swift song choice.

And our almost-but-not-quite kiss.

Because I know them.

If I told them *that*, they'd have a field day with it, making it out to be a bigger deal than what it is, bringing up a conversation I am more than happy to not revisit.

Because I don't want to explain to them for the millionth time that I do not have a crush on Fraser.

Especially since I'm, like, eighty-five percent positive I actually don't.

"Sounds like it was a big day," Hannah says as we start to make our way back. "Like you finally got closure on the Bryce chapter of your life."

"I really feel like I have."

I start telling them about the conversation I had with Bryce but when I reach the part where I thanked him, they all look about as surprised as he did.

Beth: "In the interest of full disclosure, I have to say I don't understand why you did that."

Summer: "I kinda get it. It was a power move."

Beth: "How so?"

Summer: "Being the bigger person, and all that. Right, Evie?"

Me: "I don't know about that. Part of me still feels bad about making him—"

I glance nervously at Amiel, then at Hannah since she brought her here and knows her better than the rest of us.

"It's okay," Hannah says with a smile. "Amiel is one of us, too."

Summer: "She is?"

Hannah: "She is."

Beth: "Right on, sister!"

Amiel, to her credit, despite looking confused because she has no idea what we're talking about, is taking our weirdness in good stride.

So I say what I was going to say. "I hate that this is how I feel, but there is a part of me that blames myself for things ending with Bryce because I made him...wait."

We reach the bottom of the hill, and I need to re-tie my shoelace. The girls wait for me. Once I'm done, I continue walking.

Alone.

I spin around. No one has moved, and now they have *looks* on their faces.

Hannah: "You did not just say that, did you?"

I scratch my arm.

Beth: "Because we have been over this, Evie."

Summer: "A million times."

Hannah: "Looks like we might need to make it a million and one."

The girls approach me.

Hannah: "I will say this and keep saying this until it finally sinks in. There is nothing wrong about wanting to wait until you're married."

Her voice is firm.

Summer and Beth nod their heads, backing Hannah up.

Even Amiel gives me a shy nod.

The four of us have another nickname. A private one that only we know.

The Vinaigrettes.

And it's based on a common trait we share—we're all virgins.

We are not a cult. I repeat, we are not a cult.

We're just four—well, now five—girls who have made a choice that feels right for us.

It's not a judgment on anyone else, but we all have our reasons, and it's great to have a close group of friends to support you in this. It can be tough sometimes, navigating dating and other people's perceptions. I'm glad I'm not alone, that I can always count on my girls.

Oh, and if you're wondering about the name The Vinaigrettes? That's a great story...for another time.

"I know there's nothing wrong with waiting, but..." I blow out a breath. "All three of my relationships have ended at the twelve-month mark. Maybe there's something in that? What sort of guy wants to wait more than a year before getting physically intimate with his girlfriend?"

Hannah: "The right guy."

Summer: "Exactly. And you were up-front with Bryce—"

Beth: "You were up-front with all three guys."

Summer: "Exactly. They knew the deal, and they signed up. They're all adults and capable of standing by the commitment they made."

Me: "But three relationships? All ending after a year? Come on. At some point, don't I have to at least consider that it might not be them? That it's *this*. Either that or I'm cursed. Not sure which option is worse."

Hannah: "Is it something you still believe in?"

Me: "Of course. I want to wait until my wedding night. It's really important to me."

Hannah: "Well, then, that's your answer. Keep waiting, and the right guy *will* show up."

Me: "You're right." I blow out a breath. "This is exactly what I needed to hear. Thanks, you guys."

Hannah: "Anytime, babe."

Summer: "That's right. We're all in this together."

Beth: "Amiel, welcome to the circus."

Before Amiel can say anything, Mrs. Kagney calls out from the other side of the street. "Oh, hi, Evelyn. You look great in the photos!" She gives a wave before slipping into the produce store.

I turn to my friends, only to be met with blank expressions. "What was she talking about?"

"No idea."

We continue walking past the gazebo in the town square and...why is everyone looking at us?

Hannah: "Have we all got something on our faces?"

Summer: "Beth and I are wearing the exact same pair of Nike Joyrides. I knew I shouldn't have told you about the mark-down. And why did you have to get them in bright pink like me? People are noticing."

Beth: "I hardly think the townsfolk of Comfort Bay are concerned with our choice of footwear."

Hannah: "I agree. I'm sure there's a more logical explanation."

Me: "Such as?"

Beth: "Maybe the world ended while we were up at Cuddle Cove Cliff, and everyone's been turned into zombies, and they're all sensing we're the only non-zombified humans left?"

We all swivel our heads in her direction.

Beth: "Sorry. I've been branching out and getting into sci-fi lit lately."

Hannah: "There's Bear's diner. AKA safety from any possible apocalypses."

"Also the place with more coffee," I point out.

"And pancakes," Amiel adds, solidifying her place in our group with those two small words.

So that's where we head, but not before Mike the mechanic, two giggling teenagers dressed in school uniforms, and Mrs. Dunn all stare at us as we pass.

Well, not at us.

At *me*.

They're all focused on me, which is unnerving because if all five of us are non-zombies, why am I the only one being singled out?

The bell above the door jangles as we scurry into the diner.

The place goes deadly quiet, everyone stopping whatever they were doing and turning to us.

"I'm starting to think this whole zombie thing might not be so far-fetched," I whisper to my friends.

"Is something going on?" Summer asks, glaring at everyone like the high-powered lawyer boss she is. "Well?"

People slowly go back to whatever they were doing before we disrupted their morning coffee and breakfast.

Bear walks over to us. "Two things," he says in his customary curt way of speaking. "One, Summer, I'm sorry but you can't bring a dog in here."

"Oh. Of course. Sorry. I wasn't thinking. We were escaping a zombie apocalypse and seeking shelter."

Bear tilts his head. "Huh?"

"Don't worry. I'll take him outside."

"What's the second thing?" I ask.

Without saying a word, he sticks his phone out for all of us to see.

I gasp and snatch the phone from Bear, panic coiling in my belly as I take a closer look.

Images of me and Fraser dancing in the ocean yesterday are splashed across a sports news website under the headline *RADEMACHER'S NEW LOVE INTEREST?*

I turn to my friends. "This is a nightmare."

"This is amazing!" Margo announces, walking up behind me.

Shoot. I thought I'd managed to sneak into the office without her spotting me.

I wheel my chair back and pivot to face her.

She's glowing.

"I have a feeling I know what you're talking about, and I'm going to have to strongly disagree with you."

"Walk and talk time, hon. Let's go!"

I push to my feet reluctantly.

She takes out her phone. "You're trending."

I wince. "The last time I heard those words, I went into hiding for a month."

"You won't want to hide from this. Believe me."

Margo tries to give me her phone, but I resist. "I'm scared to look. Just tell me."

"Fine. The top trending hashtag in the US is currently #RademacherReturns."

"That's...not scary at all." In fact, that's really good. Fraser has returned to form.

"The number four top hashtag is #FraserWithBSG."

BSG = Breakup Sneeze Girl.

"Okay. Not as good."

"But not horrible, either. The narrative is shifting, as evidenced by the number seven top hashtag in the country. #GoodluckcharmBSG."

I roll my eyes. "I am many things, but Fraser's good luck charm isn't one of them."

"I see." Margo studies me for a moment before we veer right at the elevator bank. "So you're thinking the interview angle is better than the dating angle?"

"What interview angle? And what dating angle?"

"You know, for the story. If you'd rather interview him, I get it. Dating him makes you the story, and that's always an iffy area. I totally respect your decision, Ev."

"No, but I'm not doing a story abo—"

"This will be great for your numbers."

"Wait. Margo. I'm not—"

"Gotta dash, hon. Late for a meeting. We'll walk and talk later!"

She dashes off, leaving me by the marketing department. Gina looks over at me and smiles. I wave back before returning to my desk.

Via the snack station.

I normally don't raid this area until after lunch, but it's a snack station kind of morning.

Setting up Google notifications at the diner with the girls

this morning was a giant mistake. I've been witnessing this story get picked up by more and more outlets in real time.

Images of my private moment on the beach with Fraser are spreading like wildfire.

He must be furious.

Here he is doing a nice, decent thing, taking his best friend's sister to an ex's wedding, and this is what he gets for it. Top news story coverage.

I flop into my chair, armed with enough candy and chocolate to get me through until lunch time.

My phone buzzes.

I ignore the incoming call from my brother.

"Not today, mister. I'm angry at you."

It buzzes twice more.

I ignore it both times.

Levi: *I assume you're not taking my calls because you're in a meeting or busy and not because you're ignoring your favorite brother in the world on purpose.*
Me: *I'm actually busy dealing with the major catastrophe that is entirely YOUR FAULT!*
Levi: *Ah. So you've heard. But how is Fraser holding you in the water my fault?*
Levi: *You know what? Never mind. I don't want to know the inner workings of your mind on that one.*
Levi: *I'm reaching out because I was hoping the news hadn't reached you yet.*
Me: *Comfort Bay's courier pigeons do a remarkable job of bringing information to us from the big cities these days.*
Levi: *Okay. Sarcasm. So you're on to the second stage of dealing with a PR crisis.*
Levi: *Now, you know me, I don't like to meddle in your life...*
Levi: *But I can help.*

Me: *I don't need your help.*
Levi: *Denial. Stage three. Wow. You're moving through it fast. Way to go, sis!*
Me: *It's a good thing you're not here right now otherwise I would wrap my fingers around your neck and THROTTLE YOU.*
Levi: *Stage four. Anger. This is good. Healthy. Get it out, Evie. Get it all out of your system.*

Argh! He is frustrating me so much right now, I want to scream.

Me: *What do you want, Levi?*
Levi: *Ah. We've reached the final stage. Acceptance.*

I shake my head, fuming at the mess he's caused.

I'm about to tap out a message telling him I don't have time for this when a strange voice from behind me asks, "Ms. Freeman?"

I spin in my chair, the Snickers Bar I'd been chewing falling out of my mouth, because there isn't one flower delivery person standing there.

Not two.

Not even three.

But four.

Four flower delivery men are holding bouquets of what must be at least a few dozen yellow roses in their arms.

Another text comes through.

Levi: *I've spoken to Fraser, and he feels terrible about this.*

"So I gather," I mutter to myself.

"Where would you like these, Ms. Freeman?"

"Um, over there." I point to a spare desk nearby.

The men leave the flowers on the desk, and when the flowers don't all fit, they place the leftovers on the floor around the desk.

Me: *Please tell Fraser thank you for the flowers and that this isn't his fault.*
Levi: *He bought you flowers?*
Me: *He did.*
Levi: *That was nice of him. I really do have the best best friend.*

Can't argue with that.

Me: *Will you tell him please?*
Levi: *I would love to...but relaying messages between the two of you feels wrong. Like I'm meddling or something. And you know me, I would never do that. <smiley face emoji>*

Annnd I'm back in *Evie wants to stab her brother* mode. I do have Fraser's email address, but it doesn't feel right to send him a thanks via email.

Me: *I don't have his number, otherwise I would tell him myself.*
Levi: *Oh. Perfect!*

Hear that?
That's the sound of a wild animal stepping in a carefully laid trap.

Me: *What's perfect?*
Levi: *You just said you wanted to tell him yourself.*
Me: *I did?*
Levi: *You did. And now you can! After the home game on Wednesday.*

Levi: *He's made a reservation at GOMU. But I think the G is silent so when you read this out, pronounce it as OMU. Super fancy place. Impossible to get a table there. I'm still on the waitlist. Can you believe that? Maybe I should be sneaky and make the reservation under a WHAT NOW member's name.*
Levi: *But I digress. The point I was trying to make is you'll be able to tell Fraser yourself.*
Levi: *Over dinner.*
Levi: *And before you ask, yes, I'm sure they can make you an off-menu burger.*

The home game.

Of course, that's this Wednesday. With all the commotion today—not to mention the unnaturally early start I've endured—it had totally slipped my mind.

Not that I always see Fraser at the games.

I mean, of course I *see* him because hello, he's on the ice. But I don't always hang around to speak with him afterward.

Much less at some swanky-sounding restaurant.

But I guess we do have some stuff to talk about.

He must be hating all this unwanted press.

And Levi will be there, so that should keep things nice and normal and far, far away from talking about anything remotely related to the kiss that almost was.

Me: *Fine. I'll go. But if I were you, I'd hire security. Your little sister is THIS CLOSE to going on a rampage against you.*

8

Fraser

The opposing defenseman approaches at high speed.

I fake left with a quick shoulder drop. The defender lunges in that direction, expecting a straightforward play.

With a flick of the wrist, I cut back to the right. I guide the puck through the narrow space left by the off-balanced defender and execute another seamless deke.

I'm on fire.

The whole team is.

We're up 3-0.

Two of those goals are mine, but I'm not done yet. I can feel it. I've got a hat trick in me tonight.

The energy in the arena is electric, a mixture of anticipation and tension. I love playing for a home crowd. I love *winning* in front of a home crowd even more.

I enter the offensive zone. There's no one in my way.

The goalie is my final barrier. He shifts in the crease, tracking my every move.

I shift my weight, snapping the stick forward, and unleash a powerful shot.

The puck rockets toward the goal, aimed precisely at the tiny gap between the goalie's glove and the post.

The goalie reacts, but the puck hurtles past him into the net.

The score light flashes, and the crowd erupts in a frenzy.

There are eighteen thousand roaring fans in LA tonight, but there's only one I truly care about.

Evie.

She's here, like she is for all home games.

But there's something different about her being here tonight.

It's been three days since the wedding.

Three days since those pesky onlookers invaded our privacy on the beach.

Three days in which the story about my supposed new relationship has blown up.

Every few hours, a new hashtag starts trending on social media, or some new article pops up about how long we've 'really' been together.

That's largely due to one very dedicated fan—username: *hockey4life1989*—who has compiled a score count of every home game I've played and correlated that to Evie's presence at home games to determine that my offensive output—goals and assists—is notably better when she's in the arena.

The home-ice advantage has become known as #TheEvieEffect.

Fans are sharing theories and speculating about my personal life more than ever. The rumor is that we've been together all season, and *that's* the reason why I'm playing better. She's my good luck charm, apparently.

What on earth is Evie making of all of it?

I have absolutely no idea.

We haven't spoken.

I don't even have her number to call her because I haven't needed it before. Levi passed on her thanks for the flowers I sent, which was nice of her, but I'm itching to make sure she's *really* okay. She survived one viral scandal only to be plunged neck-deep into another.

I can't help but feel guilty, like this mess is all my fault.

That's why I invited her to dinner. We need to sit down and talk properly. Whatever it takes, I am determined to fix this.

The game ends, and even with a last-minute goal by the opposition, because of my hat trick, we win 4-1.

The atmosphere in the locker room is electric. Players

engulf each other in celebratory hugs, praising each other's performance. Adrenaline from the win mingles with relief and satisfaction.

It's still super early in the season, but we've found our form and are playing better than ever. Whatever spark was missing in the second half of last season has returned, and when six players at their peak come together on the ice, there's no better feeling in the world.

"Take it you won't be joining us?" Culver asks, flicking my back with his towel as he walks past me.

"Ow. No. And after that, especially no."

He grins slyly. "You know the press is going to have a field day with your performance tonight, don't you? Or should I say *more* of a field day? I love you, man, but even I'm getting tired of seeing your ugly mug all over socials."

"Here's some free advice. Do what I do and stay off social media. Try it. Your life will be better. That comes with a thirty-day money-back Rademacher guarantee."

"Hey, some of us are addicted, thank you very much."

I laugh.

A couple of the guys approach, and we chitchat for a few minutes while we get dressed. Even Milo, our super grump goalie who was traded onto the team this season, comes over. He doesn't say much, but he nods every once in a while, and his scowl seems a little less scowly, so...progress? If I didn't have so much on my plate, I'd make more of an effort to get to know the guy, but right now, there's only one person in the world I care about.

"I know you got plans with your girl," Donovan says. "But text us later. We'll probably still be out."

"Yeah, man. It'd be good to celebrate together," Slater adds. "And bring your girl. Friends and family are always welcome. Our days of wild nights and partying are over."

"Ain't that the truth."

Donovan and Slater high-five, but the scowl on Milo's face returns, stronger than ever. Huh. Maybe the guy's nursing a broken heart? Might be why his general demeanor is a little on the icy side.

Slater makes an interesting observation, though. Apart from myself, Culver, and possibly our grumpy new goalie, the rest of the team have wives and girlfriends. Some are even starting to have families.

That's something I want, too.

I've never understood why it's called settling *down*. That makes it sound like it's a bad thing. For me, a wife, kids, a home—it's my idea of heaven. If anything, it should be called settling *up*.

"I'll be in touch later," I tell them.

But first, I have a dinner date to get to.

And yeah, I probably should have corrected the guys when they referred to Evie as *my girl*, but I guess like everyone else in the world, they believe the crazy stories that have been coming out about me this week.

Besides, Evie being called my girl has a nice ring to it. Why do something crazy like bring facts into it?

I make my way out of the locker room, discreetly kiss Evie's bracelet three times before placing it in my gym bag, then head to the family lounge where Evie—wearing her Dad's *81* jersey, of course—Levi, and one of their sisters, Harper, are waiting for me.

Levi spots me first, and when he does, he taps Evie on the shoulder. She turns around, and when her eyes land on me, a luminous smile spreads across her face, lighting up her features, and I get a rush of tingles up and down both arms.

"Oh, my gosh, Fraser!" She runs over to me and jumps into my arms.

I think quick, dropping my gym bag to the floor just in time to catch her.

"You were amazing. A hat trick! I'm so proud of you."

Is...is this real?

Or did my teammates knock me out in the locker room and this is all one giant hallucination?

Evie has wrapped herself around me, and I don't ever want to let her go.

I close my eyes and inhale her sweet perfume.

When I open my eyes, Levi and Harper are standing right next to us.

And, yep. This is real, all right.

I gently guide Evie to her feet before giving Harper a peck on the cheek. When Levi and I exchange our customary bear hug, he whispers in my ear, "You were great, but lifting me up into your arms won't be necessary."

"You sure?" I chuckle. "Wouldn't want you getting jealous that you're missing out on the full Fraser experience."

"Believe me. Not jealous at all," he says, smiling. "Also, for future reference, I have absolutely zero interest in knowing what the full Fraser experience is."

We start chatting.

I see Harper even less frequently than I see Evie, so I ask her how the reality TV show she's producing is going. She tries to tell me about it, but it's a little hard when a certain someone keeps interjecting with a play-by-play of her favorite moments from the game, as well as going through the notes she compiled on her phone.

I don't mind the interruptions at all. It's nice, actually. A small reminder that some things never change.

"So, should we go for dinner?" I ask.

"Sure."

"Sounds great."

"Let's go."

Uh-oh.

They all answered because they must think we're all going out to dinner together. My bad for giving them that impression.

"So, um, guys." I scratch the back of my neck. "There's something I feel bad about."

"Your face?" Levi asks, deadpan. "Is it your face?"

"His face is better than your face, doofus," Harper shoots back, and yep, we've just traveled back fifteen years in time.

"What I was going to say is that I made the dinner reservation for two."

"Oh."

"Oh."

"Oh."

I didn't know Harper would be here tonight, and I assumed Levi and I would catch up later.

Okay, those aren't the real reasons.

The *real* reason, the purely selfish reason, is that I want to spend time alone with Evie.

"I can give the restaurant a call to see if they can—"

"It's fine," Levi jumps in. "Harps and I can hang out while you two raging lovebirds—Owww!"

"Oops." Evie smiles sweetly. "Did your arm just get in the way of my fist?"

Levi rubs his bicep. "As I was saying, Harps and I can do our thing while you two non-raging, non-lovebirds can have dinner and discuss all the things you need to discuss. There. Better?" he asks Evie.

She gives a firm nod. "Better."

Works for me, but I try to downplay my excitement at having Evie all to myself.

"Well, if you're sure," I say casually.

"I'm sure. Now, go. Shoo." Levi starts waving us off. "Have a lovely, completely non-lovebirdy dinner."

"Would it be weird if I told you you look beautiful?" I say once we're seated in a private corner of the dimly lit restaurant with the scared-to-mispronounce name. I know one of the letters is silent, just not which one. Everyone keeps telling me something different. At this point, I'm wondering why they even bothered with a name at all.

Evie lowers the leatherbound menu, resting it against the edge of the table. "Depends."

"On?"

"What if I said yes? That it would be weird. Would you still say it?"

"Well, no."

"Why not?"

"Because I wouldn't want to make things awkward."

"Even if that means you aren't saying something that you want to say?"

"Um. I think I have a concussion."

Evie smiles warmly. "I'm just teasing. It wouldn't be weird. In fact, I've been wondering if you'd even noticed."

"Uh, yeah. I think I'd actually have a serious concussion not to notice you getting changed out of your dad's jersey into what I'm assuming is another seven-thousand-dollar dress. You're a knockout, Evie."

She laughs if off, but I'm not kidding. She looks stunning, dressed in a chic, form-fitting burgundy cocktail dress with a scalloped pattern around the neckline. Her hair is down, loosely flowing over her shoulders, and she's wearing just the right amount of makeup to highlight her beautiful features, her light freckles visible on her nose. Earrings sparkle from her ears, occasionally catching the light from the candle on the table.

"Not a seven-thousand-dollar dress, but thank you for noticing. And for the totally non-weird compliment. I'll take it."

"I like bantering with you," I say, lifting my menu.

"Same," she says. "Have you decided what you want?"

"Uh..."

To eat, bonehead. She means have you decided what you want to eat.

"Might go with the steak. You?"

"I'm having a hard time choosing something."

I fold my menu and place it on the table. "Let me guess. You want a burger?"

She looks across the table and treats me to an adorable smile/wrinkled-nose combo. "Is that bad?"

"Why would it be bad?"

"This place has a Michelin star, and I'm going to, what, ask for a double bacon burger with fries?"

"At least you know they'll be Michelin star fries."

"The chef will have a heart attack."

"The chef will do their job and give the customer what they want."

"If you say so."

The waiter arrives. He's young, looks bored, and has a trace of a French accent.

Evie mouths, "You first," so I place my order. When I'm done, Evie glances up at the waiter and asks, "I have some allergies."

"Could you pleez specify which allergiez you have? I'll make sure to inform ze kitchen team so we can accommodate your needs and provide you with meal options that are safe for you."

His words came out in one long monotone drawl, like it's something he's recited a thousand times before.

"My allergy is kind of...unique," Evie says, resting her elbows on the table.

He sighs. "I'm all ears."

"Well, see, I'm basically allergic to most food groups that aren't a burger."

"A boor-gair?"

"Yes. It's a very specific allergy. Only affects the tiniest amount of people in the world. We actually have a support group. Meet once a month online to discuss all the challenges and stigmas that we face. It's cathartic, actually, and I feel like I'm really growing and accepting that my allergy is a part of me, but not all of me. I won't let it define who I am."

Thankfully she stops because I am *this close* to bursting out laughing.

Frenchie isn't amused.

"Let me see if I understand you correctly. You would like me to ask ze chef to prepare for you a boor-gair?"

Evie nods. "With crispy fries. Or onion rings. I don't mind either way. Whatever they feel inspired to make."

"I see. Will that be all this evening?"

"You know what?" I say, snapping my menu shut. "I've changed my mind. Forget the tomahawk. I'll have a burger, too. Extra bacon. Extra cheese. With fries. Please."

Frenchie gets a vague look in his eyes, like he'd rather be anywhere else but here. He takes a deep breath, scoops the menus off the table, and mutters something under his breath in French. He's probably questioning the life choices he's made to wind up working in a posh restaurant with an impossible to pronounce name, serving burgers to Americans whose idea of refined dining is swapping out fries for onion rings.

"So, how has your week so far been?" I ask once he leaves, easing into the conversation we need to have.

"Dull. Incredibly uneventful. Bordering on boring. I've actually been hoping some scandal would erupt and I'd be right in the middle of the firestorm just so I'd have something to obsess over."

Man, I love how her mind works. Most people would answer a straightforward question like that with a simple reply.

But not Evie.

She uses words the way a hockey player carves up the ice, ducking and weaving on the way to giving a proper answer. She makes you work for it, sifting and sorting through her at times jumbled stream of consciousness to get to the heart of what she actually means.

And I love that.

It feels like what I wish all conversations I have with all people would be like. Maybe if they were, I'd feel like talking more.

"How have you been?" she asks, before I can follow-up.

"Fine."

"I've been worried about you."

"You have? Why?"

"Because you hate the press."

"Believe me, that opinion hasn't changed these past few days."

"And you've gotten a lot of it. Because of me. How are you handling it?"

"It's not because of you, Evie," I say, setting the record straight. I hope she hasn't been blaming herself for any of this. "I'm the one who asked you to go to the beach. I'm acutely aware I'm a target for people's attention, once I put myself out in public. That's on me. Not you."

"You still have a right to privacy."

"Sure. In theory. But in reality, you and I both know that's not how it works."

"And you're okay with that?"

"I have to be. Like anything in life, it's a trade-off. I'm living my dream, playing the game I love. A lot of people would kill to be in my shoes. If it means I get noticed in public and have to limit some of the things I do, then so be it. I can throw myself a pity party and cry about it in my multimillion-dollar mansion, right?"

"You're still a person."

"I'm a hockey player first, though. Person second. At least as far as the public and media are concerned."

Evie doesn't look pleased about that.

"Look. I'm used to it. With Mom's career comeback and Clayton being on every celebrity reality TV show that will have him, I've learned how to navigate this fame thing. Somewhat. As long as I have privacy where and when it matters—at home, with my family, with my friends—that's all I care about. I can handle the rest. I knew I was taking a risk when I took you to the beach, and I'm sorry I didn't protect you better."

"What? Are you kidding me? Of course you protected me. Once you saw that people were taking our picture, you totally shielded me from them. You were like my knight in shining armor, without all the problematic baggage that example brings with it."

"Really?"

"*Really*. They've stopped referring to me as Breakup Sneeze Girl and started using my actual name."

"That's...good?"

"Anything is better than Breakup Sneeze Girl."

"Fair enough. But how are you handling it?"

"I'll be honest. It is a lot. I'm used to people in town recognizing me from being on TV and being Monterey-County-famous. This story is blowing up big, though, and it's a little reminiscent of the last time I blew up big."

"I'm sorry. Is it triggering?"

"I'd be lying if I said it wasn't. But the narrative is different with this story, Fraser. I'm being treated like a person."

"You'll have to explain that one to me."

"Well, thanks to the passionate hockey-loving online sleuths out there, people have discovered who my Dad is. That's earned me some street cred, and now no one would dare refer to me by my former hashtag, at least not anyone truly in the hockey fandom, for fear of peeving off the almighty Alex Freeman. And thanks to *hockey4life1989*, I've somehow become a good luck charm. Which I know we know is ridiculous, but people are going with it."

"They are. And it is ridiculous, but you know hockey players. We're a superstitious and odd bunch."

"Oh. Believe me, I know." She smiles briefly before continuing. "Don't get me wrong. This is still *way* more publicity and scrutiny than I want or am comfortable with, but at least this time, with this story, I'm not the biggest joke on the internet. And then there's the last thing."

"What's that?"

She hesitates for a moment. "My numbers have been through the roof this week."

"That's great."

"It is."

Our eyes meet.

The air between us crackles, charged with tiny little sparks of energy.

Evie looks beautiful in the glow of soft candlelight, and I take a moment to consider everything she's just said.

She seems to be managing. It is slightly out of her comfort zone, as it is mine, but I think I can lay off the non-stop worrying about her. She's doing okay.

I decide to take a chance.

"I don't regret it," I tell her. "The beach. The dancing. I'd do it all again."

"You would?"

"In a heartbeat."

Her hazel gaze meets mine. "I've been thinking about something."

"Go on."

"Something that I think maybe almost happened between us but got interrupted."

Oh. She's going there.

"Do you mean—?"

"Your boor-gair, madam. The chef was *inspired* to make onion rings as your side dish. I trust this will be to your liking."

Evie drags her eyes away from me. "Yes. Thank you."

"And your boor-gair, sir. Extra bacon. Extra cheese. With fries. Enjoy."

I lean over once he disappears. "And by *enjoy*, he means *choke on it*."

"Possibly. Or he means *enjoy the spit the chef flavored it with*."

"That's gross, Evie."

She laughs. "It really is."

We start eating.

"Looks like we got interrupted again," I say.

She nods. "Maybe that's our thing. We get interrupted all the time, and we're left with all these questions that we then spend hours, days, weeks, months, obsessing over, dangling in our subconscious like..." She looks down at her plate. "Like onion rings."

"Like onion rings dangling in our subconscious?" I check.

She nods. "It's a little out there, but also quite a strong visual statement. Don't you think?"

I chuckle. "Sure. But let's not have interruptions and dangling onion rings be our thing, okay? Let's always clear things up so that we avoid miscommunication and know exactly where we stand, like..." I glance down at my plate. "Like a fry." I lift one up. "A fry is a fry. You always know what it is, right?"

"There is no mistaking what a fry is," she agrees.

"So let's be like fries. Like...Like...Like truth fries."

"Truth fries. I like it," she says, then raises her hand. "Okay. Problem."

"What is it?"

"In the interest of full disclosure and with all this talk of fries, now...I want fries. Don't suppose you want to share yours?"

I grin, pushing my plate toward the center of the table. "Happy to."

We munch away in silence, with Evie picking at my fries every once in a while. I'm pretty sure we're the only people in the restaurant eating with our hands, but who cares? I'm having the best time with my gir—with Evie.

"So," I begin. "Should we pick up where we left off?"

"Okay." Evie stops eating and puts her burger down on her plate. "I was going to ask you if we were about to kiss. There, I said it. *Kiss.*"

She looks up and keeps her neck craned at the ceiling for a long time.

"What are you doing?" I eventually ask.

"Making sure the sky isn't about to fall in on us."

"Yes."

She drops her head. "Yes, you're agreeing with me that the sky isn't about to cave in on us, or yes to the kiss?"

"Yes to the kiss."

"Wow. I like this whole *truth fries* thing." I can see her mind spinning. "Okay. Wow."

"You've already said wow."

"This is a wow moment, Fraser. You just said you were about to kiss me."

"Actually, no. What I said was that I thought *we* were about to kiss."

"Explain the difference to me."

I wipe some burger juice off my fingers with my napkin. "Evie, you'd had a tough day. You were emotional. I wanted to do something fun and light to get you out of your funk. Yes, I wanted to kiss you, but I wanted to make sure that was what *you* wanted, too. So I held back, and I let you take the lead."

Evie blinks rapidly. "The wow moments just keep coming. It's like a wow tornado over this side of the table. Someone call FEMA."

"Are you okay?"

"I am. I am. I'm just a little...overwowed. That's...that's a really sweet thing you said."

"It's what the fries want."

She visibly swallows. "It's so strange spending time with you again. Alone. Like we...like we used to. It's stirring up a whole bunch of stuff."

"What sort of stuff?"

"Feelings. Questions. All the usual fun existential stuff." She bites down thoughtfully on an onion ring. "But that's all in the past, and I'm all about moving on."

"We can...move on. If that's what you want."

"It's probably for the best."

Guilt stabs me in the chest.

I'd like to resolve things—especially the abrupt way I left. I can't tell her anything about Dawn's situation, but I at least owe her an explanation about the things I can reveal.

But if she wants to move on, I have to respect that.

So I squash the urge to dredge up the past by revisiting our teenage lives and instead focus on the matter at hand. "So what do we do about the story?"

The faraway look in her eyes vanishes, and she rallies. Back to upbeat Evie mode. "It's been a few days. Give it a few more, and people will start losing interest, we'll stop trending on social media, and the press will move on to something else."

"You really think so?"

"I do."

She does work in the industry, so I guess she'd know better than me how these things work.

"Trust me," Evie says, waving a fry in the air. "This whole thing will blow over soon, and our lives will go back to normal."

9

Evie

That whole thing I said to Fraser last night about the story blowing over?

Yeah. I was wrong.

"You and Fraser are in every single newspaper this morning," Levi says, pointing out the glaringly obvious.

I crashed at his LA apartment after last night's game. Dropping my gaze to the sports sections he collected on his morning run and has laid out on the coffee table, I let out a loud groan.

I was *very* wrong.

Fraser's return to form is getting wall-to-wall coverage, alongside photos of a certain someone yelling and cheering him on with their hair messed up and their face contorted like a lunatic.

"Do I really look like that when I watch a game?" I ask.

His eyes travel over the assortment of photos of me in various states of open-mouth, fist-pumping, face-scrunching fanaticism. "They haven't doctored the images, if that's what you're asking. So, yeah, that really is you."

"Why didn't you tell me I look hideous?"

Levi shrugs. "Because I don't think you look hideous. You're passionate about the guy. Sorry, I mean…the game. Besides, it takes the attention away from me and my total lack of interest. You're enthusiastic enough for the both of us."

"Yeah, well, now my enthusiasm is splashed across every sports section in the country."

And it's *not* my best look.

Although…it is a step up from freeze-frame memes of me in the middle of an uncontrollable sneezing fit.

"This is a nightmare." I collapse onto the sofa. "What am I going to do?"

The doorbell rings.

"I'm not meddling," Levi says all wide-eyed, before I get the chance to accuse him of anything. "He called me."

Levi answers the door. A few moments later, he returns with a worried-looking Fraser.

"Hey," he says when he spots me.

I tuck a pillow into my chest and fold my legs. "Hi."

"Have you seen the sports news?"

"Yeah," Levi replies, gesturing at the coffee table. "We have."

Fraser turns his head, taking in all the headlines. A line emerges between his brows. "Didn't know newspapers were still a thing."

I muster up a faint smile. "Well, they are."

He sits down next to me on the sofa, keeping some distance between us. "I called Levi as soon as I found out. I'm worried about you."

"Me?"

He nods. "Yeah. I know how much you want this all to blow over. To put it all in the past and move on."

Fraser looks genuinely worried as he repeats my words from dinner last night back to me. I do want to move on, but I want that even more for him, too. He's got to be hating the attention ten times more than I do.

"What about you?" I ask. "This isn't exactly your idea of heaven."

"You're right. It isn't." His expression softens a little. "But I can think of worse things than being romantically linked to..."

He stops, his eyes drifting over to Levi, who's standing in the corner of the room, watching us with an unreadable expression on his face.

"Drinks, anyone?" my brother says suddenly with a clap of his hands.

I look at the time. "It's eight in the morning."

"We're celebrating," Levi counters. "Or commiserating. One or the other. Whatever the occasion, alcohol will surely make it better."

"I'm fine," Fraser says. "Thanks, though."

"Evie?"

"Nope. I'm good."

"Fine. I'll drink by myself, then. Thanks, guys." And with that, he leaves the room.

"I was going to say..." Fraser inches closer to me. "I can think of worse things than being romantically linked to the most beautiful woman in the arena last night."

Another wow moment.

The crazy thing is, I don't think he even realizes how sweet the things he's saying are.

"Oh. Before I forget..." He stands and walks out of the room.

When he returns, he's holding a bouquet of yellow roses in one hand and a tray of baked goods in the other.

No. Don't tell me he bought—

"Hope you still like malasadas?" He chews his bottom lip. "Based on last night's dinner, I'm assuming your palette hasn't changed too much these past seven years."

"Nope. It's still as unhealthy as ever." I do grabby hands. "Gimme, gimme, gimme."

Fraser chuckles, laying the bouquet over the sports pages and opening the box for me. I close my eyes and inhale the appetizing aroma of freshly fried dough and caramelized sugar.

I pick up one of the treats and take a bite. "Mmm...You are officially my favorite person ever."

"Uh, hello. Favorite brother back in the room."

I giggle and take another bite.

"What are they?" Levi asks, peering into the box.

"Portuguese donuts," Fraser tells him. "Evie used to be obsessed with them. Try one."

"Can't." He lifts his glass. "Don't think it'd pair well with vodka."

"Levi!" I cry out. "It's eight in the morning."

"Five past eight," he corrects, smirking. "And I'm kidding, geez. This is water." But then he straightens, his head snapping to Fraser. "Wait. How did *you* know Evie went through a malasada era?"

Fraser looks at me.

I look at Levi.

Oh, brother...

Literally.

⁓

Seven years ago, Evie's bedroom...

I catch a glimpse of a shadowy figure outside my bedroom window, and my heart leaps into my throat. Yanking my headphones off, I reach for my trusty umbrella, stopping when I see Fraser waving frantically at me in the window.

"Hey," he says as soon as I open it. "Sorry. Didn't mean to scare you. Please don't make me listen to punk music."

I tap my chin like I'm seriously considering it, but really I'm buying some time to slow my breathing, hoping he can't see how much of a fright I got. The last thing I want is for him to think of me as some scared little kid.

My eyes travel to what he's holding in his hands. "Is that In-N-Out?"

"It is."

He lifts the white paper bag so I can see the logo and offers a smile.

A very cute smile.

"I forgot Levi is hanging out with his music friends tonight. Don't suppose you want to share this with me? I've got plenty."

Play it cool, Evie. No need for him to know you've substituted the whole 'an apple a day keeps the doctor away' thing with burgers.

"Sure. I can eat," I say casually, waving him in.

Fraser climbs into my room, and we walk over to the seating area. He looks good in his relaxed-fit Diesel jeans, classic white T-shirt, and the latest pair of Adidas sneakers Levi is super bummed he wasn't able to get his hands on.

I sit on the couch, and he takes the armchair. Why does he always position himself so far away from me? I don't smell that bad, do I?

"Take your pick," he says.

I look at all the burgers he's laid out and grab my favorite. "Thanks."

We eat in silence for a while.

"Do you know what Levi does with his music friends?"

Fraser stops with a handful of fries in midair. "Listen to music?"

"I thought that, too, but nope. I walked in on them one day when they were over here." I rest the burger on my lap. "They sit around and study."

"Study?"

"The Billboard charts."

"Are you serious?"

"Totally. Pick a month, any month, from the last thirty years, and Levi will be able to tell you the top song and album at that time."

Fraser nods, a smile spreading across his face. "That's pretty neat, actually."

"Trust my brother to take something cool like music and turn it into something nerdy."

"Says the girl who takes notes during hockey games. And then has zero qualms about sharing said notes in great detail."

He's got a point there. "Go back to your burger, Fraser."

One of the games from last year's Western Conference Finals between the Desert Canyon Coyotes and the Silver City Miners is playing on the TV. I'd been watching it with one eye while obsessing over my latest batch of bracelets. The materials I ordered on eBay arrived today so I'd been experimenting with them before Fraser showed up.

"You'll be playing in the major leagues one day."

"I hope so."

"I know so. You're good."

He stops himself from taking a bite. "Just good?"

"If I tell you what I really think, you might get a big head and rest on your laurels. I will not be responsible for you peaking at juniors."

"Fair enough."

A patch of silence follows.

"You won't mind all the travel?" I ask.

"Nope."

"But that means..."

"I won't be here."

"Exactly."

"I *cannot* wait."

"Do you really hate it here that much?"

He finishes his burger and wipes his hands clean. "I don't hate it here, but Comfort Bay is a bubble. A sheltered, privileged bubble. I want to see what else is out there. Visit different parts of the country. Figure out who I really am. Hockey is my ticket out."

"That makes sense."

"What about you?"

"What about me?"

"You're smart. You've got to be thinking about college."

"If by *thinking about college* you mean Mom already deciding that I'll be going to UCLA, then yes, I've been thinking about it a lot."

"She's kind of scary, your mom."

I hide my smile behind my burger.

I know from Levi that Fraser is low-key petrified of Mom. Smart guy. Even though he has no reason to worry. She likes him. Guess she's got a soft spot for hockey players. She did marry one, after all.

I chew on a few fries before saying, "They say that nature abhors a vacuum. Well, nature ain't got nothing on Meredith Freeman. As soon as she sniffed out that I was wavering on where to study, she pounced. She's always wanted one of us to go to UCLA, and since none of her other kids went there, she's determined that I will."

"See? Scary."

I giggle. "She is. I think she means well, but it must come from a place deep, deep, *deep* inside."

"That sounds pretty deep," Fraser says, chuckling. "What will you study, or has she decided that for you, too?"

"Thankfully, no, even though I haven't decided myself yet. Just please don't tell her or she'll pounce."

"I won't tell a soul."

"I'm tossing up between journalism and education."

"Good options. Leaning more in one direction than the other?"

"No. Not yet. You're right, though, what you said about us

having grown up in a privileged bubble. I recognize that, too. That's why I've always wanted to do something with my life that makes a positive difference in some way. Is that...dumb?"

"Not at all."

"I do know that after college, I want to come back here. Is *that* dumb?"

"Again, not at all. Why would you think that?"

"Most kids can't wait to get away and start their own lives far, far away from where they grew up."

"You're not most kids. Do you, Evie, and don't care so much about what other people may or may not think."

"Food for thought. Thanks."

The sound of a van reversing catches our attention at the same time.

"Are you filming tonight?"

Fraser nods. "Yeah. I should get going. We're doing a dinner scene."

"But you just ate two burgers."

"So did you."

I blush. I'd been hoping he hadn't noticed.

"Which, for the record, is not a bad thing," he clarifies. "I'm impressed you can keep up with me."

"Right."

"Oh, by the way, I brought some malasadas." He points to a white paper bag on the coffee table.

"What are malasadas?"

"They're a Portuguese pastry. Similar to a donut but without the hole in the middle. I got a few different flavors. Try 'em. They'll change your life."

"Okay. Thanks."

He flashes me a smile, and then we start walking toward the window.

"Wait. Why did you eat if you're going to be having dinner?"

"We're *filming* a dinner scene. Not eating. Big difference. Mom says no one looks good chewing food, so we're under strict orders to nibble only."

"Reality TV is messed up."

"Welcome to my life."

We reach the window.

He turns to face me square on. "Should I...? Nah. Forget it."

"No, go on. Say it."

"It's nothing." He averts his gaze, and if I'm not mistaken, he looks kinda sheepish.

"*Fraser.*"

"Fine. I was just going to ask if maybe I should get your number so I don't, you know, scare the life out of you when I come over again. I'm developing a stress ulcer thinking about what you're capable of doing to me with that umbrella."

I miss his joke, my mind unable to move past anything after *when I come over again.*

He wants to see me again!

Play it cool, Evie. Play. It. Cool.

"Exchanging numbers is so mid-2010s. What if..." My breath catches in my throat, but I'm determined to keep playing it cool and get the words out. "What if we make a no-numbers-exchanged pledge instead and just agree that you come over every Wednesday? That way you won't give me a rare but not completely unheard of teenage heart attack, and there'll be no need for me to use Rosie to commit violence against you."

His lips twitch. "Rosie? The umbrella?"

"You *don't* name inanimate objects?"

He laughs, and it rushes out of him, a deep, warm sound that makes my belly flutter.

"Fine. No exchanging numbers. I accept the pledge," he agrees, his eyes twinkling as he stoops down to move through the windowpane. He glances back and smiles. "See you next Wednesday, Evie."

"You know me, I'm the king of remembering the most random things," Fraser responds lightheartedly to Levi's question about how he knows about my high school obsession with malasadas.

He is the one who got me hooked on them, after all.

"The two of you will fight to have me on your team come trivia night," he adds, and I hope it's enough to satisfy Levi's curiosity.

For a moment, it looks like Levi's going to say something in response, maybe press for more information, but for whatever reason, he drops Portuguese-donut-gate and moves on.

"So, have you two given any more thought to how you're going to handle…" He tips his head toward the coffee table, his eyes widening a fraction when he spots the flowers covering the newspapers. "That?"

"No. I honestly expected this thing to blow over," I reply. "I thought it was just a silly online story, that it wouldn't go much farther than social media. But it seems that my presence at last night's game has only solidified the dating rumors. And with the team's victory, it's given credence to the whole good luck charm angle."

I pick up a pastry and take a bite. "What do you think we should do, Levi?" I ask around a mouthful of malasada.

"Well, you know me, I don't like to meddl—*Oof!* Ow. What was that for?"

He scowls at Fraser while I high-five him. If he hadn't

thrown that cushion at my brother, I would have.

"You meddle," Fraser says matter-of-factly. "It's a known genetic condition affecting everyone born within a twenty-mile radius of Comfort Bay. Come on, man. We need your help. I don't want Evie to go through…"

He doesn't have to finish that sentence for all three of us to know exactly what he meant.

He doesn't want me to go through another round of public humiliation.

The mood in the room shifts.

Levi drops down on the couch opposite Fraser and me. "I don't think this situation is the same as the…*unfortunate incident.*"

He really thinks calling it that is better. His intention is sweet.

Misguided, but sweet.

"We're dealing with an entirely different scenario here. If anything, this could be a win-win."

"How so?"

"Well…Fraser *is* playing better, even if we all know it has nothing to do with your presence. Sorry, Evie."

I stuff a mouthful of donut into my mouth. "I'm soh ohfendid."

Levi rolls his eyes. "Every single time. We go through this every single time."

Fraser chuckles.

Levi continues, "So it'll stop the media from speculating and linking him romantically to every woman he shares air with. And as for you, Evie, yes, this brings media attention onto you as well, but—dare I say it, it's the good kind? It is helping your numbers, right?"

With my mouth still full, I give a thumbs up.

My numbers have never been higher. Not even after my

first viral video.

I downplayed it with Fraser last night because I don't want him thinking I'm enjoying this attention or milking it for career gain. I'm honestly not. It's nothing more than an unexpected bonus.

"What are you getting at, Levi?" Fraser takes up the question I was going to ask.

"What I'm getting at is that you two should date for a while. Fake date, I mean. Otherwise, that would be monumentally weird."

He pulls a face, and I have the sudden urge to fling another cushion his way.

"Let the media run with the story. Eventually, you'll lose a few games, they'll get over it, and then you can quietly fake break-up. And that'll be that."

"That'll be that." Fraser mutters the words under his breath, his expression darkening.

This is absurd.

Someone has to be the voice of reason here, and even though I have literally zero experience in that role, it looks like I have to be the one to put a stop to this.

"I don't think this is a good idea. You obviously don't want to do this, Fraser."

"That's...not true." His intense blue eyes swing my way. "My only concern is you."

I find myself choking slightly as a piece of donut goes down the wrong way.

This guy and his words.

His brow furrows. "You okay?"

"Yep." I smack my chest a few times. "All good."

He waits for me to fully recover before saying, "I'm serious, Evie. I won't even consider this unless you are completely comfortable with it. And also, if we do go ahead with it, I want you to know you can change your mind and back out of it at any time."

"How would it work?" I direct the question toward my totally non-meddling brother.

"Well..." he begins, glancing at the litany of newspapers covering his coffee table. "It seems you two already have some momentum established. So I say, keep it simple. Evie, fly out to a few games so the media can get some photos of you in full-on game mode. Fraser, take Evie out for food somewhere public where you're bound to be seen. Visit her a couple of times back home, and honestly, I think that should be enough to get the media to buy it. The one upside of declining media standards."

"I don't hate it," Fraser says, with a slight nod. "I mean, if we're going to do something as wild as fake dating, I think a low-key approach is the way to go. What do you think, Evie?"

Hmmm...Let's see here.

I get to spend more time with Fraser.

See a few more games, too.

My numbers are likely to stay high, so that's helpful on the work front.

Fraser remembers my two main food groups—burgers and donuts.

He's keeping my apartment well-stocked with my favorite flowers.

And I do owe him one for coming to Bryce's wedding with me.

Aside from all that, I actually *want* to do this.

Good thing, then, that I'm over my crush.

Yep, it's totally gone...I'm, like, seventy-three percent sure.

I brush the sugar off my fingertips, smile at Fraser, and announce, "Looks like you've got yourself a new girlfriend, buddy."

10

Fraser

Getting to spend one day with Evie—even if it was at jerkface's wedding—was a bonus.

Dinner alone with her after the game? Another bonus.

Seeing her at Levi's the following day? Yet another bonus.

And now...my bonus just scored a bonus, and I'm officially the most bonusfully blessed guy in the world.

Trust me when I say I wasn't expecting any of this. I fully believed Evie when she told me over dinner that interest in us would all blow over in a few days.

That dinner was two months ago.

Since then, the story of me and Evie dating hasn't blown over—it's *blown up*.

What's surprising is that I don't actually hate the persistent media attention anywhere near as much as I thought I would.

Most of that comes down to taking Levi's low-key approach.

The press is off my back, no longer speculating and gossiping about every woman I'm seen with. They seem content to snap photos of Evie in the stands whenever she can fly out to a game.

So far, we've gone out on three public dinner outings. Each time, we get spotted by fans who post the photos online, and then voila, the next day, it hits the mainstream media.

Who knew that two people eating burgers could generate so much interest and such a variety of hashtags?

I will *never* understand social media, and I am one hundred percent okay with that.

The team is doing well.

Our record so far for the season is 14-4-2. Fourteen wins, four losses, and two overtime losses. My personal stats are thirteen goals and twenty assists. Even though it's still early, we're in a good position within our division and are on track to secure a playoff spot.

I actually don't mind the few losses we've had as much as I normally would. I have this secret fear that once we inevitably lose a game or two, the press might turn on Evie. The good luck chalice can quickly turn poisonous. I've seen it happen before to other players' girlfriends, and I don't want it happening to my girl.

Yes, I said *my girl*. I'm aware.

In my private thoughts, that's how I think of her.

Thankfully, Evie hasn't been blamed for any of our defeats. Maybe it helps that she wasn't in attendance at two of the four games we lost. Or maybe the halo effect of being Alex Freeman's daughter grants her a degree of immunity. Who knows? I'm just happy the media and fans are still on her side and that we're pulling this whole fake dating thing off.

All in all, the plan is going swimmingly.

And I haven't lost the thing I value the most—my privacy.

Because my day-to-day life has stayed pretty much the same. I still play and train like normal. I still avoid interviews —really, any interaction with the press—like the plague. I'm still perceived as guarded and aloof.

Importantly, though, my family's secret remains safe.

I'm coming back from spending a few hours with Dawn and Oakey in the mountains. As long as they're protected, I'm fine with everything else.

And I'm more than fine with what's about to happen tonight.

Because, without a doubt, the best part of this whole fake dating thing has been getting to spend more time with Evie.

I'm standing outside her apartment, yellow roses in hand, grinning to myself like an idiot. This was never part of the

Levi-plan, but it's something Evie and I just, I don't know, fell into.

Having time together. Privately. Alone.

No cameras.

No deliberate attention-seeking.

No pretending.

The time we spend like this feels very, very real. Like how it used to feel back in high school.

I don't know what it is, but there's something about Evie that loosens me up. Dismantles whatever guardrails I have.

All without even trying. It just...happens.

Which means I have to tread carefully here. Something else I am acutely aware of.

I can't forget this is a limited arrangement. I'm already way luckier than I have any right to be, getting to spend this much time with her.

I have to make the most of whatever time we have left, because at some point, she'll want to end this craziness and return to her regular life, and I'll go back to being alone.

Which is fine.

Whatever.

I'm okay with that since I'm clearly not cut out for relationships, judging by my dating track record up until this point.

I ring the doorbell and mentally brace myself for that tingly feeling that randomly pops up whenever we're together.

She opens the door and smiles brightly. Right on cue, my chest tingles.

"Fraser, hi! Oh, my gosh, you bought flowers. Again. You know, I was just wondering whether you would. But then I said to myself, *Evie, stop it. The man is not obligated to bring you flowers every time he sees you.* But then I countered that with, *But, hey, if your fake boyfriend likes bringing you flowers, let him.*

But then I thought I should probably tell you that you don't *have to* bring me flowers. I don't want it to feel like an obligation or a chore. So, wait...um, I've lost my train of thought. I did have a point to all this rambling."

I laugh, handing her the bouquet. "My key takeaway is that you like it when I bring you flowers. Correct?"

"Correct."

"And I like bringing you flowers, so there's no issue."

I give her an all too brief peck on the cheek and step inside her apartment. It's my first time here. Given the hectic season schedule, all the time we've spent together has been when Evie has flown out to see me play away games.

Our private hangouts have always been in hotel suites, where we devour room service burgers, then rearrange the furniture, lie down on the floor, stare up at the ceiling, and talk...like we used to.

I've got a mandatory bye week this week, so I've snuck in a quick trip to Comfort Bay for two days. I've already gotten to see Dawn and Oakey. I'll do the obligatory family thing tomorrow, but right now, the only thing that matters is getting to spend some time with Evie.

"So this is Château Evie," I remark, taking it in.

The place is quintessential Evie. Charming. Eclectic. Colorful. Slightly chaotic, with artfully stacked books, an assortment of vibrant plants by the massive window, and a collage of framed posters.

I smile when I notice they're a lot like the ones she had in her bedroom, a mix of hockey players and punk music album covers. The last frame displays four prominent women in hockey today, just like the four-in-one photo she used to have back in high school.

"It's a mess, and if you were an actual boyfriend, I'd make up some lie about it."

"What sort of lie?"

"You know, like, *Oh, I've just been so busy at work, I haven't had time to clean*, or, *Normally I'm not this messy*." Her hazel eyes meet mine. "But it's you..."

She pokes my chest with her finger...and yep, tingles.

"...and I'm sure you remember how messy my teenage bedroom was."

"You think yours was messy? You should've seen mine. Teenage boy rooms are the worst. And the smell. Don't even get me started on the smell."

She starts laughing as we head toward her kitchen. She grabs a vase, fills it with water, and starts arranging the yellow roses.

"So, how have you been?" I ask.

I am genuinely interested to know, but I also genuinely need something to distract me from how amazing she looks. She's in a dusty-pink loungewear set of drawstring joggers, a knitted tank top, and a cardigan that drapes loosely over her body, falling down past her hips.

I've never dated anyone who can pull off effortless chic as well as Evie does.

Okay, that last thought is a clear sign my brain is in trouble. I need to remind myself that none of this is real. We're fake dating, that's it. Get it together, man.

Shut down. Restart. Reactivate listening mode.

"...and so, I don't know, with my numbers at work flatlining despite all the attention we're getting, I'm just feeling a little *blerg*."

Wait. Her numbers are falling?

"How is that possible? The guys are always ribbing me at practice about some new meme featuring the two of us."

She leans against the counter. "Apparently, it's nothing personal, which I'm finding harder and harder to believe. We went through another round of focus group testing, and people just aren't into the type of stories I present."

"Are you kidding me? Yesterday's story."

"Don't talk to me about yesterday's story." Evie starts fanning her eyes. "I'll start crying."

She won't be the only one.

It was one of her best ever, about a dad who passed away from cancer when his daughter was twelve. Before he died, he prepaid a florist to deliver flowers and a note from him every year on her birthday. It's one of the most thoughtful and touching things I've ever seen.

"How can people not like your stories? It baffles me."

"Thank you for saying that. Now, if you could please stream my segments eighty-seven thousand times, that might make the network happy."

"I don't understand why your numbers are declining. Isn't the media obsessed with us?"

"Interest *is* starting to fade a bit," she explains. "And even though we still get a lot of traction on social media and gossip sites, that's not translating to people tuning in to my segments anymore."

I huff out an annoyed breath, hating this so much. She's so freaking talented, and her stories are so freaking good.

"Is there anything I can do?"

With a playful twinkle in her eye and a roguish grin, she begins, "Well—"

"Besides streaming your segments eighty-seven thousand times?" I cut in since that's where I know she's heading. "Something that's, you know, actually doable?"

She hesitates for a moment, then says, "There isn't, but thank you for the offer. Come on. Let's go into the living room."

"Uh..."

She stops walking. "Uh, what?"

"Aren't you making dinner?"

"I am."

"Doesn't dinner-making normally take place in the kitchen? Or do normal food-preparation rules not apply in Evie Land?"

"Oh, Fraser."

She comes over to me and slides her fingers against my cheek, lightly running her thumb over my scar.

Tingle, tingle, tingle.

"You don't need pots and pans and ovens to make food. That's so 1950s. All today's modern gal-on-the-go needs is one of these." She waves her phone in front of me. "Why, in just a few taps, I can *make* whatever food you like magically appear."

I grin. "And by *whatever food you like*, I assume you mean…"

We say *burgers* at the same time.

"I placed the order right before you got here. Should be arriving in about ten minutes."

Our eyes meet. Hers sparkle in the soft glow of string lights she's hung up along the wall above her posters.

"Wanna watch a game?" she asks predictably.

"Can you ever not have a game on in the background?"

She reaches for the remote control, then tilts her face at me. "I could. But why would I want that?"

I chuckle. "Fair enough."

While Evie browses for a game to put on, I notice a familiar sight on the desk in her work nook. I wander over, thread a piece of material around my finger, and spin around.

"You making bracelets again?"

"Oh. Yeah." She settles on a game and walks over to me, eyeing all the fabrics strewn over the desk. "I tried getting back into it during my, uh, first viral moment, but I didn't enjoy it. To be fair, I wasn't enjoying much at the time. Even burgers weren't hitting the same."

"Yikes. That's some serious stuff."

She bumps into my side, and it takes all the restraint I have in me not to wrap my arm around her and keep her there.

"But lately..." She shrugs. "I don't know. I seem to have gotten back into it."

"That's really cool." A few finished bracelets are laid out. Her style has changed since high school, and these look nothing like the one she gave me.

Should I mention that? Slip the topic we haven't even come close to broaching once into the conversation like it's no big deal?

No. I can't do that.

Because it *is* a big deal.

I stalk over to the window, needing to put some space between us.

I'm not even sure if I properly thanked her for making it for me. I'd like to think that I did, but so much about that night is a blur, I honestly can't remember.

And then to top it off, I disappeared the next day without saying goodbye.

That I do remember, and I hate myself for doing it.

But amidst all the chaos, with my dad kicking the crew out of the house, and Dawn in hysterics, my brothers and I had to do what we were told.

Shut everything down.

Act normal.

Don't speak to anyone.

And in my case, leave for training camp as if everything had been pre-planned, like our entire world hadn't just been changed forever.

That's not something you slip into a conversation. That's something a coward like jerkface would do.

No.

If...*when*...the time is right and Evie and I have that conversation, I'm going to do it properly.

"You ever think about selling them?" I ask, staying a safe few feet away from her. "I'm sure people would buy 'em up."

"Nah. It's a passion project. Nothing else."

"Keep it in mind," I say. "If it's something you enjoy, why not make a living out of it? That way work won't ever feel like work."

She shoots me a peculiar glance.

"Sorry. I flicked through a bunch of Hallmark cards while I was waiting at the flower shop on my way over. The cheesiness must have rubbed off on me. Don't worry, Hannah already roasted me for it. Said she had to get a few jabs in on your behalf. Something about girl code."

"You know it's rare..." Evie moves away from the desk. "Incredibly rare, actually..." She gets closer to me. "For me to meet someone on my level of..." She narrows her eyes and looks up at me in concentration. "Quirkiness. But you, Mr. Rademacher. You're up there."

I take a step toward her. Barely a few inches separate us. "I take it that meets with your approval?"

"It does."

"I like the way we banter," I say, aware that I've told her this a few times already over the course of the past few months.

She brushes her hand down the side of my arm. "I like the way we banter, too."

I move in closer, curl my fingers around the back of her neck, and widen my stance.

Her face tilts up.

My face angles down...

The doorbell rings.

Evie lets out a squeal and jumps back. Her pupils are blown out, her lips are parted, and she's breathing heavily.

And dammit, we didn't even kiss.

"Food," she croaks.

"Uh-huh." I run my hand through my hair as she dashes out of the room to answer the door.

Okay, so much for reining in my feelings for Evie.

Maybe getting interrupted is a sign.

A confirmation that I shouldn't do anything that even looks like I'm pursuing Evie—aside from whenever we're in public, when we hug after a game, or walk hand-in-hand from the arena.

Because every time we almost kiss, we get interrupted.

That's twice now, for those keeping score.

First at the beach after jerkface's wedding, and now, tonight.

Every single other time we've hung out, I've tested the limits of my self-restraint, and all we've ever done is talk like we did back in the day.

I've never wanted to mess with the good vibe we've got going, and maybe I'm imagining things, but I'm picking up that Evie might have some boundaries when it comes to intimate contact like kissing. I can't explain it. It's just a feeling I've got.

All the more reason to keep my hands—and my lips—to myself and stay on the correct side of the imaginary line I've drawn in my head.

Evie and I are fake dating. Even if the friendship forming between us is every bit real.

"I come bearing burgers and truth fries," she proclaims with a wide smile, carrying what looks like two very full takeout bags.

I jolt myself back to reality. "Awesome. I'm starving. Where do you want to eat?"

"If you actually were my boyfriend, I'd say something like,

let's eat at the table like adults. Or, if the relationship was going really well and I felt secure enough, I might suggest sitting on the floor and eating at the coffee table and make it appear like that wasn't my preferred—no, wait, my sole—way of eating."

"So floor it is, then," I say, taking the bags from her.

Her face lights up. "I knew Levi kept you around for a reason."

We sit down and dig in. Evie's eyes flit between the TV, the food, and me. She deftly keeps the conversation light, and it's like almost-kiss number two never happened.

Maybe that's how she'd prefer it? To leave it behind. She is all about moving on, isn't she?

But that doesn't stop me from being curious about how she's doing.

How she's *really* doing.

I'm not normally one to pry, but I decide to use this situation to my advantage and perform a deep-fried power play.

I pick up a fry and extend it toward her. "Do you, Evie Freeman, solemnly swear to follow the fry oath and tell the truth, the whole truth, and nothing but the truth so help the gods of deep fried food and baked goods?"

She drops her burger and lifts her hand by the side of her face. "I do…if I can have that fry."

"Why would you want a fry from me?" I drop my gaze. "Oh. You ate yours already, huh?"

"I did."

She seems a little uncomfortable, but not as all-out embarrassed as she was the first time this happened.

Or the second.

Or even the third.

"How about from now on, we only get large fries so we can share them?"

Her lips curve into a smile. "Deal."

How weird, on the Rademacher scale of weirdness, is it that I think it's sexy that she likes to eat?

I slide my fries into the center of the coffee table.

She takes one and nibbles on the end. "So what is it you want to know that requires pledging allegiance to the almighty fry?"

"Well, we've been hanging out a bit."

"We have."

"We talk."

"Mainly me, but sure, we do."

I smile. "But we haven't talked about one topic. In fact, we've avoided it altogether."

"What topic might that be?"

"Love."

"Oh." She adjusts how she's sitting. "What would you like to know?"

"Well...apart from jerkface, have you been in any other serious relationships?"

I know for a fact that she has, but every time Levi's brought it up, I've quickly changed the subject. He probably took it as a sign that I wasn't interested in his little sister's dating life, when the truth was, I simply couldn't handle knowing about it.

Hearing about the girl you're in love with—the girl you've been in love with for so many years and can't get over—dating someone else is about as much fun as a colonoscopy.

Especially when that girl happens to be my best friends' younger sister. Yeah, that's a whole world of pain I'm not ready to deal with. I don't even want to think about Levi's reaction. Given how protective he is of her, he'd likely go ballistic and probably never speak to me again. But that's a problem for future Fraser.

Current Fraser is blocking everything else out and giving Evie his undivided attention.

"I had two serious relationships before Bryce," Evie says, her features settling into a somber expression. "Both lasted about a year. Same as my relationship with Bryce. And then they ended. I got dumped. Something happens around that pesky twelve-month mark. An invisible, relationship-ending button must go off in their heads and, poof, end of relationship. I'm starting to think I might be cursed."

You're not cursed. They're just idiots.

I want to tell her that.

I want to assure her there is absolutely nothing wrong with her. That she's funny and smart and the best person ever to hang out with.

More importantly, I want her to believe it.

To have the self-doubt clouding her eyes vanish. To see the worry leave her face for good. To have her know on a deep, soul level that the issue wasn't her. It couldn't be—because she's perfect.

But I also have to be careful here. Praising Evie is a lot like buying flowers for her—once I start, I don't seem to be able to stop.

I realize my next question may be pushing the limits of the fry oath, but I ask it anyway.

"Were any of the guys 'the one'?"

"Heck, no."

No hesitation there at all.

My chest expands in...relief?

Relief for her, I mean. It's good that her *'one'* didn't get away.

"And are you okay now, how things are with...everything?"

She shoots me a friendly smile. "Is that your way of asking

if I'm over Bryce without saying his name or calling him jerkface?"

"I have zero qualms about calling him jerkface," I remind her. "But yes, it is."

"I am over it. I got over it at the wedding. When I went over to speak to him, I realized that what I needed from that day was closure. And I got it."

"That's good. I'm happy for you."

"Besides, we really weren't right for each other."

"Oh."

"He was a vegetarian."

I scoff. "First red flag. Nothing against vegetarians. Dawn is one. But you're like a butcher shop, with all the burgers you consume."

"I know, right?"

She giggles playfully, and the sweet sound sends a ripple of tingles cascading down my spine.

"It was other things, though. He didn't get my humor. In fact, I think I kind of exhausted him. He was naturally a morning person. He hated farmer's markets. He liked my parents. He bought me the one and only type of flower I'm allergic to. I mean, I couldn't have asked for clearer signs from the universe that we just weren't meant to be."

Listening to Evie rattle off all of jerkface's faults has got me gritting my teeth so hard, I'm surprised they haven't been crushed yet from the sheer force.

"And there were some other ways we were incompatible."

A slight blush rises up her neck, and I get that feeling again that maybe she's hinting at something to do with her boundaries.

Definitely won't be pressing her on that. If she wants to tell me, she can, but only if and when she's ready.

She picks up a fry and dangles it in front of my face. "And

now do *you*, Fraser Rademacher, solemnly swear to follow the fry oath and tell the truth, the whole truth, and nothing but the truth so help the gods of deep fried food and baked goods?"

"I do," I reply, dipping my head earnestly in agreement. "Anything you want to ask, just ask. I'm an open book."

Evie giggles again, and once I hear what I just said, I start chuckling, too.

"You are many things, but an open book? Hardly."

My cheeks get a little warmer. "You're right. I'm not. I don't know why I said that."

Maybe because when I'm around her, those words actually ring true. Evie could ask me anything, and I'd tell her.

Well, apart from the family secret, but that's only because we all agreed we'd keep it. If I wanted to change that rule, I'd have to run it past my family. It sucks because it's the one thing —the only thing—I can't be fully truthful about with Evie.

"What's your dating story?" she asks. "Have you found 'the one' yet?"

I have, and she's sitting on the floor across from me, chomping down on a fry, completely oblivious to my feelings because I'm too much of a coward to tell her how I feel.

"I, uh...guess not. Not yet, anyway."

"It wasn't Tori?"

"It *definitely* wasn't Tori."

"I didn't think she seemed like your type. She was a little, uh, outgoing."

"If by outgoing you mean she would have done anything for press, including selling our private vacation photos to an online entertainment website, then yes, you're right."

Evie winces. "I had no idea she did that. I'm sorry."

"Thanks. I seem to be a magnet for that type of girl, you know? They don't really care about me, they're only interested in dating a pro hockey player. The attention. The lifestyle. All the frivolous stuff that I couldn't care less about but that comes with being a pro athlete."

I stop talking, aware I might be playing the victim when I'm not. I just attract women who crave the limelight.

Tori never once asked me about my favorite book. Or whether I like cats or dogs. Or even really delved into my family or childhood.

We weren't on the same wavelength.

Oh, and the banter between us? Non-existent.

Tori once asked me if I was having a mild stroke when I went on a mini-rant about the unusual way the cashier was bagging groceries at the store.

But Evie?

She would've jumped right in there with no hesitation, riffing off me and probably bringing in the checkout dividers —which I'm sure she would have given names to—and it'd be something we'd spend the rest of the day talking and laughing about.

I clear my throat. "I still haven't forgiven Dawn for setting me up with her."

As if sensing I'm keen to change the subject, Evie asks, "How is Dawn doing these days?"

Of course Evie's got no idea that's a topic I want to talk about even less than my less-than-stellar dating life.

My shoulders tense. "She's fine."

"I heard she's living nearby. Up in Cedar Crest Hollow?"

Mom is still friends with Evie's mom, so it makes sense she'd know that.

"That's right."

"It's beautiful up there. I haven't driven up the mountain in ages. Maybe we could go sometime? I'd love to see Dawn."

"Uh, sure. You all done?"

Evie nods, and I scoop up all the wrappers and toss them into the bags.

Not exactly being subtle that I don't want to talk about my sister, but I can't help it. The topic of Dawn always puts me on edge. I failed to protect her once. I can't let her down again. Even if it means withholding the truth from Evie.

I take the bags into the kitchen, and when I return, we lie on the floor to watch the game. Yes, she has a couch we could be sitting on, but why waste a perfectly good floor? It totally takes me back to old times.

At the end of the night, Evie walks me to the door.

"Thanks for the burgers," I say.

"Thanks for sharing your fries with me."

"No problem." I waver for a moment. "I've been thinking, since we've already broken our no-numbers-exchanged pledge and have been texting each other to make plans..."

"The pledge we made seven years ago when we were next-door neighbors and didn't need phones to communicate with each other?"

I grin. "That's the one. Since we already have each other's numbers..."

"Yeah?"

"And since our schedules for the next few weeks are brutal and we won't be able to see each other, what if..."

Come on, man, just spit it out already.

"What if we have some chat dates?"

Evie scrunches up her nose in confusion. "Chat dates?"

"Yeah. See, there's this neat function on your cell phone. Apparently you just press a person's name from your contact list, and then somehow—don't ask me how because it's well above my paygrade—a few seconds later, you hear that person's voice on the other end of the line."

"I've never heard of this before."

"Apparently it's something people used to do all the time in the dark ages."

"You mean the '90s?"

"Exactly."

Evie taps her chin. "Chat dates, eh?"

I chuckle nervously. "Are you up for it?"

"Yeah." A smile blooms across her face. "I'd really like that."

11

Evie

"I have to admit, I thought this would be weird."

"Weird, how?" Fraser's smooth, deep voice drifts through the speaker on my phone, while I'm finishing off some bracelets.

"Like, I thought it would feel like I'm talking to myself."

"Don't tell me you never talk to yourself? You're a prime candidate for self-talking."

"What's that supposed to mean?"

"It means you love to talk. You talk back to the TV."

"When I'm watching a game."

"Oh, well, in that case..." Fraser lets out a rusty chuckle. "I've seen you talk to your flowers."

"Yes, and notice how they always last for a long time? I'm convinced plants respond to kind words."

"I bet they do. But what I'm getting at is that I think it's interesting you find talking like this, over the phone, so novel. Don't you call your friends all the time?"

"Nope. We have a group chat."

"Levi?"

"Texts, mainly."

"Your mom?"

"I have dinner with my parents every Thursday, which gets me out of having to call her during the week."

"Right. So this whole phone-talking thing *is* new for you."

"It really is."

"Well, you're doing remarkably well."

I smile even though he can't see it. "Thank you."

It's our first chat date, and I'm acing it, apparently.

This was such a great idea.

I can't make it to any of Fraser's games for the next few

weeks because I'm needed at work, and since my numbers are back to anemic, I'm in no position to ask for time off to fly around the country to watch my boyfriend play hockey.

Oops, fake boyfriend. I keep slipping up on that.

I lay down the bracelet I've been working on. "So, what now?"

"Nothing. We just keep talking. I'm a classic man, favoring the traditional back-and-forth method where one of us says something, the other listens, and then we switch. But I'm also open to the Evie Freeman method."

I smile and sit up taller. "Enlighten me please."

"Well, I have to say it's evolved over time. It used to be harsh hockey critiques sprinkled with occasional musings on a variety of random topics."

"The random musings are still trademark Evie."

Fraser laughs. "They are. But there's been a shift. Hockey feedback has mellowed. I no longer have my therapist on speed dial."

"Speed dial. Talking on the phone. This is all so '90s. Are you sure you're really twenty-five and not a freakishly young-looking forty-five-year-old man?"

"I may have the knees of a forty-five-year-old man, but I can assure you I am, indeed, twenty-five."

"Gosh..." I pick up a piece of fabric and twirl it between my fingers.

"Gonna need more than that, Evie. See, the thing about chat dates on the phone is that I can't see what your face is doing."

"My face is grinning. And the *gosh* was me remembering when you being two years older than me felt like this massive age gap. Now it's nothing."

"It's totally nothing."

"And I have to say, this whole fake-dating thing is going better than I thought it would."

"How so? Oh, and for the record, because you can't see me, I need to tell you that I'm lying on the bed in my hotel room."

"Not brave enough to venture onto the carpet?"

"No. There are...stains."

"I don't want to know."

He laughs. "Me neither."

I get up from my desk and lie down on my stain-free floor. "Well, for the record, because you can't see me, I need to tell you that I've moved from my desk and have joined you in the lying down thing. Although, I'm on my floor since, well, I was going to say my floor doesn't have stains, but that wouldn't be entirely true. But at least I know I'm the one responsible for all of them. Well, me and the food companies I use to make all my meals."

Fraser laughs again, and the rich, warm sound settles in my chest. I love being able to make him loosen up like this.

"So tell me why you're liking this fake dating thing more than you thought you would," he says.

"Well, my social media numbers have skyrocketed."

"And I know how obsessed you are about that."

I bring out the most Valley Girl voice I can. "It's, like, literally the most important thing ever."

I'm treated to another laugh.

"I'm loving how well the team is doing," I continue, a little more seriously now. "Plus, it's great to get flown out to see more games. But I still think nothing beats the atmosphere of a home crowd, if you ask me."

"I wholeheartedly agree with you on that one."

"The me being a good luck charm thing has worn off, which I'm very glad about. It was a weird pressure to have to bear."

"Also in full agreement with you on that."

I hesitate for a second. "But do you want to know what my absolute favorite thing is?"

"I do. Tell me."

"This."

"Define *this*, please. For all I know, you've looked under your couch and found a half-eaten pack of Oreos."

"Fraser! I would never"—I cast a quick glance under my couch. Nothing. Damn—"do that. What I mean by *this* is this. Hanging out with you privately. Actually, hanging out with you in public isn't that bad, either. But when we're alone it feels…it feels really nice."

"At the risk of repeating myself, I couldn't agree with you more."

Actually, it's more than nice, but I'm not ready to tell him that just yet.

Being with Fraser is unlocking parts of me I hadn't even realized I'd locked away.

I guess I've always felt a little on the backfoot for not wanting to progress to anything more intimate than kissing with the guys I've dated, so I tried to make up for it in other ways. I suppressed who I was—or tried to, at least—toning down my quirkiness, my messiness, my lack of food making-ness.

It never worked, clearly.

But fake dating Fraser means I can just be me. Even the parts of me that aren't the greatest. I mean, he didn't instantly dismiss the idea of me eating a newly rediscovered half-eaten packet of Oreos…and yet, even if that's what I had been doing, I get the feeling he wouldn't have minded. It's as if he likes all of me, which is probably why my walls are starting to crumble and my crush is returning.

Big time.

But unlike in high school, this time it's different. Because this time, it's not just a one-way thing.

I'm confident Fraser feels something happening between us as well.

We almost kissed again when he came over to my place.

He's opening up to me like he used to, even if he got oddly guarded when the topic of Dawn came up.

And he's the one who suggested these chat dates.

That has to mean something...doesn't it?

Fraser

"Wow. Two calls in two days."

I wince. "It's too much. I'm calling too much, aren't I?"

Silence hangs in the air.

I pull my phone away from my ear.

The call is still connected. Evie's still there. Probably trying to find a diplomatic way to reply to that.

"It's fine," she says eventually. "More than fine, actually."

"Really?" I double check to make sure.

"Really. I'm usually so exhausted by the time I get home I don't have the energy to do anything. I wouldn't say I'm lonely, but it's nice having someone to talk to while I chill out in a face mask and sweats."

Picturing Evie in a face mask and sweats should not set my imagination on fire. What is wrong with me?

"How was your day?" I ask, settling into a comfortable position on the bed.

She tells me about the ridiculously early start she had today to join her friends on a sunrise walk, which, according to her, should be renamed to a pre-sunrise walk for accuracy reasons since she needed to drag herself out of bed while it was still dark to make it to their favorite vantage point in time to see the sun rise.

I smile and listen as she tells me more about her day, loving hearing her voice, feeling like she's close to me when in reality, we're on opposite sides of the country.

I've been thinking about her all day.

During the bus ride from New York to Philadelphia, when I caught up on a bunch of her segments I'd missed.

Throughout practice.

Training in the gym.

While I was having a massage.

Evie was all I could think about.

Which isn't good.

My self-restraint is slipping.

Let me rephrase that. My self-restraint has bolted out the door, left the building, and is now five blocks away, looking back at me and laughing maniacally.

I shouldn't be doing this.

The control I've kept tightly woven for years is unraveling, and yet...I'm the one who suggested these chat dates because the thought of having no contact with her during this busy period wasn't okay. I couldn't let that happen.

I feel like I'm on borrowed time anyway.

We can both see that the media's focus has shifted from us, laying the groundwork for a quiet breakup and an end to this whole fake dating thing.

But I don't want it to end.

As selfish as it may be, I want to keep this going for as long as possible. Time is slipping away, and I may not get to share many more moments like this with her ever again.

"So," Evie says, her voice taking on an unmissable firmness. "Let's talk about your game tomorrow. I have some notes."

I smile, staring up at the ceiling. "Tell me everything I need to know."

Evie

"This is a surprise," is how Fraser answers my call.

"Sorry, I realize I'm calling in the middle of the day."

"No. I mean, that you know how to make a call. I'm impressed."

"Ha. Ha." I've ducked away into an empty meeting room. Fraser has a game tonight, so I figure we won't be able to talk later. Even though we did only speak last night. "Are you busy?"

"We've just finished our game day skate. I'm about to take a shower, and then we're heading out for a team meal. But I've got a few minutes."

"This won't take long. I just wanted to wish you good luck."

He doesn't say anything.

"For the game."

Still nothing.

"That you're playing. Tonight."

I can't spell it out any clearer, can I?

"Um. Thank you. That's really nice of you, Evie."

"What sort of girlfriend would I be if I didn't call to wish my boyfriend all the best?"

He chuckles, but it comes out a little garbled. Must be a bad connection.

"Look, I won't keep you," I say since Fraser sounds like he's in pre-game mode, and the last thing I want to do is break his focus. "Have a great game. I'll be watching."

"Yeah...Thanks for calling. I mean it."

"No worries. Bye, Fraser."
"Bye, Evie."

Fraser

"Oh my god, you were amazing! Another hat trick! I am so freaking proud of you."

I'm still riding the post-game high.

Another big win—5-2—against Philly, who beat us every time we played them last season, making tonight's victory even sweeter.

I'm back in my hotel room after celebrating with the team. It was good to blow off some steam with Culver and the rest of the guys, but when I saw Evie had been texting me, I decided to call it a night. I couldn't wait until tomorrow to hear her voice again.

"Thanks. The guys did incredible."

"Don't be so modest. So did you. You were the star. I haven't heard Dad yell so loud in a long time."

It makes me happier than it should knowing Evie watched the game with her old man. Alex Freeman is a personal hero of mine. Not just a living legend of the game, but one of the best men I know off the rink, too.

He's dedicated his post-game life to contributing to scholarship funds to help young people pursue their educational goals. It's inspiring and makes me want to follow in his footsteps when I leave the game.

"Hang on a minute." I glance over at the clock on the nightstand. "What time is it there?"

It's almost one on the east coast, which means...

"It's five to ten."

"And you're working tomorrow, right?"

"I am."

I grimace, hating that I'm calling when she should probably be sleeping. Start times in morning TV are ridiculously early. "Sorry for calling so late."

"It's fine. I couldn't fall asleep anyway."

"Why not?"

"It's nothing."

"What's wrong?"

"Nothing. I don't want to be a downer on a night like this. We should be celebrating your win."

"*Evie.*"

"Fine. My boss wants to speak with me tomorrow."

"Why are you making it sound so ominous?"

"Because she scheduled the meeting in my calendar."

"I may never have worked in a corporate setting before, but isn't that something normal people who work in offices do?"

"It is. But Margo isn't normal people. Her meetings are impromptu walks around the office. Or chats in the cafeteria. Occasionally, the toilet stalls, if you're really unlucky."

"Do I want to know?"

"Believe me, you don't."

She lets out a sigh, and it tears me up being so far away and completely powerless to do anything to help her.

"It must be serious if she's calling me into her office," she says.

We've spoken a few times about her low ratings, so I'm guessing it's probably got something to do with that. Unable to offer any specific assistance or advice, I go with, "Look, whatever it is, you're strong, Evie, and I'm sure you'll be able to handle it."

She yawns, and as much as I want to keep talking and reassuring her, it's late.

"You need to get some rest."

"I really do. I'll need it for tomorrow."

"Let me know how it goes, okay?"

"All right. I'll text—"

A guttural growl bubbles up in my throat.

She must hear it because she stops, then amends. "Fine. I'll call."

"Good—" I grunt, then snap myself out of my unexpected detour into caveman land.

Since when am I a grunter?

"Goodnight, is what I meant to say."

"Uh-huh. Okay. Goodnight, Fraser, and congratulations again on an awesome game."

Evie

I head toward Margo's office, my belly fluttering with nerves. Despite feeling a bit better after Fraser's assurances last night, I get the feeling I should prepare myself for some bad news.

Margo's been in LA all week, meeting with the network bigwigs. It's not a coincidence she's scheduled a meeting first thing in the morning on the day she returns.

I stop before reaching her open door, take a deep breath, remind myself that I'm strong and can handle whatever comes my way, and step inside.

"Hey, Margo."

"Hey, hon."

She gets up, and I assume she's coming over to greet me with a hug, but nope, she walks right past me and closes the door instead.

Yikes. A scheduled *closed-door* meeting. This is serious.

She gestures toward the L-shaped sofa in the corner of her office. I plop down on the couch, and she joins me a few moments later.

"I have some bad news, I'm afraid."

"You went ahead with that hideous back tattoo and now you're regretting it?"

She has the grace to smile at my weak attempt at humor. "We can revisit my pre-midlife-crisis plans some other time. As you know, I've been in LA."

"I do."

"What you may not be aware of is that ad revenue is down across the board, affecting almost every show."

"How bad is it?"

"Terminal. The network needs to make some cuts."

"Oh no." I cover my mouth. "I'm getting fired."

"Not yet. I managed to buy you some time."

"How much time?"

"A month."

"A month? That's...that's nothing. I may as well start packing up my stuff now."

"It's not nothing, Evie. It's a chance. Your last chance to make a splash. You *need* a big story."

My shoulders slump. "Why are you doing this? Why are you battling so hard for me?"

"Because I hired you, so I'm personally invested. But more than that, because I believe in you. Not just in the stories you're telling, but also, your approach."

"My approach?"

Margo gets up and wanders over to the big window. "When I was young, all I wanted to do was to get out of my small outback town in the middle of nowhere—which, in Australia, we have a lot of nowhere—move to the city, and make something out of myself. My drive, hard work, and persistence took me to Sydney, then Singapore, followed by stints in Paris, London, New York, and finally, Comfort Bay."

"I feel so bad for all those other places. They've got nothing on Comfort Bay."

She smiles and sits back down next to me, a little closer this time. "They really don't. I spent my twenties and a good chunk of my thirties chasing my dreams, reaching my dreams, only to realize dreams coming true aren't so great when you've got no one to share them with."

"You're talking about your husband Hamish?"

"I am. Fifteen-year-old feminist me would die knowing that I'd give up my glamorous, jet-setting career, where I was making serious headway to becoming the head honcho, to settle down in a small town for a man, pop out a couple of kids, and run a local breakfast show."

"I've always admired you for that very decision, Margo. When my mom gets on my case that I should pursue a 'real career,' I think about what you did. Your decision to give it all up for a small-town life. That inspires me so much."

"Thank you. But here's the thing, hon…It doesn't feel like I gave anything up. I still love what I do for work. It's just that now I have a husband who supports me and two children who fill my life with more meaning than I ever thought possible."

She gives my knee a gentle press. "I can't speak to where your mother is coming from because believe me, I know a thing or two about overbearing parents, but I can tell you this. I admire your decision to pursue the type of career *you* want."

"Even if no one tunes in?"

She shrugs. "I don't know what's going wrong, Evie."

"What about the Rademacher effect?" I ask. "Why isn't that working? I am still the girlfriend of one of the—correction—of *the* hottest player in the NHL."

"You know the press as well as I do. It's old news now. You

and Fraser have been together for months, so the novelty of the redemption story and the good luck charm angle has worn off."

I drop my head. "So what do I do?"

"I'll tell you what you don't do. You *do not* give up, Evie. You have a month. That's enough time to convince that hunky hockey-playing boyfriend of yours to sit down for an exclusive interview."

"I can't." I angle my head to face Margo. "Fraser will never go for it."

"Have you asked him?"

"I don't need to. I know him."

"True. But...for someone who hates the press, he's also dating someone who *is* the press."

"Your point?"

"My point is that maybe whatever blocks or issues Fraser has with the media could be sidestepped if *you* were the one conducting the interview."

"I highly doubt it."

"There's only one way to find out. Why don't you put a package together, something that you can present to Fraser so he sees for himself that he won't be exploited or taken advantage of, that addresses whatever his reasons are for not trusting the media. If he sees that, he might change his mind."

I huff out a despondent breath. "That's my only option?"

"Well, no. The network needs you to pull out something big. Personally, I think an interview with Fraser is your best bet for achieving it, but if you can come up with something else, then by all means, go for it. But Evie?"

"Yeah?"

"You only have one month left."

At home that night, I take out my phone and open The Vinaigrettes group chat.

Evie: *I need some advice. Is anyone around?*
Hannah: *I'm here.*
Beth: *I'm here.*
Summer: *I'm here.*
Amiel: *Me, too.*
Evie: *Okay, the full complement. Excellent. My boss wants me to do something I don't think is a good idea.*
Hannah: *Does it involve a dead body?*
Beth: *Is it singing in public?*
Summer: *Or dancing in public?*
Beth: *Ooh, yeah. That's definitely worse. Amiel, Evie has zero rhythm.*
Amiel*: Noted. Thanks for the heads-up.*
Evie: *It's none of those things, thank you very much. This is serious. Margo wants me to do a story about Fraser.*
Hannah: *But he'd never go for that.*
Evie: *I know that. But I need something big. Something to attract massive ratings. I'm conflicted.*
Summer: *Have you spoken to him about it?*
Evie: *No.*
Summer: *Why not?*
Evie: *Because I KNOW he'll say no. I should just leave it, right?*
Hannah: *Is that what your gut is telling you?*
Evie: *It is.*
Hannah: *So, yeah, leave it. For now, at least.*
Beth: *You can always revisit things later.*
Summer: *I concur. Keep it as a backup plan.*
Amiel: *That sounds like a reasonable approach.*
Evie: *Excellent advice. Thank you, ladies!*

That really is solid advice.

I can put the Fraser story on the backburner, and in the meantime, try to come up with something that doesn't involve him.

That feels like the right thing to do.

Evie: *How are you settling into Comfort Bay, Amiel?*
Amiel: *I looove it here. I work in the mornings and spend my afternoons at the beach. This is the life I always dreamed of.*
Beth: *What are you doing at the beach? Because if you want to pick up hot, rich, eligible men, the marina is where you want to be.*
Amiel: *Ha. As if a hot, rich, and eligible bachelor would be interested in me. No. I lie under an umbrella, try not to tan—well, peel, since I am a redhead—and get through the pile of great books someone hooked me up with.*
Beth: *They are pretty great, aren't they?*
Amiel: *The best. Especially the hockey romances. I love that they're clean and sweet but are still so emotional and funny.*
Summer: *Speaking of hockey players...*
Evie: **ducks for cover**
Summer: *Come on, girl. Spill. What's happening with you and Fraser? Give us the latest.*

As I think about how to answer that, another message comes through.

It's from Fraser.

Fraser: *Can you please call me when you're ready? Want to hear how your meeting went.*

I jump back into the group chat.

Evie: *I have to go. Fraser just texted.*

Beth: *Oh, I see how it is. You're that girl who dumps her friends the second her hot high school crush texts.*
Evie: *I am not.*
Evie: *Wait. Okay, maybe I am.*
Evie: *A little.*
Beth: *Hahaha. I'm just teasing. We'd all do the same thing in your shoes.*
Hannah: *100%.*
Amiel: *For sure.*
Summer: *But before you go, a quick update. Please! I feel like I haven't seen you in forever.*
Evie: *Sorry. Work has been hectic, and his schedule is insane. So we've been chat dating every night.*
Beth: *What on earth is that?*
Hannah: *I believe it's using the device we're all currently on but, like, talking into it? Am I right, Evie? <smiley face emoji>*
Evie: *Exactly. And you know me, I love trying new things.*
Summer: *How has it been?*
Evie: *Incredible. Fun. Sweet.*
Evie: *Even if I keep having to remind myself it's meant to be fake.*
Beth: *Let me guess, it's not feeling fake?*
Evie: *Not. At. All.*
Hannah: *Your crush is back?*
Beth: *Did it ever really leave?*
Hannah: *I don't think this is one-sided, you guys. He is ALWAYS buying her flowers. My revenue is way up!*
Summer: *I saw the latest photos of them having dinner online. He looks genuinely smitten.*
Amiel: *I saw those photos, too. Nothing fake about the look in his eyes.*
Beth: *Are you talking about the photos where Evie has ketchup on her chin?*
Summer: *Yep. They're the ones.*

Beth: *Ooh, I missed them. Send me a link?*
Evie: *Guys, I'm right here.*
Beth: *Oh, are you? I thought you were abandoning us. <smiley face emoji>*
Evie: *Well, I am now!*
Evie: *Thanks again for the work advice.*
Hannah: *Anytime, babe.*
Beth: *<love heart emoji>*
Summer: *<love heart emoji>*
Amiel: *<love heart emoji>*

Smiling, I exit the chat and give Fraser a call.

12

Fraser

"And you didn't believe her?" my sister asks, as I give Oakey a push on the swing set in the park.

"Not for a minute. I know Evie well enough to know when she's pretending to be happy. And last night, she was not happy."

"Moooore!" Oakey cries gleefully.

I apply a bit more force to his swing. "Hang on, buddy!"

"Wheeeee!"

I smile through my exhaustion.

It was worth catching a cross-country flight to spend some precious time with my sister and my nephew. Even if this is a brief pit stop before my final destination.

Evie.

I give Oakey another push and take a proper look at my sister. Gone is the decked-out-in-all-black goth girl she used to be—including her jet-black hair; she's back to her natural auburn color—and in her place is a beautiful, smiling, happy wife and proud mom-of-one.

"You're looking well," I say, before returning my attention to Oakey.

"That's because I am well."

"Mooore!" Oakey cries out again, so I make some grunting noises behind him to make him think I'm pushing him harder. I'm already swinging him pretty high.

I miss the little guy so much when I'm on the road. I love seeing how he's growing and developing every time I come for a visit.

Being an uncle is awesome, but it's got nothing on what I really would love someday—kids of my own with the woman I love.

I glance around the pretty park, nestled in the heart of the small town of Cedar Crest Hollow. The January air is crisp, carrying the fresh scent of pine from the nearby forest. Snow caps the distant mountain peaks. While a few locals are wandering about, we're the only ones crazy enough to be using the playground equipment.

I never pictured Dawn settling down in a place like this. She and I spent so many nights dreaming about leaving Comfort Bay. I was sure she'd end up in a big city like LA or New York. Maybe even Chicago. Not a tranquil, picturesque small mountain town.

"Is this enough for you?" I ask.

It's a blunt question, but the thing about Dawn and me is that even though we aren't natural talkers, when we do talk, we get straight to the point. We say what we mean, and we never sugarcoat anything.

"Life is what you make it, Fraser," she says, taking over swing-pushing duties. "And if someone wants to make their life about chasing money or power or success or whatever, then that's fine. More power to them. I've chosen to make my life about people. My husband. My son. My family. That's more than enough for me."

Warmth fills my chest. "I'm so happy for you."

"Thanks." A smile spreads across her face as she looks my way. "What about you? Are you happy?"

"Yeah. I guess. The season's going great."

"True."

"No issues with the family. Everyone is doing well."

"Also true. But what about love?" When I struggle to find an answer, she hedges, "You know that thing, when you're in something and can't make sense of it, but it's actually pretty clear to someone else on the outside observing the situation?"

I kick the ground. "Yeah. Sort of."

"Would I be overstepping if I shared with you my observation about what might be going on with you?"

"It would be, but you were born in Comfort Bay, so it comes with the territory. Go ahead."

"I only say this because I recognize it as something I went through, the tension that comes from wanting to desperately protect your heart at all costs and yet, at the same time, longing for the type of connection that only comes from being truly vulnerable. Am I in the right ballpark?"

Nail, meet head.

"You got it in one."

"You and me, Fraser, we're different from the rest of the family. We're introverted, naturally reserved. We need time to establish trust and really get to know someone on a deeper level. And even with the people closest to us, the ones we love and trust the most, we still don't always find it easy to open up. Right?"

"Right."

"But if Evie is your person, I really think you should—"

"Whoa, whoa, whoa...Hang on a minute." Dawn is the only person I've told that Evie and I aren't actually dating. But she still has no idea that I've been secretly in love with Evie for years. "This whole relationship thing is fake, remember?"

"Is it, though?" Her blue eyes meet mine. "Because if I'm being honest, it's kind of obvious you have a thing for her."

I sag against the swing set. "Not you, too."

She smirks. "Who else picked up on it? Levi?"

"No. Of course not. Levi's clueless. I don't think I'd be standing here with both legs intact if he knew I was in love with his sister. It's one of my teammates. Culver."

The smirk on her face expands. "I see. Well, at least you're not denying it."

"No one else knows, right? Mom, Dad? Trace? Clayton?"

"They're all as clueless as Levi," she assures me. "Come on, munchkin, time to go home."

"But I don't wanna go."

"You can jump on my shoulders," I offer.

"Yaaaay."

Dawn helps Oakey off the swing, and I crouch down as low as I can. He swings one leg over each shoulder.

"Hang on to my beanie," I say, and he does, latching onto it with his small hands.

I hoist myself up, make sure Oakey's gripping me tightly, and we begin walking through the snow-covered streets back to Dawn's place two blocks away.

"So what's the occasion for surprising Evie with a visit?"

"She sounded really sad on the phone last night."

"Wait." Dawn spins around, walking backward next to me. "You convinced your coach to give you time off to fly across the country during a game week because *Evie sounded sad?*"

"*Really* sad," I emphasize since maybe I'm not making it clear enough. "She sounded *really* sad."

"Oh, man. You got it bad." She grins at me. "Worse than I thought."

I don't reply to that because, yeah, she's absolutely right. I do have it bad.

We reach Dawn's house.

Her husband Tim greets us at the door. He's not the tattooed teenage punk he once was. He's turned his life around and is working hard getting his plumbing business off the ground. I carefully lower Oakey off my shoulders.

"Hey, man, good to see you," Tim says, giving me a hug before turning his attention to his son. "You—upstairs now, mister. Bath time."

"Do I have to?"

"You do."

"Fine."

Oakey stomps down the hallway. Tim looks at me. "Great season. Stanley Cup could be yours this year."

"Fingers crossed."

"You sticking around?"

"Nah. Need to head off soon."

"I'll get the little guy clean. Can you wait so he can say goodbye to you?"

"Of course."

Tim follows Oakey to give him his bath, leaving Dawn and me alone.

And like all good sisters, she can't resist picking things up where we left them as soon as we sit down in the living room.

"So what's the plan?"

"What plan?"

"Fraser. Come on. You're fake dating the girl of your dreams. You have to have a plan. Please tell me you have a plan."

I hug a cushion into my chest. "Nope. No plan."

"Why not?"

"Because what's the point? Nothing can ever come of it."

"Again, why not?"

"You know why." My gaze shifts beyond her, trailing down the length of the hallway.

"No. No, no. Don't do that," she says.

"Do what?"

She gets up and sits on the same sofa as me, lowering her voice. "I appreciate everything that you, Mom, Dad, Trace, and Clay have done for me. I really do. More than I'll ever be able to adequately express in words. But I need you to please, please, *please* stop putting your life on hold for me."

"It's not just you. It's Oakey, too."

She leans back. "We can't protect him forever, Fraser."

"We can try."

"No," she says firmly. "You've done everything you can."

"But it's my fault. I let you down. I should have done a better job of keeping you safe."

"It was never your job to monitor me twenty-four-seven. You have to stop blaming yourself for my actions as a sixteen-year-old kid. And besides, I was safe. I wasn't sneaking out to go to parties or drink or take drugs. I was sneaking out to be with my boyfriend who I knew even back then I wanted to marry. And believe it or not, Tim and I did use protection. It just didn't work. And I'm sick of being this secret that everyone in the family has to keep."

"We don't have to keep this secret. It's our choice," I correct her.

"Well, it doesn't feel like a choice *to me*. It feels like a family decision we made seven years ago that made sense at the time. Mom and Dad didn't want it to get out that their teenage daughter was pregnant. So Dad pulled the plug on the show, and everyone's done their best to keep the attention off me. I appreciate it. I really do. But it's different now. I'm twenty-four. I'm married to the father of my child. My angsty, emo days are long behind me."

That manages to draw a small smile out of me.

"I'm okay. I really am." Her lips twitch. "Besides, if I recall correctly, I wasn't the only one sneaking out back then."

My cheeks get warmer. "You knew about that?"

She nods. "I knew you were as desperate to get out of filming that horrible show as I was, but I had no idea where you were going. I thought you'd be off doing something stupid like smoking pot in the pool house. So one night, I decided to follow you. I saw you climb into Evie's room."

"Nothing ever happened, I swear."

"I know."

I drag my fingers through my hair. "And what about Oakey?"

"He has Down Syndrome, Fraser. That's not something we need to hide from the world."

"I beg to differ."

Her eyes land on me. "I know you had a bad experience a few years ago."

"That's putting it mildly," I scoff, a knot of tension forming in my gut as that awful memory comes rushing back to me.

It was my first year playing in the majors, and the Swifts were visiting a children's hospital. We spent time with the kids, hanging out, talking, playing some b-ball with those who were up to it. The press were there covering it. It was meant to be a simple puff piece, some good PR for the team while raising awareness for the hospital.

When the story came out, I read it online and made the fatal mistake of scrolling down into the murky waters of the comments section.

The vast majority were positive—

Heartwarming to see my favorite team taking time out of their busy schedules to bring joy and smiles to the sick children.

What an incredible gesture by the team! I'm sure the kids and their families appreciate it.

The Swifts rock! The players are great role models, both on and off the ice.

Unfortunately, a small section of comments weren't.

I will *never* be able to erase from my memory the vile, disgusting things I read. What sort of sick, deranged individual makes jokes about sick kids or uses derogatory language I wouldn't even think, much less have the gall to express?

After that, I doubled down on my efforts to do everything in my power to protect Oakey and make sure he never has to experience anything like that.

"The majority of people are good, Fraser. We can't let our lives be dictated by the tiny percentage who aren't. If people are truly so messed up that they'd make fun of a kid with an intellectual disability, that says everything we need to know about them."

"I understand. Logically. But I don't want Oakey to ever have to go through that. He's an innocent kid. He doesn't deserve it."

"I agree. But we can't shield him forever. What we can do is make sure that if or when something bad happens, we're there for him. Say what you want about our family, but we are always there for each other."

"Yeah. We are."

"You can't keep living your life with these walls up. You have to let people in."

"I let people in," I lie, and she clocks it instantly.

"That's not the way Tori sees it."

I take full advantage of the opening to deflect away from myself for a moment. "I still haven't forgiven you for setting me up with her, by the way. What made you think we'd be a good match?"

"She's nice, pretty, and down-to-earth...for an influencer."

"Big caveat-slash-red flag right there."

"I'm sorry. I had no idea she'd morph into such a publicity-hungry monster. But stop deflecting and deal with what we're talking about."

"Which is?" I pretend not to know, smiling goofily.

"You and your guardedness." She punches my arm softly. "There's taking time to get to know someone and build up trust, and then there's...well, you. You move at the pace of a tortoise with two broken legs."

"It was never going to work out with Tori," I say.

"Why?"

Because she's not Evie.

"Because I wasn't in love with her," I answer honestly. "And we wanted different things, aside from our approach to publicity."

"I know."

"Huh?"

Dawn drops her head. "She told me."

"What?" I straighten, my heartrate kicking up a notch. "What do you mean she told you?"

There is no way Tori would betray me like that. She swore she wouldn't tell anyone.

My brain snags on something Dawn said earlier. "Before, when I said nothing ever happened when I would sneak into Evie's bedroom, you said 'I know.'"

"I did."

Yep, that confirms it. My sister knows.

I shake my head. "I can't believe Tori told you."

"I, uh...may have led her to believe I already knew."

"What?"

"Please don't be mad. She was upset about the breakup, and I was consoling her. She alluded to this big secret you had, and I panicked. I worried she was referring to something bad, like you were into drugs, or...punk music."

"Now is not the time to be bringing up my well-known dislike of punk music."

"Anyway, when she told me you were a, uh..." Dawn sighs. "When she told me that you wanted to wait until you got married, I felt relieved. And instantly guilty for knowing. I didn't mean to pry. I just wanted to make sure you were okay. Are you okay, Fraser?"

"My sister just told me she knows I'm a virgin. How great do you think I'm feeling right about now?"

"Hey. You've never judged me for the choices I've made in

my life, and I am not judging you for yours. In fact, I think it's great."

"You do?"

She nods enthusiastically. "Totally. It's old-school romantic." She pauses. "Can I ask why you're waiting?"

I've given this a lot of thought over the years, so my answer comes easily.

"Because of Mom and Dad. They were each other's first loves. And Nan and Pop." Mom's parents. "High school sweethearts. And when Mom told me the story about her grandparents growing up next door to each other, it sealed the deal for me. I like the idea of only being with one person. I want that one big love. I just wish it would hurry up and get here."

Dawn smiles knowingly at me. "I have a feeling it's already here. You just need to be brave and open up to Evie. You trust her, right?"

"I do. She's the only person I've ever truly opened up to."

"Is that what you guys did when you snuck into her room?"

"Yeah. We used to lie on the floor and talk. Eat food. Watch games. She used to make bracelets."

"I wish I hadn't been so stuck in my emo, *I hate everything and everyone* ways and had made more of an effort with her. She seemed like a great person."

"She still is."

"I'd love to see her."

"She'd like to see you, too."

"Awesome. Let's set it up." When I open my mouth to say something about how that would be impossible, Dawn beats me to it. "And I'm calling a family meeting so I can come out of hibernation. I am done being hidden from the world. I'm not saying we do an exclusive sit-down with *60 Minutes* anytime soon, but if my story comes out, it comes out. I'm a grown woman. I can handle it."

She takes a breath, then continues. "Clayton is a clown appearing on every reality TV show he can get on. Mom is basking in the glory of her back-to-back Emmy wins. Dad and Trace are killing it running the family business. Everyone has moved on with their lives except for you, and I don't want you to feel like you have to hide me away like I'm some dirty little secret."

"I've never thought of you like that."

"I know you haven't. But it's time, Fraser. It's time for you to move on."

She's right. About everything. She is an adult, and a strong and capable one at that. I have to stop using her and Oakey and the whole situation as an excuse to stop myself from living my own life.

"Fine. Call the family meeting."

Oakey runs into the living room in his dinosaur pajamas, full of energy, his sandy-blond hair still damp, and leaps onto my lap.

"I need to get going, kiddo."

He gives me an almighty hug. "I love you, Uncle Fras."

"I love you, too, buddy."

As I get into my car and the three of them wave me off, Dawn mouths the words, "Open up."

I think about it on the thirty-minute drive down the mountain into Comfort Bay.

I've always been a reserved person, even as a kid. Making friends has never been easy for me. It isn't that I'm shy, I just don't have a natural way around people.

I'm not outgoing and charismatic like my oldest brother Trace, who can walk into any room and strike up a conversation with anyone. He's got the gift of making you feel like you're the only person in the world when he's talking to you.

And I didn't inherit Mom's incurable need to be the center of attention like Clayton did. He laps up people's attention like the 'Best in Show' winner at a dog show.

My only talents in life are shooting a puck into a net and keeping up—or trying to—with Evie and Levi's non-stop banter.

Once I get into town, I stop by the flower shop to get Evie some more yellow roses, exchanging a few words with Hannah.

I make the short drive from the shop to Evie's place, pulling up in front of her apartment block. It's a rustic two-story building with wood and stucco exteriors painted in warm, earthy tones and a classic Spanish-style tile roof.

A grin spreads across my face as I stride into the building.

She has no idea I'm coming, and I can't wait to see the look on her face when she sees me.

I reach her door, take out my phone, and press the green button next to her name. Whatever music she'd been playing—not punk, thankfully—stops, and she answers.

"Hey, Fraser."

My heart drops because in those two words alone, I can feel her not-okayness through the phone. The meeting she had with her boss today mustn't have gone well. At least it justifies my crazy decision to fly across the country to be with her.

"Hey, Evie. What's up?"

"Oh. You know. The usual life of a modern gal living it up in Comfort Bay on a Wednesday night. It's all very glamorous. Sipping on a cocktail while deciding what seven-thousand-dollar dress to buy next to add to my collection."

I knock on the door.

"Sorry. Can you hang on? There's someone here." I hear her shuffling toward the door. "I wonder who it is. I haven't ordered any food."

I'm smiling so hard my cheeks hurt. "No problem. I'll wait."

She unlocks the door, and it swings wide open.

Her mouth falls open, and she stares at me in sheer horror, almost dropping the ice cream carton she's carrying in one hand and the hot glue gun in the other.

"Oh, my gosh, Fraser! What are you doing here?" is what I think she means to say, but because of the spoon in her mouth, it comes out more like, "Oh, mmmph gosh, Frah-sa! Wha' ah yew doin' 'ere?"

Good thing I'm well-versed in Evie-speak.

"Surprising you, of course." I lift the bouquet of flowers in front of me and flash her a wide smile. "Surprise!"

13

Evie

I'd clasp my chest in shock if I weren't cradling a tub of ice-cream in one hand and holding a hot glue gun in the other.

Fraser doesn't flinch as he takes me in, and a big smile spreads across his face, even though I must look like a mess. Hardly sipping on a cocktail while picking out a new dress, that's for sure.

My hair is slick due to a deep-conditioning treatment, I'm wearing an old hockey jersey and sweats, and I've got a spoon dangling out of my mouth. At least I've washed off the bright-blue face mask I had on earlier and applied some moisturizer.

"This takes me back," he says, still grinning.

Maybe his brain is having a delayed shock response to the hot mess he's stumbled upon?

I extract the spoon from my mouth and spear it into the ice cream. "Takes you back to what?"

"That time I came over for a late-night chat and you had one of those sheet facemasks on that made you look like a ghost. Apart from making me listen to punk music, that's the only other time you've actually scared the life out of me. Remember that?"

"No. I'd successfully blocked that from my memory from my subconscious, but thank you for bringing it back."

"Are you...okay?"

Is he being serious?

"Are you being serious? Look at me."

He has the gall to actually look at me, running his piercing blue eyes up and down the length of me.

"You look great."

"Did you bump your head? Is that why you're here? To tell me you've sustained a serious head injury and won't be able to play for the rest of the seaso—? Wait. Why are you here? You're meant to be in Raleigh. You have a game tomorrow. What's going on?"

"All great questions. Mind if I come in?"

I wince. "Of course. Sorry. The leave-in conditioner has seeped into my brain and erased my manners. Come in, come in."

Fraser steps inside, sporting a huge smile, waving a bright yellow bouquet of roses in front of me.

He bought me flowers.

Again.

I've lost count how many times it's been. Maybe I should ask Hannah if she's keeping track. She probably is.

"Since your hands are full, I might just leave these here," Fraser says, placing the bouquet on the kitchen counter.

"Thank you." I drop the hot glue gun and ice cream tub there, too. "I love them."

"Mission accomplished, then."

"I still have so many questions, but I need five minutes. Give me five minutes, okay?"

"Sure. Take your time."

I race into the bathroom to wash out the hair treatment. Then I throw on some jeans, a tank top, and the cashmere sweater Levi bought me for Christmas last year. Slightly more company-appropriate than the jersey and sweats I was wearing when I opened the door.

I don't have time for makeup, but my face has a fresh glow after the mask, so I should be okay on that front.

"All right, I'm back, and this time I look human," I say, announcing my arrival in the living room.

Fraser spins around from the bracelets he'd been studying, laid out all over my desk in my work nook.

And boy, he cuts a fine figure.

When I board a plane, I go through an invisible force field that instantly wrinkles my clothes, frizzes my hair, and makes me put on five pounds in water weight.

Fraser looks like he just stepped off a runway in Paris or Milan, not schlepped in on an American Airlines cross-country flight.

His zip-up black hoodie opens to reveal a dark-gray shirt, his form-fitting denim fits his form very nicely, molding to his muscular legs, and he's wearing white low-tops. The look is quintessential Fraser—athletic, comfortable, and undeniably sexy.

"Feel better?" he asks.

"Yes, but more importantly, I *look* better."

He makes his way to the couch. "I liked your look from before. Wet hair is all the rage these days."

I laugh. "Unlike the term *all the rage*, which very much is not."

"Hey, I'm secretly a forty-five-year-old dude who wishes he could time travel back to the '90s, remember?"

I smile, but it quickly disappears when I notice my laptop left open on the coffee table. I quickly shut it as we take a seat, and I tuck it into the side of the couch. I can brainstorm ideas to save my career some other time.

"Start at the beginning. Why are you here?"

"I was worried about you."

"Me?"

"Yes. I've developed a sixth sense for picking up on when you're pretending to be happy even though you're not. It happened at jerkface's wedding. You do it whenever the subject of your mother comes up. And you did it over the phone last night when we talked about your meeting with your boss."

"That just proves you're an Evie-whisperer. It doesn't

answer my question about why you flew halfway across the country to see me."

"It totally does."

"No. It doesn't." I lift my chin. "I can pretend I'm fine over the phone just as well as I can to your face."

"My, my, my. How little faith you have in me, Evie." His lips curve into a suggestive smirk. "You honestly didn't think I'd come here on my own without reinforcements, did you?"

I blink. "Actually, I did."

There's a knock on the door. Fraser shoots to his feet. "I'll get it."

"Sure," I mutter to myself since he's already out of the room. "Don't mind me. I just live here."

What is happening?

Surely he can't be serious—that he bailed in the middle of a game week to fly all this way and see me.

Can he?

"Evie, close your eyes," he says from the entryway. "I don't want you seeing my secret weapon until I'm ready."

I close my eyes, trying not to smile at the absurdity and kookiness and loveliness of it all.

"Fine. My eyes are shut."

"No peeking?"

"No peeking."

"All right, then."

With my vision gone, my other senses pick up. Specifically, my sense of smell.

"You didn't...?" I begin, my eyes still firmly closed.

There's a beat of silence before I hear, "You can open your eyes."

I do, and Fraser is standing in front of me, holding up a serving of large fries in his hand.

"Truth fries!"

He's grinning hard. His deep blue eyes are sparkling and bright, and it instantly shaves a few years off him, reminding me of how he used to look back in high school.

He shakes the fries, and the delicious smell wafts into my nose.

"I had a feeling you might be less than forthcoming, so I knew I had to call in some backup. You can hide from me all you want, but I know you'd never dishonor our pledge to the almighty fry."

I break out into a fit of giggles because this is all too much. In the best way ever.

Fraser hands me some fries and takes out another serving for himself. Then he crosses his legs, sits on the floor at the edge of the coffee table, casts a glance my way, and says, "Whenever you're ready. I've got all night. And by *I've got all night*, I actually mean I have to be at the airport in three hours to get on my red-eye. But hey, no pressure."

I'm so overwhelmed by this, *by him*, I can't even eat.

"My meeting didn't go well," I say, getting straight to it since we don't have a lot of time.

"Why not?" Fraser sets his fries down on the coffee table. "What's going on?"

"Same old story. My segments aren't generating the kind of numbers the network is looking for."

He blows out a frustrated breath. "People baffle me. Your latest story about Comfort Bay's oldest resident made me smile all day. Coach was worried something was wrong with me."

I don't know what to say to that.

Or to the flowers.

Or to him coming all this way to see me just because he *suspected* I was having a rough time and might have been in need of some cheering up. How is he so finely tuned to me?

"I'll be fine," I say, drawing on some of the confidence Margo has in me. "I have a month to turn things around."

"And what if you don't turn things around in a month?"

"Then I guess I'll be looking for a new job."

His jaw clicks. "What can I do to help?"

Margo's words echo in my head. Could Fraser's distrust of the media be overcome if I were the one interviewing him?

His eyes are fixed on me with a deep focus. I can *feel* the words right there, tickling the tip of my tongue...but I just can't bring myself to say them aloud. I can't ask him for this favor. I just can't. It's too much.

"You being here is amazing. Unbelievable, actually." I take a breath. "I'll...I'll figure out my work stuff on my own."

His unwavering gaze remains fixed on me. "Okay. But if I can do anything to help, let me know."

"I will."

A brief silence ensues.

"There's another reason I came," Fraser says, his voice carrying a husky rasp that wasn't there a moment ago.

"What's that?"

He hauls himself off the floor and joins me on the couch, sitting so close our knees almost touch.

"I've been doing some thinking."

"What about?"

"You. Me."

I suck in a breath between my teeth. "Oh."

"I know this isn't real, Evie. That this whole fake dating thing started because some random fan called you my lucky charm online and it helped your numbers at work—and it stopped the press from endlessly speculating about my love life."

"Uh-huh."

"The press is no longer hounding me about my romantic life, but the first two things are no longer applicable."

That's true. I haven't been considered his good luck charm for months now, and my numbers at work have plummeted back to earth.

His brow furrows, and I wonder where he's going with this. An uneasy inkling settles in the pit of my stomach that it might not be leading to something good.

He takes a breath. "I guess what I'm trying to say is that I understand if you want to start thinking about how we end this fake relationship. Just tell me when you want to do that, and I'll pull the pin."

My heart sinks with disappointment. "That's not what I want."

It's literally the *last thing* I want.

Does he, though? Has he had enough of this and wants to go back to his normal life?

"What about you?" I ask.

"What? No way. I'd rather take you on in a chili dog eating contest than end this. I'm just letting you know—the eject option is always there. Just tell me when you've had enough of all this."

"I will," I say, giving a slight nod as relief washes over me.

But I won't.

I'm enjoying fake dating Fraser way too much to put an end to it. This is, hands down, the best, healthiest, and most fun relationship I've ever been in. I'll psychoanalyze how pathetic that makes me sound some other time.

"So...we're good?"

"We're good," I confirm.

The strain in his neck loosens. "In that case, there's something I've been wanting to do for a while now. I've been unsuccessful on the first few attempts, but I'm determined not to let anything get in my way this time."

"What is it?" I ask, suddenly realizing my whole body is angled toward him like I'm the Leaning Tower of Pisa.

Without warning, he gets up and stalks over to the window and closes the curtain.

He collects our phones from the coffee table and takes them into the kitchen.

Finds the remote and turns off the game I'd been watching.

"Fraser." I grab him by the arm to stop him moving. "What are you doing?"

His Adam's apple bobs in his throat. "I want to kiss you, and I don't want any interruptions."

My poor heart jolts into overdrive. I've gone from thinking he wants to end things to him wanting to kiss me. It's a lot to take in.

But I am here for it.

I am *so* here for it.

"You're not wearing anything that will beep or buzz or go off, are you?"

"No. All my beeping and buzzing clothes are in my laundry hamper."

He snickers and comes closer. "Good."

"No food deliveries coming?"

"I ate already."

I stand up.

Our eyes meet.

He traces his fingers delicately across my cheek. "I've tried so hard to resist you, Evie. And I've waited so long for this moment."

I tilt my head up. "You have?"

"You have no idea. I want to kiss you so bad. Can I?"

"Yes."

He leans in closer, sliding his hand around my waist, and gently brings me closer to him. There's a slight pause, as if he's checking in to make sure I'm okay. I bob my head, and he continues.

Our mouths meet for the very first time.

Tentatively.

Tenderly.

In the softest of collisions.

The gentle brush of his lips against mine sends a yummy warmth radiating throughout my entire body.

Gradually, the kiss deepens.

He grows more confident, curling his fingers around the back of my neck and taking control.

I part my lips, an invitation he accepts.

His tongue sweeps into my mouth, a melding of warmth and wonder, a show of strength and sensitivity.

I surrender to it.

To him.

To this moment teenage me wanted so badly but thought would never come.

To this moment adult me tried to convince herself she didn't want and thought she had gotten over hoping for.

"Hi," he says, as the sweetest kiss of my life ends, and he delicately strokes my cheek.

"Hi," I manage.

"That was amazing." His voice is low and coarse.

"Worth traveling all this way for?"

"Definitely." He exhales. "I hate that I have to leave so soon."

"Don't be silly. You have to go. I can drive you to the airport if you like?"

"Thanks. But I rented a car. You can walk me to your front door."

So I do.

We kiss again.

I watch as he walks down the stairs until he's gone, then I race back inside, tugging the curtain wide open.

He stops walking to his car and looks up at me.

I wave.

He waves back.

I don't leave my spot by the window for a good five minutes after he's driven off.

At the end of the night, I get ready for bed, unable to get my mind off him.

It's official.

My crush on Fraser has returned with a vengeance.

Truth be told, it may never have really left.

Forcing myself to get some shut-eye, I find myself reminiscing about the past, my thoughts floating back to the night I first realized I had a crush on him...

Seven years ago, Evie's bedroom...

Fraser and I are in what's become our usual position—lying on my bedroom floor.

I got sick of him always sitting so far away from me, so a few weeks ago, I lay down on the floor after a meal, and he joined me.

This is our go-to position for whenever he comes over now. It's nice...and a little odd at the same time.

We're closer, but still never touching. I'm starting to suspect Fraser's keeping some space between us on purpose, which is gentlemanly of him. I can respect that, I guess.

But I like being near him.

We're currently staring up at the ceiling, passed out after gorging on an In-N-Out and malasada feast.

Ever since he introduced me to those delicious pastries, I've become addicted. I've hunted down the best malasadas in the county. They're in a bakery two towns over. Fraser drove there just to fetch them for me before coming over.

It's a Wednesday night.

Our sixth Wednesday, not that I'm counting or anything.

This is the pattern we've fallen into.

He brings the food, I show him the bracelets I'm working on.

I give him a few pointers I picked up from watching him at practice—and yes, I'm being nicer and more considerate of his feelings...or at least trying to.

He fills me in on whatever stuff has been going on with him.

I mainly talk.

He mainly listens.

But he's starting to open up, too, telling me about some of the stuff going on at school, at practice, with his brothers and Dawn.

We laugh and have a good time.

No one's the wiser.

Not Levi. Not my parents. Not anyone from Fraser's family.

It's our little world. Our little secret world.

"Up for a lightning round of questions?" I ask.

He turns his head, looking at me side on. "Uh, sure."

Six weeks ago, he would have hesitated. Maybe even said no. He's come a long way.

"Great. We'll take turns asking each other questions. Want to go first?"

"Nope. You can."

"Okay. Favorite book, assuming you read."

He scoffs. "I read, thank you very much."

"Sorry. I didn't mean it like that. I know you're *capable* of reading, I just didn't know if you like to do it for pleasure. Or even if you have the time. You're pretty busy with hockey."

"That's true. But I like to read before I go to sleep. It relaxes me."

"Cool. And again, I apologize. So, what's your favorite book?"

"That's a tough one. There are too many to choose from."

"Okay. I'll make it easier for you. Favorite book that you've recently read?"

A few moments pass, then he responds with, "*The Sympathizer* by Viet Thanh Nguyen. I hope I'm saying his name right."

"What's it about?"

"It's a spy story that explores identity, politics, and the Vietnam War from multiple perspectives."

"No wonder it puts you to sleep."

"Hey." He gives my arm a playful squeeze.

"Your turn," I say, secretly wishing he'd keep his hand there longer, but unfortunately, he pulls it away.

"Um. Okay. Let me think. Okay. I've got one. Why do you like punk music?"

"Why can't I like punk music?"

"You absolutely can. I'm just curious. Someone like Dawn liking punk music makes sense. Someone like you, not so much."

"What does that mean?"

"Ah, ah, ah, I believe I'm the one asking the question."

"Fine." I stare up at the ceiling as I formulate an answer. "It's like, I'm not an angry person, but I guess I have a little rage within me. Like we all do. Listening to punk lets me tap into some of those emotions I usually ignore without, you know, doing anything that will see me getting twenty-five to life."

"That's a good answer."

"You're happy with it?"

"Is that your question for me?"

"It is."

He smiles. "Yeah. I'm happy with that answer."

"Why? And before you can accuse me of asking two questions in a row, this is a related follow-up, so it counts as one, and you have to answer. Don't make me get Rosie."

"Oh, no. Not your glittery pink umbrella."

"Hey. She can do some major damage."

"I bet she can."

We laugh.

Fraser folds his hands over his chest. "Um, I like your answer because it explains a bit about you. You're an upbeat and optimistic person, and normally I can't stand upbeat and optimistic people. But you do it in a way that isn't offensively sweet. Don't get me wrong, you are sweet, but I'm not going to catch diabetes by hanging out with you."

"Gee, thanks. Also, not sure it's possible to *catch diabetes*."

"But you get what I'm saying, right? You're...cool."

"Thanks. I think?"

He laughs.

His face is lit up by the blue glow from the TV, and I notice just how perfect his teeth are.

"My turn again," he says. "Are you a cat person or dog person?"

"Can I be both?"

"Sure."

"Okay. So I'm both. What about you?"

"Dogs. Big dogs."

"So, no dogs that could fit in a purse?" I tease.

"Definitely not." He grins while he mulls over his next question. "Have you decided what you want to study?"

"No final decisions have been made, but I'm leaning toward journalism."

"Permissible follow-up question coming...Why? Why not teaching?"

"I'll allow the follow-up," I say. "I figure this way I might be able to reach more people. And I have this idea. A potentially very crazy idea."

"My favorite kind."

"I want to share good stories. Uplifting stories. The world sometimes feels like it's a dumpster fire, and I want to give people a sense of hope. Because I think that deep down, there's more that unites us than divides us."

"That's not all that crazy. Sign me up. I'll watch. Or read. Or subscribe. Just don't ask me to share anything on social media because I avoid it like the plague."

"Noted." I smile. "Thanks for your support. I guess there's no point in me asking what you want to do, is there?"

"Only one way to find out."

"Oh, come on. It's obvious you've always wanted to be a hockey player."

"Actually, that's not entirely true."

"Really?"

"Yeah, really. Everyone assumes it's been my only dream in life, to play. And while I do want to make it into the majors, and I think it's my best ticket out of here, there's always been a part of me that's wanted to coach."

"You can always go into coaching when you retire."

"Nah. Don't think so."

"Why not?"

"I'm not like you, Evie. I'm not great at peopling."

"I don't know about that. You seem to people well with me."

We turn our heads at the exact same moment.

Our eyes lock.

A wild thought enters my head.

Will he kiss me?

Almost as quickly as it blew in, it evaporates into thin air when Fraser asks his next question.

"What sort of wedding do you want?"

"Excuse me?"

"It's my turn to ask you a question, and that's what I'm asking." When I don't say anything, he tries to explain with, "Don't all girls dream about their wedding day?"

"Have you asked Dawn about her wedding day?"

"My sister isn't like most girls."

"Neither am I. I haven't given it much thought, in all honesty, but I know I don't want anything big. I'd be perfectly happy with something small and no fuss. Or, I don't know, maybe getting hitched in a chapel in Vegas. Have Elvis or Marilyn officiate."

"Isn't that a bit...tacky?"

"Oh, it's totally tacky. But that's why I love it. Funerals should be serious, but weddings are meant to be fun. Grandma always says that. I'd want everyone to have a great time, and *I* want to have a great time. When Mom shows me photos of her wedding to Dad—which, by the way, she puts gloves on so her finger oils don't damage the album."

"You're joking."

"I'm deadly serious."

"That's insane."

"That's my mother. Anyway, the photos are gorgeous. It was a grand and beautiful and very expensive affair. But when I look at her eyes, or Dad's eyes, despite them smiling and putting on the appearance of being happy, they just look...

tired. I don't want that. I want to be rested and alive and in the moment."

"You should have opened with that."

I giggle. "I was workshopping ideas. What sort of wedding do you want?"

"I don't really care."

I'm about to tease him for giving the most boy answer ever, but before I can, he goes on. "As long as my wife-to-be is there and happy, that's all I care about."

And we've gone from the most boy answer ever to the most perfect answer ever in less than three seconds.

It takes me a few moments to recover from that.

"You know," I say, nudging the side of his hand with my pinky. "I don't think you're as bad at this whole peopling thing as you think you are."

He doesn't move his hand. "Thanks, Evie."

I stare up at the ceiling, my heart beating faster in my chest.

How is it that I'm only now just realizing that Fraser is the total package?

There's so much more to him than the aloof next door neighbor with insane hockey skills.

Yes, he's exceptionally talented on the ice, but he's also smart, reading books I haven't even heard of.

He's thoughtful, always keeping me well stocked with food, even if it means driving two towns over to bring me my favorite pastry.

He listens when I speak, and he remembers what I say, like about me deciding what to study, and then asks follow-up questions.

And he's cute. Like, really, *really* cute.

And wow, okay...I think I've got a crush on my brother's best friend.

14

Fraser

"Dammit," I grumble, as we lose control of the puck again.

We've squandered a 2-1 lead to be trailing the Philly Panthers 4-2 with only a couple of minutes left in the game.

For whatever reason, we just haven't been able to get in the zone tonight.

Myself included.

Despite having scored both of our goals, I've also missed twice.

Something's off, and I don't know what it is.

Evie's in the stands, having flown out earlier today. Losing always sucks, but knowing she's here, seeing the team unravel in person, only makes it hit harder.

The guys are tiring.

Where we used to be sharp and confident, now every pass, every play, is hesitant. We're out of sync, and the opposition is pouncing on every opportunity we hand them.

A swift pass sends the puck gliding toward the offensive blue line where Kingsler, Philly's star forward, picks it up. Accelerating, he weaves through our defenders like a hot knife through butter.

I curse under my breath.

Kingsler barrels down the ice, crossing into the attacking zone. Culver shifts his weight, preparing to leverage his body in a textbook defensive move. Kingsler fakes out at the last second. Culver tries to pivot but catches on something in the ice, twisting awkwardly as he falls to the ground.

The game comes to a halt.

Officials signal for medical attention as my teammates and I speed over to him.

I reach him first. "You okay, man?"

He grimaces in pain, trying to get up, but can't.

"Stay down. Stay down. Let them look at you."

The medical team arrives, and the guys and I move out of their way. I keep a close eye on Culver, watching anxiously as he's assessed by the medics before they help him off the ice.

Turns out he's strained his knee. It's not catastrophic, but it's enough to sideline him for the rest of the game.

Great. Just what we need. Losing our best defenseman. But at least he's all right, and hopefully it's nothing too serious.

We end up losing 5-2.

The mood in the locker room after the game is subdued. Frustration and disappointment hang heavy in the air. The usual banter is replaced by reflective silence or hushed conversations about what went wrong.

I get showered and dressed fast, keen to get an update on Culver's condition.

Before heading out, as always, the last thing I do is kiss Evie's bracelet three times. I wonder if I should tell her I still have it?

For all the things we've talked about these past few months, neither one of us has broached the subject of why I left and what happened all those years ago.

Dawn has scheduled a family meeting to discuss things, which will pave the way for me to finally tell Evie everything.

But there's something else I want to discuss with Evie tonight.

Something important.

I leave the locker room and hunt down the assistant coach, who tells me Culver has been taken to the Hospital of the University of Pennsylvania.

So that's where I head.

Via a quick stop at the club box.

"Hey," Evie says, rushing over to me the moment she spots me entering the lounge.

I don't know what sort of greeting I was expecting, but it certainly wasn't her looping her arms around me and just... holding me.

I breathe in the sweet vanilla scent I've grown used to and run my fingers through her silky soft hair.

"That was brutal, but you did great."

My body tenses, and Evie must feel it, because she pulls apart, latches both hands onto my shoulders and gives a firm squeeze. "You did great, Fraser," she repeats with such conviction, I almost believe it.

But I'm in a post-game losing funk, and it's hard to break through it. The scoreboard doesn't lie. Not to mention Culver getting injured.

"How's Culver?" she asks, as if reading my thoughts.

"Don't know. He's been taken to the hospital. They're running some scans on him. I'm sorry, but I need to go see him."

Evie frowns. "Why are you sorry?"

"You flew all this way out here for the game, and I don't know how long I'll be, but I'd feel bad if I didn't—"

Her soft, sweet lips cut me off.

It takes my brain a second to click into gear, but once it does, my hands find their way to her lower back, and I press her in closer to me.

"You were saying?" she murmurs against my mouth.

"I was speaking?"

I feel the hum of her giggle vibrate through my body.

"If you don't mind, I'd like to tag along. I want to make sure Culver's okay, too. Hannah's going out of her mind."

"I bet she is."

Culver and Hannah are childhood friends. Their families

have known each other going back four generations. She must be sick with worry.

"I told her I'd give her an update as soon as I could."

"Let's go, then."

Twenty-five minutes later, we're in Culver's hospital room, waiting for the results of the tests. He's resting and no longer in pain, so that's good.

Evie has ordered food and updated Hannah. Her phone dings. "Food's here," she tells us. "I'll go get it."

"Want me to come with you?" I ask.

"No, stay." She smiles. "Give you two a chance to talk about how great I am."

"She's definitely a keeper," Culver says once Evie is out of the room.

"Because she's broken down the food pyramid into three main food groups—burgers, fries, and pastries?"

Culver smiles. "Nah, man. Because she's terrific and because of the way you look at her. Reminds me of how my old man used to look at Ma. Like she hung the moon in the sky. Except, you have a much goofier face."

"Hey, leave my goofy face alone."

Evie reappears with the food, and the three of us eat as she gives us her very detailed take on what went wrong in the game and what we need to improve on.

Maybe I've grown immune to it, but her delivery has improved so much since she was a feisty twelve-year old barking critiques at me whenever I was over at her house, hanging out with Levi. Even back then, she knew the ins and outs of the game like a pro. Guess that's her dad's influence rubbing off on her.

"You weren't lying, man," Culver says with a grin once she's done. "She's tough."

I finish chewing my burger. "This is nothing. You should

have heard what she was like when she was younger. It's taken me years of therapy to recover."

Evie throws a fry at me. "Stop it. You're exaggerating...You are exaggerating, right?"

I laugh. "I am."

Kinda.

"I get it from my dad. You should hear half the stuff that comes out of his mouth."

"I bet," Culver says. "The man is a legend. He's earned the right to say what he wants to say."

"And as the daughter of a legend, so have I."

"You ever consider playing?" Culver asks, wiping his fingers clean on a napkin.

Evie shakes her head. "No. Those who can, play. Those who can't, critique. I'm firmly in the second camp."

"True. But it's a shame to let your insight go to waste. I bet what you told us tonight will be what coach tells us tomorrow. Right, Fraser?"

"Totally. And for what it's worth, I think she'd make a great coach or assistant or whatever role she chooses to pursue."

"Thanks, guys. But I'm sticking with reporting. For now."

She drops her head after she says that.

Culver gives me a small nod, and I take the cue. "We should let you rest up, buddy."

"Thanks for checking on me. Appreciate it."

"No worries. Let me know if you need anything."

We exchange fist bumps, then Evie and I leave.

"You okay?" I ask, wrapping my arm around her as we head to the elevator bank.

"Yeah. Fine. Sorry. I shouldn't have mentioned work. It's depressing, and I didn't want to bum you guys out even more. It's been a rough night for both of you."

I press the button. "You can bum me out anytime you want

to. Use me as a sounding board during our chat dates, if you want."

She smiles, but the sparkle doesn't reach her eyes. "Thanks. I appreciate that. I've actually come up with an idea for a story."

"Care to share?" I ask as we step into the elevator.

"Not yet. But it's gonna be big."

"I'm intrigued."

"Good."

"All right. Be vague and mysterious, then."

"I intend to. I will say this, though. It airs in two days, and I *strongly* recommend you try to catch it live."

"I'll have to see where I'll be and what I'll be doing, but I'll do my best."

We're mostly quiet on the ride back to the hotel room.

I'm worried about Evie. I can tell when she's masking her problems, and she's masking big time tonight.

I'm concerned for Culver, too.

He's two years older than me, and while twenty-seven isn't ancient in normal-people years, the average retirement age for hockey players is between twenty-eight and thirty. An injury at his age could spell the end for his career, which I'm sure is the last thing he wants. Hockey is his life.

And I'm nervous about what I want to bring up with Evie. But it's a good nervous, if that makes sense?

Spending time with her, whether it's in person or on our chat dates, is changing me. I've taken Dawn's advice to heart, and I'm opening up to Evie even more. It feels good. A bit strange since I'm not used to being like this, but good.

"What floor are you on?" I ask her once we're in the hotel lobby.

"Fourteen. You?"

"Sixteen."

We hop into the elevator and ride up without a word.

I'm exhausted. Physically and mentally. Tonight's been bruising, and I have an early-morning flight to catch tomorrow, headed to Florida for our next game.

When the doors ping open on the fourteenth floor, I step out with her.

She turns to me, clearly surprised. "What are you doing?"

"Escorting you to your room, naturally."

"Right. Because the fourteenth floor of The Four Seasons is renowned for being a place no young lady should walk unescorted."

"Especially at this late hour," I play along.

She rolls her eyes and giggles as we head toward her room.

"This is me," she says once we get to room 1409.

"There's actually something I wanted to talk to you about."

"Okay," she says, opening the door and gesturing for me to follow her inside.

I turn to face her and take a deep breath. "As you know, you and I have...kissed."

"I'm aware."

"And I just wanted to check in with you to make sure you're cool with it."

Her eyes narrow. "Are you asking me to rate you on a kiss scale of one to ten where one is accidentally kissing your grandma on the lips and ten is sipping hot chocolate by the fireplace on a cold winter night?"

I chuckle. "That couldn't be any farther from what I'm asking. And since you're not taking this seriously, I'm calling in a backup."

I pull out my backup from my pants pocket and hold it up in front of her.

"Ew. What is that?" Evie asks.

"A fry. From the hospital. I snuck it into my pants when you weren't looking. Yes, it got smooshed, but its outward appearance doesn't lessen the impact of its presence. I'm summoning the universal fry laws for this conversation."

"You're summoning universal fry laws because you want to have a *serious* conversation? Do you hear the contradiction in that sentence?" she teases lightly.

"Don't mock the fry laws, or you will pay a severe price."

"Okay, serious talk. I'm activating serious-mode *now*."

I drag a hand through my hair and glance down at the sorry excuse for a fry I'm holding. "Okay. So. I'm not super great at this, but I wanted to make sure you're okay with the kissing since I'm pretty sure it was never part of the rules."

"Actually, I've scoured the *How to Fake Date Your Best Friend's Sister* rulebook, and there's no mention of real kissing."

"But did you check the *Guide to Fake Dating Your Brother's Best Friend* companion guide?"

"I did. Nothing in there, either. The only reference I could find that vaguely relates to our situation was something about both parties being willing participants in anything else that may occur while in said fake relationship."

"Uh-huh." My eyes lock on hers. "And are you? A willing participant?"

"I am. Are you?"

"Very much so."

She reaches out and runs her hand down my chest. "I do have a question for you."

"Go ahead."

She looks down. "And I will remind you that you are holding a truth fry, so I expect nothing but complete honesty from you."

"Always."

Her hazel eyes darken. "Before we kissed at my apartment, you said something about waiting so long for this moment.

What did you mean by that? Have you been wanting to kiss me for a while?"

"I have."

"How long?"

"Years."

Her eyes widen. "Years?"

I nod, glancing down at the truth fry, then blow out a breath before saying, "Since my senior year."

"When you used to come over?"

I nod again. "I would never have acted on it, then. I was much older."

"You're still much older," she says with a smile.

I meet her eyes, and despite the inclination I have to stop talking and retreat into my shell, I push ahead. "I wanted to kiss you then. Not right away, just so we're clear. That was never my intention when I first started coming over. But as we started hanging out, the way I saw you started to change...and the way I liked you started to change, too."

Evie's soft hands slide over mine, and she takes the fry from me. "I wish you'd kissed me back then, but I totally understand and respect why you didn't. And even though it's taken you seven and a half years, I'm glad we're kissing now."

I smile. "I'm a slow mover."

"Tell me about it."

"I also need you to know something else, Evie."

"What?"

"I would never kiss someone unless it means something. This isn't a game for me. I'm not trying to make up for something I've wanted to do since high school. I have genuine feelings for you."

Her eyes bore into me. "Do you really mean that?"

"I do." My fingers skim down the curve of her arm. "I don't

know where we go from here, but I wanted to let you know how I feel."

Her eyes are darting about, and I can tell she's processing it. It's a lot to lay on her, I realize that. More than what she signed up for.

So, I add, "I don't expect anything from you, and you don't have to say anything back."

"I'm holding a fry, Fraser. I'm kind of obligated to say something."

I crack a tiny smile. "You really don't. We can make a one-time exception."

"But I want to," she says, and I pick up on a trace of that unmistakable Evie determination. "I have genuine feelings for you, too."

There have been times in my life when I've been lucky enough to live out a long-held dream. Getting drafted into the NHL. Scoring my first game-winning goal in overtime. Being awarded the Calder Memorial Trophy for Rookie of the Year.

In all those moments, I had an almost out-of-body experience. Like I was watching them happen to me rather than them being things I was going through.

But hearing Evie saying those words, words I've wanted to hear her say for so long, I've never been more *in* my body.

Every blink.

Every breath.

Every heartbeat.

Every second that passes, I am here.

I've never felt more alive.

"I don't know what we should do next, either." She looks up at me and smiles shyly. "Maybe we just keep going with this whole fake dating thing for a while longer and see where it leads?"

"That makes sense," I agree.

Her smile grows. "A *try before you buy* arrangement, if you will."

"Oh, is that what you're doing now? Sampling the goods while you can still return them?"

"You caught me. And here I was, thinking I was being all cool and stealthy about it."

"You're not being stealthy at all."

We kiss again, and there's a heady mix of newness and familiarity about it.

I close my eyes, committing to memory every sound, every taste, every smell.

We don't know what our future holds, so I want to remember these details about her for the rest of my life.

"Fraser. No."

"Awww, come on, Evie. Gimme a clue."

"No."

"First letter?"

"No."

"Rhymes with?"

"Still no and will always be no."

With an exasperated sigh, I flop down onto the hotel bed, drained from last night's loss, the early flight this morning, worrying about Culver—he's out for the next game but will hopefully return after that—and squeezing in a gym session after we checked into the hotel here in Tampa.

"Fine. You win," I concede before letting out a silent yawn.

"Sorry. The line broke up. What was that?"

The line did not break up.

"You win," I repeat, only so I can hear the satisfaction in her voice, when she shoots back with, "Has such a nice ring to it, doesn't it?"

I laugh through my tiredness, then try my luck again. "So what are you doing in LA?"

"Fraser! I know what you're doing."

"What am I doing?"

"Trying to get me to reveal what my segment tomorrow is about. Nice try, buddy."

"I have no idea what you're talking about."

"I can *hear* the smile in your voice."

I bite my lip, but it doesn't work. I'm grinning from ear to ear.

I've spent the last fifteen minutes trying to pry something—anything—out of Evie to get a clue about the subject of her segment.

But yeah, I've well and truly lost that fight.

I yawn again, not so silently this time.

"I should let you go," she says.

Normally, I'd fight her on it, but my eyes are already getting heavy. "Okay."

"Rest up. Oh, and Fraser?"

"Yeah?"

"If you can, I strongly recommend you catch my segment live. It'll be worth it."

"I've already scheduled it in my calendar," I reply. "Goodnight, Evie."

"'Night, Fraser."

15

Evie

The thing I always seem to forget about a Vinaigrettes group chat is that they can go on for a very long time. That's why it's best to start them early. Because if you text late in the evening, you're almost guaranteed to get to bed way past your normal bedtime.

But the chats are always fun, and I'm in LA and I need to remind everyone to tune in and watch my big segment tomorrow.

We've already been talking for a while when Amiel brings up an interesting question.

Amiel: *So, ladies, I have to ask...The Vinaigrettes. Where on EARTH did that name come from? It's been driving me crazy not knowing.*
Hannah: *Over to you, Evie. It's your story.*
Evie: *It was the fourth of July weekend a few years ago. I was in college and had just started dating a guy (we went on, like, three dates). He came back with me to Comfort Bay for the fireworks and a party on the beach.*
Summer: *That guy was a jerk. No offense, Evie.*
Evie: *None taken. I agree. He was. (Date number four never happened.)*
Evie: *Anyway, I'd told him how I wanted to wait, and he seemed fine with it.*
Evie: *Until he had a few too many beers.*
Evie: *He comes over to me by the bonfire and makes it clear he wants to do stuff. I tell him no. So then, in front of everyone, he yells, "Why do you want to be a vinaigrette for the rest of your life?"*
Evie: *He meant to say virgin, but he was so hammered, he got his words mixed up.*

Evie: *It was hilarious, and I started laughing. Hannah, Beth, and Summer came over and joined in, and we've claimed it as our secret name ever since.*
Amiel: *I LOOOOVE that story.*
Beth: *Me, too. It's empowering.*
Summer: *As it should be. It's our decision to wait, and we should celebrate that.*
Beth: *Here, here.*
Hannah: *Don't suppose it's come up with you and Fraser yet?*
Evie: *No. We have been talking a lot but never about that.*
Beth: *What have you been talking about?*
Evie: *Everything and nothing. We laugh and have so much fun together. It's awesome. Fraser's opening up. It reminds me of how things were back in the day.*
Amiel: *Back in the day?*
Hannah: *Fraser used to come over for late-night chats and food and malasadas when Evie was a sophomore in high school. They used to be next-door neighbors.*
Amiel: *Okay, cool. Thanks for explaining to the newbie. Also, how great are malasadas?*
Beth: *THE. BEST!*
Summer: *That's a minor miracle about Fraser opening up to you again, Evie, given how closed-off he normally is.*
Evie: *I know, right?*
Beth: *Let's circle back to the vinaigrettes issue for a moment—are you nervous about bringing it up?*
Evie: *A little, yeah. I'm not sure if it's the right time to mention it.*
Hannah: *Why not?*
Evie: *Well, we agreed to keep going with this fake dating thing, which is good.*
Hannah: *That is good.*
Beth: *Very good.*
Summer: *Very, very good.*

Amiel: *Adding this so I'm not left out: Very, very, very good. <smiley face emoji>*

I giggle to myself, loving how very, very, *very* goofy my besties can be.

Evie: *But we're not officially dating, so I'm thinking maybe I should wait and see what happens before I come out with it.*
Hannah: *Not that there's anything to feel ashamed or embarrassed about, right, Evie?*
Evie: *Of course not. It's not shame or embarrassment, I promise. It's more that I'm trying not to get too carried away.*
Summer: *Why not? All the signs are pointing to this having a happily ever after. Right, Beth?*
Beth: *Oh, totally. You guys have all the hallmarks of a fake dating, best friend's brother, hockey player romcom. <love heart emojis x3>*
Evie: *I hope so. I'd love a happily ever after with Fraser. It's just, well, there are a few things standing in our way.*
Hannah: *Such as?*
Evie: *He doesn't want to live in a small town.*
Hannah: *He said that years ago. He could have changed his mind since then.*
Evie: *True. He's away for most of the year.*
Summer: *Long-distance is manageable. You're making it work now.*
Evie: *Also true.*

I blow out a breath and tap out the biggest reason of all, the thing that's holding me back from getting swept up in how great things are between Fraser and me.

Evie: *He left once before. He could do it again.*

A few seconds pass before the next message comes through.

Beth: *That is a possibility. It's good to be prepared for the worst.*
Hannah: *I agree that it's good to be ready for any outcome. Don't close yourself off to the possibility of having a future with him based on what happened in the past.*
Summer: *Exactly. Things are different now. You've both grown a lot.*

I want to believe what Hannah and Summer are saying, but my heart is battling with my head.

While I know Fraser would never do anything to hurt me intentionally, I still have to be careful and not get involved with someone who doesn't want the same things I do, like live in a small town or wait until marriage.

Been there, done that—and trust me, it's no fun.

I blow out a heavy breath, letting my thoughts swirl in my head. After a few moments of wallowing, I decide to lighten the mood a bit.

Evie: *At least when we fake break up, I know Fraser will be a gentleman about it.*
Summer: *Don't joke like that. It's not funny.*
Hannah: *I second that.*
Amiel: *Third that.*
Beth: *Fourth that.*
Evie: *Nice of you all to be ganging up on me.*
Hannah: *It's always from a place of love. We just want you guys to work out.*
Evie: *I do, too.*

Believe me, I do, too.

Summer: *Hate to say this, ladies, but it's waaay past my bedtime. I need to get some rest.*
Amiel: *Same. I need to be up and baking in a few hours.*
Beth: *Oh, any last-minute clue you want to share with your besties about your segment, Evie?*
Evie: *Nope. Like I told Fraser, you'll have to tune in tomorrow to find out!*

"Evie, are you sure you want to do this?" Margo's voice comes through loudly in my earpiece. "It's not too late to change your mind, hon. We have a backup segment we can use instead."

"Not an option," I whisper back, smoothing down the front of my jumpsuit. "It's fine. I'm fine."

I am *not* fine.

I am the thing that's the complete opposite of fine. Inside.

But outside, I'm doing everything I can to project an image of calmness and strength.

I *need* to do this.

March is Developmental Disabilities Awareness Month. I came across it while brainstorming ideas for segments. In my research, I learned that it focuses on raising awareness about the inclusion of people with developmental disabilities in all areas of community life, as well as highlighting barriers that people with disabilities still sometimes face.

This is it.

My big story.

Because I'm going to present it in a way no one would expect—by BASE jumping off a building.

It's a risk, sure. But the payoff could be big, and I don't just mean in terms of numbers. I've been working on this story for a while now, and it means so much to me. It's an important message and such a great cause. I hope people tune in.

I know a few people will. The Fast-Talking Four-slash-Five —now that Amiel's joined us—and Fraser.

I suck in a few deep breaths.

It's a beautiful morning, the sun is shining, and there's not a single cloud in the sky. I'm standing on the roof of the Wilshire Grand Center building in downtown LA with a group of four people of varying physical and mental abilities.

What am I trying to achieve?

I want to show viewers that a physical or intellectual disability doesn't have to be a barrier to living a full life. That people of all abilities can *and should* have the same access to opportunities as everyone else.

I would love it if there was a way to make that point without resorting to jeopardizing my life, but there isn't.

If I went down the more traditional, expected path of interviewing a few people or highlighting some local organizations that do great work in this area, who would watch that?

No one. It's unfortunate but true.

Evie's lovely but her segments are so boring, we usually leave the room to get ready for the day when she comes on.

That's a direct quote from a viewer in the last round of testing.

I need to do something, and it needs to be *BIG*.

And it doesn't get any bigger than me jumping off the tallest building in LA and potentially plummeting to my death, does it?

But my possible death is beside the point.

The point is, I can turn my numbers around with this story while raising some much-needed awareness.

And I'm doing it without having to rope Fraser into it.

I stand by my decision not to raise the interview idea with him. In all the time we've spent together, he hasn't once said or done anything to indicate he'd be open to it. He's as anti-press and pro-privacy as he's always been.

So, no. It's this. It has to be this.

Since there's no building tall enough to meet the height requirement in Comfort Bay, I've had to come down to LA. A bonus is that my segment will be syndicated throughout the state. Another good thing for numbers.

Who knows, I might even go viral again. *So long, Breakup Sneeze Girl, may you come back...never.*

"We've got five minutes," Margo's thick Australian accent booms in my head. "I only need one word from you to make the segment switch. Your call."

"Thanks, but I'm all set," I tell her.

There's no way I'm backing out of this now.

"How are you feeling?" I ask, walking up to Gemma.

She's in her early twenties. She has an intellectual disability that affects her cognitive functioning and adaptive behavior. I met her at the local day program she attends where she engages in vocational training that's been tailored to her interests and capabilities.

"Scared. But I'm excited. You?"

"Mainly just the first part."

"You'll do great."

"Thanks. You will, too."

"Don't look so petrified," Jared says, approaching me with a sympathetic smile. He's a thirty-six-year-old veteran who lost his left leg. He was involved with the UCLA research team who developed a prosthetic limb designed for extreme sports.

"I thought I was managing to hide it."

"Just keep breathing."

"I'll do that," I say. "This is your fourth jump, right?"

"That's right. You'll be fine. There's nothing to worry about."

"Thanks."

I look around the group, inhaling through my nose and exhaling through my mouth, and think about all the additional hurdles they face in their lives. My determination sets, harder than ever. I can do this.

I *will* do this.

We're gathered at Spire 73, which, on a normal day, is the tallest open-air bar in America. It's closed this morning while we do our stunt. I mean story.

Okay, yes, it's totally a stunt. I know that. But I need a unique angle to hook viewers. Developmental Disabilities Awareness Month is a great cause, but I'm competing for attention with wars, sports, politics, and whatever thin sliver of material Miley Cyrus calls a dress and wears to an awards show.

"How ya doing, Evie?" Mason asks with a friendly smile.

He's the safety coordinator for the company that organized this jump and got all the required permits and clearances needed for jumping off one of the tallest buildings in the country in one of the busiest cities during rush hour. I have no idea how they managed to pull it off.

"Ask me in ten minutes...assuming I'm still alive."

"It's normal to feel nervous," he says warmly. "Everything has been triple-checked to ensure safety. The equipment is top-notch and designed to keep you secure. The team here is professional and has an excellent safety record. You're in good hands."

"Thanks. How many times have you recited that speech?"

"About ten thousand."

"Okay. That's reassuring. I'm assuming everyone has survived?"

He grins. "They have. Hey, listen. Once you're back on solid ground, I don't suppose I could bug you for an autograph?"

"You want my autograph?"

He grimaces. "Sorry. I wasn't clear. I, uh, meant Fraser's autograph."

"Ah. That makes much more sense."

"It's just that my niece worships the guy. She's obsessed with hockey. You should see her. She even scribbles down notes during a game, and then reads them out to us once it's over."

I can't help but smile. "Reminds me of someone I know. The autograph will be no problem. I'll get your details after. And by *after*, I mean after the jump, not in the afterlife."

"Awesome. Thank you."

He's about to check on the others when I ask him, "Does your niece play?"

"No. She lives in Starlight Cove." That's a few towns over from Comfort Bay. "There aren't any teams for girls in that area."

Of course there aren't.

"Look. I should check on the others. Keep breathing and try to relax. Once you jump, the exhilaration is unmatched. You're about to experience something truly amazing."

"Thanks, Mason."

As he attends to the others, I slip away to the edge of the rooftop. The view is spectacular, offering a panoramic vista of the entire Los Angeles basin. The western horizon stretches out to the Pacific Ocean. To the north and east, the peaks of the San Gabriel and San Bernardino Mountains offer a stunning contrast to the skyscrapers of Downtown LA. Looking north, the iconic Hollywood Sign and Griffith Observatory are visible, nestled in the Hollywood Hills.

And looking down.

Whoa. Not a good idea.

I pull back sharply from the ledge, my heart pounding in my throat.

This is really high.

Knowing that the rooftop is eleven hundred feet above the ground and *seeing* it from up here are entirely different things.

A cold shiver rattles through my body, but I have to do it.

I need this.

My career needs this.

"Sixty seconds," Margo says, and I walk over to where we're set up to shoot.

Mark Merril, the anchor, will cross to me from the studio after the short segment I recorded about Developmental Disabilities Awareness Month runs. We'll chitchat for a bit, and then, without warning, I'll hurl myself off the building. The others will follow shortly after me. They're all lined up and in position, spaced safe distances apart from each other across the length of the rooftop. Several drones and a helicopter are circling overhead to capture the aerial shots.

"Ten seconds..."

"You can do it, Evie," I say to myself, gripping my microphone so tight my knuckles turn white.

I close my eyes and picture Fraser watching me from the other side of the country. A surge of warmth spreads inside me. It's almost as if I can feel him here with me.

"Three, two, and..."

"Good morning, Mark. As you can see, I've left Comfort Bay for something a little different this morning. I'm coming to you live from the tallest building in Los Angeles."

"We hear you have a big surprise in store for us," Mark says.

"That's right, I do." I begin walking, the camera following me. "I'm joined by some of the folks you met in the segment that just aired. And I figured it's all well and good to talk about everyone having the same access to opportunities, but I wanted to show you that it really is possible."

"I'm only on my second cup of joe, and you're being very cryptic this morning, Evie."

I smile. "I know I am. But this is a message to everyone watching at home who might be going through something tough in their lives and may be feeling like there's no easy path forward. I hope what you're about to see will show you that there really are no limits. If you change how you think about something, you can change your whole life."

And with that little nugget of Insta-worthy life inspo delivered, I stare down the barrel of the camera, do a theatrical mic drop because it'll look good on TikTok, lift myself onto the ledge of the building, and wave to the camera behind me.

With my nerves buzzing with energy, I step over the edge... and then I'm free-falling.

16

Fraser

I almost drop my coffee, my mouth flying open in shock.

I'm about to have a heart attack.

One minute, I'm watching Evie's pre-taped segment about Developmental Disabilities Awareness Month.

And the next...the next, they cross live to her from the studio. For some unknown reason, she's on top of the tallest building in the state of California. She chats with the anchor, being unusually vague, and then she HURLS HERSELF OFF THE BUILDING!

Panic seizes my chest as I stare at the TV screen. The camera pans out, capturing her tiny frame side-on plummeting toward the ground.

Yes, I can see she's wearing a harness.

Yes, I know she's attached to a cord.

Yes, I'm sure they would have taken every single safety precaution known to mankind to ensure nothing happens to her or to any of the other people doing the jump with her.

But right now, all I'm seeing is Evie plunging toward the street, and *I AM NOT OKAY*.

She stops a good fifteen, twenty feet off the ground, before rebounding back up, doing that bouncy thing that happens at the tail end of a bungee jump.

"She's okay, she's okay," I mutter to myself, reaching for a bottle of water on my bedside table.

I bring it to my lips with a shaky hand and take a few sips.

She may be okay, but she's still dangling upside down.

A couple of guys in bright-blue polo shirts run over and unclip her, carefully bringing her to her feet.

She's on the ground.

She's upright.

She's safe.

I let out the breath I must've been holding since this action nightmare scenario began ten years ago, because that's how long it feels like these past few seconds have lasted.

"How are you feeling, Evie?" Mark Merril asks.

Someone hands Evie a KCFB microphone. Strands of hair cling to her cheeks and forehead, and her cheeks are flushed a bright red.

She smiles at the camera. "Oh, my goodness, Mark. That was beyond exhilarating, but let me tell you, I am *very* glad to be back on solid ground."

"I bet. Evie, how is everyone else doing?"

Evie waves to someone off-camera. A woman walks up beside her. "Gemma, hi! How was that?" Evie asks, positioning the microphone in front of her.

"So awesome!" Gemma smiles at the camera and gives the happiest two thumbs-up I've ever seen.

I grab my phone and fire off a message to Evie.

Fraser: *Watching you live now. I didn't think there was anything scarier than being forced to listen to punk music. I now know that there is...I *think* I've recovered from my heart attack, but the doctor says I can't sustain any more shocks. I have practice now but will have a few hours free this afternoon before tonight's game. Call me to check in on the patient? <smiley face emoji>*

Through the fogged-up shower pane, I see Evie's number light up my screen. I've been keeping an eye on my phone all afternoon, waiting for her to call.

I turn the shower off, quickly dry my arms and chest, hook the towel around my waist, and answer the phone.

"Thanks for calling. You'll be glad to know all my vitals are returning to normal and my medical bill to you is in the mail."

"Great. Just send it to Levi's address, and I'll grab it off him never."

I step out of the bathroom. "What's wrong?"

"We're bantering. I just volleyed back to you. How do you know something's wrong?"

"I can hear it in your voice."

"Ugh," she sighs, giving up any pretense of being fine. "I'm totally bummed."

"Why? Are you facing a class-action lawsuit from other viewers who also had a heart attack while watching your segment this morning? Does that mean I'm not alone? Is there a support group I can join?"

Silence...and then, a tiny giggle.

It's not much, but I'll take it.

"Tell me what's wrong," I say, injecting a seriousness into my voice to let her know I'm done messing around.

"Well, it is about the segment, but thankfully, it doesn't involve lawsuits or viewer's medical conditions." She pauses. "Like always, it comes down to the numbers. Seriously, if I had a quarter for every time I've said the word *numbers* this past year, I could retire early. I'm getting so sick and tired of this."

"I'm not following."

Another heavy breath. "I was hoping this morning's segment would bring in massive ratings. Blockbuster ratings. I've been working so hard on this, thinking it was my big shot to finally get a breakout story. Maybe even go viral again. And, just as importantly, shine a light on a worthwhile cause. Show viewers that having a disability isn't a life sentence and hopefully inspiring them to live their own lives more fully."

"I loved the pre-taped segment. I donated fifty thousand to the organization in your story."

"You did? Wow. That's wonderful. Thank you so much."

"No. Thank *you*. I could tell you really care about the people you spoke with, that you're genuinely invested. I've felt inspired all day."

She has no idea how much.

Seeing those folks, hearing their stories, gives me hope that Oakey can grow up and lead a normal—or pretty close to normal—life himself.

Another sigh comes through my speaker. "Unfortunately, the segment barely moved the needle. No traction on socials. No major outlet is picking it up. It's crickets central over here."

I clench my jaw and keep my mouth shut to stop myself from blurting something about how frustrating that is. She doesn't need me telling her that—I can hear the hurt and sadness in her voice loud and clear.

"Maybe I'm not cut out for this? Or maybe I should just give in and do what Mom's been pressuring me to do and move to Washington and finally become a real reporter?"

"What do *you* want to do, Evie?"

She huffs out another sigh. "Honestly? I don't know anymore. I'm so confused. I thought this would be it. That reporting would be my way to make a difference in the world. Something that I enjoyed, was good at, and served a higher purpose. But now I think I've been deluding myself this whole time."

"You haven't. You *are* a great reporter. You work hard, you're passionate about what you do, and you are talented. So, so talented."

"Thanks. I appreciate you saying that. I've still got a tiny bit of time left, so I'll figure something out.

She says it, but she doesn't sound like she means it.

She's hurt, she's down on herself, and she's doubting her

life choices while I'm stuck in Pittsburgh with no way of flying out for another surprise visit.

I hate this.

I want to be with her more than anything. I want to be by her side, figuring this out together. I want to be someone she can depend on.

Someone she can trust.

Someone she can confide in.

And that's when it hits me...

If I want to be that person, it's time I come clean to her about a few things.

Seven years ago, Fraser's bedroom...

"Where have you been?"

My older brother's deep growl scares the life out of me.

"What are you doing here, Trace?" I ask.

He flicks on the light, illuminating my bedroom. He's standing by the door, arms folded, looking majorly peeved.

I wipe the sweat off my forehead. It's an unseasonably hot night. "Why are you in my room?"

"Answer my question."

"No. Newsflash, you're not Dad, so I don't have to tell you anything."

"Yes, you do." He marches over and fists my shirt, giving me a good shake.

I smack his hands away. "What is your problem?"

Trace is usually pretty uptight, but this is extreme. Even for him.

"Family meeting. Downstairs. Now." He stomps over to the door, then glares at me over his shoulder. "Now, Fraser."

"Okay, okay. I'm coming."

Geez.

I slip the present Evie gave me tonight into my top desk drawer and follow my irate brother downstairs.

It's a non-filming night.

The house feels oddly quiet without cameras and crew everywhere when it should just feel normal.

But nothing feels normal anymore.

Not since Mom and Dad decided to put our lives on display for the whole country to tune into every week and pick apart every conversation, every argument, every carefully orchestrated scene for their viewing pleasure.

I hate it.

Trace and I step into the living room. Mom, Dad, Clayton, and Dawn are all there, sitting around with solemn looks on their faces. I'm tempted to joke, "Who died?" but I have the good sense not to since someone might have actually died. The vibe is that gloomy.

"What's going on?" I ask as Dad says, "Where were you?"

"Nowhere."

I sit down beside Dawn. Her eyes are red-rimmed, cheeks flushed. "Are you okay?" I whisper to her, but she only turns away from me.

"Effective immediately, we are making some changes," my father's commanding voice fills the living room. "Filming is canceled."

My brothers and I stare at each other in disbelief.

"Are you serious?" Clayton cries out, visibly upset.

I'm in shock at Dad's announcement, but the last thing I am is upset.

Good riddance, I say. If I never have another camera shoved in my face again, it'll be too soon.

"We're in the middle of filming the season," Clayton carries on. "We can't just stop abruptly like this. We've signed contracts. Aren't we obligated?"

"We are," Dad replies tersely. "And the network has already threatened legal action. But I'll take care of that."

"Mom? Are you okay with this?" Clayton asks, turning to her as the obvious choice for support. Out of all of us, it's him and Mom who are the most into the show.

"I am. I agree with your father," Mom answers Clay, before she slowly makes eye contact with the rest of us. "And from now on, we're implementing a new rule. No one speaks to the press."

"No one," Dad reiterates, his voice practically a growl. "I don't care what they ask you, what they say to you, or where they accost you. You are to remain tight-lipped and say nothing. Not even a *no comment*. Nothing."

"Why?" Trace speaks up. "Why are we doing this?"

"This is going to have huge implications," Clayton says, pushing to his feet. He begins pacing, charging his fingers through his hair. "We can't stop filming. They won't let us. We're going to be in trouble. There will be repercussions."

Yeah, and you'll stop being reality-TV-famous, I think to myself because *that's* what he really cares about. But for the second time tonight, I manage to restrain myself.

"Sit down!" Dad barks.

Clayton stops mid-stride, stunned.

We're all stunned.

Dad may be the CEO of a multimillion-dollar yachting business, but he's normally a cool operator. I have never once seen him lose it. Least of all at one of us.

Clayton drops down into the nearest armchair.

Dad starts issuing orders. "Trace, you'll be in the office with me. I need to fly to Croatia to meet with a client in a few days. You'll come, too."

Trace nods. By Dad's side is his happy place, but even he can read the situation enough to know this isn't a celebration.

I don't really know what this is. I'm still confused about what's actually going on.

"Clayton, you're going to do that six month trek you've wanted to do in Southeast Asia."

"What? I can't leave now. I've almost reached a million followers on Insta—"

"That's a good point," Dad cuts him off. "No more posting on social media. In fact, delete all your social media accounts." He waves his finger at us. "All of you."

His steely blue eyes land on me. "And Fraser…"

I gulp.

"You're off to hockey training camp first thing in the morning."

"Training camp isn't until summer."

"You're going to a different camp."

"I am? Where?"

"Quebec. You'll be away for three months."

"What about school? Graduation?"

"I don't know. We'll figure something out. You'll graduate, son. Don't worry."

I'm scrambling to keep up with all of this. My whole world is getting turned upside down in front of me.

And why?

Neither Dad nor Mom have yet to give us one good reason for any of this.

I look at my father. "I leave…tomorrow?"

He nods.

The first thought that pops into my head is, *I have to go back and see Evie, tell her what's going on*. But of course, I can't say that since no one knows about our late-night chats.

I know—I'll use Levi as my cover. It's normal I'd want to

bid farewell to my bestie. Yeah, that won't arouse any suspicions.

"Okay. I'll just go over and say goodbye to Levi—"

"No. You speak to no one."

"Excuse me?"

My father's nostrils flare. Up until right now, I'd never once noticed my father's nostrils.

"What is going on, Dad? Why are you suddenly forcing us to uproot our lives and change everything?"

"Because I'm pregnant," Dawn cries out beside me, her anguish palpable.

All heads swivel in her direction.

She stands and throws her arms in the air. "I'm pregnant, okay? And I'm sorry I've ruined everyone's lives."

And with that, she storms out of the room.

17

Evie

"So, where are we off to?" I ask, buckling up in Fraser's car.

He's been mysterious since he showed up on my doorstep this morning with the biggest bouquet of yellow roses yet—Hannah must be loving this, he's setting her future kids up for a great college education—and a mission to take me out for pancakes.

How could I say no?

We'd just finished breakfast at Bear's diner, and as Fraser was settling the bill, he mentioned something about going for a drive.

"Up the mountain," he answers, pulling out onto the street, a determined look settling over his features. "We're going to visit my sister."

"*Okay.*" I didn't have that on my bingo card of people I'd be seeing today, but I'm excited to see her. "I haven't seen Dawn in years."

"I know." He drums his fingers on the steering wheel. "Just hold tight, okay? I know I'm acting a little...funny. I'll explain everything once we get there."

"Cool. I like a bit of mystery."

He glances over and smiles, and for the first time this morning, it's a proper smile, one that makes the skin around his eyes crinkle a little.

He focuses his attention back on the road, and I use the quiet time to reflect.

It's been a rough few days for both of us.

Margo called me into her office as soon as I got back from filming the LA story. It was another scheduled, closed-door meeting, making me totally regret having ever spoken badly about the 'walk and talks'—oh, how I long for those days.

She basically prepared me to brace for the worst. The network will be making their first round of layoffs shortly, and to no one's surprise, I'm on the list. I appreciated the heads-up and have amped up my efforts to do whatever I can to save my career in the short amount of time I have left before I'm forced to resort to Plan Washington.

And Fraser has been through the ringer lately, too.

Despite the Swifts getting off to a great start this season, their form has slipped. Badly. They've racked up a series of losses that have put a question mark over their shot at the Stanley Cup. At the rate they're going, they'll be lucky to scrape into the divisional playoffs.

But if I didn't know Fraser as well as I did, I'd barely know anything was wrong with him. All throughout breakfast, he kept the conversation focused on me, on how I'm doing. Anytime I'd throw it back to him, he'd somehow manage to deflect and steer the conversation back around to what's going on in my life.

Part of that is Fraser's natural reluctance to open up. But I feel like there's more to this.

He's acting strange, and it obviously has something to do with him taking me to see Dawn. We've talked a lot these past few months, but we still haven't broached the biggest mystery of all.

Over the years, I've quizzed Levi about it a million times, probing my brother for more information about what happened that made the Rademachers cancel filming their TV show midseason and Fraser disappear the very next day.

Rumors swirled immediately. With a scandal that big in a town as small as Comfort Bay, they were bound to.

I did my best to avoid them, and I certainly never believed any of them. Especially some of the nastier ones.

Like Fraser's dad having an affair.

Or that Fraser's mom went into rehab for some sort of addiction, sometimes it was alcohol, other times it was abusing prescription meds.

Or that Fraser's older brothers had done something illegal and the Rademacher clan were all in on it and covering it up.

Something obviously happened, but all those rumors were too far-fetched to be anything other than the product of people's imaginations.

But just because I didn't listen to the rumors doesn't mean I wasn't curious, so I went to the most likely source of information to try and get some information. Despite repeated attempts, I was never successful in my mission.

My conversations with Levi about it would usually start with me saying something like, "You don't have to tell me any of the specifics, but has Fraser ever told you what happened?"

He'd shake his head annoyingly. "Nope."

Then I'd say, "But you're best friends."

He'd nod his head annoyingly. "We are."

"So why hasn't he shared it with you?"

He'd shrug annoyingly. "It never comes up, I guess."

The Rademachers unexpectedly halting the filming of their show is one of the biggest mysteries in Comfort Bay history, and it's never come up? Male friendships truly baffle me. What do guys talk about, then?

On second thought, I don't want to know.

Fraser pulls up beside a small park in the picturesque town of Cedar Crest Hollow.

"I haven't been here in years," I say, taking in the pretty surroundings.

He cuts the engine. "It's a great place."

"Says the guy who's allergic to small towns."

"Not allergic." His rebuttal comes out a little quicker and more forcefully than I expected it would.

Our eyes connect.

"In fact," he continues, "I'm possibly reconsidering my stance on small towns."

His deep, low voice rumbles throughout the car—and through me.

"Seriously?"

"Yeah." He turns away and smiles.

I follow his gaze to a pretty auburn-haired woman at the swing set and the small boy she's with.

For the briefest moment, a streak of jealousy tears through my chest as my imagination concocts a wild scenario where Fraser has a secret family that he's kept hidden from the world all these years because he's not really a pro hockey player but a mafia drug lord working for the government.

Then I rein in my overactive and totally illogical imagination—*why would a mafia drug lord be working for the government, and if Fraser was needing to keep a low profile, how does being one of the biggest hockey stars in the country fit into that?*—and remember why we're here.

"Is that...Dawn?"

"Yeah. It is. She's no longer an emo teenager."

"She certainly isn't. She looks so..."

"Normal?"

I swat his chest. "I was going to say pretty. Who's the little boy with her?"

"That's her son. Oakey."

When I don't say anything, Fraser turns to look at me. He lowers his head, his blue eyes drilling into me, searching for a reaction, I guess, since I'm not usually without words for this long.

"I...I had no idea."

"No one does." He unbuckles his seat belt. "Come on. Let's go meet them."

We get out and walk over to the playground. It's spring, but there's still a distinct crisp chill in the air. I forget it's always a few degrees cooler up here.

The second Oakey spots Fraser, he practically leaps off the swing and races over. Fraser crouches down as Oakey crashes into him, wrapping his arms around his nephew. "How are you doing, buddy?"

"I'm good. Wanna push me?"

Fraser gets up, grinning. "In a minute. There's someone I'd like you to meet. This is Evie."

Oakey waves at me with a smile. "Hi. Do you wanna push me?"

"Maybe after I give her a big hug," Dawn interjects, joining us.

We hug, and it's one of those long, warm hugs that you could just melt into and stay in forever. Despite not being as close as I wish we could have been, I've always had a soft spot for her. I never understood what she was going through, but I felt this weird sort of connection to her anyway. Maybe because she reminds me so much of Fraser. Personality-wise, the two of them are practically identical.

"Oh, my gosh, Evie. You look wonderful."

"So do you. Your hair!"

"I know, right? Back to my natural color. Well, natural-adjacent."

I laugh.

"Can *someone* push me?" Oakey taps his uncle on the leg. "*Pleeease*?"

"All right. Let's do it, little man."

"Yayyy."

We walk over to the swing set, Oakey running out ahead of us. Fraser makes sure he's secured in the seat before giving him a measured swing. "We have a lot to catch you up on, Evie," he says as Dawn and I stand beside him.

"Before we get into it," Dawn says, grabbing my arm. "I just want to thank you so much for your segment last week. I was in tears watching it."

"So was I," Fraser mutters. "But probably for different reasons."

"Thanks, Dawn."

"It's so good seeing positive, aspirational representation."

She only stops talking because Oakey lets out an excited, "Wheeee!"

"Having a child with additional needs is tough. So much of the focus is on doctor's appointments and tests and worrying about them and how they're developing. I needed to see people like Gemma and the others living quality lives. I needed to be reminded that Oakey can have that kind of life, too."

"Of course he can," Fraser says with a definitive nod. "And he will. He's a Rademacher."

"Technically, he's a Graham," Dawn corrects.

"You're married?" I squeal excitedly.

"I am. Very happily." She lifts her hand, smiling proudly as she shows me her sparkling diamond.

"That's amazing. Congratulations. Okay. You guys need to start catching me up. I feel like I'm years behind."

"Go ahead, big brother." Dawn takes over swing duty.

Fraser rubs his temple. "I don't even know where to begin."

"How about one hot spring night seven years ago?"

"Right. Okay." He glances over at Dawn. "Would you mind if Evie and I sat down on the bench over there?"

Dawn's blue eyes flicker back and forth between Fraser and me, a knowing smile rising on her lips. "Sure."

We make our way over to the bench, far enough away to

give us the privacy I suspect Fraser is wanting for the conversation we're about to have.

"So..." He rests his hands on his knees once we're seated. "Truth time."

"My second favorite type of time, narrowly beaten to the top spot by *half-price ice cream* time."

He smiles, draws in a breath, and begins talking. "That night I left your room, the *last* night I left your room, when I got home it was...full on. Dad had canceled our involvement in the show while I was with you, and the family was gathered in the living room."

"Did you get into trouble for sneaking out?"

"I managed to dodge that bullet because there was much bigger news. Dawn was pregnant."

"*Ohhhh.*"

Years of wondering, of coming up with my own theories about what happened, bubble to life in my mind, but I cut all that noise out to focus on what he's telling me.

"So *that's* why your parents canceled filming?"

"It is." Fraser nods, glancing over at Dawn and Oakey. "One of the reasons they did the show was to raise the profile of Dad's yacht-building business. His clientele are...odd."

"The mega, mega, *mega*-rich usually are."

"Tell me about it. They're either super progressive, microdosing, self-made entrepreneurs where anything goes, or they're ultra-conservative people where nothing goes. I'm generalizing and oversimplifying of course, but it's true for the main part. Dad and Mom were worried how an unwed pregnant teenage daughter would look."

"I get that."

"More than anything, though, they wanted to protect her. Business reputational damage aside, they love Dawn and didn't want her situation to be subjected to the usual nonsense that takes place on social media and late-night TV shows. So, we agreed, as a family, to do everything we could to keep her from experiencing any of that."

"In my head, my memories are stuck on you leaving without saying goodbye. I forgot that Dawn left, too. I thought she got shipped off to boarding school in the UK."

"That was the official story."

"What's the real story?"

"Dawn and Tim got married quietly, and with her trust, they bought a place up here."

"Right."

I'd also forgotten that the Rademacher kids have a living inheritance. Levi told me about it once. I don't know the reasons behind it, but Fraser's dad wants his children to have access to a portion of the family money while he's still alive.

"The original plan was to pull back from all press, all publicity for a year or two. Once interest in us died down, if the story somehow made it into the media, it wouldn't be that much of a big deal. We'd be has-beens by then, and only diehard fans would really care." His eyes travel back to his nephew. "But once we learned that Oakey would have additional needs, as a family, we doubled-down."

"Meaning?"

"We had to ensure Dawn and Oakey had privacy and absolutely zero media intrusion in their lives. *Ever*."

"Which explains why you avoid the spotlight as much as you do."

"It's a very big part of it. Another part of it is something that happened two years ago…"

Fraser recounts what starts off as a great story about the LA Swifts visiting a children's hospital and ends with him reading through a bunch of vile, disgusting online comments.

"That was a horrible thing to go through with people who

weren't my family. Imagine if that was Oakey. Imagine if those comments were directed at him. I don't know what I'd do, Evie. I'd...I'd lose my damn mind."

Right on cue, the little guy lets out another happy "Wheee!" as Dawn swings him higher.

"I love him so much. We all do. Our family and Tim's." Fraser drops his head and lets out a heavy breath. "I'm not proud to admit this, but when I first heard about his condition, a part of me worried that it would change things."

"What do you mean?"

"That it would somehow make it harder to connect or even love him. I've never been more wrong in my life." He looks over at Oakey, and I can see the love he has for his nephew. "Because that kid is the heart and soul of two families. I love him so much. We all do."

Fraser wipes away an errant tear, and I do the same.

Seeing his capacity to love, hearing him open up like this, being so vulnerable, admitting his most private thoughts, I'm totally blown away. He's letting me inside to the truest, deepest parts of himself.

In fact, he's been nothing but open and truthful with me the whole time we've been fake dating.

Guilt washes over me.

I wish I could say the same...but I can't.

I haven't told him I'm a virgin, and I haven't shared the idea of running a story about him, either.

I only made the decision after my disastrous attempt, that saw me flinging myself off a building, failed to move the needle. I thought about the group chat I had with the girls, when they said to keep it as a backup option and use it when needed.

That time is now.

I'm putting together a package to show Fraser what a

potential story could look like. I'm confident he'll hate it, say no, and we can move on.

I'm hoping the v-issue will be just as easy for us to resolve.

I'd like to think it will be, but I'm anxious. Fraser has always been so respectful, allowing things to unfold between us slowly, naturally, always checking in with me to make sure I'm comfortable with everything we're doing.

But maybe the reason he's been going slow is because we're in this strange, uncharted limbo land of fake dating sprinkled with a few real kisses. Will he still be interested in me when I tell him I want to wait until my wedding night, or will it be a deal-breaker for him?

We sit in silence for a while, the squawks of a few birds overhead and the occasional holler from Oakey the only sounds in the chilly air.

I rub my arms. Fraser notices and pulls off his hoodie, placing it over my shoulders.

"Thanks."

"No problem. So...what do you think? It's a lot, right?"

"It is. I'm trying to put myself in your shoes. Or Dawn's. And I can't. I've got nothing to draw on that even comes close to what this must've been like for you and your family."

"It's not exactly a situation you can google," he says with a slight smile.

"No. It isn't. The closest family issues we have are the occasional chili-eating contests and Mom's constant disapproval of all my life choices. That's hardly in the same league as the bombshell you guys were dealing with."

"Don't underestimate how full-on terrifying your Mom can be."

"Believe me. I don't." I place my hand on his leg. "I have some questions."

"Thought you might. Go ahead."

Well actually, I have one main question. The others can wait. This question has been burning in my head since the very next day after that hot spring night.

I inhale and ask, "Why didn't you come over to see me and say goodbye?"

Fraser grimaces, scrubbing his hand down the side of his face. "I wanted to, Evie. I did. I even came up with a cover story about how I wanted to go over and say goodbye to Levi so I would have a reason to be at your house, but the idea was nixed. I'm sorry."

He turns to face me and takes hold of my hands. Squeezing them firmly, he repeats, "I am so sorry. Sorry for not seeing you. For not saying goodbye. For not thanking you for the bracelet you made."

The bracelet? He remembers the bracelet?

"I thought you'd forgotten all about that."

His eyebrows knit together. "How could I forget about it? I still wear it."

My eyes fall to his wrists. "Has it...turned invisible?"

He grins. "I wear it when I play. It's my lucky charm. I couldn't imagine being on the rink without it."

"Are you for real right now?"

"A hundred percent. Ask Culver. Ask anyone on the team. I kiss it three times before and after each game. It's a known thing."

"Wow."

"You say that a lot around me."

"That's because you're a wow kind of guy."

Fraser's cheeks turn a shade of pink.

I can't believe he's kept the bracelet all these years. I for sure thought he'd discarded it and hadn't given it so much as a second through.

But he wears it on the ice.

At every game.

Kisses it three times.

That's...That's...That's very wow.

He lets go of my hands but keeps his eyes squarely aimed at me. "I'm genuinely sorry for leaving so abruptly. It wasn't my choice, and if I could do it again, I'd defy my parents and sneak out anyway. But I was in a state of shock, and then Dawn..."

We turn our heads to her at the same time.

"I spent all night with her. I'd never seen her so scared. I felt like I'd let her down. I'm her big brother, and I didn't protect her. Which, I know now—and because she's hammered it into me a million times—is silly. There's nothing I could have really done. But that night, as I watched her cry and worry and deal with an uncertain and daunting future, I needed to be with her."

"Of course. It makes total sense that you stayed with her." I split my focus between Fraser, Dawn, and Oakey, processing it all. "It also explains your aversion to the media or any type of press."

"But not everyone *from* the press," he points out with a cute grin.

"I'm glad you could make an exception. There is one thing that doesn't fit the pieces of the puzzle I'm trying to put together in my mind."

"What's that?"

"Clayton."

"Ah, my publicity-hungry, limelight-loving brother."

"That's the one. If your family wanted privacy, how does that explain what he's been doing all these years? The guy has been on practically every single reality TV show here *and* in the UK. He even did that one in Australia where he got deported, didn't he?"

"*Almost* got deported. Dad pulled some strings." Fraser

leans back onto the bench. "As you can imagine, Clay was devastated about the show ending. After the first season aired, he became a bit of a pinup boy. The ultimate teenage girl bad-boy crush. After that night, he went traveling for a few months. When he came back, he received an offer."

"What sort of offer?"

"*Celebrity Dancing on Ice with Dogs.*"

A small giggle escapes me. "I still can't believe that's a real show."

"I know. It's ridiculous. Initially, we were all dead-set against it. But the timing of it coincided with Dawn giving birth, so we thought it'd be a good distraction. Keep the media from snooping around us by offering Clay as very willing bait to soak up the limelight. And of course, Clayton being Clayton, he proved to be exceptional bait."

"So it worked?"

"It did. Dawn had Oakey in private, and Clayton lapped up the attention and used that one appearance as a launching pad to becoming America's favorite reality TV villain."

"I see."

Clayton Rademacher has definitely got the bad boy image down pat. His shenanigans have been hard to miss, and I don't even watch reality TV.

"Is he really that awful?" I ask.

"Honestly, no. It's mainly for show, and again, it keeps all the publicity on him, which has allowed the rest of us, except for Mom, of course, to fade into the background."

"I'd hardly say you fade into the background, Fraser. You're one of the biggest names in pro hockey."

"I try to maintain as low a profile as possible." He angles his head. "With one exception."

My heart flutters. "Oh yeah? And has it been worth it? Making an exception?"

"Like you wouldn't believe."

Fraser slides closer to me, and I lean into his warm body. He wraps an arm around me, and I watch Dawn with Oakey, playing mental catch up with everything Fraser has revealed. All the pieces are finally falling into place.

Why his family canceled the show midseason.

Why he left so abruptly the following day.

Why he couldn't say anything about what happened to anyone, for all these years.

Why he continues to be wary of the media.

It even explains why his brother is the way he is...

Everything makes sense.

But still, the reporter in me has questions.

Two, specifically. One silly one, one serious one.

I opt for the silly question first.

"Follow-up about Clayton."

"Go ahead."

"He's the subject of a lot of rumors, most of which I assume are false."

"You assume correctly."

"But is it true he's a ladies' man?"

Fraser's body stiffens. "Before I answer that, *why* do you want to know?"

The possessive rasp in his voice is unmissable.

I laugh. "Not for me. For Harper."

He relaxes, letting out a chuckle. "Don't tell me your sister has a crush on my brother?"

"Fine. I won't say that, but what I will say is that it's not a coincidence that she's watched every single reality TV show he's ever been on."

"Even the ice-skating dog one?"

"Even the ice-skating dog one. She claims it's for research

because she produces reality TV, which may be true, but I'm convinced it's not the only reason."

A grin spreads across his face. "You're just as meddlesome as your brother."

He's possibly right.

I'm possibly in blissful denial.

"Stop deflecting and answer, please."

Rather than answering my question, Fraser makes the zippy-lip gesture, throwing away the key over his shoulder for good measure.

"You really shouldn't have done that," I say, resting my hand on his knee.

"Why?" he mutters, through pursed lips.

"Because I really want to kiss you. But since your lips are sealed, I can't."

"Spare key," he mumbles out the side of his mouth, producing it magically out of thin air and unzipping his lips. "My lips are all yours."

I laugh. "Are they, now?"

"If you want them."

I do. I lean forward and plant a long, closed-mouth kiss on his lips.

When I pull away, Dawn is looking at us.

She averts her gaze swiftly when I see her.

Fraser smiles. "Oh, boy. She's going to have a field day with this."

"Do you mind?"

"Not in the slightest," he says with zero hesitation.

"One last question," I warn him.

With the silly question out of the way, it's time for the serious one.

He grins. "I know you, Evie, and I don't believe that for a second. But go on."

"Okay. Last question *for now*," I clarify, before coming right out with the question that's been playing on my mind. "Why did you decide to tell me all of this now?"

He looks over at his sister and smiles before answering, "Dawn and I talked and it got me thinking about how closed-off I normally am."

"Okay."

He turns to face me again. "I know I'm not a naturally expressive guy. Talking doesn't come easily to me. But I actually enjoy opening up to you. I like the feeling I get when I let you in and tell you things I haven't told anyone else. For some reason, I've always been afraid to do that with anyone else."

"Why? What did you think would happen when you shared your feelings?"

"The universe would implode, reality would fold in on itself, and time would cease to exist."

"Makes sense." I smile at him, then find his hand and thread my fingers through his.

"You're the only person I've ever opened up to like this, Evie."

My arms erupt in goosebumps. "Wow." I feel a little dizzy. "I may need a few moments to let this sink in."

He smiles warmly. "Take all the time you need. I've dumped a lot on you."

After a few minutes of silence, I break it with, "Thank you."

His eyebrow arches. "For what?"

"For opening up to me. For sharing everything. It's not easy being vulnerable and honest."

"Tell me about it."

"You're pretty incredible," I tell him.

He squeezes my fingers. "You're pretty incredible, too."

He smiles at me, and I have officially fallen into a wow canyon.

Just when I think Fraser can't do or say anything to make him more incredible, he opens up even more and takes his incredibleness to a whole new level.

We watch Dawn push Oakey on the swings in silence until the little guy runs over and excitedly tells us about a puzzle he's working on. We spend the rest of the morning sprawled on the floor in Dawn's living room, watching Oakey put his puzzle together, helping from time to time.

I don't get to meet her husband, Tim, since he's at work. She proudly tells me about his plumbing business and their hopes of expanding their family.

I catch her up on old school friends since she's been missing in action and hasn't kept in touch with anyone.

We even take a few selfies—some with me and Dawn, a few with me, Fraser, and Oakey.

As we're leaving, Dawn says, "You'll have to come up again."

I reply, "For sure, I'd love that," and I mean it.

Who knows? Maybe by then, Fraser and I will be officially together.

I lean down to say goodbye to Oakey, and he looks up at me with his adorable big blue eyes. "Can you swing me next time you visit, please?"

"I would love that."

He barrels into me with a hug so strong, I almost topple over.

When I stand back up, Fraser is looking at me with a soft, tender expression, his normally intense eyes glimmering with a quiet joy.

"I'm so happy Dawn is settled and in a really good place in her life," I say as we begin our drive back down the mountain to Comfort Bay.

"So am I."

"Is that why you're reconsidering your aversion to small towns?"

"That's part of the reason." His eyes dart over to me. "There may be another reason as well."

"Oh. *Oh*."

I don't know what to say to that, so I stare out the window at the rolling hills, my mind swirling with all the revelations from the day.

"Where should we stop for burgers?" Fraser asks as we get closer to town.

"Bold of you to assume I'm hungry."

"Er, it would be bolder of me to assume you aren't. And I love that about you," he says, snuffing out the last vestiges of self-consciousness I have about my appetite...and my food choices.

I don't have to watch what I say, how I act, or what I eat around Fraser, and it's so freeing. He accepts me for who I am.

I shoot him a smile right as my stomach grumbles. "I know a good place."

18

Fraser

Scores are tied at two-all in the third round of the divisional playoffs, a best-out-of-seven series, with the winning team advancing to the conference championships.

We've lost two games and won once.

If we lose tonight, we're staring down the barrel of the next game being our last one this season, but honestly, my heart's not in it the way it usually is.

Don't get me wrong. I want to win.

The team and I have had a bumpy rollercoaster of a season. We've worked hard just to make it here, and as it stands, we barely scraped into the playoffs.

Culver has fully recovered from his injury and is playing some of the best hockey of his career, proving that age ain't nothing but a number, and Evie and Hannah are watching the home game from the family lounge.

It's been two weeks since I took Evie to visit Dawn and Oakey. We had a Zoom family meeting a few days beforehand to discuss things. Dawn took the lead and repeated what she had said to me. That she was done being hidden away. That while she wouldn't be deliberately seeking out attention, she also wouldn't be hiding anymore, either. We all agreed that if that's what she wanted, then that's what we'd do.

That gave me the all-clear to take Evie to see her, which I was relieved about. I didn't like keeping this part of my life from her.

I've been more honest, more open, with her than I have with anyone else in my life. And it feels right.

Like a missing piece of me has slotted back into place.

Like I'm finally becoming the man I want to be.

She now knows everything about me.

Well...except for my last remaining secret.

My virginity.

As well as a surprise I'm working on.

But I'll tell her about both things. In due course.

I intercept a pass near the blue line, then explode down the ice, leaving the defender in my wake. The roar of the crowd grows deafening as I propel myself through the neutral zone.

Suddenly, a shadow materializes from the periphery. I should have been on it, catching out the opposing player before he got the chance to cut across my path.

But my head, much like my heart, is otherwise occupied.

I miss Pietrowski's lunge with his stick, and I'm too slow in my response. There's a clash of steel on rubber, then the puck spins free from my control and into the air.

With the reflexes of a predator, Pietrowski pounces on the loose puck. The cheers of the home crowd die, replaced by a stunned silence, as he takes off toward our goal.

Our goalie, Milo, does his best to block the incoming puck, but it's no use. The net ripples, the scorelight flashes, and with my head hung low, I skate toward the face-off circle, bearing the full weight of the missed opportunity on my shoulders.

"Hey, cheer up, man. It ain't over. We still got a shot."

"Yeah, I know," I say to Culver who's sitting across the booth from me.

Technically, he's right. There is still a path for us to progress past the divisional playoffs.

But it's a very narrow one.

We're down three games, which means we need to win the next three to advance.

My lack of concentration and the silly mistakes I'm making aren't helping us.

"If it's any consolation, your stats for the game weren't *that* bad," Evie says consolingly before taking a massive bite of her burger. "Could be better, obviously, but don't beat yourself up about it. That's my job."

I turn to face her, sitting next to me, and manage a small smile. "Thanks."

I munch on my cheeseburger, determined to leave my abysmal performance tonight in the past. I need to regroup and focus for our upcoming games, and more importantly, I need to regroup and focus on what's happening right here, right now.

Evie, Culver, Hannah, and I are at one of my favorite diners in LA. It's one of those old-timey ones that looks exactly like it probably did back in the 1950s when these sorts of places were all the rage.

I seem to like it, for some reason. It's got greasy burgers and thick-cut fries that Evie loves, for all the usual reasons.

Someone looking at us might assume we're on a double date, which is only one-quarter true since technically, Evie and I are still fake dating—subtract half a point—and Culver and Hannah have been friends their whole lives, so they are firmly in the friend zone—minus one full point.

I shove a few fries into my mouth and chomp down on them as irritation paws inside my chest. I don't like thinking about Evie and me as fake dating because, apart from how it started, nothing about this relationship has felt fake.

I realize we agreed to keep things going the way they are and stick with fake dating, but it's not enough for me.

I want Evie to be my girlfriend. For real.

She and Hannah are talking at their usual breakneck speed,

and Culver and I have broken off into our plans for the summer. After his injury earlier in the season, he says he wants to keep the vibe chill and might even visit his family in Comfort Bay.

Overhearing this, Hannah drops her conversation with Evie and turns to Culver, her eyes brimming with excitement. "You are?"

"Yeah, maybe," Culver answers with a noncommittal shrug. "We'll see. Gonna play it by ear."

"If you do, let me know so we can hang out."

That's an innocent statement, right?

A friend excited by the prospect of a friend being close by so they can spend some time together.

Evie certainly doesn't make anything of it, judging by how she's listening while eating her burger.

And Culver is as clueless as ever as he demolishes his.

But me?

I spot it.

The way Hannah looks at Culver. The way she keeps one ear open to his conversations. The thrill she gets at the mere prospect of spending some time with him.

I've always had my suspicions that there was something between them, and now I see it, clear as day. Hannah's got feelings for Culver, feelings that extend way past the boundaries of friendship.

I recognize myself in her, in the way I've felt about Evie for so long, in how I tried to hide my feelings.

"I'm going to get another soda," Hannah says, getting up. "Anyone else want one?"

We're all good.

"I need to use the bathroom," I say to Evie. "Will you excuse me?"

"Sure."

She lets me out of the booth, and I follow Hannah to the counter.

We've gotten closer these past few months since I spend a lot of time either at her flower shop, ordering flowers from her online, or emailing her about flowers I'd like to order, but that doesn't mean I'm about to confront her with my suspicions.

Besides, I have another matter to raise with her.

A much more important one.

"You feeling all right?" she asks me after placing her order with the server.

"Yeah. Just have to put this game behind me and focus on what's next."

"That's a good attitude."

"Easier said than done, but I'm trying. Hey, listen, I need your help with something. Something big."

She smiles mischievously. "Okay. Is it about you-know-who?"

"Well, if by you-know-who you mean Oprah, then no. Although, I am a fan of hers, and I admire how she uses her platform to empower women and advocate for social justice. However, if by you-know-who you mean..." I lower my voice. "Evie? Then yes. You're correct."

Her smile deepens. "She's really rubbing off on you," she teases, taking a jibe at my babbling.

"She is." I look over my shoulder, double checking that Evie hasn't snuck up behind us, but nope, she's got her phone out, and judging by the look on Culver's face, I'd say she's going through a play-by-play dissection of tonight's game with him.

Good.

I mean, not good for Culver—the guy looks like he'd rather be getting a root canal—but good for me.

This has to remain a secret.

I turn back to Hannah. "This stays between us."

"As always."

"I want Evie to be completely and utterly surprised."

"Of course."

"The something big I have in mind is...Are you able to procure one thousand yellow roses?"

She lets out a gasp, covering her mouth with her hand. "Oh, my gosh, Fraser! Are you going to propo—?"

"Whoa, whoa, whoa. Hold your horses," I cut in.

I haven't even asked Evie to be my girlfriend; it's way too early to ask her to be my wife. That's definitely on my radar, but not just yet.

"What I have in mind is something different."

"Okay, okay," she says, recovering. "Different how?"

"Well, it's more of a business thing."

"A business thing?"

"Yeah. As you know, Evie's in a tricky place with the network."

Hannah's face falls. "I don't get why people aren't obsessed with her segments. I am."

"Same. They're the best thing about that show."

"One hundred percent agree."

"Since Evie doesn't know what her future holds, I have an idea for something else she might like to do. It's something she'd be great at and she's wanted to do but has never taken the risk. I'm hoping this might help her."

"Ahhh." Hannah grins knowingly. "I think I know what you're referring to. I think it's a great idea. She makes the best bracelets."

"Yeah, she does."

Before I can say anything else, Hannah rubs her hands together excitedly. "I love this for Evie, and to answer your question, yes, I can get the flowers shipped in. When do you need them?"

"My schedule depends on what happens in the next few games, so I was thinking anywhere from a few weeks to a month or so. Does that give you enough time?"

"It does. That's perfect. I'll place the order with my supplier first thing tomorrow."

"Thanks. I appreciate it."

Hannah returns to the table with her soda, while I go use the restroom. When I return, Culver and Hannah are pitching story ideas to Evie.

"Ma was telling me about this friendship bench that's popped up in Starlight Cove," Culver suggests.

Beside him, Hannah nods. "That's a great idea. Or Beth mentioned that some Comfort Bay residents have started a free library. I think it's on Peach Street. Someone's placed a box there for people to swap books."

"Guys, thank you," Evie cuts in, resting her burger onto her plate. "I appreciate what you're trying to do, but I think the writing is on the wall. Good news simply doesn't sell."

"So what are you going to do, then?" I ask as I slide into the booth and she scooches in next to me.

"I have a couple of options."

I grab her hand under the table. "Care to fill us in?"

She visibly tenses. "Uh, no. It's way too early. Wouldn't want to jinx it."

Her hazel eyes are awash with sadness...and an emotion I can't quite pinpoint. Evie's being unusually guarded—maybe I'm rubbing off on her, too?—but I don't push, despite my curiosity. I'm sure she'll tell us whenever she's ready.

The conversation moves on, but in my head, all I'm picturing is the moment I bring Evie into the locker room filled with one thousand yellow roses and reveal my big idea to her.

I hope everything works out for her at the network, I really do. But if it doesn't, or if she decides she wants to pursue something else, there's one other thing I know she's passionate about and loves. It could be the perfect second career for her.

I think back to those nights when I'd sneak into her bedroom and we'd hang out, talk, eat, watch games, and she'd make her bracelets, and I grin to myself.

Yeah, I think I've come up with a really awesome idea.

19

Evie

Even with Margo's thick Australian accent coming through the car speakers, I'm instantly transported back in time as I turn onto the street where I grew up. All sorts of childhood memories come flooding back to me.

Countless summer days spent with my sisters, riding our bikes around the neighborhood and through the local park.

Eating ice cream with Levi after a day spent on the beach.

Watching the game with Dad on our big-screen TV, him whooping and hollering and swearing like a sailor.

And as I drive past the Rademacher's house, all I can think about is Fraser and those late nights we shared.

Now that I know the truth, I'm not upset things turned out the way they did. He did what he had to do to protect his family.

I personalized it. Made it about me. Took it as a sign of rejection when him not coming over to say goodbye or acknowledging my bracelet was because he had a pregnant teenage sister to console and a training camp he got shuttled off to without warning.

It all makes sense now.

It must have been so hard for him—for all of his family—but things have turned out well. Dawn is doing great, Oakey is the coolest six-year-old ever, and Fraser's living his major league dream.

Speaking of, I'm very happy to report that after hitting a rough patch, the Swifts have rallied. They've dug deep and won their last three games, plus the decider, and secured themselves a spot in the conference finals.

Talk about an up-and-down season. If they manage to ride

this hot streak, they could go all the way and win the Stanley Cup this year.

I pull into the driveaway of my parents' house.

Margo finally takes a breath, so I switch my mind back into work mode and decide to bring up something I've been meaning to tell her.

"I've been working on something."

"What is it?"

"Well, despite my days at the network being numbered, I'm putting together a package to show Fraser what an interview segment could look like."

"That's fantastic news. I reckon you're onto a winner with that, hon. And it's not too late. I say go for it. It could be enough to save you."

"I'm not making any promises," I say, trying to reset her expectations into the realm of reality. "I'm still ninety-nine percent sure Fraser will veto the idea, but there's no harm in raising it with him, is there?"

"Exactly. Have you got an angle?"

"I do."

"Ooh," she squeals. "Do tell. Oh, no. Damn. I'm getting another call. Double damn. I have to take it. We'll talk later, yeah? You've made me very happy, hon."

The call ends, and I turn off the car, sitting silently for a few moments. "What do you think, Daisy?"

She sighs in sympathy, and I imagine her saying, "You're down to your last two choices, Evie. And a girl's gotta do what a girl's gotta do."

"Ain't that the truth."

Last choice number one—putting together a package and presenting it to Fraser.

Even if he says no—which I fully expect him to—at least when I look back on this time in my life, I'll know I did everything I could to save my career. That I didn't slink away from the challenge, and that I gave it my all.

And the angle I've come up with?

Well, since Fraser has been so closed off, he's developed a reputation for being a little...gruff. I want to change that inaccurate perception and present his softer side. And the best way to do that would be to show him with his family, especially Dawn and Oakey. He loves that kid with all his heart, and he's so great with him. *That's* the Fraser Rademacher I want the world to see.

Plus, it also allows me to slip Dawn's story into the segment—if she and the rest of the family would like to be involved, that is. It could finally put an end to the ugly rumors and speculation that have dogged the Rademachers since they pulled the plug on their show.

They'll have full control of the narrative since I have no desire to make the piece exploitative in any way.

I know Fraser is—and will always be—a private person, but in this way, he and his family are in the driver's seat. They control what and how much they want to reveal.

I still don't think he'll go for it, but it's one of the last two remaining options I have.

The other option?

I get out of the car and walk toward my childhood home. It backs onto the Pacific Ocean, and the salt-tinged air tickles my nose as I take in the stucco walls, red tiled roof, and arched doorways.

I reach the front door and press the bell, the distinctive chime echoing throughout the house.

"Evelyn," Mom says, sounding surprised as she opens the door.

"Hey, Mom." I hug her. "Why do you sound surprised to see me?"

I called and arranged this visit with her yesterday.

She gives me a once over. "It's just that you said you'd be here at two o'clock."

"Yeah, and it's two o'clock," I say.

"Exactly. I'm glad to see you've improved your punctuality. Come in."

I step into the house biting my tongue—literally. I've been late twice in the past year, once because I got held up at work, and once because I was hanging out with Hannah and the alarm I'd set to remind me to come here didn't go off.

Don't engage, Evie. You're here for a reason. Focus on that. Focus only on that. Hey, defensemen, you're awake today, Great. Something tells me I'm going to need you.

I follow her into the formal living room.

There's a tray laid out on the coffee table with a kettle, two tea cups, and a plate with an assortment of pastries.

"I wasn't sure if you'd be hungry," Mom says, taking a seat. "Two o'clock is such a strange time to meet. Have you eaten? I can get Louisa to make you something if you like."

"That won't be necessary, Mom," I say, sitting opposite her and helping myself to a mini cinnamon roll.

"Tea?"

"Yes, please."

Mom pours the tea, the aroma of citrus and spice wafting in the air. She hands me a cup and saucer adorned with a pretty floral pattern. "Here you go."

"Thanks."

She sits down and lifts the porcelain mug to her lips, her eyes never leaving me. "So, to what do I owe the pleasure of this visit? I assume you need something."

"Mom. Geez. Can't a daughter just visit her mother and hang out?"

She quirks a brow. "You want to hang out with me, Evelyn?"

"Sure. Why not? How is everything?"

"Fine."

"Dad?"

"He's fine."

"The ladies at the country club?"

"Also fine. Evelyn." The cup clinks against the saucer with a sharp ding. "You did not come here to make small talk. If you have a point, please just get to it."

"Okay, okay. Just promise me you won't get all *Mom* about it." She looks about as unimpressed as I expected that comment to make her look. "I came here today to talk to you about your contact in Washington."

She perks up. "Really?"

"Yes. Work isn't going very well."

A puzzled expression crosses her face. "Why not?"

"For a number of reasons I'd rather not get into, but mainly because my segments aren't attracting viewers."

She makes a quiet sound I can't decipher, then says, "Well, that's odd."

"Why would that be odd?"

"Because I think your segments are lovely, Evelyn."

"You...watch my segments?"

"You don't have to sound so surprised. Of course I watch them. I'm allowed to, aren't I?"

"Of course. Yeah. It's just..."

When I don't follow that up with anything, she prompts, "It's just, what?"

"Well, didn't you once say morning shows are—and I'm paraphrasing a little here—basically for morons who need to have something on while they get ready for their day?"

"I highly doubt I used the term *moron*. But to your point, while I may not be the target demographic of *The Morning Buzz*, I make sure to tune in to watch your segments. Just like I listen to that sad excuse for music Levi's band makes, and I torment myself by watching recaps on YouTube of whatever sad excuse of a reality TV show Harper is producing."

There is so much to unpack in that sentence...so of course I latch on to the most important detail. "You watch YouTube?"

Mom sighs. "I may be old, but I'm not ancient."

I crack a grin. "Louisa showed you, didn't she?"

Mom stifles a smile. "Actually, it was your father. The point remains—I support all my children. Even Laney, who for the life of me, I still can't fathom why she would choose to work as a maid—"

"She started off as a maid, but now she *runs* the hotel, Mom."

"Still. It's a waste of her intellect, if you ask me."

Which no one is, I think, but wisely kept to myself.

Two for two, guardsmen. We're on a roll today.

"But back to your request. I'd be more than happy to set up a meeting with Devlin Wilshire. I hear he's on the lookout for a political reporter."

"That'd be great. Thanks, Mom," I mumble into my tea.

I'm grateful for her help. I am. I just wish I wasn't in a position to be asking for it in the first place. Moving to Washington and reporting on politics is the last thing I want to do.

But what other choice do I have?

I've even been considering taking Fraser up on some of the not-so-subtle hints he's been dropping lately and taking a business course so I can sell my bracelets online.

I slurp my tea and finish off the rest of my pastry while Mom sits there, assessing me.

"What's the matter, Evelyn? You don't seem happy. This could be a great opportunity for you. A steppingstone to a real reporting career."

I wipe my hands on the sides of my pants, which earns me a look of mild disgust. "And what if I don't want to be a real reporter?"

"What is that supposed to mean? Why wouldn't you want that?"

"I don't know. Maybe because being the reporter I am now doesn't feel as good as I thought it would. Maybe because I'm starting to question if journalism is even the right career for me. Maybe because I just feel this constant, nonstop pressure from you to wear the right clothes, and go to the right college, and wipe my hands on all the right surfaces. It's...It's too much, Mom."

She stills, save for her eyes, which are doing that darty thing they do whenever she's busy thinking.

Or scheming.

"You feel pressure from me?"

I nod.

"Really?"

"Yeah, Mom. All the time." I pause, placing a hand on my heart. "I just...I just want your approval."

"You have my approval...mostly."

"I want it *unconditionally*. Even when you don't understand or agree with what I'm doing. I know moms are always gonna mom, but I need you to trust me. You and Dad raised me well. I'm smart. But I will make mistakes. I'll have stuff I'll need to figure out. I just want you to be there for me. Not if I say or do or wear the things you want me to, but regardless."

She places the cup and saucer on the coffee table and squares her shoulders. "I'm going to tell you something I've never told you before."

"You and Dad are lizard people and only eat time-traveling vegetables."

"Excuse me?"

"Never mind. Continue. Please."

"What I was going to say is that I only want what's best for you, Levi, Harper, and Laney," she begins.

"I know that, Mom."

She folds her hands neatly in her lap, trying to mask her discomfort. Mom is the queen of chitchat and can make polite small talk with anyone.

But talking about real things? This is way outside her comfort zone.

"As you know, your father and I got married quite young."

"You were twenty, right?"

"I was. Just turned. By the time I turned twenty-one, I had dropped out of college, gotten married, and had my first child."

This much I know.

"Do you know which university I dropped out of?"

"I have no idea—Wait. No. Don't tell me. UCLA?"

"Correct. And would you like to take a guess at what I was enrolled to study?"

"No way. Journalism?"

Mom nods. "That's right. Now...Listen carefully because I don't want you to misunderstand what I'm about to say."

"I'm listening. Carefully."

"Being a wife and mother is, by far, the biggest blessing of my life. I love your father with all my heart, just like I love all my children. *However*...I have also put my own life on hold for my husband and my children. It was a little different once you and Levi were born, but for the first few years with Laney and Harper, I followed your father around the country as he played. I never went back to college to get my degree. I devoted myself to raising my children. I didn't pursue a career. My path was laid out in front of me. I never got to make mistakes and figure stuff out on my own. And while I'm very happy with my life and everyone in it, I want you to have what I never did. Choices."

I take a few deep breaths, processing everything she just said. I look up at her and say, "Mom, I hear what you're saying. Things make a lot more sense now, like why you pushed so hard for me to go to UCLA and study journalism, but if you want me to have the ability to make choices, you have to step back and let me make them, and..." I add this last part as delicately as I can. "They have to be *my* choices."

"I realize that. It's just that I've had four children. I wanted one of them to go to a university. Does that make me a terrible mother?"

"It doesn't make you a terrible mother," I say, offering her a smile. "But Levi and Harper did go to school in LA."

"Oh, please. One-year diplomas from some ridiculously overpriced media entertainment school don't count," Mom says with an unimpressed eye roll.

Normally, I'd defend my siblings and say that it still counts as an education, but right at this very moment, I let it slide. Because I get what Mom's saying, even if it is all sorts of messed up for her to be laying all her unfulfilled expectations on me.

I'm the youngest. Shouldn't she be over parenting by now and just be glad I'm alive and not in jail? Why did my siblings fail me and not tire her out? Oh, that's right—because none of them attended an approved four-year college, that's why. Thanks, guys.

I hang around for another ten minutes or so before telling her I should get going.

"Oh, I almost forgot to ask," Mom says as we reach the entryway. "How's Fraser?"

"Uh, he's great."

"And how are things with the two of you?"

"Also great."

Mom's still under the impression we've really been dating this whole time, and I have to say, she seems to be on board. I guess that's because Fraser ticks off all her potential husband requirements. Plus he's a hockey player, and I suspect that since she married one, that might sweeten the deal even more.

"Excellent. In that case, can you please extend an invitation to him to join us for a family dinner next week?"

"Really?"

"Yes, really. I know he feels like part of the family already because of Levi, but if he's an important part of your life, I'd like to make more of an effort to get to know him better. Bring it up with him next time you see him, and let me know what he says."

"I will. Bye, Mom."

"Goodbye, Evelyn."

I sigh into the speaker of my phone during my chat date with Fraser that night. "Do you think we'll ever get to a point where we don't feel like we're a major disappointment to our parents?"

"Maybe once they're dead?" Fraser offers.

"Normally I'd agree with you, but I think it's unlikely in my case."

"Why is that?"

"Well, knowing Mom, and with the way AI is advancing, I'm sure she'll find some way to express her displeasure at my life choices from beyond the grave."

"So I take it that your time with her today didn't go well?"

"It actually wasn't as bad as I thought it would be. We

talked about some...interesting stuff. But still, I hate having to ask her for anything, much less something I don't really want."

I've told Fraser about how Mom is going to set up a meeting for me with her Washington contact, who happens to be the husband of one of the women she used to be on the Winter Carnival Planning Committee with until they left Comfort Bay and moved to D.C.

I may have also grumbled, for possibly not the first time, about how much I do not want to be pursuing this option.

"Oh. That reminds me," I say.

"Yeah?"

"You're invited to a family dinner next week."

The line goes quiet.

"What is it? What's wrong?" I ask when the silence stretches for too long.

"Nothing. It's great. I'd love to go."

"But?"

"But will there be chilis?"

I laugh. "Probably. But don't worry, I'll get Mom to ask the cook to go easy on you."

"Thank you." He lets out an audible sigh of relief. "So, in what capacity exactly have I been invited to the family dinner?"

Before I can answer, he says, "Actually. Can I call you back in literally one second?"

"Uh, sure."

We end the call and a second later, my phone buzzes, but this time it's not a voice call from Fraser.

It's a video call.

I reject it and text him.

Evie: *Nope. Not happening.*
Evie: *Not talking on video.*

Evie: *I look terrible.*
Fraser: *Is that why you rejected the call?*
Evie: *It is.*
Fraser: *But you look beautiful.*
Evie: *You haven't seen me tonight, so you have no way of knowing that.*
Fraser: *Actually, I do.*
Evie: *How?*
Fraser: *Because you're always beautiful.*

How?

How does he always know the most swoon-worthy thing to say?

But still, I will not allow myself to get sidelined by Fraser's swooniness.

I press on.

Evie: *Why do you want to switch to a video call?*
Fraser: *Well, because we're about to have 'the conversation'.*
Fraser: *And before you make some crack like: and by 'the conversation' do you mean why do people in Britain butter their bread for a sandwich?*
Fraser: *I want to be serious for a moment.*
Fraser: *Because by 'the conversation' I mean talking about us.*
Fraser: *Specifically, there's a question I've been meaning to ask you.*

I almost drop my phone.

It's happening! It's happening! It's happening!

Fraser is going to ask me to be his girlfriend.

My instincts may have let me down in the past, but I *know* I'm right about this. I've been sensing him skirting around the topic for a while now.

He's finally going to do it...and my chin is dripping in

Häagen-Dazs ice cream, and I haven't changed out of my workout gear from my Pilates class this afternoon.

Fraser: *I think that conversation warrants some face-to-face time. Don't you?*
Evie: *Give me five minutes.*
Fraser: *Normally I wouldn't rush you, but I have been waiting YEARS for this moment.*
Fraser: *So...I've started a timer.*
Fraser: *<smiley face emoji>*
Fraser: *<stopwatch emoji>*
Fraser: *<red heart pulsing emoji>*

For not the first time, I scramble to make myself look presentable for Fraser.

I throw on a clean sweater, wash my face, tame my hair into a ponytail, and slap on some lip gloss and blush.

It's not perfect, but it'll do.

The screen is lighting up as I walk back into the living room.

Wow. He wasn't kidding, he really was timing it.

I plop myself in an armchair, lift the phone up to above chin height, and take the call.

"Hi, and thanks for calling Paul's Pizza and Pasta Pie Shop. We bake 'em, you take 'em. How can I help you today?"

Fraser leans back in his armchair. "Is this your idea of being serious?"

"Hey, my head's spinning. I had to make myself presentable in under five minutes. A weaker woman would have crumbled, but not I."

"No. Definitely not you." He licks his lips. "You look great, Evie, though I suspect you looked great before, too."

I wave my hand in the air, grinning. "You're just saying that because you didn't see the state I was in. I was giving facemask high school Evie a run for her money."

He shakes his head, his blue eyes sparkling. "Got it all out of your system?"

"Yes." I give a firm nod. "Ready to commence seriousness."

As soon as the words leave me, my stomach swoops, just like when you go over the top crest of a rollercoaster and have that second or two before you commence the descent.

Because if I'm right, when Fraser opens his mouth, we're going to enter completely uncharted territory.

"Evie, getting to know you again these past few months has been incredible. I've never met anyone like you because I don't think there is anyone like you on this planet. You're smart. Funny. Beautiful, especially when you wear sweatpants and *ugh* boots."

A giggle bursts out of me. "Don't forget the wet hair."

He grins. "How could I forget?"

Then he sucks in a breath, his eyes darken, and I can tell this is it. The moment he's been building up to.

"Evelyn Freeman, will you be my girlfriend?"

My heart swells in my chest. "Oh, Fraser."

I honestly never thought this day would come, that my high school crush, the guy who left without saying goodbye, would be asking me out.

"Of course I'll be your girlfriend."

20

Fraser

It's real.

I'm in a real relationship with Evie.

And right now, I'm really kissing my real girlfriend.

For real.

"We're gonna be late," Evie mutters, managing to wrestle her lips away from mine.

"Don't care. Making out like teenagers is more fun."

"My mother will kill us."

I pull apart immediately. "True. We should get going."

Mrs. Freeman has always low-key terrified me, but I think I've done a pretty good job of hiding it over the years. I've heard enough stories from Levi—and more recently from Evie—to know she is not a woman to be messed with.

Her intimidation has this weird effect on me, making me super polite around her, which I think in some weird way has endeared me to her. But I am *not* willing to risk ruining that by showing up late to my first family dinner as Evie's boyfriend.

I push to my feet and extend my arms to help her up.

"Wow," she says with a laugh, sliding her palms into mine. "Can't believe you're still scared of Mom. I would've thought you'd have grown out of it by now."

"I am not scared of your Mom," I white-lie, pulling Evie to her feet.

I lean in for another kiss.

She ducks her head out of the way. "You so are. 'You look beautiful, Mrs. Freeman,' 'Can I get you something to drink, Mrs. Freeman?,' 'You're just so wonderful, Mrs. Freeman.'"

"There's nothing wrong with having a healthy respect-slash-fear of your girlfriend's mother."

Evie flashes me a dazzling smile. "Say the second-to-last

word in the previous sentence again. Non-possessive form."

I lower my voice to just above a whisper and trace my fingers along her neck. "Girlfriend."

Evie's eyes flutter to a close.

I brush my fingers along her jaw. "Girlfriend."

Around her ear. "Girlfriend."

Across her soft cheek. "Girlfriend."

She's not the only one who likes the sound of the word. I do, too.

I'd been working up to asking her to be my girlfriend—for real—for a while, but getting the timing right proved tricky. Ideally, I would have liked to have done it in person, but our schedules have been crazy busy lately.

Her bringing up the invitation to a family dinner during a chat date last week was the opening I needed. I switched the call to video, waited the longest five minutes of my life while she got ready, and then I found myself asking the only girl I've truly loved to be mine.

I lower my hand into the arch of her lower back and tug her in closer to me.

A breath shudders out of her as she lifts her head and opens her eyes. "For the record, if this is my punishment for teasing you, expect a lot more teasing to come your way."

"Oh, I do."

I expect a lifetime of it.

But first, I have to survive a Freeman family dinner.

It's been a while since I've been to one, and I'm pretty sure not much has changed. I know what I'm in for. Plenty of fast-talking. Mrs. Freeman expressing her opinions freely. Mr. Freeman being totally laid-back and relaxed as ever.

And chilis.

"Hey, did you get a chance to request a *low-spice, would still like to feel the roof of his mouth by the end of the evening* option for me?" I ask as we drive the short distance from Evie's place to her parents'.

"I did."

"And?"

"No luck. Mom said the food will be what the food will be. That's all I remember her saying. I zoned out when she started rambling about messing with her dinner theme."

"Uh, okay."

"Look, if it's too spicy for you, don't eat it, okay? Don't feel pressured to keep up with us. Especially when Mom starts laying it on. Be strong, Fraser, and resist the almighty Meredith Freeman."

I let out a chuckle, hoping it conceals my nerves.

Evie's playing it off, but the Freemans are crazy intense when it comes to chilis. Levi once didn't talk to me for a whole week because I refused to split a jalapeno with him.

I come to a stop before reaching the Freeman's house and take in my old family home. Mom and Dad sold it a year after *that night.* They wanted a fresh start, so they bought a beautiful house in the hills, halfway between Comfort Bay and Dawn in Cedar Crest Hollow.

"Walking down memory lane?" Evie asks, placing her hand on the center console.

"I'm just taking a minute."

I gaze at the house where I grew up, then turn to face Evie, threading our fingers together. She looks stunning in a chic form-fitting emerald-green dress that perfectly contours to her figure and accentuates her eyes.

"I have a question," I say.

"What is it?"

"Well, I fell in love with you back in high school. Did you… did you not fall for me, too?"

She reaches out and strokes my cheek. "Oh. I definitely had

a crush on you. I made you a tacky bracelet, after all."

"Not tacky. It's the best lucky charm ever."

She smiles, her hazel eyes sparkling in the low light. "And I was heartbroken when you left which"—she raises a finger when she sees me open my mouth to say something—"I now realize wasn't what I made it out to be in my head."

"I still feel bad about it."

"Well, then, stop it. Please. It wasn't your fault. You did what you had to do for your family. That's actually really admirable."

"I just did what anyone would've done."

"I don't know about that. You put their needs ahead of your own. You spent the night comforting your sister when she would have been terrified and vulnerable and needed you more than ever. And you kept your end of the bargain all these years, shunning the spotlight and just focusing on being great at the thing you're great at."

"I think you're making me sound better than I am."

"Nope. I'm making you sound exactly the correct level of awesome that you are. I'm talented like that."

I can't help but grin. "Thanks, Evie."

I drive up the Freemans' driveway and park next to Levi's bright-blue Chevrolet Corvette. He came up from LA with Harper, so I'm assuming the other car belongs to Laney.

Everyone's here.

"Have you spoken to anyone in your family about our change in status?"

"Haven't had the chance," Evie says as we get out of the car. "Besides, everyone except for Levi thinks we're dating anyway, so I figure there's really no need."

"True." I walk next to her. Which brings us neatly to..."What about Levi, then?"

"Are you worried?"

"A little, yeah. He's my best friend. You're his little sister. He could get kinda weird about it."

"How would you feel if the situation were reversed? If Levi was dating Dawn?"

"Very weird given that she's married."

Evie rolls her eyes. "Pretend that she wasn't. Would it be strange for you?"

"I don't know." I shrug, reaching the front porch. "Probably at first it would be. But once I got over the initial surprise, I guess I'd be fine with it. Levi's an awesome guy, and as much as I don't want to think about my sister's romantic life...ever, I'd want her to be with someone awesome. So yeah, I'd find a way to be cool with it. Eventually."

"Well, then, there's your answer. I'm sure Levi will be cool with it."

"You're sure Levi will be cool with what?" the man of the moment asks.

I missed the front door opening, but there he is, leaning against the doorframe in ripped jeans and a Metallica T-shirt. How long has he been standing there?

"Oh, nothing," Evie dismisses, dashing up the porch steps to give her brother a hug.

"It wouldn't have anything to do with your so-called fake relationship, would it?" he asks me before giving me a hug.

And he hugs me hard.

Real hard.

Way harder than usual.

And he's not letting go.

Oh, man, is he trying to suffocate me by hugging me to death? Is that a thing?

"What do you mean so-called fake relationship?" Evie asks, once he relieves me from his grip, and I'm...I'm still breathing.

Maybe he injected something into my skin through my

jacket? No. I'm being paranoid. If Levi is going to kill me for dating his sister, I'm sure he'll do it like a man and kill me to my face. Yeah, that makes much more sense.

"Oh, come on, you guys." He closes the door behind him to give the three of us a bit more privacy. "When did you crack?"

His eyes dance between Evie and me, a mischievous glint sparking within them. He's enjoying this way too much.

"What are you talking about?" I ask, playing dumb, but inside, my heart rate is skyrocketing.

It would kill me if this great thing happening between me and Evie cost me my friendship with him.

He pats me on the shoulder. "Come on, man. You've been getting heart eyes every time I mention Evie's name for years. And whenever I talked about anyone she was dating, you'd get all grouchy and silent. Correction, more grouchy and more silent than normal."

A giggle escapes out of Evie.

Levi faces her. "Oh, and don't think this is all one-sided either, missy. Your crush on Fraser is as impossible to ignore as the inflatable T-Rex costume you wore for Halloween when you were ten."

"I was going through a dinosaur phase," she explains to me while smacking Levi's arm.

I step in closer, standing squarely between my best friend and my girlfriend. "What are you saying, Levi?"

I'm pretty sure I already know but I want him to confirm it.

"What I'm saying is you guys are meant for each other. Why else do you think I set this whole thing up?"

"Because you love to meddle," Evie and I respond in unison.

"Ugh. Now is not the time for facts. I was hoping that one date would get you guys to see what you could have."

"Really?" I say. "This whole thing, you set it all up?"

"Yes, really. Dude, you're the best guy I know. And I know that no matter what happens, you'll never treat Evie like..."

He stops, shaking his head, and I'm glad he does. If I never think of jerkface or any of the other idiots dumb enough to squander their shots with Evie ever again, it'll be too soon.

"You'll treat her well," he continues. "I know this because I know you. You're the most loyal and decent guy. Unless Dad has opened the door and is standing behind me."

I grin. "Coast is clear. No Dad."

"Okay, good." Levi turns to his sister. "And Evie, you're my favorite sister. Unless Harper and Laney are standing right behind me, in which case, you're in my top three favorite sisters."

Evie smiles. "No one is standing behind you."

"Great. So you're back to being my favorite." He takes us both in. "So why wouldn't I want the two people I love most in the world...unless Mom is behind me...to be together?"

"I'm gobsmacked," I say, as a wave of relief washes over me.

"Gobsmacked and dumbfounded," Evie concurs.

"Ooh, dumbfounded, that's a good one."

"Bamboozled is also a good word," she says.

"Highly underused, if you ask me."

"Should we try to bring it back? I think we could bring it back."

"You guys are...You know what? I don't think a word's been invented to describe what you guys are." Levi snickers. "I'd hoped you two would get your act together at Bryce's wedding, but I get it. It might've been too emotional an occasion. I was scheming up some other way to force the situation, but you beat me to it. Well, the media beat me to it, which for once, I'm grateful for the intrusion. But then I was getting concerned that your relationship wasn't progressing. I mean, how long was I expected to wait for you guys to make it real? Come on."

Evie and I look at each other. "Still gobsmacked?" I ask her.

She nods. "Yeah. And all the other words. You?"

"Yep. Same. Also, very grateful to still be alive."

Levi places one hand on my shoulder, one on Evie's, with the biggest, smuggest smile stretching his lips. "But when I saw you both tonight, I knew."

"Knew what?" I ask.

"That you'd finally gotten your act together and crossed the line to something real. You guys have this really cool energy. I can't describe it. But it's not something you can fake."

I glance over at Evie, take her hand in mine, and smile. "No. It isn't."

She returns my smile before turning her attention back to Levi. "Wait. Why were you spying on us? That's creepy."

"I needed a momentary reprieve. Mom's in a mood."

"I take back the creepy comment. It all makes sense now. Why is Mom in a mood?"

"We don't have five years to unpack that, Evie. But don't worry, she'll be fine once Fraser arrives. Fraser can do no wrong in her eyes."

Evie pokes her tongue out at me. "Told you you're a suck up."

"I am not. Also, just a quick reminder, we are all adults, and this conversation isn't very adult-like." I punctuate my statement by sticking my tongue out, and the three of us chuckle like the adults we are.

"Bottom line," Levi says, looking between us. "I honestly couldn't be happier for you. On one condition."

Evie frowns. "What's that?"

"I hear absolutely no details about anything romantic, romance-adjacent, or within a thousand-mile radius of romanceville."

"Deal," Evie and I say at the same time.

"Great. Now come in. Mom should have simmered down, but you don't want to be late."

I glance at my watch. We're thankfully still two minutes early, despite the unexpected conversation with Levi.

But he's cool with us.

That's one barrier down.

Now I just need to pull off my big plan, confess that I'm still a virgin, and who knows, I might actually be in with a shot of keeping Evie.

We follow Levi into the formal living room, where the rest of the Freeman clan are seated. I head straight for the matriarch.

"You look wonderful, Mrs. Freeman," I say extra loudly for Evie's pleasure, knowing full well she'll mock me mercilessly for it later.

"Fraser. So lovely of you to join us."

I kiss her on the cheek, and if she was in a mood before, I certainly can't spot any signs of it now. She's as polished and well-dressed as ever in a fitted black turtleneck sweater, tailored high-waisted trousers, and a belt adorned with a gold buckle.

I go over to Evie's dad-slash-hockey legend. "Mr. Freeman."

"Fraser." He stands and gives me a solid handshake.

The man is the epitome of California cool. He's still in great shape, with a thick head of sandy blond hair and warm hazel eyes. For how elegantly dressed Mrs. Freeman is, he's his usual super casual self in a plain white T-shirt, board shorts, and flip-flops.

He and Mrs. Freeman couldn't be any more different, and yet, they seem to be as happily married as my folks are.

"I was going to say we need to talk about your last game, but I assume you've heard anything I was going to say from Evie."

"About a hundred times."

She shoots me a faux-murderous look across the room. "Heard that."

"And I love hearing her notes every single time."

"Correct answer," Mr. Freeman stage whispers to me with a chuckle. "Also, call me Alex." He glances over at his wife. "But stick with Mrs. Freeman until she gives you the green light."

"Roger that."

I move on to the sisters next, giving them each a kiss on the cheek.

"How's the world of reality TV treating you?" I ask Harper since it's been a few months since I last saw her.

"Still as brutal, backstabbing, and cutthroat as ever. And that's what happens off-camera."

"Oh."

She waits a beat before adding with a grin, "And I love every single second of it."

"That's great." I turn to Laney. "I assume the world of hotel management in Comfort Bay is a little less cutthroat."

"You'd think that, wouldn't you? But let me tell you, there is a whole underbelly in the hotel world that would blow your mind."

"Oh."

"That would actually make for a great reality TV show," Harper says.

"It totally would," Laney agrees.

They start cackling in laughter, and yep, I'm officially with the Freemans.

I know I'm going to be behind the eight ball all night. Might as well get comfortable, settle in, and hold on for dear life. I suspect that's how someone as laid back as Mr. Freem—Alex survives in such a high-energy family.

"Dinner is ready, if you'd like to make your way to the dining room," Mrs. Freeman announces.

I take Evie's hand, and she sways into me as we walk. "How are you doing?" she whispers.

"So far, so good."

We sit down next to each other, and I can't help but notice Mrs. Freeman smile approvingly when I hold Evie's chair out for her.

Evie clocks her mother's glance, too, and yep, that's another item she'll be adding to her *I'm going to rib Fraser about this* list. For the record, I always hold her chair out for her because that's how a man should treat the woman he loves.

The first course comes out, served by two butlers in fancy uniforms. I know the Freemans have domestic help, but I'm pretty sure these two were brought in for tonight only. Say what you want about the woman, but Mrs. Freeman knows how to throw a dinner party.

"Oh, no spice?" I say, concealing my relief as I take in the spice-less seafood chowder being placed in front of us.

"We're saving that for the next three courses," Alex tells me.

"We're having Indian tonight, but somebody felt like chowder," Mrs. Freeman explains, shooting a look at her husband that spells out in no uncertain terms who that certain someone is.

"Guilty." Alex raises his hand by his face, "So, it's my fault and no one else's that tonight's dinner lacks thematic consistency."

"I never said that, Alex. Never mind." Mrs. Freeman forces a smile, and okay, I think we've stumbled upon what might have set her in a bad mood before our arrival. Here I was thinking it might have been something serious when it turns out it was about *dinner thematic consistency*.

"Welcome to the madhouse," Evie whispers as she reaches over for the sourdough bread.

"Hope you're ready to handle some heat, Rademacher," Alex says, smiling at me from across the table.

"I'm sure his tolerance has increased since he was a teenager," Mrs. Freeman adds, then mutters something that sounds an awful lot like, "At least I hope so," under her breath.

"So, girls, what's been happening?" Alex asks his daughters, and the first lightning round conversation of the evening gets underway.

Levi, who's sitting on my other side, taps my leg and leans closer when the next course is brought out. "Avoid water and heap an extra spoonful of yogurt onto your plate. That will help you when you overheat."

"You said when, not if," I whisper back to him.

He claps me on the back. "Oh, Fraser, my man, you have no idea what you're in for, do you?"

He's absolutely right. I don't.

Because over the next three courses, the dishes get progressively hotter and hotter. Levi's tip to load up on yogurt seems to be doing the trick, though, even if Mrs. Freeman casts the occasional odd look my way. Not sure you're meant to be consuming spoonfuls of yogurt the way I am, but if it gets me through this meal, that's all I care about.

"You're doing really well," Evie says, wiping beads of sweat off her brow with her napkin. "I thought the vindaloo would be your limit."

"His tolerance has matured," Mrs. Freeman says with an approving smile. "Should I get them to bring out some more yogurt, Fraser?"

"Yes, please. That'd be great, Mrs. Freeman."

After dinner, Mrs. Freeman invites everyone back into the formal living room. Evie excuses herself to use the powder room, so I take the opportunity to have a quiet word with Mr. Freeman.

There's something important I need to discuss with him.

After about an hour chatting in the living room, Evie yawns and suggests, "Should we make a move?"

My stomach started making some strange gurgling sounds about ten minutes ago, so I'm happy to go. "Sure."

We say our goodbyes to everyone, and once we get in the car, the gurgling noises amplify.

"I'm so sorry," I say, completely embarrassed. "My body isn't used to handling so much spice."

"I was surprised at how well you kept up."

"Can't take all the credit. I downed about a gallon of yogurt. Levi's suggestion."

Evie smiles. "He's always looked out for you. You're the brother he never had. I'm so glad he knows the truth about us and that he's happy for us."

I'm about to say something when a pain rips through my gut accompanied by the loudest rumble yet. I clutch my stomach with my non-driving hand.

"Are you okay?"

"No. I'm not. I need to go to the bathroom. Stat."

The plan was to hang out at my place for a bit before dropping Evie back at her apartment, but her building is literally just around the corner.

"Let's go to mine," she says.

"I was just thinking the same thing."

I screech to a stop outside her block. We race out of the car. Evie opens the front door for me, and I sprint into her bathroom.

I'll spare you all the gory details—because believe me, they're gory—but the pain is unlike anything I've ever experienced.

The Fake Out Flex

From now on, the hottest thing I'm eating is mild salsa. The Freemans can laugh at me all they want. Including Mrs. Freeman. Nothing is worth this kind of agony.

After a few minutes, there's a tentative tap on the bathroom door. "Fraser. Everything okay in there?"

My stomach chooses that very moment to twist painfully, and even though there's a door between us as well as the humming of a ventilation fan to conceal the unpleasant sounds emanating from my body, I don't want Evie near any of this.

"I'm fine!" I call out.

"Can I get you anything?"

"Nope. Thanks."

"Should I call the doctor?"

"Also no."

"Hannah's been raving about a naturopath who's apparently helped her with—"

"Evie!" I yell out. "I love you, but can I have some privacy please?"

"Oh." A brief pause, then, "Okay. Sure. I'll leave you be."

"Thank you."

After an agonizing few minutes that feels more like a few hours, I'm finally feeling okay-ish.

I begin washing my hands and splash some water on my face when it hits me.

What I said to Evie.

Well, blurted out, actually.

I freeze—Macaulay Culkin in "Home Alone" style—my wide eyes staring back at me in the mirror.

Oh, no.

No, no.

No, no, no, no, noooooo!

21

Evie

Fraser loves me.

He did just say that, didn't he? I didn't mishear him.

Granted, he is recovering from a dinner with my family, so maybe he's not in the right mental state to be making such an important declaration.

Or the best physical state, either.

He looked like he was in considerable pain in the car, and the way he hotfooted it into the bathroom—he moved faster than he does on the ice during a game.

But surely yelling out something along the lines of, *I'm going to murder the chef*, or *I'm never getting dragged to another Freeman family dinner ever again* would have been more appropriate, wouldn't it?

Admitting you love someone when you're in the throes of major stomach pain? Is that even a thing? I need to find my phone and do some googling.

Before I can, I'm stopped in my tracks. A still squeamish-looking Fraser is resting against the wall.

"Are you standing like that because you can no longer feel your legs?"

"Almost. I am so, so, *so* sorry you had to witness that."

"It's all good. I once had a guinea pig who used to poop everywhere all the time."

Fraser cocks his head to the side. "Is that supposed to make me feel better?"

"Yes. Question mark?"

He manages a small smile. "And I'm also sorry that the first time I told you that I love you was when I was sitting on the toilet."

Houston, we have confirmation.

"Wow."

When I leave it at that for a few beats too long, Fraser takes a tentative step toward me. "Good wow? Bad wow? *Get out of my house I never want to see you again* wow? Help me out here, Evie."

"The first option."

Now, I've seen Fraser smile before.

When he scores a goal.

When his team wins a game.

When he's with Oakey.

But I have *never* seen the type of joy that's radiating off him right now.

He looks like he just won the Stanley Cup, the lottery, and the Super Bowl all at once.

"Does that mean I get a do over?"

"You totally get a do over. In fact, I insist on one. We're going to need a much better story to tell people."

"Very true."

He bridges the gap between us in one swift motion, meeting me as I get up from the sofa. His big palm cups my cheek, and his fiery gaze holds me spellbound before he dips his head so that our foreheads touch. With his breath fanning out across my face, my whole body floods with warm anticipation.

"I should have stepped up and said this years ago. It's long overdue."

"Better late than never," I say, breathlessly, smoothing my hands down his ridiculously solid chest.

He pulls his head back, aims those two intense blue orbs at me, and says the words I thought I'd never hear him say. "I love you, Evelyn Freeman. And the more time I spend with you, I fall deeper and deeper in love with you."

"Oh, Fraser." I drape my arms around his neck, pulling myself closer to him. "I love you, too."

I lift onto my toes and bring my mouth to his.

Our lips meet, sealing our words, and I lose all track of time. Nothing else exists except for Fraser and me and this kiss.

He loves me.

Which means...

I pull back sharply.

"Everything okay?" Fraser asks. "My breath's not funky, is it? I did consume an inordinate amount of yogurt tonight."

"Your breath is fine," I assure him as my heart breaks out into a gallop in my chest.

"Well, what is it? I can tell something's up."

Everything about this relationship with Fraser has been so topsy-turvy, from the way it began right up to this very moment, that usually, I would have told him I'm a virgin and planning on waiting until I'm married a lot earlier.

I have to tell him now. He has a right to know.

"I've got something to tell you."

His jaw visibly tightens.

"It's nothing bad. Just...important. And also kind of embarrassing. But also necessary. Very necessary. You need to know this, and for the record, if after hearing what I have to say, you want to take back your *I love you*, I won't be mad."

"I would never do that," he says, swiping my cheek with his thumb, his eyes back to their usual laser-focused intensity. "But tell me what it is, please, because I'm starting to get worried."

I take a deep breath, do my best to ignore the unsettling sensation coiling in my chest, and reveal, "I'm a virgin."

His head tilts to the side. "Oh."

I press on. "Normally, I'm up-front and say this much earlier. But our relationship hasn't exactly been conventional."

"No. It hasn't."

"Our timeline has been all out of whack. It all started with us doing it just for show."

"It was never just for show for me," he says, his voice so low and husky it burns right through me. "I tried to pretend that it was. I went along with it because it gave me the chance to spend some time with you. Alone. I thought I could control my feelings, rein them in. But I couldn't. From the first time we hung out together, I was a goner."

"Does...does what I just said change anything for you?"

He shakes his head, a lock of hair falling onto his forehead. "It does."

My eyebrows shoot up. "It does?"

When he shook his head, I assumed he'd say no.

"It only makes me love you even more because, Evie..." His breath hitches. "I'm a virgin, too."

"You are?"

He swallows. "Yeah. And I've been in knots about telling you, hoping it wouldn't be a dealbreaker for you."

"Oh, Fraser."

I slide my hand over his face, running the tip of my finger delicately over the scar on his left cheek.

"It might sound sappy, but I only ever want to be with one girl. It's kind of a thing in my family. I want to wait until I'm married before taking that final step."

"If that's sappy, then I'm the biggest sap there is." I stare into the eyes of the man I love. "Because that's exactly what I want, too."

A smile rises on his lips. "So, we're on the same page?"

"We're in the same sentence."

We kiss again, and my heart brims with so much joy, it

feels as if it could explode at any moment. I can't believe this is real. It's better than any of the possible reactions I'd pictured in my mind.

When our impromptu make-out comes to an end, I pull back and say, "I hate to break the moment, but I need to use the bathroom."

Fraser lets go of me. "No problem."

I hurry away, floating on air, swept up in the beauty of our first *I love yous*—the official version, not the actual first *I love you* which shall never be spoken of again—as well as the amazingness of being on the same page.

The same sentence.

When I return a few moments later, the change in vibe hits me instantly.

Something is off.

There's a palpable tension in the air.

Fraser is standing over my desk with his back to me. My heart begins to race as I walk up behind him.

His ears prick, and he spins around. "What is this?" he asks, his voice laced with anger.

I glance down at my desk, at the notes and photos and old newspaper clippings scattered about everywhere.

"It's not what it looks like."

"Really?" A deep line emerges between his eyebrows. "Because it looks like research. Are you...are you doing a story on me?" He lifts one of the selfies I'd printed out, the one of him and me with Oakey, and shakes it angrily in his hand. "Are you doing a story about my family?"

"No. I'm not. At least not yet. I was just—"

"I can't believe this."

He storms past me.

I reach out, trying to grab his arm to make him stay. To make him understand that I was just putting together a pitch for a story. To explain that I would never, ever in a million years do anything without his and his family's full permission.

But it's too late.

The door slams shut with such force that it shakes the walls of my apartment.

I want to chase after him and not let another second go by without clearing this up, but I have *never* seen Fraser this angry.

As much as it kills me, I need to give him some time to cool off.

I run to the window, every cell in my body on fire, watching as he storms to his Range Rover.

Look up, look up, look up, I silently will him.

But he doesn't.

There's no look.

No smile.

No wave.

Nothing.

He climbs into his car, slamming the door shut. The lights come on, the engine roars to life, and with a screech of tires, he speeds off down the street.

I watch from the window, waiting until he turns the corner and disappears from view.

And then I turn, back onto the wall, and slide all the way down to the floor, ribbons of tears running down my face.

What have I done?...

"I'm sorry about the change of plans, you guys," I mutter, before loudly slurping the last of my strawberry milkshake through my straw, as Hannah, Beth, Summer, and Amiel pile into the booth.

It's my third milkshake. Not that I'm counting.

Because yes, I am that girl who group-texted her friends last night and hijacked this morning's sunrise walk to instead drown her sorrows with all the dairy and pancakes Bear can supply.

I drizzle an unhealthy amount of maple syrup over my second stack—which I'm also not counting—and let out a depressed groan, "I'm a mess."

"We can tell, we have eyes," Beth says bluntly, as only Beth can.

"Tell us everything that happened," Hannah instructs. "Start at the beginning, and leave nothing out."

I wave my empty frosted glass at Bear, who gives a nod of understanding, and I proceed to fill my friends in on the events of last night, starting with Levi's super cool reaction to Fraser and I being together for real before the family dinner.

I tell them that, despite the food being way too spicy for him, Fraser did a decent job keeping up with us, that the conversation flowed well, and that all in all, it was a great evening.

I omit the specifics of his first *I love you* and leave it at, "He probably won't be in a rush to eat spicy food any time soon."

And then I move on to the pièce de résistance. The first official *I love you*...which was swiftly followed by our first fight.

"I excused myself to the bathroom for a moment, and when I returned, he was looking at the story pitch I've been working on," I say glumly. "He was furious, you guys. I've never seen him like that before."

"What did he say?" Amiel asks.

"Nothing. He just stormed out." I drag my hands across my sleep-deprived eyes. "And you know what's even worse than Fraser being angry at me?"

They all shake their heads.

"*I'm* angry at me. That I didn't just come out and tell him my idea. Fraser would have nixed it immediately, and that would have been that. Case closed. Move on. Now? Now it looks like I've deliberately gone behind his back and deceived him. He already has trust issues and a hard time letting people in. And then I go ahead and do something stupid like this. He must be feeling so betrayed right now."

In one of only a handful of instances in all of human history, the Fast-Talking Four-slash-Five are actually silent.

I feel horrible. Like pond scum. Worse than pond scum. I feel like whatever looks at pond scum and thinks, *That's an upgrade.*

Until recently, I was the one who had doubts about Fraser, that he wouldn't stick around. That because he'd left abruptly once before, he could do it again.

And now it turns out, I'm the one who's created a problem that gives him a reason to leave.

I wouldn't blame him if he did. I'd be just as mad as he was if the situation were reversed.

"Who died?" Bear asks, delivering my next milkshake.

His eyes swing between us, and even in the state I'm in, I can't help but notice how they linger on Summer.

"Man troubles," Beth explains.

"Say no more." Bear backs away. "Let me know if you need anything else."

"Just keep everything coming," I say, bringing the straw to my mouth.

I take a few slurps of my milkshake, stuff some pancakes into my mouth, then say, "Wuh-at am I guh-onnah do?"

All heads turn to Hannah, since she's known me the longest and is well-versed in Evie-with-her-mouth-full speak.

"She asked, 'What am I going to do?'" Hannah translates for the group.

"You're kind of asking the wrong girls," Summer says delicately. "We're hardly experienced in the love department."

"True. But one of us has read about a lifetime's worth of romance novels," Hannah counters, and we all fix our attention on Beth.

Beth turns to me. "Do you really want to plot your next course of action based on what I've gleaned from reading romance novels?"

I slurp noisily on my milkshake, then sigh. "That's currently my only, and therefore best, option."

"Okay. Well...I'll tell you what you *don't* do," Beth says, sitting up taller. "Hear me loud and hear me clear, ladies."

We all lean in.

"Do. Not. Leave it," Beth says, wagging a finger through the air to emphasize each word. "Do not let Fraser get on that plane this morning without resolving things, because if there's one thing that makes romance readers want to hurl their books or Kindles at the nearest wall, it's the overused, clichéd, third-act breakup due to miscommunication. That has been done to death. Don't be that girl, Evie. You're better than that."

"I'm currently on my fourth milkshake and second plate of pancakes," I point out. "So maybe I'm not better than that."

"Yes, you are. You have the truth on your side," Summer reminds me. "Once you explain everything to him, I'm sure Fraser will understand."

"He's head-over-heels about you," Hannah adds. "My profits have been through the roof since you started dating."

"And the way he looks at you," Amiel sways back into the booth, clutching her chest. "I'm basing this purely on the images I've seen online, but believe me, I'd love for a guy to look at me that way."

"Resolve this," Beth reiterates. "The more time that passes, the worse it gets."

"You're right. You guys are absolutely right."

I shovel in a few more forkfuls of pancakes, swallow it down with an almighty swig of my milkshake, *wait* until I finish chewing this time, then leap to my feet and announce, "I'm not going to be an overused, clichéd, third-act breakup basket case. I'm going to fix this."

I knock on Fraser's wood-paneled front door and inhale sharply.

I'm a mess.

I haven't slept.

I've been stress-eating.

And I may or may not currently be wearing the clothes I slept in...which also happen to be the same clothes I wore yesterday.

And the *ugh* boots are back.

Don't judge me.

Or do judge me, I deserve it.

I'm too exhausted to care.

But I have to do this. I have to set the record straight.

Fraser may still be angry and hurt when he finds out I was planning on pitching him the story—which he's entitled to be—but at least he won't be under the wrong impression that I had any intention of betraying him.

Bottom line: I wasn't honest with him, and I fully own that. I'm prepared to deal with whatever consequences may come.

Well, as prepared as anyone can be when it comes to potentially losing the person they love after they just finally got together with them.

The door swings open, revealing a messy-haired,

crumpled-looking Fraser with two prominent bags under his eyes that weren't there yesterday.

"I come in deep-fried peace," I say, holding up the fries I picked up at the diner.

He looks at my lame peace offering, then at me, then says, "Come on in."

I follow him into his living room.

There are two big suitcases open on the floor, and he's midway through packing. He pushes them out of the way with his foot and gestures toward the sofa. "Can I get you anything to drink? Soda? Juice? Water?"

"I'm okay, thanks."

I sit down on the couch.

Fraser sits down on the other end. Not all the way over, but leaving way more space between us than he normally does. It feels like we're back in our high school days again.

"How's your stomach?" I ask.

"Slowly returning to normal. He's issued a strict Freeman family dinner ban. Effective immediately and for eternity."

"I'm glad you're feeling better." I smile.

He's keeping things light. That's a good sign...I think?

I decide not to waste any more time.

"I know you're hurt and probably really angry at me right now, and you have every right to be, but if you give me five minutes, I can explain everything."

"All right."

I lift up a fry. "Let me tell you the fried truth, the whole fried truth, and nothing but the whole fried truth..."

I start with what he already knows. That my numbers had been tanking despite our high-profile relationship and my jumping-off-building antics to rectify it. That Margo had warned me my head was on the chopping block when the network announces their first round of cuts shortly.

Then I bring in some new information. "She's actually been bugging me for months to do a story on you."

"She has?"

"Yeah. And for a long time, I resisted."

"Why?"

"Because I know you, and I was positive you wouldn't be interested and you'd turn it down. I also didn't want to bother you with it or make you uncomfortable, especially since you'd already done me one giant favor by going to jerkface's wedding with me."

That draws the tiniest smile out of Fraser. "Glad you're finally using his correct name."

I carry on. "After exhausting all my options, I was left with just two. As you know, I caught up with Mom and asked her to set up a meeting with her Washington contact."

"Even though that's not something you want to do?"

I lift a shoulder. "Desperate times call for desperate measures. I have to be realistic. I'm good as gone from the network. I need to have a plan B."

"That being a story about me?"

The words stall in my throat, but I push them out. "Yes. I was still convinced you wouldn't go for it, but I thought if I pitched you an idea that allowed you, and your family, to tell your side of the story your way, you might at least consider it."

"And what if, after considering it, I still said no?"

"Like I said, I fully expected that. I wasn't counting on this story ever happening. I just wanted to bring the idea to you and have that conversation. It wouldn't have changed anything if you'd said no. Honestly."

He breathes out through his nose.

"I'm sorry I kept this from you. That was wrong of me. I should have mentioned it earlier, you would have made some joke about me being out of my mind, and that would have been the first and last time the topic was discussed. Instead, I did something that made it look like I was being deceitful or underhanded when I really, truly wasn't. I apologize. I own what I did because I can see that's exactly how it looks."

He exhales again. "Thank you. I needed to hear that. I've had the worst night. Seeing those photos and newspaper clippings on your desk triggered my two biggest vulnerabilities—my distrust of the media, and my desire to protect my family. I got hit with a double whammy of pain."

"I feel so awful about that."

He tunnels his fingers through his hair. "I tossed and turned all night, running it over in my head. I tried to be logical about it, knowing deep down that you would never use me for a story. I kept trying to come up with some way of explaining it. But unfortunately, the logical part of my brain got hijacked by insomnia, late-night home shopping network ads—side note, you and everyone I know will soon be receiving the latest state-of-the-art food dehydrator—and...fear."

"Fear? Fear of what?"

"Of losing this thing that we have." He sets his eyes on me. "This is everything I've ever wanted in a relationship. I don't mean to sound cruel or unkind, but I've never had anything like this with any of my previous girlfriends. With them, I was never able to truly open up and be myself. It felt like...like there was something there, a barrier, that prevented me from accessing those parts of myself. I felt broken, like something was wrong with me. Which wasn't fair to them."

"Wasn't fair to you, either," I gently point out. "And you're not broken, Fraser." When he makes a sound like he doesn't believe me, I say, "You're not. I know you. Yes, you're guarded, and you really need to get to know someone well before you feel safe enough to open up to them, but that's just who you are. Just like being kind and thoughtful and a great listener are also things that make you who you are. I've spent a lot of time with you, so I speak from experience. I'm not just saying it. You are not broken."

"Yeah. Maybe...but with you, Evie, without effort, without trying, it just happens. I can be myself. Fully myself. It started in high school, and it's been the same these past few months."

"I feel the exact same way. My previous boyfriends never really understood me, so I found myself changing to fit into who I thought they wanted me to be."

"I don't want you to change anything about yourself, Evie. I love everything about you. Even the things you think I might not."

I've always wanted to be with a guy who I could be myself with. Someone who loved all of me, and I didn't have to hide or change any part of myself to make him feel more comfortable with me.

Fraser *is* that guy.

I feel it and know it with every part of me, from the tips of my fingers to the depths of my bones.

He thinks I'm beautiful when I'm a mess.

He loves it when I eat like a horse.

He doesn't mind my messiness.

Or my detailed notes about his hockey performance.

Or my rambling and quirky sense of humor.

He gets me.

He loves me.

All of me.

I just hope I haven't ruined everything.

"I've never loved anyone as much as I love you. It's..." He lets out a long, deep breath. "It's scary."

"Most relationships are. At least at the start."

"You saying it gets easier?"

"I'm saying I have no experience in relationships longer than twelve months, so I'm not the most qualified person to answer that. But when I look at my parents, or yours, or anyone who has been in a long-term relationship, then yeah, it seems like it does get easier. You know each other better. You build up trust. And you make sure you have healthy ways of resolving any disagreements or miscommunications that arise. Mom and Dad have a rule that they never go to bed angry, that if something happens that day, they deal with it that day."

He smiles. "I like that."

"I want you to know something else." I shuffle over, closing some of the distance between us. "I would never, ever betray you. No part of us being together was ever part of some covert attempt at getting a story about you or your family. I *need* you to really hear that."

"I do. I know you would never do anything that underhanded or sneaky. That's not who you are."

"I couldn't." A tear slides down my cheek, but I quickly brush it away. "I honestly couldn't."

He scooches down a bit closer to me, our knees almost touching. "I'm sorry I stormed out like I did. That wasn't very mature of me."

"Totally understandable given the circumstances."

"Can I make a suggestion? Two, actually."

"Go for it."

"One." He takes my hand, curling his thick fingers around it. "From now on, we take a page out of your parent's book and we don't go to bed without resolving things. Or in our case, since we don't share a bed, before we go to sleep. If it happens that day, we deal with it that day."

I nod. "Deal."

He gives my hand a firm squeeze. "And two, no more secrets. *Ever.*"

"Deal again." I rub his forearm. "So...are we okay? Because I really don't like it when you don't like me."

"We're okay." He wraps an arm around my waist. "Want to know something really messed up?"

I lift my chin. "Always."

"Even when I'm meant to be mad at you, I still like you. It kept me up all night and drove me crazy."

"I have been known to have that effect on people."

We kiss, and it's soft and tender, and it feels like the best kiss we've ever had because everything is finally out in the open.

No more secrets.

No more not communicating.

No more leaving things unresolved.

I hate that it took us having a fight to get here, but it feels like we're on the right track. Nothing can stop us now.

22

Fraser

I'd love to say that working things out with Evie this morning has translated to having a great game tonight.

But if I did, I'd be a liar.

Because we are getting *smashed*.

Despite having advanced to the third round of finals, we're currently at 3-0 in the best-of-seven series and down and 4-0 in this game. If we lose this tonight—which we most likely will since I don't see us having a miraculous turnaround in the remaining ninety seconds—it'll be a wrap on the season, and we can kiss our chances of competing for the Stanley Cup goodbye.

It's been a wildly inconsistent season for us. We've had short runs of great games, but we haven't been able to ride that momentum.

To top it off, Culver called a medical time out in the first period, his ankle flaring up this time, and he's been sidelined pending medical clearance.

I haven't been performing at my best tonight, either. The lack of sleep, the loss of electrolytes after last night's dinner, and the stress of having missed my connecting flight today—I almost didn't make it to the stadium on time—is wreaking havoc on my body.

Not to mention my heart's not really in it, either.

How can it be after everything that's happened? The only thing I can think about is Evie.

I *hated* the feeling I had last night when I discovered she'd been working on a story about me and my family. It was betrayal mixed with anger...and confusion.

How?

How could she do something like that?

I'm not proud of my behavior, storming off the way I did, but I needed to get out of there. If I had stayed, I risked saying something stupid or hurtful, something I'd regret once Evie got the chance to explain. I needed to cool off and get my head right.

And man, I'm so glad she came 'round this morning. I was deciding whether to give her a call before my flight since I hated leaving things unresolved, but her showing up was so much better.

Deep inside, I knew there had to be an explanation for what she was doing.

And there was.

It sucks that we had to have our first fight on the night we said our first *I love yous,* but I guess love never runs smoothly, does it?

Besides, we have plenty more *I love yous* ahead of us...and hopefully not that many arguments.

And it's gotten us to a good place. We've agreed to never go to bed being mad at each other, and we'll never keep secrets from each other, either.

I am fully on board with both of those things...but does a surprise count as a secret?

I'll have to check on that with Evie *after* I surprise her with the big plan I've been working on.

The game clock runs down the final seconds, and yep, that's it. The LA Swifts' season is officially over.

The only upside to losing?

I get to fly back to Evie and put my plan into action sooner than expected.

∼

"Where are we?" Evie asks as I gently guide her with one hand pressed into her lower back, the other holding her hand. "This place smells funky."

She sniffs the air. She's blindfolded, so she's using her sense of smell to try to determine where I've taken her. This place is old and has essentially been abandoned for the better part of ten years, so yeah, the air in here isn't exactly fresh.

"And not the good kind of funky," she continues. "I'm talking bad funky. Like sweat and dirty socks and other bodily functions I don't want to mention aloud." She takes a few more whiffs. "Can I get a hint? Please?"

"You'll find out soon enough," I say, carefully steering her around the corner of a bench. "Be patient."

Yeah, right, I think just as she says, "Yeah, like that's gonna happen."

I smile even though she can't see me.

Everything is set, and I have to say, I can't believe I've actually pulled this off.

It was a longshot.

A lot of work.

And a ton of money. Good thing I have a trust fund I can tap into.

It's a crazy idea that I've somehow managed to turn into reality. All without her suspecting a thing.

I'm hoping that, a) she likes it and jumps on board, and b) that if she does, it might be something she wants to do together.

With me.

I can totally see us killing it.

Because Evie's not the only one facing the prospect of an uncertain future, career-wise.

I'm not ready to give up playing just yet. My body has

another one or two seasons left in it, fingers crossed. And I'd love a shot at winning the Stanley Cup.

But after that, who knows?

This could be the start of the next stage of our lives.

Before I picked Evie up, I swung around here to make sure everything was perfect. Hannah has been working since the crack of dawn, positioning one thousand yellow roses in every single nook and cranny of what really isn't that big a space.

She's done a terrific job, transforming a musty locker room that hasn't been used for a decade into a beautiful oasis, even if she was distraught that there was a mix-up with the order and the roses she got weren't fragranced, hence the pervasive, less-than-nice boy smells wafting in the air around us.

"Are you comfortable?" I check.

"Oh, yeah. This is great. I love it. I'm thinking blindfolds could be a new trend alert."

"Ah, your sarcasm. One of the many things I love about you."

"Ah, your unintended swoonyisms. One of the many things I love about *you*."

I'm ninety-five percent sure *swoonyisms* isn't a word, but just like in high school, I'm not confident enough to challenge her on it.

"Okay, so before you see where we are, I need to warn you that this is quite an outlandish thing I'm doing."

"Really? Because the blindfold and driving me to a mysterious, smelly location totally made me think you've got something super boring and mundane lined up."

I chuckle. "This is just an idea. I hope you like it, but you're not under any pressure or obligation to go through with it. I have a Plan B in place."

"Can you please be *more* vague?"

I grin. All right, enough toying with her. "I'm going to take this off now…"

"Finally."

I reach toward the knot securing the blindfold. Evie's breath goes shallow with anticipation. I carefully untie the knot, and the blindfold loosens.

This is it. I'm about to reveal my big surprise.

There's no going back now.

I lift the blindfold away and step into a prime viewing position so I can see her face.

There's a moment of hesitation, and then her eyes flutter open. She blinks a few times, adjusting to the light.

She looks at me.

I smile nervously.

Slowly, she turns, her eyes roaming over all one thousand roses dangling from the ceiling, fixed to the walls, wrapped around any surface they can be wrapped around.

"Oh, Fraser." She brings her hand to her heart. "This is… The flowers are amazing. Thank you. But why did you blindfold me and bring me to an old, and by the smell of it, super gross locker room to give me flowers?"

Our eyes meet again, and I smile, growing a little more hopeful that this might actually work.

"I didn't just get you the flowers," I tell her, then wave my hand around. "I got you this."

She's thoroughly puzzled. "You got me a stinky locker room?"

"Well…yeah. Kinda." I grasp both of her hands in mine and announce, "I bought you a hockey team, Evie!"

23

Evie

I must have misheard him.

Or maybe I misunderstood.

Maybe the stench from the locker room has seeped into my ears and messed up my hearing.

Because Fraser couldn't have possibly said what I think he said...Could he?

I'm still so in awe at the stunning sight of all these yellow roses that I need to double-check, make sure I'm not losing my mind.

"You did what now?"

"I bought you a junior hockey team." He sits down on the bench. "Let me explain."

"Please do. Start at the beginning. And talk slowly, please."

He smiles, nods, and then launches into it. "I got the idea a few months ago driving past this old stadium."

"Wait. Is this...Are we in Harbor View Arena?"

"Good guess. Yeah, we are."

"You used to train here, but it got shut down like seven, eight years ago."

"Ten, actually. I contacted the owner, and they were open to selling it."

"Right."

"So I bought it."

He says it casually, like someone might say, *I bought a loaf of bread at the grocery store today.*

"You...own this stadium?"

"I do. Although, the plan is to transfer ownership to you. But we're getting ahead of ourselves."

"Ya think?"

"After securing the stadium, I moved on to the next phase

of my big plan—starting a junior league team. But I didn't want it to be just any junior league team. I wanted it to be open to all kids, regardless of their gender or physical needs."

"Oh. *Wow*."

"As you know, there aren't enough girls in the game…"

"No. There aren't."

"Well, on this team, on *your* team, you can change that. I haven't named the team yet, but it's registered in the Western States Hockey League."

"Wow. That's a tier two league."

The most common junior hockey teams are either Tier 2 or Tier 3. The main difference between the two tiers lies in the level of competition, player development, and exposure to higher levels of play. Tier two is the higher, more advanced tier.

My mind races ahead, picturing a team composed equally of boy and girl players. How awesome would it be to see that? And who knows, maybe one day there could even be an all-girl team to take on the all-boy teams.

Fraser drops his head and takes a breath. "Then I looked into kids with different needs, both mental and physical, and unfortunately, they're ruled out of playing in the junior league. But I wasn't going to let that stop me."

"What did you do?"

"Well, I kept digging into it and since you own the stadium, there's nothing to prevent you from offering training to any kids you want. You can create a program that includes everyone, including kids like Oakey."

He smiles when he mentions him, and I can tell how much it would mean to him for Oakey to be included and treated just like everyone else.

"There's a para ice hockey junior league which provides opportunities for young athletes with disabilities to participate in competitive hockey. That could be something to look into in the future."

"That sounds amazing."

"It is. There's a lot to do. The stadium needs work, not to mention everything involved in setting up a junior league team and getting them ready for competition. And of course, the team is going to need a coach. Someone who knows the game inside out. Someone who's tough but has also learned to be kind. Someone who wants to make a positive difference in the world."

His eyes swing to...

"Me?"

He nods. "I realize this is a lot to take in, Evie, especially considering it's come out of left field. This is a humongous, crazy undertaking, but if anyone can make it work, you can. You're at risk of losing your job, and I know you don't really want to pursue Washington. And even though you enjoy making bracelets and you could possibly start a business selling them, it doesn't light you up from the inside the way hockey does." He lowers his head and bites his lower lip. "Nothing lights you up like hockey does."

"Well," I quirk a brow. "Maybe one thing does."

He smiles bashfully. "Was hoping you'd say that."

My gaze travels around the locker room.

I'm trying to take it all in—Fraser's announcement, the flowers filling my vision everywhere I look—but it's almost too much for my brain to handle.

"This is...This is definitely a wow moment," I say. "And believe me, you and me, we've already had a few of those."

"You're allowed a wow," Fraser says with a soft grin on his lips.

I nod, my mind still reeling. "This might even be a double-wow moment. A possible contender for a triple—or even quadruple—wow."

He braces my shoulders, and when I stare into his eyes, all I see is love and excitement and support.

"Evie," he says. "I would never force you into doing anything you don't want to do. The stadium is yours, and the team is yours, but only if you want them. All the paperwork and legal stuff is currently in my name in case you don't. I didn't want to be presumptuous or for you to feel trapped or guilted into taking this on. This is a big decision, so take all the time you need to think about it. I've spoken with your dad, and he's happy to step in as interim coach, and you know, I can help out since I know a thing or two about hockey."

I create a small gap between my thumb and index finger. "You know this much."

He chuckles. "Yeah. Give or take."

I get up and start pacing the length of the room, running my fingers over the flower petals fixed to the wall.

Fraser's right.

Nothing ignites me like hockey does.

When I was a girl, I wanted to be a coach so badly, but not seeing any representation meant that it felt like a pipedream, completely unattainable.

By the time I got to high school, that dream had been replaced by more 'realistic' options like teaching or reporting.

That's why I framed that photo of the four women I admired so much and hung it alongside my favorite players. My dream may have been over before it even began, but the photo was a small reminder, a link to a part of myself I had given up on a long time ago.

But Fraser never gave up on it.

And now...now he's *BOUGHT ME A HOCKEY TEAM!!!*, and

I can actually do it. I can pursue a dream I never in a million years thought I'd be able to.

Best of all, I can coach a team made up of young girls and all kids, regardless of their abilities. I can make sure every child has an opportunity to pursue *their* dream.

I spin around and take in the kindest, most loving, thoughtful, amazing man. I know he said I could take time to think about it, but I don't need any. My mind is already made up.

"It's...It's...It's perfect!"

"Are you sure?" He scrutinizes me intently. "Because you just *it's-ed* me three times."

"Yeah, well, get ready for number four. I *it's-ed* you three times because *it's* a lot for me to get my mind around. This has always felt like such an unattainable thing. I didn't even try to seriously pursue it because I put it in the same category as, like, wanting to grow up and lead the first human expedition to Mars."

"Hockey still has a long way to go, but there are some incredible women breaking through."

He lists off the names of a few women as well as the roles they currently have in the NHL. It's impressive how seriously he's taking this. It's not a tokenistic gesture. He really believes in this.

He believes in *me*.

"And they're only the beginning, Evie. More women can and will come through. If it's something that you want, you can be one of those women. Women in hockey should not be in the same category as humans colonizing another planet."

I glance once more around the flower-filled locker room. With each passing second, I grow even more certain that this is what I want. "I want this. I really, *really* want this."

"In the absence of having something to physically give you to signify your ownership of the stadium and the team—"

"What? This place doesn't come with a key?"

He chuckles. "No it doesn't. I'm going to lend you something instead."

He lifts the cuff of his dress shirt and peels a bracelet off his wrist. I recognize it instantly. It's the one I made him all those years ago.

He hands it over to me. "I will need this back as soon as preseason games start, but I want you to have it for now."

I take it from him and throw my arms over his shoulders. He slides his hands around me, and we hug, his warm, firm body pressed against mine, the love between us so strong, so right.

When we break apart, his hands stay anchored on my waist. "Being with you has shown me that I am capable of opening up and talking more. That being closed off isn't the only way to be. I don't think I'll ever be Mr. *Sunshine Who Likes to Talk Everyone's Ear Off*, but thanks to you, I'm also not going to be Mr. *Don't Go Near That Angry Looking Man*, either. You... you make me a better man, Evie." He brushes the backs of his fingers across my cheek. "I love you with all of my heart. And I know you'll make this work. Take a chance and believe in yourself."

"I've officially reached quadruple-wow status," I breathe out because wow, has he hit the nail on the head or what. "*That's* been the missing piece this whole time," I say, as a lifetime of unspoken feelings crash into me. "I've never fully trusted myself or my instincts. I've always been swayed by what I thought other people wanted me to do. Like Mom with Washington, or Margo with the story about you."

"To be clear, I'm not trying to sway you, either. Despite having bought you a stadium and a hockey team. I just want you to realize for yourself that you are brilliant, Evie. You don't need anyone's approval or to change any part of yourself for anyone."

"Even my love of hot food?"

He grimaces.

"Or my collection of vinyl punk albums?"

"Is it too late for me to take that last statement back?"

"Totally. You said it. It's on the record." I smile, bring my lips to his, and murmur, "What you've done is beyond amazing, Fraser. I cannot tell you how much I'm looking forward to starting this next chapter of my life."

"And you're absolutely sure?"

"I am."

I open my mouth to say something else, but the words stall in my throat. But then I think about how much Fraser has opened up to me. How hard he's worked on himself. This incredible thing he's done for me...

I find the courage to ask, "So what does this mean *for us*?"

"Well, I've got another season, maybe two, left in me. And then after that, I guess I'll move back home, and if I'm *reaaally* lucky, the most successful coach in the junior league might put me to good use as her assistant coach."

Something he said in my bedroom all those years ago comes back to me "You've always wanted to coach, too."

With a shy grin, he says "I have. But I thought I lacked the people skills."

"You definitely do not lack the people skills." Then my mind processes the other implication of what he just said. "Wait. Does that mean you're going to move back here? To Comfort Bay?"

He nods. "I'd like to, yeah."

"What about eighteen-year-old Fraser who couldn't wait to get out of here?"

"Yeah, well, almost twenty-six-year-old Fraser has found a reason to come back."

"A reason, eh? Do I know her?"

"You do," he says, releasing a warm chuckle. "I don't know what my post-hockey life will be like. All I know is, I want it to be with you."

EPILOGUE
EVIE

Four months later...

"Something fishy is going on here," Beth says, eyeing the ballroom suspiciously.

"Sorry, it's a little hard to take you seriously when you're dressed as Marie Antoinette," I say with a giggle.

"I agree with Beth. I mean, Marie," Elizabeth Bennet from *Pride and Prejudice*, aka Hannah, chimes in beside me, sipping on her champagne. "I mean, why would Fraser throw a historical romance themed party? Something doesn't add up here."

"To be perfectly honest, ladies, I share your suspicions. My boyfriend is definitely up to something."

"Sorry, didn't quite catch that," Amiel, who's wearing a medieval-style dress with flowing sleeves and a cinched waist, says with a gleam in her eye, because she totally did catch that.

"Oh, you mean when I said my boyfriend?" I raise my voice. "*My boyfriend, my boyfriend, my boyfriend.*"

The five of us laugh, because yeah, I'm that girl who will never tire of hearing myself say those two words.

Fraser didn't have the entire summer off, but we spent every single day of his free time in the offseason together. I had a lot of extra time on my hands, since, to no one's surprise, I got fired from *The Morning Buzz*.

But now that I'm the proud owner of the Harbor View Arena and a junior league hockey team, I didn't have any spare time to cry about it.

You know when everything just feels like an uphill battle?

That's what my reporting career felt like. I kept trying to find an audience that wasn't there. People just aren't interested in good news stories, and I've finally—*finally*—accepted it.

But do you also know the feeling of when life gives you all

the green lights, and things feel easy, and everything just falls into place?

That's how it is with the junior hockey league team I own and will start coaching in the fall.

Even though there's been, and will for the foreseeable future be, a never-ending amount of work to do, everything is progressing smoothly.

Starting with the stadium itself.

Initially we thought it might get by with just a cosmetic makeover, but once we looked into it properly, it quickly became apparent it needs a complete overhaul. It's been vacant for so long, and prior to that, years of neglect and poor management have left it in a rundown and dilapidated condition.

Fraser has stepped up and taken the lead on that side of things, organizing structural repairs to fix the damaged roofing, replacing the outdated HVAC system, resurfacing the ice, upgrading the cooling system, installing new boards and glass, and basically making the stadium a place people would want to come and bring their families and friends to.

We've hired a small team to help with spreading the word about the two teams we'll be putting together, because yes, I want the teams I coach to be available to *all* kids. One team will be for boys and girls, and the other team will be for any child who wants to play, irrespective of their physical or intellectual abilities.

Support personnel are handling operations, admin, logistics, marketing, and communications.

My focus has been on getting ready to coach. Luckily, I know a guy who knows a thing or two about the game.

No, not Fraser.

My dad.

Hockey has always been the thing that's connected us, and

I love that he's involved in this venture, too. It's been great spending time setting up the team together with him. He's been an invaluable source of information for me, allowing me to run my ideas by him, and he really does give the best advice.

I also enrolled in a USA Hockey coaching education program. Because while, yes, I know the game inside out, and yes, I have a lifetime of practice in doling out feedback, I'm determined to take this seriously. Just because I'm coaching junior and para teams doesn't mean I'm not going to be the best coach I can be. These kids deserve it.

And of course, I had to come up with a name for the team.

It took me a while to land on something special.

I'll never forget Fraser's face when I told him what I'd settled on. I was worried he'd think it was stupid, or might not want me to use it, but he got all choked up, hugged me, and said it was the best team name ever.

So what name did I choose?

Why, that would be...*drum roll please*...The Comfort Bay Oakeys.

It's perfect, don't you think?

I've never been as excited about anything like I am this. For the first time in my life, I believe in myself, and I've got the support and love of the most incredible guy ever. What more could I ask for?

"And why aren't you dressed up?" Summer asks, snapping me out of my thoughts. "It's a little strange how the only person *not* in a costume is the girlfriend of the guy who's throwing the party."

I smile, because yeah, being referred to as Fraser's girlfriend will never grow old, either.

"Guys, I am just as much in the dark about this as you are. Fraser gave me strict instructions not to dress up in costume. That's all I know."

Hannah: "And you didn't ask him why not?"

Me: "Of course I did. I asked him about a million times. I badgered him on a level that would make Mom proud."

Beth: "And?"

Me: "And nothing. That man is like a vault. I couldn't get anything out of him."

Summer: "So you really have no idea why Fraser has gathered pretty much everyone the two of you know—"

Beth: "Which is pretty much everyone in Comfort Bay."

Summer: "Right, and asked us to wear these ridiculous costumes, but allowed you to wear that amazing dress, which I am so borrowing from you?"

Me: "I honestly don't know. And thank you, you can borrow it anytime you like."

Summer: "Thanks."

Beth: "And why is he throwing a historical romance-themed party? Does Fraser even like historical romance?"

Me: "That would be a hard no."

Hannah: "Guys, look, let's give Fraser some credit here. I'm sure he's got something amazing planned. After all, he did pull off the all-time most epic romantic gesture in Comfort Bay's history by buying Evie a hockey stadium and a junior team."

Beth: "Did you get that verified?"

Hannah: "That it's the all-time most epic romantic gesture in our humble small town's history?"

Beth: "Yeah."

Hannah: "I did. Scoured through the town records and everything. Sorry, Mr. Cooper from the late 1800s, but the love letters you wrote and left all over town have been surpassed."

Summer: "Is that...for real?"

Hannah: "No. Of course not. Why does no one think I'm capable of sarcasm?"

Beth: "It's not that your sarcasm is bad, it's just that mine is so much better. There's really no comparison between the two."

Amiel: "Think we're getting a little sidetracked here."

Beth: "Agreed. Let's go back to grilling Evie."

Me: "Guys, I really don't know what Fraser has in store or why he picked this theme for everyone to wear except for me, or even why we're having this party in the first place. I'm just as clueless as you all."

Amiel: "I believe you, Evie."

Me: "Thanks, Amiel. You may be the newest member of the recently renamed Fast-Talking Five, but you're already my favorite."

Hannah: "That's sweet but unfortunately not possible."

Me: "Why not?"

Hannah: "Because she's *my* favorite."

Beth: "I believe I called dibs on favoriting Amiel on our walk last month."

Me: "I wasn't on that walk."

Beth: "Doesn't matter. It still counts. Which reminds me..."

Me: "Uh-oh."

Beth: I know you're all loved up and everything, but you haven't seen a sunrise in a very long time, missy."

Me: "I know. I'm sorry. I've been super busy. But I'll make more of an effort. Promise."

Beth: "Good."

Hannah: "Good."

Summer: "Good."

Amiel: "I'm just chiming in so I don't get left out...*Good*."

"Oh, no. It's a disaster," Margo's thick Aussie voice cuts in from behind us.

We all spin around.

"We're both Marie Antoinettes," she says, pointing at Beth. "Except I'm way more busty."

She's not wrong.

Margo's cleavage is, uh, very ample and very much on display. Gravity-defyingly so.

"You made it," I say, giving her a warm embrace.

Having to fire me was hard for her, too. She really did everything she could to keep me. I'm glad we've remained friends, and I'm happy she's here.

"Of course I made it. Wouldn't miss this for the world, especially when you said the entire LA Swifts team would be here."

"Are you a hockey fan?" Summer asks.

"I'm a hockey *player* fan, hon. I even bought my husband an entire hockey outfit. The jersey. The shoulder pads. The helmet. The gloves."

I'm surprised to hear her say that. "Oh. I didn't realize Hamish plays hockey."

"He doesn't." Margo takes a sip of her cocktail through her straw, her cheeks swelling with a mischievous smile. "Notice how I didn't say I bought him any pants? Let's just say it's added a whole new level of spice to our nocturnal activities."

For only the second time in recorded human history, the Fast-Talking Five have been reduced to silence.

Thankfully, my brother, decked out as a Scottish highlander complete with a tartan plaid kilt, sporran, and Jacobite shirt, swoops in to save us from the awkwardness.

"Aye, it's a pleasure to see ye," he says, followed by a dramatic bow. He grins goofily. "And that's all I've got as far as pretending to be Scottish goes."

"What a shame," Beth responds dryly. "I was so looking forward to hearing more of you butchering the Scottish accent."

"See," I hear Summer whisper to Hannah. "*That's* how you deliver sarcasm."

"Oh, so you're the brother, ay?" Margo asks, stepping in toward Levi.

He takes a polite half step back because, uh, cleavage, and answers, "The one and only."

"I heard you do a neat party trick." When his expression remains blank, she adds, "You're a music charts savant, apparently."

He rolls his eyes. "Geez, Evie. Is there anyone you haven't told about this?"

"About you being a music geek? Uh, no. Everyone knows. Including Amiel now."

Amiel smiles, and Margo takes another sip of her cocktail, then picks a random date. "March 1999. Go."

Levi shoots daggers at me for another few seconds before his inner music nerd breaks through, and he turns to Margo. "Early 1999 was an interesting time on the Billboard Top 200 mainly due to the *Titanic* soundtrack dominating the album charts. The biggest casualty? Madonna. Because despite her seventh album *Ray of Light* being critically lauded, Celine stopped it from reaching number one. I guess her heart really did go on...and on...and on."

"I've forgotten he's able to do that," Hannah says as she flags down a waiter and swaps out her empty champagne glass for a new one, which is very unlike her. One drink is usually her limit.

We haven't been able to hang as much as I would have liked to over the summer. I've been flat-out with the stadium, and she's been spending most of her spare time with Culver.

The two of us watch as Levi regales Margo with way more chart trivia than I think she was anticipating. He finally finishes ranting, and she grabs Hannah and hastily retreats back to the girls while Levi wanders over to me.

"Margo couldn't wait to get away from you," I observe with a smile.

"Well, then, stop telling people about my talent."

My smile grows. For all his meddling and general annoyingness, I really couldn't have asked for a better brother.

"Where's Fraser?" he asks, scanning the ballroom.

"No idea. You haven't seen him?"

Levi shakes his head. "Nope. Although, I gotta say, this theme is wicked. It's too bad kilts aren't a thing. It's so...freeing."

"Please stop talking."

He laughs.

A waiter carrying a tray of goblets walks past. Levi grabs two glasses, and we move a little bit away from the girls, who have engulfed Margo in another fast-talking tornado.

"Cheers," he says, lifting his glass.

"What are we cheersing to?"

"To you being happier than I've seen you in a very long time. Possibly ever. And to me for being the best brother in the world by setting you up with my awesome best friend."

"Fine." I tap my glass against his. "I suppose you did play a very small role in Fraser and me getting together."

"Very small role, ha. Yeah, right. If it wasn't for my meddling, you'd still be harboring a crush on the guy, and Fraser would still be secretly in love with you from a distance. I deserve an award."

"I'll call the UN first thing in the morni—" I latch onto Levi's arm, my mouth hitting the floor. "O...M...G."

He follows my gaze, and something a lot less PG than OMG flies out of his mouth. He waves Mom, Dad, Harper, and Laney over to us.

"Mom, what are you wearing?" Levi asks, since I'm too stunned to say anything.

"There was a little mix-up at the costume store," Dad explains since Mom—excuse me, *Wilma Flintstone*, is not looking very cheery at the moment.

I'm not entirely sure who Dad's meant to be, but at least he's in the right theme, donning a distinguished Victorian gentleman's outfit, complete with a waistcoat and top hat.

Mom-slash-Wilma folds her arms. "A mix-up that we would have had time to rectify if *someone* had picked up the costumes yesterday like they were meant to and not today on the way over here, leaving me with no other option but to wear this ridiculous outfit."

There's a momentary hint of guilt in Dad's eyes, but it's quickly replaced by a smile aimed at me. "Someone's been keeping me very busy."

I smile back at him.

"You've got nothing to be embarrassed about, Mom," Levi says, trying—and failing—to hide how funny he's finding this. "You have amazing legs."

A giggle escapes me.

Mom glares at the two of us, but it's a little hard to take her seriously, standing there in an asymmetrical, knee-length white tunic dress, chunky stone necklace, and red bob wig topped off with a white bone hair accessory.

Say what you will about Meredith Freeman, but when she commits, she commits.

"You could have just not worn a costume," I mention.

"Don't be ridiculous, Evelyn. Who shows up to a fancy dress party not wearing a—?" Her eyes narrow. "Wait a minute. Why are you dressed like that? Why aren't you in fancy dress like the rest of us?"

"Don't know." I shrug. "Fraser's orders. He told me to wear normal clothes."

She gives an unimpressed *hmph* as she surveys the packed ballroom. "Oh, no," she groans. "There's Anita Bickmore."

"Who's that?" Levi asks.

"She's on the hospital board with your mother," Dad answers.

"Arts and cultures committee," Mom corrects. "She's been hounding me incessantly to let her sister join. Now I'm going to have to spend the whole evening trying to avoid her."

"At least you're not wearing anything that will make you stand out," I point out helpfully, but strangely, I'm on the receiving end of a very unimpressed glare.

"Soooo..." I decide to move on and address my sisters, "Who are you guys meant to be?"

"We're both Juliettes looking for our Romeos," Harper answers.

"So, art imitating life, then?" Levi teases, earning himself a very deserved smack across the back of the head from Harper...who proceeds to totally non-discreetly cast her eyes over the ballroom.

Fraser's brothers, Trace and Clayton, are coming tonight, and my money is on Harper being keen to spend some time with Clayton, AKA America's favorite reality TV villain.

"Any idea why Fraser is throwing this party, Evelyn?" Mom asks me.

"No idea. I was just telling the girls I'm completely in the dark abou—"

Before I can finish speaking, my words are drowned out by the jangle of an old-fashioned bell.

The room falls quiet, and then there he is. Fraser, standing on a stage at the end of the ballroom.

Everyone makes their way over to him.

I do, too, unable to take my eyes off him. He's so handsome, dressed in a tailored three-piece suit. His hair has grown out over the summer break and is styled neatly, and he's smiling, something he's been doing a lot more of these past few months.

"Evelyn Freeman," he says into the microphone, his deep voice reverberating throughout the ballroom. "Please make your way to the stage."

"Coming through," I call out as people move out of my way.

As I get closer to him, the rapid thud of my heart echoes in my ears.

What is he up to?

I climb the stairs at the side of the stage, and by the time I reach him, he's beaming. He places his microphone on the lectern, takes hold of my hands, and says, "You look stunning, Evie."

"Thanks. You don't scrub up so badly yourself. Now would you like to tell me what on earth is going on?"

"All shall be revealed."

I sniff the air a few times. "Do I smell fries?"

He grins mischievously, then picks up the microphone, and turns to address the crowd.

"Ladies and gentlemen, I regret to inform you that I have gathered you all here under false pretenses."

A hushed murmur breaks out.

"You see, next Saturday will be exactly one year to the day since I was set up on what was supposed to be one date with Evie. But I'd been keeping a secret. I've been in love with Evie for a very long time. And I knew, deep in my heart, that one date would never be enough."

A chorus of sighs and *awwws* cascades throughout the ballroom.

"Which brings us to tonight. I wanted to do something memorable. Something unusual. Something that would throw you all off so that no one would suspect what I'm about to do."

"Yeah, you've done that," Beth yells out.

Fraser smiles. "Excellent."

He reaches underneath the lectern and produces a microphone which he hands over to me, as well as a...

"I *knew* I could smell fries," I say, which draws a few surprised and probably confused chuckles from the crowd.

Fraser shakes the packet. "I bought them this morning."

"Um, okay."

He looks sad for a moment. "They're cold now."

"Forget about the fries, Fraser. It's fine."

He looks up at me and sticks his lower lip out adorably. "Don't suppose I could interest you in one?"

"A cold fry? No thanks."

"Not even one?"

"No, really. I'm fine."

"Not even, like, the top one?"

I stare out into the audience and am met with a sea of blank faces. What is he doing? Why is he so insistent on me eating a cold fry?

I glance down at the packet in his hands and almost drop the microphone. "Oh, my goodness!" I gasp.

Fraser drops to his knee, plucks out the top fry, and discards the rest on the floor.

There's a ring, a deep, vivid, canary-yellow diamond center stone accentuated by smaller white diamonds, sparkling on it.

He takes it off the fry and reaches for my hand. "Evie, it may have taken me almost eight years to ask you to be my girlfriend, but it took me about eight seconds to realize I needed to buy this ring and put it on your finger the second I saw it."

"Where did you see this ring?"

"In a jewelry store in New York."

"You were just casually walking down the street in New York and decided to pop into a jewelry store?"

"Correct."

"This something you do on a regular basis?"

"Evie, you're overthinking it."

"I'm just curious about your big-city shopping habits. This is important information for me to factor into the decision I'm about to make."

"You're not going to have a decision to make if I don't get the chance to ask the question."

"Good point. Continue, please."

"Thank you. I know this is sudden and maybe a little too soon, but I also know with everything I have in me, that I want you to be my wife. The mother of my children. The assistant coach to your junior league and para hockey teams." He swallows. "I want to share the big moments of life with you, but also all the small, ordinary, even mundane ones, too."

It takes me a moment to catch the reference. "'Sweet Nothing,'" I whisper, holding his gaze, remembering our dance at the beach.

He nods. His normally piercing eyes have become misty.

So have mine.

Because for all his grand gestures—like this amazing proposal, like buying me a hockey stadium and team, like flying across the country just because he had a hunch I might be feeling bad—so many of my favorite moments with him have been simple ones.

Like lying on the floor talking.

Like laughing as we eat burgers and way too many malasadas.

Like just being together and *knowing* that this is right. That we belong together.

"You make me a better man, Evie, and I want to be the best man I can be for you every day for the rest of my life."

He looks at me and smiles, and I honestly don't think I've ever felt happier than I do right now.

"We don't have to get married this year, or even next year. We can have the world's longest engagement if that's what you want." He takes a small breath, then resumes, "So, with all that said, Evelyn Willow Freeman, will you do me the honor of being my wife...someday?"

"Yes! Of course I will. Yes!" I sputter into the microphone.

My hand trembles and tears start to fall down my face as Fraser eases the ring onto my finger, the grease from the fries helping it slide on effortlessly.

The crowd—oh, that's right, we're standing on a stage in front of a ballroom filled with people, I'd completely forgotten—erupts in cheers and applause.

Fraser gets to his feet and kisses me. "I love you, Evie," he mumbles into my lips.

"I love you, too, Fraser," I mumble back into his.

We step off the stage and stand hand in hand as people come over to congratulate us.

Starting with...

"Uncle Fraser!"

Fraser lets go of my hand to scoop up Oakey in his arms. Dawn and Tim follow close behind.

"Congratulations, you guys!"

"Thank you," I say as Dawn grabs my hand and inspects the ring.

"Good choice, Fraser," she says, and there's a sparkle in her eyes that makes me think he might have consulted her about it.

Dad and Wilma—sorry, Mom—are next, both of them a little misty-eyed.

"Now, as happy as we are for you both, unfortunately we can't stay," Mom informs us.

"Why not?" I ask with a grin, knowing full well Mom will be wanting to escape from here as soon as it's socially acceptable to do so. Literally everyone is staring at her outfit.

"You're not as funny as you think you are, Evelyn."

Fraser's parents are up next. "You're going to have gorgeous babies. I'm friends with a fabulous photographer. He doesn't normally do baby photo shoots—"

"Mom," Fraser interrupts his mother. "First, we're not even married yet. And second, no baby photo shoots."

"Oh, sweetie. I'm not saying it'll happen now. Pedro is booked out years in advance."

Fraser lets out an exasperated sigh.

I thread our fingers together, and once his parents have left, I whisper, "I love that your family is just as crazy as mine."

His brothers are next. "Congratulations, little bro," Trace says, and boy, he's looking and even sounding more like their father every time I see him.

Clayton greets me with a hearty hug, lifting me off my feet. "I'm so freakin' happy. Thank you, Evie, for taking this lug off our hands."

All three Rademacher brothers are ridiculously tall and handsome men, but I definitely lucked out and scored the handsomest.

Still, that doesn't mean I've completely forgotten about my sister.

"Have you guys seen Harper, by any chance?" I ask, directing the question more toward Clayton.

"Can't say that I have," he replies.

"He's been too busy taking selfies with fans," Trace supplies.

Clayton shrugs and flashes a bright smile. "Gotta give the fans what they want."

It's so wild to me how different Fraser and his brothers are.

Trace is super serious, business-focused, and travels all over the world. Clayton has a seemingly boundless supply of energy and adores living his life in the public eye and playing into his bad-boy persona.

While Fraser values his privacy and wants the same thing I do—a simple small town life filled with hockey, love, friends, family...and malasadas.

"Well, she's keen to say hi, so make sure you catch her," I say to Clayton, which is followed by a gentle poke from the man standing beside me.

"You're officially more of a meddler than Levi," he whispers once they leave.

I repeat what I said to Clayton to Harper when she and Laney come over, but reverse it, saying Clayton is keen to see her. Watching her eyes almost pop out of her head made the harmless lie totally worth it.

Then Hannah comes over, nursing yet another drink, joined by Culver. They spent most of the summer together. If they weren't lifelong besties, I'd be starting to suspect that something was going on with them. But surely not. They're so deep in the friend zone, they're practically family at this point.

"Congrats, man."

"Thanks, man."

Hannah and I giggle at the display of bro-ness as she bundles me in a big, warm hug.

"I am so happy for you, Evie," she says, rubbing my back, then letting out a small hiccup.

"Thanks. I'm happy for me, too."

I want to check in and make sure she's okay since I've only ever seen her tipsy twice in my life, but more people are making their way over to congratulate us. At least she's with Culver, who wraps his arm around her as they head toward the dance floor.

After what feels like forever, we've finally spoken to everyone.

We move away from the side of the stage. The band is playing a mid-tempo number, so Fraser lifts my hand, presses a gentle kiss onto it, and asks, "May I have this dance?"

"Sure."

His eyebrows shoot up.

"Why are you so surprised?"

"I was counting on having to ask at least seven times. I even have notes on my phone outlining reasons why you should dance with me."

I swat his chest. "You do not...Do you?"

He grins. "Even though there are no truth fries to be found, I can't lie to you...Yes, I have notes. And yes, they're thorough."

I throw my head back and laugh. "Hey, if you want to risk public humiliation by dancing with me, who am I to stand in your way?"

"That's the spirit."

He leads me onto the dance floor, wraps his hands around my waist, and we start swaying to the music.

"What a year it's been," he says.

"Oh, yeah. Anything interesting happen?"

He chuckles. "Let's see. It started with a fake date..."

"And ended with a real proposal."

"It sure has. I meant what I said up on that stage, Evie. You make me want to be a better man."

"You already are the best man ever. I mean it. You're so much more open than you were a year ago. I mean, hello, a public proposal. Last year Fraser wouldn't have done that at all."

"You don't mind I did it so publicly?"

"Not at all. I love that all our friends and family were here to share the moment with us."

"That's what I wanted, too. And you don't mind that I did it a week before our one-year anniversary?"

"Why would I mind that?"

His eyes darken. "You know, the curse and all."

"What curse—*ohhh,* the twelve-month curse. You know, it totally slipped my mind."

Guess that's what happens when you find yourself a great guy and are in a stable, honest, and healthy relationship. You don't worry about silly things like getting dumped after a year.

"Good. I'm glad. That's why I wanted to do this a week *before* our one-year anniversary. I wanted you to go into that special day feeling secure, knowing I would never leave you."

This. Man.

Can he get any swoonier?

"The curse is broken, Fraser. You're my forever person."

His face lights up with a bright smile, and then we kiss.

With all my heart, with every fiber of my being, I know Fraser is an incredible, kind, thoughtful man who would never deliberately hurt me or deceive me.

Or dump me after a year of dating.

Or publicly humiliate me by breaking up with me on live TV.

That all feels like a lifetime ago.

He lowers his voice so no one dancing near us can hear. "And are we still all good on the waiting thing?" he asks.

"Of course. Why? Have you changed your mind?"

"Every single day about a hundred times a day," he replies jokingly. "I want you so much, Evie. You're the most beautiful woman in the world. But I know it will be so much more special if we wait."

His words ebb through me like a slow-moving river, and I feel the soul-deep rightness of this decision for us. Because part of me wants to race ahead, too, but like he said, it'll be so much more special if we hold off until our wedding night.

"You mentioned something about a long engagement?" I say.

"I did. I don't want you to feel pressured or rushed."

"You know, I'd still be happy with eloping to Vegas."

He chuckles. "So that hasn't changed since high school?"

"Nope." I smile, then reconsider. "Let's put the tacky Vegas wedding into the maybe pile."

"Fair enough."

"Just promise me we'll get married the way *we* want to get married, okay? If we want something small and intimate, then that's what we'll do. I can just picture our mothers getting together to organize the wedding of the decade, and that's literally the last thing I want."

"Same here. Although, when it comes to your mother, I'll let you handle her."

"Awww, you still scared of her?"

"Completely. Even dressed as Wilma Flintstone."

"That was a terrifying sight." I slide my hand through his hair. "I realize we haven't exactly done things the traditional way. But I wouldn't go back and change a single thing."

"I would...The family dinner, hello."

"Oh. Yeah. That was bad."

"Horrifically bad. I can't even look at a jalapeno without breaking into a sweat."

"Don't worry. I have a lifetime to get you used to handling a little heat."

"Nope. That one is totally non-negotiable."

"We'll see." I smile, staring into those beautiful blue eyes I'll get to stare into for the rest of my life. "I love you so much."

"I love you even more, Evie." Fraser leans in and kisses me, long and hard. "I can't wait to spend the rest of my life with you."

The night flies by in a blur.

We dance with family and friends. We talk. We laugh. We drink. It's the most magical evening ever.

And then it's all over.

The cleaning staff start moving in as Fraser wanders over to me, his jacket casually flung over his shoulder. "Do I need to get you home before midnight or else you'll turn into a pumpkin?"

"No. But you do need to get me to an In-N-Out or I'll turn into something worse."

He laughs.

"What can I say?" I continue. "Dancing burns a lot of calories. I am famished."

Fraser smiles, extending his hand to help me up from my seat. "That's my girl."

My whole body flushes with happiness.

He doesn't do it often, but I love it when he calls me his girl.

It's an intoxicating combination of strength and possessiveness. It doesn't make me feel weak or less than. If anything, it fills me with a sense of empowerment, like I can do and be and achieve anything I set my mind to.

We hold hands as we make our way toward the exit when a high-pitched giggle rings out in the air.

Fraser glances over at me. "Was that you?"

"Yes. A hidden talent you have yet to uncover about me is that I'm a ventriloquist. Did you see my lips movi—"

The giggle rings out again, louder this time.

Fraser points toward the corner of the room. "It's coming from over there."

We walk toward the sound coming from behind a row of tables and chairs stacked in the corner. We reach the end of the tables and peer over.

"Whoa," I exclaim.

"No way," Fraser says, breaking out into a huge grin.

Because there, lying on the floor, side by side, laughing hysterically—possibly because they're both tipsy—are our two best friends, Hannah and Culver.

THE END

ABOUT ASH KELLY

The Fake Out Flex is Ash Kelly's debut novel.

For more information about Ash,
please visit - **www.ashkellyauthor.com**

Made in United States
Troutdale, OR
05/22/2024